Music and Science

Music and Science provides an introduction and practical guidance for a scientific and systematic approach to music research. Students with a background in humanities may find the field hard to tackle and this accessible guide will show them how to consider using an appropriate range of methods, introducing them to current standards of research practices including research ethics, open access, and using computational tools such as R for analysis. These research methods are used to identify the underlying patterns behind the data to better understand how music is constructed and how we are influenced by music. The book focusses on music perception and the experience of music as approached through empirical experiments and by analysing music using computational tools spanning audio and score materials. The process of research, collaboration, and publishing in this area of study is also explained and emphasis is given to transparent and replicable research principles. The book will be essential reading for students undertaking empirical projects, particularly in the area of music psychology but also in digital humanities and media studies.

Tuomas Eerola is Professor of Music Cognition in the Department of Music, University of Durham.

"Empirical music research has quite a history, and it is a joy to see its history, accumulative knowledge and current tools assembled in one concise publication. The author is a true expert and an inspiring teacher, providing students with all the knowledge and tools they need to contribute to this exciting field, where there is still a lot to explore."

Henkjan Honing, *Professor of Music Cognition, University of Amsterdam; author of* Music Cognition: The Basics *(Routledge, 2022)*

"Eerola's *Music and Science: A Guide to Empirical Music Research* offers an up-to-date and clearly organized introduction to the field. Balancing theoretical and practical approaches, it serves as an invaluable resource for any student or researcher getting started with empirical work on music."

Elizabeth Margulis, *Professor, Director, Music Cognition Lab, Princeton University*

SEMPRE Studies in The Psychology of Music

Series Editors
Graham F. Welch, *UCL Institute of Education, UK*
Adam Ockelford, *University of Roehampton, UK*
Ian Cross, *University of Cambridge, UK*

The theme for the series is the psychology of music, broadly defined. Topics include (amongst others): musical development and learning at different ages; musical cognition and context; applied musicology; culture, mind and music; creativity, composition, and collaboration; micro to macro perspectives on the impact of music on the individual – from neurological studies through to social psychology; the development of advanced performance skills; music learning within and across different musical genres; musical behaviour and development in the context of special educational needs; music education; therapeutic applications of music; and affective perspectives on musical learning. The series seeks to present the implications of research findings for a wide readership, including usergroups (such as music teachers, policy makers, leaders and managers, parents and carers, music professionals working in a range of formal, non-formal and informal settings), as well as the international academic teaching and research communities and their students. A key distinguishing feature of the series is its broad focus that draws on basic and applied research from across the globe under the umbrella of SEMPRE's distinctive mission, which is to promote and ensure coherent and symbiotic links between education, music and psychology research. There are now over 45 books in the series.

Teenage Boys, Musical Identities, and Music Education
An Australian Narrative Inquiry
Jason Goopy

Recorded Music in Creative Practices
Mediation, Performance, Education
Edited by Georgia Volioti and Daniel Barolsky

Music and Science
A Guide to Empirical Music Research
Tuomas Eerola

For more information about this series, please visit: www.routledge.com/music/series/SEMPRE

Music and Science
A Guide to Empirical Music Research

Tuomas Eerola

Routledge
Taylor & Francis Group

LONDON AND NEW YORK

Designed cover image: Created by Tuomas Eerola with Midjourney.

First published 2025
by Routledge
4 Park Square, Milton Park, Abingdon, Oxon, OX14 4RN

and by Routledge
605 Third Avenue, New York, NY 10158

Routledge is an imprint of the Taylor & Francis Group, an informa business

British Library Cataloguing-in-Publication Data
A catalogue record for this book is available from the British Library

ISBN: 9781032277097 (hbk)
ISBN: 9781032277066 (pbk)
ISBN: 9781003293804 (ebk)

DOI: 10.4324/9781003293804

Typeset in Times New Roman
by Newgen Publishing UK

This book is dedicated to my family.

This book is dedicated to my family.

Contents

Figures

Tables

Preface

Why did I become interested in the scientific approach to music? Before embarking on an academic path, I was a clarinet player. Although nothing beats the feeling of performing in front of a live audience, becoming an instrument tutor and musician felt restricted. After A levels, I heard that one can pursue music at university in a discipline called *musicology*, which seemed appealing. At the least, gaining wider knowledge of music in its all varieties seemed to be a useful investment for any future career in and around music.

In the early 1990s, music research and training at university was still very much focussed on scores, history, and interpretation of compositions within their cultural context in the humanities tradition. But there was also the emergence of computers as a viable tool for analysing music, the internet (and the invention of the MP3 format), and the MIDI protocol, all of which influenced and shaped new areas of music consumption, music making, and eventually musicology as well. At the time, all these technical developments aligned with my interests. I started my studies in an intriguing programme that promised to approach all music as an equally valuable object of study. This statement was penned by Professor Jukka Louhivuori at the University of Jyväskylä, Finland. He was at the forefront of a new paradigm of music research that tackled the question of how the mind processes music, and this question borrowed methods from cognitive psychology and computer science. Our Bachelor of Arts training included – and this sounds incredibly advanced and naive at the same time today – training chord sequences with neural networks that learnt to recognise tonal centres and common tonal functions in music. It was mind-boggling to see little icons to strengthen the connections between the nodes of pitch-classes in the *MacBrain* software when it was exposed to a dozen (!) nursery tunes. The notion that no genre of music was deemed to be above the others was radical at the time when you recall that teaching at the conservatoires, where I had accrued my knowledge of music, clearly laid out a hierarchy of values, where Western classical music was at the top, followed by Western jazz, and folk and popular music or music from other cultures was something not considered properly under the education system at the time. As an omnivorous music listener, I relished the idea that this field could tackle anything from corny songs by Manowar to the trashy lyrics of Finnish pop or to the complex harmonic and timbral textures of

Björk. Due to Louhivuori's interest in folk music and the focus of his star students, such as Petri Toiviainen, on jazz improvisations, these orally transmitted traditions were used as case studies to understand the processes involved in music making that did not rely on scores. It was refreshing, departing suitably from the world of music conservatoires and the classical canon, and profoundly shaped my thinking about music scholarship.

In the 1990s, one also had to learn how these rather primitive technologies worked (one had to write actual html code, rely on MIDI standard, and create sounds or excerpts of music through rather unwieldy synthesis software and so on). When computers were introduced as an option to analyse music, this area was titled *cognitive musicology*. This area kept the focus on the listener and performer, not just what the machines/computers could do with music. This was a healthy distinction, since it kept the focus on issues that have direct relevance to the listener, how they perceive music, what happens emotionally, how the 'hardware' itself (the ear, the auditory periphery, the brain, and the body) shape our perception and experience. We also learnt to avoid advocating approaches where the interest was in pure mathematics or numerology without a close connection to empirical reality. The field also regarded musical processes mainly as cognitive activity, which was in retrospect too narrow a view as it ignored the body and all kinds of embodied, motor, emotional, and physiological processes.

In the late 1990s, when I became more involved in research, my interest moved to the intersection of culture and biology in the processing of music. Again, I was lucky to be in the right place at the right time and volunteered to assist an eminent music psychologist, Carol Krumhansl, in her research project. This concerned psychological aspects of melodic expectations that she carried out in Finland due to availability of specialist participants who had exposure to very specific collections of music (Sami yoikers and a sect of Finnish beseechers). Exploring musical expectations of these specialist participants and comparing them to non-specialists provided materials that addressed both the cultural and hardwired aspects of music. However, it was more influential to see how this experienced and enthusiastic scholar operated and made research engaging, fun, and intellectually stimulating. I expanded these research ideas into comparisons of participants from non-Western cultures (e.g., Pedi people in South Africa) and of course got caught by the usual difficulties of cross-cultural research (translations, applying Western ideas and values to non-Western music to name just some). However, this was excellent education and provided important lessons about perception, cultural conventions, and the Western domination of musical influences. There was a sense that many exciting possibilities were available. I wish to pass on and regenerate some of these sentiments by offering the examples in this book and hope that others seize the opportunities that this rich field has to offer.

Acknowledgements

Thanks to everyone who helped and inspired me to complete this book. My wife Päivi-Sisko offered brutally critical reading of most chapters, but also gave me positive encouragement on some topics that I initially felt insecure about. My daughter Lilli proofread half of the book and she and my son Paavo asked some very good questions along the way. This book took inspiration from the work of my father Untamo in broadcasting and the career of my mother Maisa in teaching the English language. Annaliese Micallef-Grimaud has been the ideal graduate teaching assistant for teaching music and science to undergraduates, and she has monitored how students get on with online code examples, data collection, and analysis tasks concerning replication projects. I am also grateful to Juan Sebastián Gómez-Cañón for his experience with online solutions and the promotion of Python as a serious candidate for computational music research. Peter Harrison offered numerous concrete proposals and pointers about what he would like to see in a book such as this, and his ideas about sharing the code were invaluable. Peter also raised standards and inspired me to tackle some topics that I was not initially including in the manuscript. Thomas Magnus Lennie has been wonderfully patient and pedagogical with the early variants of music and science teaching. Fabian Moss gave several inspirational talks that encouraged me to include a computational music analysis section in a book that initially steered clear of the topic area. He also gave me numerous knowledgeable comments about music analysis and corpus analysis, which substantially improved several chapters. I am grateful to Scott Bannister for allowing me to use his pioneering research on music and chills in several examples. Imre Lahdelma spared me from several embarrassing moments by providing patient corrections to music-theoretical discussions. He was also my sparring partner on several topics, often related to his interest in consonance and dissonance and more generally to his broad knowledge of music theory and history. Mats Küssner suggested numerous improvements, especially concerning the history sections, and many times suggested a more diplomatic phrasing of an idea. Ian Dickson generously guided me on the topics related to music analysis. Brian McFee nudged me in the right direction concerning the audio analyses. David Huron inspired numerous topics within the book by his own pioneering research involving many topics (computational analysis, music and emotion research, methods, transparency in research, etc.) as can be seen from the frequent citations within this book. I am also indebted to Martin Clayton who has consistently demonstrated the broad need for empirical music research in his own research related to entrainment. He has pooled together impressive empirical datasets, and he has broadened the menu of relevant questions to be asked and explored. Kelly Jakubowski has been an ideal colleague and has influenced the activities within our *Music and Science Lab* at Durham University, which in turn have guided the choice of topics for this book. I also wish to thank Liila Taruffi for her ideas on the research culture in this field.

Heidi Bishop at Routledge was very supportive throughout the process and two anonymous reviewers gave numerous useful suggestions, particularly relating to the idea of diversity of music and sources. I am thankful to Graham Welch and Adam Ockelford for supporting the inclusion of the book in the series *SEMPRE Studies in The Psychology of Music*.

Series Editors' Preface

SEMPRE Studies in The Psychology of Music
Series Editors
Graham F. Welch, *UCL Institute of Education, UK*
Adam Ockelford, *University of Roehampton, UK*
Ian Cross, *University of Cambridge, UK*

There has been an enormous growth in research across recent decades into the many different phenomena that are embraced under the psychology of music 'umbrella'. This increase is evidenced in new journals, books, online sources, wider media interest, and an expansion of professional associations (both regionally and nationally, such as in Southern and Eastern Europe, Africa, Latin America, and Asia), as well as by increasing and diverse opportunities for formal study globally. Such growth of interest comes not only from psychologists and musicians, but also from colleagues working in the clinical sciences, neurosciences, therapies, acoustics, in the lifelong health and well-being communities, new technologies and informatics, philosophy, musicology, social psychology, ethnomusicology, and education across the lifespan. There is also evidence in several countries of a wider political and policy engagement with the arts in general and music in particular, such as in arts-based social prescribing for mental and physical health – addressing a need that became more acute in 2020 with the global pandemic and which shows no sign of abating. Research into the potential wider benefits of music for health and well-being, for example, seems to be particularly apposite at this time of global health challenges.

As part of this worldwide community, the *Society for Education, Music and Psychology Research (SEMPRE)* – having celebrated its 50th Anniversary in 2022 – continues to be one of the world's leading and longstanding professional associations in the field. *SEMPRE* is the only international society that embraces formally an interest in the psychology of music, research, and education, seeking to promote knowledge within and at the interface between the twin social sciences of psychology and education in combination with one of the world's most pervasive art forms, music. *SEMPRE* was founded in 1972 and has published the journals *Psychology of Music* since 1973, *Research Studies in Music Education* since 2008, and the fully online *Music and Science* since 2018. The three journals are produced in partnership with *SAGE* (see www.sempre.org.uk/journals) and we use the income as a charity to support national and international conferences and research initiatives through a small grants programme.

As a Society, we recognise that there is an ongoing need to promote the latest research findings to the widest possible audience. Through more extended publication formats, especially books, we believe that we are more likely to fulfil a key component of our distinctive mission, which is to have a positive impact on individual and collective understanding, as well as on policy and practice internationally, both within and across our disciplinary boundaries. Hence, we welcome the strong collaborative partnership between *SEMPRE* and Routledge.

The Routledge (formerly, Ashgate) *SEMPRE Studies in The Psychology of Music* series has been designed to address this international need since its inception in 2007 (see www.routledge.com/SEMPRE-Studies-in-The-Psychology-of-Music/book-series/SEMPRE). The rationale for books in the series is explained on the series information page.

This particular volume in the *SEMPRE* series is a single-authored volume by Tuomas Eerola titled *Music and Science: A Guide to Empirical Music Research*. It derives from Tuomas' long-term interest in the application of science to the world of music. The text draws on his personal research journey to engage the reader in his joy at exploring empiricism in order to understand how musics globally make sense to people within and across different social and cultural settings. The narrative introduces a sense of history, including strengths and weaknesses in empirical studies in music, whilst also providing illustrations of how a variety of research methodologies and methods can be applied in our studies of the art form, such as through the systematic application of computational models. There are also core chapters which explore the ways that we might annotate the ingredients of music and how to make sense of emergent music-related data. A common thread in the book is the elaboration of key principles, processes, and concepts in order that the reader is enabled to build deeper insights into the ways in which the human species engages with music, such as through music listening and performance. Given the huge rise in our access to music through digital media, Tuomas' book offers very timely, research-based insights into how modern musicology studies are enriched through the application of an empirical mindset.

Professor Graham F. Welch, UCL Institute of Education,
London, 24th April 2024

Online Resources

See links on website: https://tuomaseerola.github.io/emr/

1 Introduction

Music is a powerful source of experiences for many of us. We also know that music itself is extremely diverse, from visceral Taiko drumming to subtle *sul tasto* passages performed by a world-renowned string quartet. To appreciate the breadth of music will require investment of time and opportunities of engagement before one can appreciate the richness offered, which not only brings the cultural and wider meanings but also a host of ephemeral and subtle corporal and cognitive associations. Similarly, to study music, one needs a broad knowledge of the subject and the methods that bring this subject within the grasp of scrutiny.

Music research is traditionally conducted within arts and humanities, although there has always been an emphasis on scientific perspectives on music. These range from psychoacoustics, through neuroscience to perception and learning. Many of these fields of study view music as a rich domain of human activity that can reveal how the auditory system operates, how the brain works, or how learning and experience accumulate. It has also been a common trend in academia to focus on music within studies of history, media, or culture. These studies are not necessarily connected to musicology, as music is an activity that can encapsulate individual behaviours, values, and identities, but also collective beliefs, political changes, and cultural shifts.

Can music be studied in a way that satisfies the criteria for objective, systematic, and empirical research? Of course it can, and these ideas in the scholarly study of music are not entirely new, as much of Western scholarly history has touched upon music when the brightest minds have pushed forward our understanding of the world. Not many scholarly disciplines can boast a link to great thinkers such as Plato, Galilei, Rousseau, Wundt, and Helmholtz, who all had novel and systematic ideas about the essence of music and how to capture and describe it. This book aims to give the reader the background in which the current scientific approach to music can be understood as a continuation from the empiricists of the 19th century, and the core ideas of contemporary scientific musicology and empirical music research are offered and contrasted with what I will call humanistic musicology (music history, theory, cultural musicology).

What can be done with the heaps of data and sophisticated tools that allow us to analyse audio signals or thousands of musical scores? Such tools have become

DOI: 10.4324/9781003293804-1

readily available in the last decade, but the training and awareness for the possibilities they allow remain low. The use of these tools is transparently demonstrated in the example analyses. In many cases, the code and data are also offered to give the reader a transparent and reproducible research pipeline.

The aim of this book is to show how to approach the study of music empirically, systematically, and in an objective fashion. This is done by offering examples and clear blueprints for studies and outlining the powerful research designs that allow for the posing of direct questions and verifying assumptions or hypotheses about music. This work will also help to analyse data that are music-specific, whether it is the acoustic signal itself, the notational symbols in a collection of scores, or the actual movements of a performer. In this way, the purpose is to introduce several key contemporary data analysis approaches to music scholarship and guide the reader into topics and approaches with concrete examples. While embarking on this journey in scientific music scholarship, links are frequently made to map these operations to the landscape of music research as a historical activity and how humanistic disciplines such as music history, music theory, and analysis are tackling similar questions from a slightly different perspective.

This book introduces concepts, techniques, and skills that guide you through conducting empirical music research that tackles questions that are relevant for musicology, music theory, music perception, and music psychology. Methods of empirical research cover everything from research planning to research designs, data collection, analysis, and reporting. I will also focus on how to analyse actual music – whether it is a score, a captured performance, or an audio recording – in a separate section. All themes are delivered in a way that promotes transparency and reproducible research; the analyses and examples covered in the book are available as online notebooks that utilise open-source software such as *Python* and *R* and relevant libraries dedicated to the analysis of music.

Who Will Find This Book Useful?

The book is written to be readily understood and consumed by music undergraduates and postgraduates; postgraduates studying music psychology or related disciplines; and students studying digital humanities, media studies, and data sciences involving music. I have imagined my readers to be primarily humanities students and scholars and not engineering or psychology students. Humanities students will benefit from an exposure to scientific methods and approaches, but of course if your background already includes such approaches, seeing how they are wielded towards music and musical behaviours is still valuable.

What Does This Book Cover?

This book begins by contextualising **the history** of empirical research on music and moves on to explain the **core principles and values of empirical music research**. There is considerable emphasis on **methods**, including **research processes**, **research designs**, and **sources of information**. I will cover **data analysis and**

reporting principles with plenty of examples and illustrations from existing research and practice. After these methodological chapters, I will turn the attention towards music. First, we focus on **annotations** and cover the basic concepts and approaches, and then move on to empirical research into **scores, performance**, and **audio,** as well as **corpus studies** using computational tools. In the final part, we will discuss what this empirical approach can offer to music scholarship in general.

Availability of Data, Software, Code, and Materials

There are some sections that come with computer codes. These are mainly in the *R* language for quantitative analysis and in *Python* for music analysis. I have organised the codes into *Jupyter* notebooks that can run the code in a browser. For many of these notebooks, they can be run, copied, and edited on a cloud service called *Colab* or 'Colaboratory' just by following the link in the notebook. This allows anyone with a browser and online access to try out the analysis options and start learning without any technical requirements or installing software. Code sections are meant to give examples of the analyses and will look like this:

See Chapter1 R code at https://tuomaseerola.github.io/emr/

When short code snippets are embedded into the text to explain a particular technique, they look like this:

```
# Code 1.1
library(MusicScienceData)          # loads library w data
data <- MusicScienceData::soundtrack  # pick data
cor.test(data$Energy,              # calc. correlation
         data$Tension)
##
##  Pearson's product-moment correlation
##
## data:   data$Energy and data$Tension
## t = 7, df = 108, p-value = 4e-11
## alternative hypothesis: true correlation is not equal to 0
## 95 percent confidence interval:
##   0.437 0.690
## sample estimates:
##    cor
## 0.577
```

An online repository https://tuomaseerola.github.io/emr/ contains links to all notebooks that can replicate the analysis operations in either R (mainly statistics) or Python (mainly analysis of music).

I will give the minimum information necessary for understanding and using these codes, but to really learn coding (R or Python), you should consult some of the excellent resources available (see the links in the online repository for details). A brief tutorial on operating the basic analyses in *RStudio* is also available in the online materials.

2 History

DOI: 10.4324/9781003293804-2

Early History

> Musicke I here call the Science, which of the Greeks is called Harmonie ....
>   Music is a Mathematical Science, which teacheth, by sense and reason, perfectly to judge, and order the diversities of sounded hye and low.
>   (John Dee, 1570, from Fauvel et al., 2006, p. 1)

Music and science have long been intertwined in engrossing and intimate ways; Pythagoras built a whole foundation of Greek music theory on ratios and mathematics of music (Papadopoulos, 2002), which have resonated and impacted the research and history of music in Western societies. As a founder of mathematics, he captured the nature of why some intervals sound pleasing (e.g., an octave, which has a 2:1 ratio, or a fifth, which has a 3:2 ratio) while others do not (e.g., a major second with a 9:8 ratio, or a minor second, which has a 10:9 ratio) by explaining these differences with ratios that related to underlying integers. Later authors such as Nicomachus (Zbikowski, 2002) put forward a claim – unfortunately, a fictional one – that Pythagoras observed the sounds coming from a blacksmith's workshop, where hammers were beating on anvils. Some of these sounds were consonant and some were not. After investigating the actual weight and size of the hammers, he realised that it was not the particular place nor the velocity of the hit that produced different frequencies, but the relative weights of the hammers. He was claimed to have constructed his own experiments that used not only hammers but also strings and blowing through hollow tubes to explore how frequency and intervals are generated by differences in the physical properties of the instruments (see Figure 2.1). Interestingly, many of these experiments, such as suspending weights from strings at one end, do not provide evidence for the simple ratios, since such ratios are squares of fractions of the lengths of the strings. This was only realised in the 16th century by Vincenzo Galilei. Nevertheless, during antiquity, the powerful narrative captured by the simple ratios, such as 2:1 for an octave, 4:3 for a fourth, and 3:2 for a fifth, formed a powerful link between mathematics, nature, and music.

Despite the lack of veracity of the story about the hammers, the insight into ratios and intervals led the Greeks to assume that these discoveries are manifestations of the unseen order of the cosmos that are simply expressed in numbers, giving a

Figure 2.1 Pythagoras exploring the ratios of tones with a monochord. Engraving by Theo Gafurius, 1492. Milan, Italy (copyright Tarker / Bridgeman Images).

great and powerful narrative of how music lies at the epicentre of science. This notion persisted into the Middle Ages and Renaissance (e.g., Boethius) and has kept several eminent scientists across the centuries interested in the acoustical aspects of music (Tenney, 1988). I'm also tempted to say that I sometimes recognise the obsession with numbers and ratios in contemporary music scholarship, so the appeal of this narrative has never truly disappeared. Richard Parncutt and Graham Hair (2018) have provided a succinct overview of the historical account of intervals as ratios and persuasively countered these mathematical or physical accounts of intervals considering overwhelming psychoacoustic and cultural evidence about how intervals are perceived.

Aristotle and Plato were influenced by the discovery of ratios and intervals attributed to Pythagoras. They developed the idea into a more pragmatic and even – in a contemporary sense – perceptual direction, by promoting a detailed account of music as something that has vocal motion and intervals as the central elements. These ideas were later systematically charted by Aristoxenus (Mathiesen, 1999), who put another pivotal concept forward by defining melodic intervals either as *concordant* or *discordant*. Although this account of music does not hold a prominent place in contemporary music scholarship, it demonstrates one aspect of our cognitive processing, namely categorisation, which is fundamental to cognition. Categorisation is one of the fundamental processes we use to interpret the world around us (for a longer discussion, see Zbikowski, 2002). The categories which Aristoxenus addressed as concordant and discordant are nowadays debated under the terms *consonant* and *dissonant*, which strictly speaking do not exist simply due to the numerical ratios of the intervals but because the intervals are related to our experience of consonance, the way the auditory system operates, and the physical properties of sounds (Parncutt & Hair, 2018).

In the 15th century, an influential debate shaped the way music was regarded to reflect the fundamentals of the universe. The actors in this drama were Vincenzo Galilei (the father of Galileo Galilei); music theorist, composer, and performer, who brought a new style of music that heralded the beginning of the Baroque in music; and another Italian music theorist, Gioseffo Zarlino. Initially Zarlino claimed the octave as the origin of all intervals and distinguished thirds and fifths as fundamental building blocks of composition (Zarlino, 1968). He derived the distinction of major harmony from the notion of harmonic, where the length of the string in a monochord is divided into six ratios (1, 1:2, 1:3, 1:4, 1:5, 1:6) which correspond to unison, octave, fifth, fourth, major third, and minor third (C_2, C_3, G_3, C_4, E_4 G_4), see Figure 2.2. The minor mode is obtained from the arithmetic division of six ratios (1:2:3:4:5:6), where the denominator is constant (6:6, 5:6, 4:6, 3:6, 2:6, 1:6), creating a fundamental, minor third, fifth, octave, fifth, fifth (C_3, $E\flat_3$, G_3, C_4, G_4, G_5). While the emphasis on *six* ratios was defended by an esoteric explanation (six planets, six days of creation) (Cohen, 1984), this system elevated major and minor thirds to a special status that became the hallmark of Western music (major and minor modes and triads). Zarlino also explicitly mentions how major and minor chords create either happy or sad expression; although he was not the first to point out this association, it solidified the system of scales and intervals for Western music.

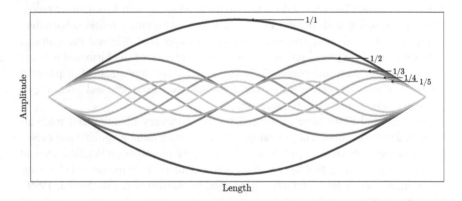

Figure 2.2 Division of a string where 1/1 is fundamental (110 Hz), 1/2 = octave (220 Hz), 1/3 = fifth + octave (330 Hz), 1/4 = two octaves (440 Hz), and 1/5 = major third + two octaves (550 Hz).

Zarlino, who was also Galileo's former master, endorsed the Pythagorean system – which he modified slightly – that upheld the abstract ideals of ratios and used them to explain modes and interval combinations such as triads. This set of ideas was to become the backbone of Western music theory, but the fundamentals of the framework were disputed by Vincenzo Galilei. Over a series of letters and writings about the exact nature of the ratios that best serve vocal and instrumental music, Galilei sharply criticised Zarlino's reliance on simple ratios and stacked empirical evidence against these ratios. He first rejected the notion that some special intervals can be called 'natural' just because they may be based on simple ratios. Galilei also enquired why we, as listeners, tolerate some imperfections from the pure ratios, or why the ratios do not always bring the desired intervals. Galilei had experimented with the length of strings and had found that when we compare the *tensions* of the strings rather than the *lengths* (which was the past practice) to obtain the octave, one must increase the tension by a factor of four instead of two (i.e., $1:2^2$). Together with another Italian mathematician and physicist, Giambattista Benedetti, the reasoning against number ratios was a devastating attack and toppled the dream of working out systems that would retain the simple ratios in the centre of any musical theory. The reason behind the acerbic debate was that Zarlino still subscribed to the numerological world view, while Galilei and Benedetti represented the new ideology of progressive empiricism. The empirical approach not only tried to test the ideas with experiments, but the whole idea of considering the topic allowed them to put more weight on experience (Cohen, 1984). Despite the critique and gradual disillusionment with simple ratios, Zarlino's influence on music theory was more profound than that of any of the empiricists.

It was not easy to relinquish long-held ideas about intervals and simple integer ratios. Several other prominent thinkers in the early modern period were influenced by the elegance of the ratios; for instance, the French mathematician and philosopher Marin Mersenne upheld the notion of ratios as fundamental building blocks and also partially supported Plato's view of the nature of the universe in his main work *Harmonie Universelle*, published in 1636 (Mersenne, 1636). Mersenne's position was rather nuanced, but he was nevertheless challenged to a debate on the objective nature of dissonance by René Descartes (Mace, 1970). Interestingly, this debate was not only about the ratios, but it brought the concept of subjectivity to the debate. Descartes expressed this radical notion in a letter to Mersenne in 1630:

> In order to determine that which is more agreeable, it is necessary to assume the ability of the listener, which changes, like taste, according to each person; thus some prefer to hear one voice only, others a whole chorus, etc., exactly as one prefers that which is sweet, and another that which is a little sharp or bitter.
>
> (René Descartes, 1630, from Mace, 1970, p. 9)

Mersenne established a formula for the calculation of vibrations (Schneider, 2018) and he was able to separate the fundamentals and the partials using mathematics. He was sceptical about the universality and naturalness of consonance, since it seemed to be elusive in general, influenced by subjective notions, and clearly swayed by experience. Before jumping to the contemporary perspective on this topic, it is worth saying that currently both biological and cultural elements are acknowledged to contribute to dissonance and consonance (Harrison & Pearce, 2020; Lahdelma & Eerola, 2020). At the same time as theorising about consonance was going on in the early modern period, composers and performers were exploring the imperfect consonances. For instance, Monteverdi's fifth book of madrigals (1605) or Gesualdo's fifth book of madrigals (1611) provide exquisite masterpieces which are ripe with minor sixths, major seconds, and other intervals that were certainly assumed to be dissonant intervals at the time. It is safe to assume that the theoretical discussion and practical music making had a fruitful dialogue, since the tuning systems and building of enharmonic instruments designed by Mersenne were known among musicians and other theorists (Lindley, 1980).

In 1687, Isaac Newton published his main book *Philosophiæ Naturalis Principia Mathematica* (Newton, 1687), which provided the foundation for developing mechanical accounts of vibrating strings. He cited a pioneer in the acoustics, Joseph Sauveur (1701), in his *Principia*. Sauveur had proposed that harmonics could be constructed with organ pipes and that the underlying principle of these sounds was harmonic series. This directly inspired Jean-Philippe Rameau, who is responsible for much of the centrality of major and minor chords in Western music theory. For Rameau, the major triad was the ultimate chord that was natural and captured the essence of (Western) music. His magnum opus, *Traité de l'harmonie Reduite à ses Principes Naturels* (Rameau, 1722), drew ideas from Sauveur, Zarlino, and Mersenne, and outlined a system that allows composition according to natural laws derived from acoustics. The influence of Rameau's writing on music theory was profound, as he established a tonal theory in which keys are related to each other through motions of roots, and this was a more graded way of dealing with harmony and consonance, and made its way long into the early 20th century, to the writings Heinrich Schenker and Paul Hindemith (Tenney, 1988).

These laws include an octave that holds a special function that allowed him to regard intervals within the octave as the basis for all interval combinations. He adopted the division of the fifth as a basis for the major and minor triad ($1{:}3{:}5$ and $1{:}1/3{:}1/5$). He argued that some intervals, such as the octave, fifth, and major third, are central in music and in nature due to natural laws (harmonic vibration). Rameau particularly advocated the combination of $15{:}5{:}3$ which was the ut-mi-sol in his system. His idea of collapsing the chords across the octave became the norm, and he labelled the inversions (root position, first inversion, and second inversions) in a systematic fashion. To be fair, he was not the first to suggest this system, as Lippius had offered similar ideas about a century earlier (Dahlhaus, 1990). The terms 'basse fondamentale', 'dominant', and 'leading note' are all Rameau's proposals (Tenney, 1988) that continue to be drilled into every music student, even now, 300 years later.

Rameau proposed to tune the instruments into equal division across the octave (known as *equal temperament*), which became the standard tuning around the 19th century. He explored his ideas through empirical experiments where he listened to organ pipes that were either played separately or simultaneously to test the ideas of octaves and the ratios underlying the overtones and undertones. His revolutionary

Harmonic	1	2	3	4		5	6	7	8		9	10	11	12		13	14	15	16
Freq (Hz)	55	110	165	220		275	330	385	440		495	550	605	660		715	770	825	880
Cent dev.	0	0	−0.2	0		+2.2	−0.4	+7.0	0		−1.1	+4.4	+17.3	+38.5		+25.0	+14.0	+5.6	0

Figure 2.3 The harmonic series from A_2.

concept was to express that when one tone resonates, there are simultaneously strong overtones that also resonate. These overtones follow harmonic series that are easily defined by multiples of the initial frequency (f, or F_0 as used in later chapters), where the five first overtones are $2f, 3f, 4f, 5f, 6f$. If we assume that the fundamental frequency f is 55 Hz (cycles per second), the overtones would be 110, 165, 220, 275, 330 which correspond to notes $A_2, E_3, A_3, C\sharp_4, E_4$ (see Figure 2.3). The discovery or formulation of the overtones was not an original invention by Rameau, but he used the overtones to create a systematic theoretical framework for explaining tonality in his *Traité de l'harmonie Reduite à ses Principes Naturels* (1722). In his theory, he was able to derive the qualities of most chords from the overtones and this extended beyond the triad, which still retained the appealing mathematical aspects of music from Zarlino (who was influenced by Pythagoras). There was another aspect that has contributed to the establishment of Rameau as the leading theorist and a reference until today; he was also very keen to defend his theory against anyone who dared to express any doubts about it. His vehement attacks on eminent philosophers and encyclopaedists such as Jean-Jacques Rousseau and Jean Le Rond d'Alembert who expressed detailed critiques of Rameau's theory make riveting reading, where all the tools of rhetoric are wielded to pound the opposing view and also its proponents (see Christensen, 1993).

19th Century Foundations

Ernst Florens Chladni (1802) provided the first systematic account of acoustics in a comprehensive manner that was rooted in empirical observations. His work explored scales, temperament, and tuning, and he invented new instruments to measure tuning more precisely than any of the previous inventions had allowed. At the same time, the anatomy of hearing began to be understood. Italian anatomist Alfonso Corti discovered in the 1850s how the cochlea and auditory nerve are laid out by dissecting hundreds of animal and human cochleas. He reasoned that the frequency of notes is linked to the shape of the cochlea, although a more refined understanding of the inner workings of the cochlea needed another half a century to be unveiled.

A person who made a lasting and extraordinary impact on 19th century scholarship in science, physics, and philosophy of science, as well as a few other areas such as vision and acoustics, was Hermann von Helmholtz.

Helmholtz was educated as a military physician and was trained in experimental methods and medicine, which also included philosophy. Early in his career, he formulated a sign theory which tried to pin down the link between sensations and objects by proposing that these are learnt inferences rather than innate links between the senses and their configurations, as the prevailing view had it (Cahan, 1993). Helmholtz's bold proposal put experience and learning at the centre of perception and, in some ways, framed the process in what would be called *predictive processing* (Swanson, 2016) in contemporary scholarship. Helmholtz created these theoretical ideas when thinking about vision, but he also developed an interest towards biological matters, particularly about the way energy is consumed by living organisms. In this line of work, he also debunked the idea of perpetual motion machines by compiling evidence from physics and mathematics. He managed to formulate some of the central theorems of fluid dynamics, which seemed to lead him to explore sound and acoustics in more detail.

This interest resulted in a seminal book on music, acoustics, and music theory, *On the Sensation of Tone as a Physiological Basis for the Theory of Music* (1875). In the book, he takes the reader through the fundamentals of acoustics, how sound is generated through vibration and how frequency is dependent on the thickness and size of the membrane. He made many empirical experiments and devices to measure the frequencies of sounds. The most well-known devices are the small resonators that he constructed from glass and metal, which could be held next to the ear (see Figure 2.4). If an external sound has the same frequency as the resonator, the listener hears the sound in an amplified fashion, whereas all other frequencies are attenuated. These resonators are physical filters and allowed Helmholtz to unpick the fundamental and the frequencies of the partials of complex sounds. He applied the insights from these experiments with his knowledge of physiology to develop ideas about how sound and, specifically, these arrays of frequencies are processed.

The perception of dissonance and consonance is a good example of Helmholtz's insights in the late 19th century. He outlined the mechanism by which fundamentals close in frequency create mechanical interference in the cochlear fluid and along the basilar membrane that is felt as beating, dissonant, and mildly unpleasant (see Figure 2.5). He also uncovered the dissonance created by the partials of sounds,

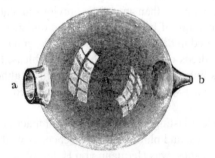

Figure 2.4 Helmholtz resonator made out of glass (from Helmholtz, 1875, p. 43).

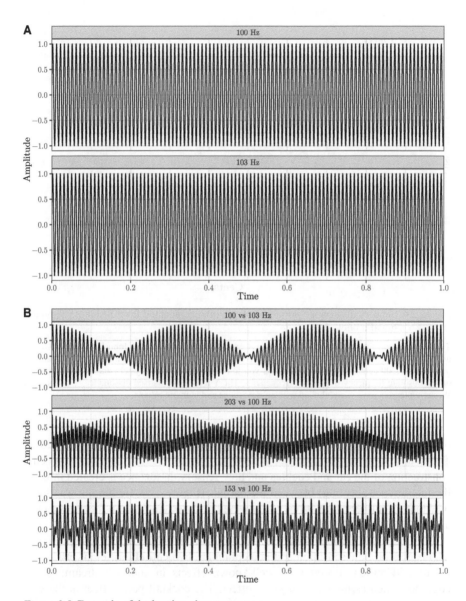

Figure 2.5 Example of the beating phenomenon.

Panel A shows separate sine waves at 100 Hz and 103 Hz. The upper signal of Panel B displays how these two are summed together forming 3 Hz amplitude fluctuation (beating). The middle signal of Panel B shows the interaction between 100 Hz and 203 Hz sine waves, which still reveals the difference of 3 Hz fluctuation through every other period (octave difference) and the lowest sub-panel displays the summed 100 Hz and 153 Hz sine waves, where the 3 Hz beating is just about visible across the amplitude differences.

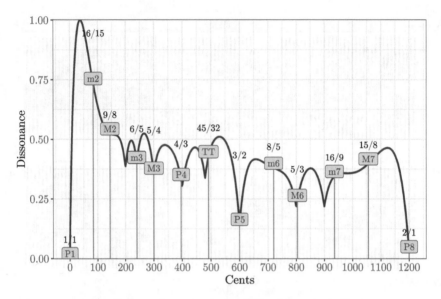

Figure 2.6 Sensory dissonance initially after Helmholtz, adapted from Sethares' computational model.

The X axis represents an octave (1,200 cents). Cents, defined by Alexander John Ellis in 1880, are a useful unit of measure for the ratio between two frequencies, where one semitone is 100 cents and an octave has 1,200 cents. This measure allows you to measure any tuning system and is not dependent on the absolute frequency of the two frequencies. The Y axis is normalised dissonance. The common Western intervals have been labelled with abbreviations and numeric ratios.

by characterising the summation tones – which had been briefly characterised by Tartini and Sorge earlier (Lohri et al., 2011) – that are created through the specific construction of the ear and cochlea and how sensory dissonance is created through the interference (beating) between the partials (Figure 2.6). Helmholtz was sceptical that the numerical relations really were the underlying reason for consonance, and convincingly debunked these older explanations.

Helmholtz's experiments were initially guided by physics, but he also presented his insights on how sensation and perception are two entirely different processes. He also identified several now well-known effects in auditory streaming and cognition, such as the *cocktail party* effect. The cocktail party effect is the way we can tune in to a specific speaker in a noisy room full of speakers, and it also describes the uncanny phenomenon whereby we perk up upon hearing our name (or other highly charged words for us) among the gibberish of discussions around us. Although the effect was properly studied in the 1950s, Helmholtz reasoned that the effect is consistent with the way he had outlined how vision must operate where learning, automaticity, and attention play a strong role.

Helmholtz regarded music as an art form based on patterns of sound and, in particular, pitch structures, and he believed that significant progress in understanding music can be made by unravelling the components of perception. The impact of his work on acoustics and psychoacoustics in the 20th century was profound; it was all empirical, based on his own observations and experiments, and it outlined a coherent programme of research and a clear programme of how to tackle the questions of hearing, psychoacoustics, and rudimentary auditory perception (Fauvel et al., 2006).

Early 20th Century

At the turn of the century, Helmholtz's strong influence and German scholarship in general formed the basis for empirical research on music. Carl Stumpf absorbed and acknowledged most of Helmholtz's theories, but also criticised his concept of consonance and dissonance (Stumpf, 1898) because it was only based on acoustics and psychoacoustics and lacked a psychological dimension. Stumpf was a philosopher by training and worked on phenomenology, epistemology, and experimental psychology. He also had a solid training in music as part of his upbringing. He pointed out that one needs to consider musical tradition and 'habituation' (we would say familiarity or exposure) more seriously. Even more prophetically, he argued that confining research to European art music is not going to be a convincing coverage of the rules related to musical processing. By doing this, he invented a completely new paradigm, comparative musicology (*Vergleichende Musikwissenschaft*), which was an important precursor to ethnomusicology. He pursued this notion by studying non-Western music recorded for the first time in the field and in Berlin (e.g., in 1900, he recorded a Thai ensemble in Berlin) and carried out small experiments and interviews with Thai musicians and reported how an entirely different tuning from Western standards seems to operate. In the case of Thai music, the tuning system was based on an equiheptatonic scale, which requires the octave to be divided into two equal parts. An avid user of state-of-the-art technology, Edison had a phonograph and a Danish telegraphone to capture the sound to be analysed and occasionally transcribed (Stumpf, 1926, see Figure 2.7).

In the early 20th century, a group of German scholars such as Robert Lach and Kurt Koffka, although they worked mainly on vision, used music as an example of *Gestalt*, which they referred to as 'form/whole/configuration'. The idea was that any perceptual phenomenon is best regarded as something organised and structured as a whole, as opposed to the notion of dissecting everything into separate elements. Music suited the idea of *Gestalt* well, as the listener is not really paying attention to separate notes or intervals, but instead grasps the melody as a *Gestalt* (Koffka, 1935; Lach, 1921). The visual analogy would be the Kanizsa and Ehrenstein illusions (Figure 2.8). In the former, you will see a white triangle in the middle, although it is just a product of our perceptual system filling out the missing information since the triangle is not really there, but just cued by the black shapes. In the latter, circles emerge between the grid lines similarly implied by the empty space (Walter Ehrenstein published his illusion in 1951 and Gaetano Kanizsa his in 1955). Even though *Gestalt* psychology did not survive as such into contemporary psychology or music research, it was revisited several times at the end of the 20th

Figure 2.7 A cylinder from 1916 to which Carl Stumpf recorded experimental vowel sounds.

Copyright: Ethnologische Museum der Staatlichen Museen zu Berlin – Preußischer Kulturbesitz, photograph by Albrecht Wiedmann.

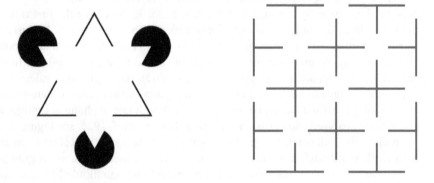

Figure 2.8 Kanizsa and Ehrenstein illusions.

century when computational and sub-symbolic approaches (e.g., self-organising maps) brought the concept back into music research (Leman, 1997).

In the early 20th century, there was clearly an appetite for transforming music scholarship into scientific exploration along the lines proposed by Robert Lach and Carl Stumpf. Guido Adler was persuaded by the same arguments and was a friend of the founder of the *Gestalt* school (C. von Ehrenfels), but Adler did not agree that Western music should be dropped from its privileged position when adopting this scientific and systematic line of research. Adler's lasting contribution was to divide musicology into historical and systematic branches (Adler, 1919), which has remained a significant division until now, but he retreated from the systematic approach himself, although it influenced his studies of Western music history (Weber, 1997).

Systematic musicology grew from the elements laid out by Stumpf. Two colleagues – Otto Abraham and Erich von Hornbostel – who worked at the Berliner Phonogramm-Archiv founded by Stumpf in 1900, published several studies involving non-Western music (Japan, India, Africa) (Hornbostel, 1910). Hornbostel also began to conduct experiments on tonal distances and brightness inspired by the differences observed across cultures (Hornbostel, 1926). Eventually he became the director of the Berliner Phonogramm-Archiv and amassed a massive collection of recordings in experimental Edison cylinders (see Figure 2.7). He also started to collaborate with Curt Sachs, which led to the system of instrument classification (Hornbostel & Sachs, 1914) that formulated a system based on sound-production principles that is suitable for all cultures and types of instruments.

The collaboration between musicologists and psychologists in Germany had been productive and gave rise to several new topics of music research. Most importantly, these ideas pioneered the approach called systematic musicology at the time. This fertile period ended abruptly with the rise of the Nazi regime in 1933 and many of the scholars, including Köhler, Sachs, and Hornbostel, emigrated outside Germany.

At the same time, in the US, one scholar brought innovation to empirical music research by proposing empirical tests to capture musical ability and the nuances of performances that are not visible from the score (timing, dynamics). This scholar, Carl Seashore, worked in Iowa and was focussed on the measurement of musical ability (Seashore, 1915), a topic which later generated an industry of musical ability tests that are still being developed today. The question of ability was fashionable, and other abilities (IQ, different mental abilities, but also specialist skills such as typing) began to be measured and applied in various ways. Perhaps more profoundly for empirical music research, he invented a way to capture expression in performance, initially for piano. He and his team at the University of Iowa built an *Iowa Piano Camera*, which let light through to moving photo-sensitive paper that had the amazing temporal resolution of 10 ms. The system could also capture dynamics to some degree. The impact of such a system, which was reported in his book, titled *Psychology of Music* (Seashore, 1938), was immense. It could demonstrate how top-level performers consistently altered the timing of music to generate appealing and natural expression of music. He also asked performers to play without expression, which was revealing since it demonstrated that although the deviations from the correct timings were reduced, the performers were, in fact, unable to perform music in a mechanically accurate or even fashion. This was the starting point for music performance science, which only began to get traction in the mid-1970s when the development of music technology created standards and tools (e.g., MIDI) that allowed recording and transformation of music performance data. Sadly, Carl Seashore's influence and intellectual engagement sphere also included eugenics, which appear to have profoundly shaped his views on the heritability of musical ability, and this controversial and unethical worldview contributed to his efforts to reform the US education system (Koza, 2021).

Late 20th Century

After World War II, research in social sciences was shaped by a rise in the use of computers in research. Computers and the workings of the human mind received a great deal of attention during the war when scholars of psychology and engineering had turned their attention towards making better radars, detection systems, and encryption. Cognitive psychology was continuing to map how the elements work, instilling the model of the human mind working as a computer – an idea still recognised today. At the same time, related disciplines such as linguistics, computational linguistics, and neuroscience also tackled similar questions and charted the boundaries of what the architecture of the information processing system would look like.

During this time, topics in scientific studies of music largely reflected the broader interest of cognitive sciences; attention turned to expectations (Meyer, 1956), memory processes (Francès, 1958), and rhythm (Fraisse, 1956). Leonard Meyer was a great translator of new concepts such as linking emotion to expectations and rephrasing elements of structural analysis as something that should reconcile the perceptual limitations from cognitive psychology to musicology. The importance of his contribution to musicology and to the evolving disciplines of music psychology and cognition cannot be overstated. His landmark book, *Emotion and Meaning in Music* (Meyer, 1956), was the inspiration for several American scholars (Robert Gjerdingen, Fred Lerdahl, and Eugene Narmour) who went on to redefine how the analysis of music should embrace ideas from information processing, and the knowledge of memory structures and gestalts that bind these concepts together. Meyer also suggested how rhythms could be organised and analysed with these ideas in mind (Cooper & Meyer, 1963). Soon after World War II, French psychologist Paul Fraisse began an impressive systematic research programme on the psychology of rhythm using rigorous empirical experiments. He was the first to capture sensorimotor synchronisation, observing how people have difficulty tapping in anti-phase (off-beats) and that this difficulty is directly related to tempo (Fraisse & Ehrlich, 1955).

Although Fraisse also offered several conceptual insights into synchronisation and rhythm, it took time for the anglophone world to catch up after the English translation of his book *Psychologie du Temps* (1957) in 1963. It took until the late 1970s when cognitive psychologists such as Mari-Riess Jones addressed how rhythms are attended to (Jones, 1976), Dirk-Jan Povel showed how the perception of beat intervals can be modelled (Povel, 1977), Diana Deutsch demonstrated how durations are encoded (Deutsch, 1986), and Caroline Palmer and Carol Krumhansl provided empirical evidence to show how beat structures are hierarchically organised in the minds of Western listeners (Palmer & Krumhansl, 1987).

Another emerging theme of scientific studies of music focused on sound and timbre (Erickson, 1975; Grey, 1978). The growth of interest in sound was not only relevant because computer processing started to allow computing and creating sound synthesis but was also due to the expansion of experimental music and sound generation and production technologies. The history of sound synthesis technology and experimental artists is intertwined in a fascinating fashion. For instance, Max Matthews and Jean-Claude Risset, pioneers of sound synthesis and analysis, collaborated with Edgard Varèse at Bell Laboratories in the 1960s (Risset, 2004). By the early 1970s, computers were harnessed more and more frequently for sound generation (Roads & Strawn, 1985) and since the 1980s, signal processing and the newly established MIDI standard have allowed precise communication between digital instruments (see Figure 2.9). These technologies were to be integrated into music and science activities and allowed new topics such as performance expression (Clarke, 1989) and timbre space (Wessel, 1979) to be studied more deeply than had been possible before. The availability of the MIDI standard was naturally important for musical creativity and advanced music production, but it also opened a completely new area of research for music: performance. Before this, the nuances of live performance were difficult to capture despite the attempts of past scholars such as Carl Seashore to do so. From the 1980s onwards, pioneered by Henry Shaffer (1981), a stream of studies was carried out which detailed how professional pianists breathe life and interpretation into music and how musical structure, interpretation, and expression work together. This line of work continues

Figure 2.9 Atari music workstation of the 1980s with MIDI capability.

to this day, but perhaps the culmination point was seen in an impressive summary of a body of research by Bruno Repp (1990).

In the symbolic domain of music, linguistics informed music research by offering parallels between music and language (Patel, 2010). In the 1970s, new units (phonemes) of analysis had been defined (Chomsky & Halle, 1968) and generative linguistic theory (Chomsky, 1972) gave inspiration to the analysis of music as a language. These innovations led music scholars to articulate grammar, syntax, and musical logic (Laske, 1973; Roads & Wieneke, 1979) that were assumed to be the key to understanding musical structure. Adapting syntax and grammar even in a superficial way from language to music is not without problems, and the debate went on about how these concepts could best be operationalised and continued until the 1980s (Nattiez, 1977; Ruwet, 1972). Even if the debate was not fully resolved, some powerful insights emerged that used these elements. John Sloboda approached music as a cognitive process, exploring how people encode contour and other attributes of the melody, and how musicians engage in score-reading. His book, *The Musical Mind: The Cognitive Psychology of Music* (Slododa, 1985), is the first summary of all relevant findings in how we process music, and this handbook has been widely translated and used in teaching. Fred Lerdahl and Ray Jackendoff defined a comprehensive model of the kinds of structural relations an experienced listener may rely on when listening to music. Their book, *A Generative Theory of Tonal Music* (Lerdahl & Jackendoff, 1983) gave rise to a new wave of empirical studies of grouping (Deliège, 1987), hierarchy (Bharucha, 1984), metre and phrasing (Palmer & Krumhansl, 1987), and reduction (Todd, 1985), where this influential framework has been empirically tested. In most cases, the empirical results supported the ideas put forward in generative theory, although improvements and clarifications were proposed to the details of some elements of the model. Carol Krumhansl brought attention to pitch structures and tonal hierarchies that she empirically established with Edward Kessler in the 1980s. Her book *Cognitive Foundations of Musical Pitch* (1990) was a rigorous psychological and mathematical characterisation of the core concepts related to pitch processing, schemata, and tonal hierarchies. As a psychologist, she brought a rigorous approach to music research, one that allowed computational approaches to test the theories empirically. For example, she and Mark Schmuckler established a key-finding algorithm based on the theory of tonal hierarchies. The research by Krumhansl with music theorist Fred Lerdahl on tension and segmentation (2007) brought music theory and psychology together in a way that had not been done previously. Krumhansl also expanded the scholarly perspectives on these topics in acquisition and cultural differences.

As an emerging discipline, the late 1970s and early 1980s saw an unprecedented rise in music-related empirical research. A host of specialised journals such as *Psychology of Music* (1973), *Psychomusicology* (1981), and *Music Perception* (1983) were established. These journals strengthened the identity of the new discipline and allowed better dissemination of ideas. Several international societies were also formed during this period of expansion, such as the *European Society for Cognitive Sciences of Music* (1991) and the *Society for Music Perception and*

Cognition (1990). Furthermore, universities started to offer specialisation modules and courses that had the ring of systematic musicology, music acoustics, or generative theory of music to them (Parncutt, 2007). In short, the field was getting institutional recognition which effectively funnelled new generations of scholars towards the field.

The neural aspects of the human mind, measurable since the invention of EEG in the 1930s, began to be wielded towards the question of musical processes in the late 1980s. A novel paradigm that allowed probing the brain response to isolated sound events, called mismatch negativity (MMN) (Näätänen & Picton, 1987), was easily applicable to musical events such as changes in chords, pitches, rhythms, and timbres. Event-related potential (ERP) is a robust index of how the brain detects changes in the signal. For this reason, a wide variety of empirical, music, and sound-related questions were turned into MMN paradigms; detecting pitch deviants, contour deviants (Brattico et al., 2001), patterns (of intervals) (Trainor et al., 2002), and timbre (Crummer et al., 1994), to name a few using this paradigm. What was exciting about this line of work is that the MMN paradigm could not only pick up some subtle changes in the audio signal that the listeners were sensitive to but, more significantly, the detection was shown to be sensitive to the patterns encoded and learnt by listeners. This, of course, allowed it to be used as an index to probe a variety of acquired mental structures related to music in more detail, and it led to a major breakthrough in how we still think the acquisition of musical expertise and skills is empirically traceable in the neural responses across the development.

Around the same time as neuroscientific methods started to bridge the gap between music theory, music psychology, and understanding of neural underpinnings of sound processing, computational sciences had entered a new phase. In the 1980s, much of the scholarship in music and science relied on the metaphor that the mind is either a computer or at least a device calculating statistical inferences using symbols (MIDI or another score-based notation). These symbols served as an adequate solution to build representations that helped us understand how these structures could emerge and function. The problem was that this approach typically left out timbre, dynamics, and timing details (Leman, 1999) that are deemed to be quite central to our musical experience and appreciation of music. To counter this lack of nuance in representations, a sub-symbolic approach was proposed (Bharucha, 1987; Leman, 1993; Todd & Loy, 1991), where it was assumed that our mental representation is much richer than just the symbols (notes, chords, sequences), and that we hear the music internally. Therefore, the make-up of computational models should not be based on high-level symbolic abstractions but on actual acoustic signals, although the idea did also meet opposition, particularly in terms of whether we learn something useful from the neural networks and other sub-symbolic models in music (Leman & Carreras, 1997; Rahn, 1994). See Figure 2.10 for an example of how such a self-organising map establishes tonal centres that loosely resemble the circle of fifths after being trained on Bach preludes. Nevertheless, the work that went on to utilise the rich information embedded in regularities of the audio signal did lead to curious and

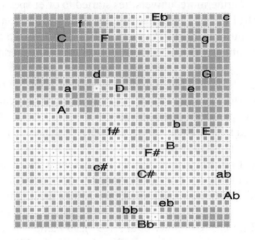

Figure 2.10 Sub-symbolic representation of tonal centres of Preludes of Book I of Bach's *Das Wohltemperierte Clavier* performed on harpsichord by Kenneth Gilbert (CD ARCHIV 413439-2).

The topological map shows the surface of a torus (the upper and lower border are connected and the left and right border are connected) that displays activations on a (30 x 30) network of neurons that have been trained with Bach Preludes and probed with Shepard tones. The labels show the locations of the highest response of each probe tone to this self-organising map (SOM), which loosely resembles the circles of fifths. The grey boxes show the activation of the neurons to the probe tone C. The figure is from Leman & Carreras (1996, p. 5).

fundamental insights about how sub-symbolic models were able to explain signifi-
cant parts of the basic elements of Western music such as tonal hierarchy (Leman, 2000), segmentation (Rossignol et al., 1999), or rhythm (Desain, 1993). These models never became fully adopted by the whole field, since the interpretation and utilisation of them was perhaps challenging and requires in-depth expertise.

Another turn in the road was an emerging emphasis on the body and embodiment in understanding musical processes. More broadly, these notions were influenced by ecological perception, which were articulated for music by Eric Clarke (2005). The emphasis on embodiment took the bodily responses (locomotion, arousal, tactile aspects of senses) as a vital influence on the perception and playing of music. More profoundly, the role of the body moves the focus of research from pure cognition in the perception of music to cognition in interaction with music (Godøy, 2006). Here the fundamental observations were that all activities involving music are related to our bodies, whether it is learning, memory, or prediction, and our bodies do influence the way we process music (through actions and analogies). This approach not only capitalises on the sub-symbolic turn in the field as it embraces sonic patterns in the form of physical and acoustic arrangements but more importantly puts the interaction between the perceiver and the environment under the focus of attention. Sensorimotor principles have been shown to govern many of the fundamental

principles, such as dancing (Naveda & Leman, 2009) and movement to music (Phillips-Silver & Trainor, 2005). From these principles, a new field emerged, *embodied music cognition*, spearheaded by Marc Leman (2007), which not only brings in the body and patterns from sub-symbolic data (movements, sounds, physiology), but sets up intentionality or *enactment* (Krueger, 2009; Leman et al., 2018) as the fundamental foundation that shapes all our interactions with music. The patterns of musical signals and our engagement with them only make sense if there is a sense of value and reward that we get when we engage with these patterns. The idea of patterns has been expanded to encompass culture and better contextualisation of gestures as historical and cultural patterns that usually also denote hierarchies and expertise level differences between musicians (Clayton & Leante, 2013; Moran, 2013). Over the recent years the field also includes evolution of musical ability and comparative studies with animals (Honing, 2018), and how different senses or modalities interact in the perception of music (e.g., Eitan & Rothschild, 2011).

Coda

The early history of music research was linked with scholarly interest in ratios and explanations of the origins of tuning systems. As the understanding of the perceptual system emerged, 19th century scholars started to root the earlier accounts of musical principles to what could now be called empirical music and science. Hermann von Helmholtz laid the groundwork for psychoacoustics, acoustics, and music cognition, although the next generation of scholars criticised him for not taking the psychological aspects of listening and comprehending seriously enough. In the 20th century, the emphasis was clearly on working out how the human mind creates and grasps patterns in music, and the rise of interest in music ethnology and non-Western musics broadened the scope for what kinds of musical phenomena needed to be explained. In the late 20th century, cognitive psychology and rapidly progressing music technology both influenced the research profoundly.

Discussion Points

1. Can you still see the influence of early accounts of consonance and dissonance and number theories and ratios in music training?
2. The early history of music and science can be seen as an evolution of technologies that allowed concrete tracing and testing of aspects of musical phenomena (using strings, resonators, phonographs, computers, etc.). Have you ever explored any musical phenomena with concrete objects (dividing a string to get intervals, finding fundamentals with resonators, or computer spectrograms) and what did you learn from these exercises?
3. From the 1960s onwards, computers have been the central tool for analysing, but have also been relevant for creating music and new sounds. In

what kinds of situations do you use a computer to create music and analyse it beyond notation?

4. Two emerging research areas – timbre and embodiment – have been
   incorporated into empirical studies in the last 15 to 30 years. What are the
   common difficulties that musicians may find in talking about these topics
   or bringing insights from research into their practices?

Further Reading

Fauvel, J., Flood, R., & Wilson, R. J. (2006). *Music and mathematics: From Pythagoras to fractals*. Oxford University Press.

Leman, M. (1997). *Music, gestalt, and computing: Studies in cognitive and systematic musicology*. Springer.

Parncutt, R. (2007). Systematic musicology and the history and future of Western musical scholarship. *Journal of Interdisciplinary Studies of Music, 1*(1), 1–32.

References

Adler, G. (1919). *Methode, der musikgeschichte*. Breitkopf & Härtel.

Bharucha, J. J. (1984). Anchoring effects in music: The resolution of dissonance. *Cognitive Psychology, 16*(4), 485–518.

Bharucha, J. J. (1987). Music cognition and perceptual facilitation: A connectionist framework. *Music Perception, 5*(1), 1–30.

Brattico, E., Näätänen, R., & Tervaniemi, M. (2001). Context effects on pitch perception in musicians and nonmusicians: Evidence from event-related potential recordings. *Music Perception, 19*(2), 199–222.

Cahan, D. (1993). *Hermann von Helmholtz and the foundations of nineteenth-century science*. University of California Press.

Chomsky, N. (1972). *Language and mind*. Harcourt.

Chomsky, N., & Halle, M. (1968). The sound pattern of English studies in language. In N. Chomsky, & M. Halle (Eds.), *Computer Science*. MIT Press.

Christensen, T. (1993). *Rameau and musical thought in the Enlightenment*. Cambridge University Press.

Clarke, E. (2005). *Ways of listening: An ecological approach to the perception of musical meaning*. Oxford University Press.

Clarke, E. F. (1989). The perception of expressive timing in music. *Psychological Research, 51*(1), 2–9.

Clayton, M., & Leante, L. (2013). Embodiment in music performance. In M. Clayton, B. Dueck, & L. Leante (Eds.), *Experience and meaning in music performance* (pp. 188–207). Oxford University Press.

Cohen, H. F. (1984). *Quantifying music: The science of music at the first stage of scientific revolution 1580–1650* (Vol. 23). Springer Science & Business Media.

Cooper, G. W., & Meyer, L. B. (1963). *The rhythmic structure of music*. University of Chicago Press.

Crummer, G. C., Walton, J. P., Wayman, J. W., Hantz, E. C., & Frisina, R. D. (1994). Neural processing of musical timbre by musicians, nonmusicians, and musicians possessing absolute pitch. *The Journal of the Acoustical Society of America, 95*(5), 2720–2727.

Dahlhaus, C. (1990). *Studies on the origin of harmonic tonality* (trans. by R. O. Gjerdingen). Princeton University Press.

Deliège, I. (1987). Grouping conditions in listening to music: An approach to Lerdahl & Jackendoff's grouping preference rules. *Music Perception: An Interdisciplinary Journal, 4*(4), 325–359.

Desain, P. (1993). A connectionist and a traditional AI quantizer, symbolic versus sub-symbolic models of rhythm perception. *Contemporary Music Review, 9*(1–2), 239–254.

Deutsch, D. (1986). Recognition of durations embedded in temporal patterns. *Perception & Psychophysics, 39*, 179–187.

Eitan, Z., & Rothschild, I. (2011). How music touches: Musical parameters and listeners' audio-tactile metaphorical mappings. *Psychology of Music, 39*(4), 449–467.

Erickson, R. (1975). *Sound structure in music*. University of California Press.

Fauvel, J., Flood, R., & Wilson, R. J. (2006). *Music and mathematics: From Pythagoras to fractals*. Oxford University Press.

Fraisse, P. (1956). *Les structures rythmiques: Étude psychologique*. Publications Universitaires de Louvain.

Fraisse, P. (1957). *Psychologie du temps*. Presses Universitaires de France.

Fraisse, P. (1963). *The psychology of time*. Harper & Row.

Fraisse, P., & Ehrlich, S. (1955). Note sur la possibilite de syncoper en fonction du tempo d'une cadence. *L'annèe Psychologique, 55*(1), 61–65.

Francès, R. (1958). *La Perception de la Musique*. Vrin.

Godøy, R. I. (2006). Gestural-sonorous objects: Embodied extensions of Schaeffer's conceptual apparatus. *Organised Sound, 11*(2), 149–157.

Grey, J. M. (1978). Timbre discrimination in musical patterns. *The Journal of the Acoustical Society of America, 64*(2), 467–472.

Harrison, P., & Pearce, M. (2020). Simultaneous consonance in music perception and composition. *Psychological Review, 127*(2), 216–244. http://dx.doi.org/10.1037/rev0000169

Helmholtz, H. L. F. (1875). *On the sensations of tone as a physiological basis for the theory of music* (trans. by A. J. Ellis). Longman.

Honing, H. (2018). On the biological basis of musicality. *Annals of the New York Academy of Sciences, 1423*(1), 51–56.

Hornbostel, E. M. (1910). Über vergleichende akustische und musikpsychologische untersuchungen. *Zeitschrift für Angewandte Psychologie, 3*, 465–487.

Hornbostel, E. M. (1926). Handbuch der normalen und pathologischen physiologie. In A. Bethe (Ed.), *Handbuch der normalen und pathologischen physiologie* (Vol. XI) (pp. 701–730). Springer.

Hornbostel, E. M., & Sachs, C. (1914). Systematik der musikinstrumente. *Zeitschrift Für Ethnologie, 46*, 55–90.

Jones, M. R. (1976). Time, our lost dimension: Toward a new theory of perception, attention, and memory. *Psychological Review, 83*(5), 323–355.

Koffka, K. (1935). *Principles of gestalt psychology*. Harcourt.

Koza, J. E. (2021). *"Destined to fail": Carl Seashore's world of eugenics, psychology, education, and music*. University of Michigan Press.

Krueger, J. (2009). Enacting musical experience. *Journal of Consciousness Studies, 16*(2–3), 98–123.

Krumhansl, C. L. (1990). *Cognitive foundations of musical pitch*. Oxford University Press.

Lach, R. (1921). Gestaltunbestimmtheit und gestaltmehrdeutigkeit in der musik: Bei-und nachträge zu höflers abhandlung "tongestalten und lebende gestalten". In A. Höfler (Ed.), *Naturwissenschaft Und Philosophie: Vier Studien Zum Gestaltungsgesetz-2. Tongestalten und lebende Gestalten* (pp. 127–154). Alfred Hölder.

Lahdelma, I., & Eerola, T. (2020). Cultural familiarity and musical expertise impact the pleasantness of consonance/dissonance but not its perceived tension. *Scientific Reports*, *10*(8693). https://doi.org/https://doi.org/10.1038/s41598-020-65615-8

Laske, O. E. (1973). In search of a generative grammar for music. *Perspectives of New Music*, *12*(1/2), 351–378.

Leman, M. (1993). Symbolic and subsymbolic description of music. In G. Haus (Ed.), *Music processing* (pp. 119–164). Oxford University Press.

Leman, M. (1997). *Music, gestalt, and computing: Studies in cognitive and systematic musicology* (pp. 42–56). Springer.

Leman, M. (1999). Relevance of neuromusicology for music research. *Journal of New Music Research*, *28*(3), 186–199.

Leman, M. (2000). An auditory model of the role of short-term memory in probe-tone ratings. *Music Perception: An Interdisciplinary Journal*, *17*(4), 481–509.

Leman, M. (2007). *Embodied music cognition and mediation technology*. MIT Press.

Leman, M., & Carreras, F. (1996). The self-organization of stable perceptual maps in a realistic musical environment. *Journées d'Informatique Musicale*, île de Tatihou, France.

Leman, M., & Carreras, F. (1997). Testing the hypothesis of psychoneural isomorphism by computer simulation. In M. Leman (Ed.), *Music, gestalt and computing: Studies in cognitive and systematic musicology* (pp. 144–168). Springer.

Leman, M., Maes, P.-J., Nijs, L., & Van Dyck, E. (2018). What is embodied music cognition? In R. Bader (Ed.), *Springer handbook of systematic musicology* (pp. 747–760). Springer.

Lerdahl, F., & Jackendoff, R. S. (1983). *A generative theory of tonal music*. MIT press.

Lerdahl, F., & Krumhansl, C. L. (2007). Modeling tonal tension. *Music Perception: An Interdisciplinary Journal*, *24*(4), 329–366.

Lindley, M. (1980). Mersenne on keyboard tuning. *Journal of Music Theory*, *24*(2), 167–203.

Lohri, A., Carral, S., & Chatziioannou, V. (2011). Combination tones in violins. *Archives of Acoustics*, *36*(4), 727–740.

Mace, D. T. (1970). Marin Mersenne on language and music. *Journal of Music Therapy*, *14*(1), 2–34.

Mathiesen, T. J. (1999). *Apollo's lyre: Greek music and music theory in antiquity and the Middle Ages*. University of Nebraska Press.

Mersenne, M. (1636). *Harmonie universelle: Contenant la théorie et la pratique de la musique*. Editions du centre national de la recherche scientifique.

Meyer, L. B. (1956). *Emotion and meaning in music*. Chicago University Press.

Moran, N. (2013). Music, bodies and relationships: An ethnographic contribution to embodied cognition studies. *Psychology of Music*, *41*(1), 5–17.

Näätänen, R., & Picton, T. (1987). The N1 wave of the human electric and magnetic response to sound: A review and an analysis of the component structure. *Psychophysiology*, *24*(4), 375–425.

Nattiez, J.-J. (1977). Under what conditions can one speak of the universals of music? *The World of Music*, *19*(1/2), 92–105.

Naveda, L., & Leman, M. (2009). A cross-modal heuristic for periodic pattern analysis of samba music and dance. *Journal of New Music Research*, *38*(3), 255–283.

Newton, I. (1687). *Philosophiæ naturalis principia mathematica (mathematical principles of natural philosophy*. Royal Society, London.

Palmer, C., & Krumhansl, C. L. (1987). Pitch and temporal contributions to musical phrase perception: Effects of harmony, performance timing, and familiarity. *Perception & Psychophysics*, *41*(6), 505–518.

Papadopoulos, A. (2002). Mathematics and music theory: From Pythagoras to Rameau. *The Mathematical Intelligencer*, *24*(1), 65–73. https://doi.org/10.1007/BF03025314

Parncutt, R. (2007). Systematic musicology and the history and future of Western musical scholarship. *Journal of Interdisciplinary Studies of Music*, *1*(1), 1–32.

Parncutt, R., & Hair, G. (2018). A psychocultural theory of musical interval: Bye bye Pythagoras. *Music Perception*, *35*(4), 475–501. https://doi.org/https://doi.org/10.1525/mp.2018.35.4.475

Patel, A. D. (2010). *Music, language, and the brain*. Oxford University Press.

Phillips-Silver, J., & Trainor, L. J. (2005). Feeling the beat: Movement influences infant rhythm perception. *Science*, *308*(5727), 1430.

Povel, D. J. (1977). Temporal structure of performed music: Some preliminary observations. *Acta Psychologica*, *41*(4), 309–320.

Rahn, J. (1994). Musical transformation and musical intuition: Eleven essays in honour of David Lewin. In R. Atlas & M. Chelan (Eds.), *Musical transformation and musical intuition: Eleven essays in honour of David Lewin* (pp. 225–235). Ovenbird Press.

Rameau, J.-P. (1722). *Traité de l'harmonie reduite à ses principes naturels: Divisé en quatre livres*. Ballard.

Repp, B. H. (1990). Patterns of expressive timing in performances of a Beethoven minuet by nineteen famous pianists. *The Journal of the Acoustical Society of America*, *88*(2), 622–641.

Risset, J.-C. (2004). The liberation of sound, art-science and the digital domain: Contacts with Edgard Varèse. *Contemporary Music Review*, *23*(2), 27–54.

Roads, C., & Strawn, J. (1985). *Foundations of computer music*. MIT Press.

Roads, C., & Wieneke, P. (1979). Grammars as representations for music. *Computer Music Journal*, *3*(1), 48–55.

Rossignol, S., Rodet, X., Soumagne, J., Collette, J.-L., & Depalle, P. (1999). Automatic characterisation of musical signals: Feature extraction and temporal segmentation. *Journal of New Music Research*, *28*(4), 281–295.

Ruwet, N. (1972). *Langage, musique, poésie*. Editions du Seuil.

Sauveur, J. (1701). *Principes d'acoustique et de musique: Ou, système général des intervalles des sons*. Editions Minkoff.

Schneider, A. (2018). Springer handbook of systematic musicology. In R. Bader (Ed.), *Springer handbook of systematic musicology* (pp. 1–24). Springer. https://doi.org/10.1007/978-3-662-55004-5

Seashore, C. E. (1915). The measurement of musical talent. *The Musical Quarterly*, *1*(1), 129–148.

Seashore, C. E. (1938). *Psychology of music*. McGraw-Hill.

Shaffer, L. H. (1981). Performances of Chopin, Bach, and Bartok: Studies in motor programming. *Cognitive Psychology*, *13*(3), 326–376.

Slododa, J. A. (1985). *The musical mind: The cognitive psychology of music*. Oxford University Press.

Stumpf, C. (1898). Konsonanz und dissonanz. *Revue Philosophique de La France Et de l'Etranger*, *46*, 184–188.

Stumpf, C. (1926). Zur physik und physiologie der sprachlaute. In C. Stumpf (Ed.), *Die sprachlaute* (pp. 349–373). Springer.

Swanson, L. R. (2016). The predictive processing paradigm has roots in Kant. *Frontiers in Systems Neuroscience*, *10*, 79.

Tenney, J. (1988). *A history of consonance and dissonance*. Excelsior.

Todd, N. (1985). A model of expressive timing in tonal music. *Music Perception: An Interdisciplinary Journal*, *3*(1), 33–57.

Todd, N., & Loy, G. (1991). *Music and connectionism*. MIT Press.

Trainor, L. J., McDonald, K. L., & Alain, C. (2002). Automatic and controlled processing of melodic contour and interval information measured by electrical brain activity. *Journal of Cognitive Neuroscience, 14*(3), 430–442.

Weber, M. (1997). Empiricism, gestalt qualities, and determination of style: Some remarks concerning the relationship of Guido Adler to Richard Wallaschek, Alexius Meinong, Christian von Ehrenfels, and Robert Lach. In M. Leman (Ed.), *Music, gestalt, and computing: Studies in cognitive and systematic musicology* (pp. 42–56). Springer.

Wessel, D. L. (1979). Timbre space as a musical control structure. *Computer Music Journal, 3*(2), 45–52.

Zarlino, G. (1968). *The art of counterpoint: Part three of le istitutioni harmoniche, 1558* (trans. by G. A. Marco & C. V. Palisca). Yale University Press.

Zbikowski, L. M. (2002). *Conceptualizing music: Cognitive structure, theory, and analysis*. Oxford University Press.

3   Empirical Music Research in the 21st Century

To move on from the historical context of music and science, let us attempt to clarify the specialist disciplinary terms that are related to this broad area and then focus on the distinctive elements that define contemporary music and its scientific research.

In the late 1990s, the music scholarship that used methods from the sciences and social sciences carried different labels such as cognitive musicology, music cognition, psychomusicology, and empirical musicology. Tracing back the logic of these terms highlights the historical and geographical trends (Parncutt, 2007), where European tradition produced distinctly different terms, mainly *systematic musicology* from German 'Systematische Musikwissenschaft', whereas North American scholarship adopted *music cognition* and *cognitive musicology* due to closer links with the cognitive sciences and the pioneering work of other American scholars involved in language cognition. *Empirical musicology*, though very much favoured by some American scholars such as David Huron and David Butler (the pair founded the journal *Empirical Musicology Review* in 2004), has been boosted by British scholars Eric Clarke and Nicholas Cook (2004), although the idea that this field is the only empirical one in music scholarship has naturally encountered resistance (e.g., Becker, 2009; Huovinen, 2009). The rise of empiricism in music research has been characterised in a more diplomatic fashion by David Huron. He concedes that 'empirical' is not only under the umbrella of science but is equally present in social sciences and in the humanities – to some extent. But it is an organic part of music scholarship that is 'motivated by the desire to learn as much as possible from information available to us' (Huron, 1999, p. 29).

Marc Leman's definition of musicology as a 'science of musical content processing' (Leman, 2003) also marries the values of sciences to music scholarship by grounding it in the evidence coming from computational modelling, psychology, and biology. This call for the general reorientation of musicology was not as persuasive as it could have been since the tone of his writing was rather provocative. Leman characterised the opposite approach in musicology as 'post-modernist verbal gymnastics and endless introspective argumentation about the justification of personal musical experiences' (sec. 3.1). Nevertheless, Marc Leman explicitly linked scientific approaches and how the insights from these need to be embedded

DOI: 10.4324/9781003293804-3

in a cultural environment. In other words, he espoused the view that an individual interacts with his physical and cultural environment and that these interactions are governed by different timescales and processes. Music scholarship should study how the different domains and conditions (sensory, cognitive, affective, motoric) work to enable listeners and performers to engage in this multifaceted phenomenon we call music. Although Leman's call for a change in the direction of music scholarship was perhaps overly strongly worded as a fair description of some of the extremes with which humanities researchers can engage in their research, it also challenged those who already worked within the sciences to take culture and its complexity more seriously.

Whereas Huron and Leman have stressed the possibilities brought by the methods and approaches adopted from the sciences to music research, Richard Parncutt offers a useful comparison of the values and aims of these broad scholarship pathways in his analysis of systematic musicology:

> Scientific systematic musicology, or simply scientific musicology, is primarily empirical and data-oriented. It involves empirical psychology and sociology, acoustics, physiology, neurosciences, cognitive sciences, and computing and technology. These various strands are united by epistemologies and methods that are characteristic of the sciences.
>
> (Parncutt, 2007, p. 5)

Parncutt draws attention to the fact that *scientific musicology* attempts to understand general questions about music: what is music, why are we obsessed with it, how does it work in general; whereas *humanistic musicology* (historical musicology and ethnomusicology) aims to understand the specific issues of music: how is this piece of music composed, what is the context of the composition or the specific performance and how does this context (social, musical, situational) influence the interpretation, reception, and promotion of the music. It is useful to distinguish these opposite aims of different approaches (see also Honing, 2006; Huron, 1999). The term *systematic musicology* has perhaps generated more confusion in English-speaking countries than the field has been able to solve. In systematic musicology, the term systematic stands for consisting of multiple *systems* (in other words, the term should be *systemic musicology*) as it captures a complex interacting system of subdisciplines (Parncutt, 2007; Schneider, 1993). This nuance is lost on the critics of the term, who feel that any scholarly discipline must be systematic in order to be credible and carry out research in an orderly and organised fashion. Parncutt suggests that the best revision of systematic musicology would be *scientific musicology*, although he concludes that this term is saddled with negative connotations from the war of 'two cultures' characterised by Charles Snow (1959). I would assume that the opposition of the humanities and sciences has at least partially evaporated as scholarship within science and humanities has become more multicultural and interdisciplinary (Van Dijck, 2003; Van Noorden et al., 2015) since the 1960s, but these views may still be embedded in the training and values held by many active scholars. There have also been notable promoters of dialogue between the humanities and social sciences; Adam Ockelford (Ockelford, 2013; Ockelford & Welch, 2020) uses intentionality and influence in communication to bind together meaning and psychological processes involving music. His tracing of musical development, and what constitutes exceptional musical abilities, utilises a close reading of observations and experiments and spans the divide between the sciences and humanities. Ockelford captured his notion of how sonic elements operate in his *zygonic theory*, where the label itself is a nod to similarity and imitation as it is derived from the Greek word 'zygon', meaning yoke and suggesting the union of two similar items. This theory draws from imitation and elaborates how the communication of affect is achieved through musical structures, and describes how narratives are constructed through patterns of sound; and these operations can be traced empirically from compositions and improvisations, as well as from musical interactions between children and adults.

Scientific vs Humanistic Musicology

To illuminate the distinctions between the two paradigms of scientific musicology and humanistic musicology, let us compare their goals, topics, methods, and approaches and also refer to the relevant disciplines (Table 3.1).

In this summary, the difference between scientific and humanistic musicology lies in the goals of scholarship activities: whereas the former attempts to identify and model – and thereby understand – the laws and regularities of how we process music, humanistic musicology attempts to delve deeper into the details and specifics, and determine how each individual constructs meanings and values for the specific musical activities that are deeply situated and contextualised. The topics are therefore also different and often read as the curriculum syllabus of a music degree, where the dominant part is usually allocated to styles and traditions including musical techniques, with occasional courses of perception or the meaning or social issues of music. It is perhaps trivial to point out here that proponents of scientific and humanistic musicology agree that the distinct topics outlined earlier

Table 3.1 Focus of attention in humanistic and scientific musicology.

	Humanistic musicology	Scientific musicology
Goal	Detailed understanding of subjective phenomena	Derive laws, explain phenomena objectively
Topics	Styles, composers, works, performers, traditions, values	Perception, comprehension, origins, how elements of music operate
Methods	From history, anthropology, and culture studies	From social sciences (psychology) and sciences (acoustics, neuroscience)
Approach	Case-oriented, descriptive, theory-generating, data-oriented (interpretative)	Data-oriented (inferential), theory-testing
Disciplines	Music history, music theory and analysis, cultural musicology	Music psychology, systematic musicology, empirical musicology, psychoacoustics

may be closely linked; how we perceive music may have shaped the way music tends to be created and performed, or vice versa, the way we perform or create music may have shaped the way we decode and extract meaningful units from sonic structures. Nevertheless, scholarship activities do not tend to bridge the gap as a rule, because it is not only the topics and perspectives that drive a wedge between the two; the values of how to get reliable information about these topics through methods and approaches are the real driver of the distinction. In scientific musicology, methods tend to be borrowed from other disciplines such as psychology, linguistics, or acoustics, whereas humanistic musicology owes a great deal to methods in history, anthropology, and cultural studies. To be fair to humanistic musicology, music analysis is an exception since it is unique to music, although it bears some semblances to the analysis of Western texts, architecture, or paintings.

Moving onto the differences of approach across the two perspectives, scientific musicology stresses the importance of data and uses it to critically test claims and theories, whereas humanistic musicology tends to build a narrative around case studies as the best way of providing an explanation for the phenomenon in question. Humanistic musicology usually does not seek to test or reject competing theories. Instead, it often proceeds to propose new or potential explanations or analogues that enable scholars to capture more nuances of the complex reality that is being tackled. One implication of this difference is that scientific musicology tends to be incremental and progressive, where past theories get replaced with newer ones, whereas humanistic musicology typically builds chronological networks of ideas that represent past endeavours as a narrative and engages in critical evaluation of the success of the past theories or ideas, but this is done conceptually rather than empirically. Although historians of science have advocated that scientific progress is not linear but takes place through a paradigm of revolutions (Kuhn, 1962), the rationale that the more recent theories are more accurate than the old ones holds true for scientific progress. Note that the use of computers, so-called objective measurements, or statistical analyses, do not ensure or even imply objectivity as such, since all these steps are subject to interpretation, biases, and other issues such as selectivity. To claim so would be to fall into the 'lure of objectivity' as Rieder and Röhle have dubbed the tendency to bring measurements into the digital humanities (Röhle, 2012). Here the purpose is not to claim that everything on the side of musicology is subjective and the other objective, but to highlight the emphasis and tendency by which the two musicologies have a set of contrasting values of scholarship.

The table describing the two musicologies paints a rather simplified picture of the fundamental differences between them in terms of their aims, goals, and approaches. The substantial differences stem from values that are much more deeply rooted in the principles of scholarship and philosophy of science, such as realism, naturalism, or reductionism. Some of these concepts, such as reductionism, have strong negative connotations in the humanities, and there are examples in music theory where opposites such as complexity or holism are promoted (Rahn, 1983, p. 197). To make headway into the differences, it is worth discussing some of the epistemological concepts briefly. Scientific musicology subscribes to *realism*, which is a framework in which the material world exists despite human perception and consciousness. The material world is very much tangible (music that we hear is the movement of molecules in the air that is transferred to our brain through a series of mechanical operations), and *epistemological realism* assumes that we can gain solid knowledge of all sorts of physical, chemical, and biological processes that rule all aspects of this reality. *Naturalism* is a related notion, where the world is governed by natural laws that can be discovered by science. The laws are complex and embedded into systems and subsystems, but these can still be described, understood, and captured by specific principles, laws, and models. In essence, naturalism uses the scientific method and empirical observation – including controlled experiments and modelling – to make progress in understanding the ways in which the natural world operates. This is the standard paradigm in social sciences and therefore a fundamental part of scientific musicology. Naturalism necessitates that the question and scope of the investigation are reduced to deal with the details of the issue without getting confused and hampered by other, usually broader issues. This narrowing of the focus of research is the source of much criticism from humanities scholarship community and usually goes under the label of *reductionism* or *positivism*. In other words, reduction of complex topics risks overgeneralising, where something is established as true for a population, but it is not necessarily true to everyone, as any music phenomenon generally is shaped by culture and environment.

Instead of valuing reductionism for its ability to eliminate unnecessary factors masking the research question, humanistic scholarship sees reductionism as something that merely reduces a question or phenomenon into smaller elements and pursues solutions to these without being able to account for the whole complex issue as a holistic entity. This type of critique of reductionism accuses it of boiling everything down into physics, and any attempt to resolve issues at higher levels (chemical, biological, cognitive, cultural) is just not going to be useful. This is of course an exaggeration of how reductionism is normally used in social sciences, where it is simply utilised to deal with complex topics by reducing the number of variables or dimensions to study the essential aspects of the topic. Reductionism is merely a way of facilitating the study of a complex topic by introducing a level of control by isolating factors – or controlling the potential confounding factors – that can confuse or hide the way the core question operates. A good example in music would be the question of timbre, which is a complex, multidimensional topic. The perception of timbre has been reduced into separate dimensions such as changes in the amplitude envelope, brightness, and transients of high frequency components (Grey, 1977). These dimensions, in turn, have been separated into the physical characteristics of the signals and isolated from other factors, such as dynamics or pitch, that also influence timbre in various ways. The perceptual research of timbre initially focussed on expert listeners (Grey, 1977) but has also been expanded to include non-experts (Kendall & Carterette, 1993). Similarly, timbre was initially studied by focussing on a small number of Western instruments that were synthesised (Grey, 1977; Wessel, 1979) but later research expanded into artificial, hybrid instrument sounds that swapped the spectral envelopes of instruments (Grey

& Gordon, 1978). The act of reduction has allowed timbre research to tackle the role of timbre in perception of music in a controlled and systematic manner and has given us an understanding of how timbral contrast is able to form separate auditory streams and how instruments are able to blend or stand out. In other words, scientific musicology studying timbre has worked out the precise laws and models which have in the past been summarised as rules of thumb by classical orchestration manuals. David Huron's classic paper on the perceptual principles that underlie voice leadership is a great example of such a summary (Huron, 2001). In addition, a systematic analysis of the language and terms used in orchestration treatises has found some interesting convergence between the perceptual studies of timbre and the linguistic accounts of timbre in the tradition of classical music (Wallmark, 2019).

   Going back to reductionism, it not only operates at the level of breaking down the focus of research and sub-topics within the topics, but it has also been taken into a more concrete direction at different junctures in history. For instance, in cognitive sciences, reductionism led scholars to distinguish modules in the mind that specialise in certain functionalities (Fodor, 1983). This was inspired by a similar distinction in numerous anatomical designs of the human body. For example, the rod and cones in the eye specialise in different light conditions, are differently distributed in the retina, and serve two sets of functions ('what' versus 'where'). A discovery of areas of the brain that appear to serve a specific function (e.g., Broca's area for speech) in the 19th century is another example of a reduction operating at the level of neural mechanisms. In music and neuroscience, this has led to the search and identification of the modules and areas dedicated to processing musical information such as contour, metre, and tonality (Peretz & Coltheart, 2003). When such specialisations or modules are applied to neural processes, we have known since Lashley's experiments in the 1950s (Lashley, 1950) – where he caused lesions in rats' brains without discernible effects on their memories – that modules or memories might not be so neatly localised in the brain but distributed over the network and subject to plasticity and further learning. Nevertheless, the focus on specialised brain areas has been one of the ways that has allowed people to probe whether the elements of music are processed in localised areas in the brain. In contemporary neuroscience, the focus has moved on to study the interactions between different brain areas, taking a more holistic approach in comparison to the modular approach.

   The word epistemology refers to the theory of knowledge and is a branch of philosophy (see Williamon et al., 2021, for a recent discussion on epistemologies in empirical music research). For our purposes, it is a convenient term to describe why scientific and humanistic musicologies have an entirely different set of beliefs about where and how knowledge can be obtained. In the sciences, it is typical to adopt a stance where theories are falsified and discarded; generally, the methods are designed to poke holes in theories and claims through hypotheses, which in turn are implemented through research designs, analysed with statistics, and then interpreted with understanding of the design, hypotheses, and limitations of the study. The underlying principle of this process is to avoid pronouncing something as true if it is in reality false. The opposite tendency may be seen among humanities scholars, who will retain theories, ideas, and interpretations because they might help us to interpret the object of study. This approach is prone to amplify coincidences and chance observations, which are systematically removed in scientific methods through design, sampling, and inferential statistical reasoning. The important point to note is that humanities scholars are no less critical about their research, but their interpretative stance creates more options, narratives, and explanations, some of which turn out to be implausible, and this might be a natural consequence of having a restricted number of observations available in the first place. Much of music history provides only a very limited set of observation sources, and there is simply no way of retrieving more observations or providing more manipulations to explore the effect of different elements or factors of the theory. In these circumstances with finite or even very limited amounts of data, it is understandable that the epistemological criteria for discarding scholarly ideas would not survive if only supported ideas were kept and all unsupported ideas were discarded. However, this does not mean that this justification can and should be maintained as a principle. There are many topics in humanities musicology that could be subjected to systematic observations (e.g., music analysis, meanings of music, topic theory, gestures in music, performance practice, etc.), and computational analysis and corpus studies are one way of bridging this gap between the humanities and the sciences, which is already happening (see Chapters 9, 10 and 11 for a full account).

Scientific Musicology as a Subset of Empirical Music Research

After comparing the two paradigms in music research, let us focus more on empirical music research and what its core values are. Here, I am switching from the term scientific musicology to a broader term of *empirical music research* as it is more inclusive and allows one to focus on the approach rather than the strict disciplinary orientation. It may be that various projects in history or music theory – which are clearly within the fold of humanistic musicology – aspire to utilise empirical methods. Or strands of ethnomusicological research will need to delve into the measurement of specific aspects of performances (timing, tuning, or pitch content). In these cases, the fundamental values brought about by the term 'scientific' could work against the research objectives and values of such projects, although they would still capitalise on empirical approaches. For this reason, it is easier to call the shared area 'empirical music research' than to go for the narrower definition of scientific musicology. Note that I have opted for *empirical music research* rather than *empirical musicology* to widen the scope of the definition and to allow disciplines that are traditionally not part of musicology (e.g., psychology, acoustics) to be more easily included within the term. It is a change from a disciplinary definition to an approach-based definition. However, the intention of this emphasis is not to devalue humanistic musicology, as humanistic approaches enable us to tackle the richness and nuance of musical experiences, which are challenging to capture in a strict scientific and quantitative approach. Moreover, the interpretative humanistic approach may be able to show insights into musical phenomena that are extremely challenging or impossible to pin down using the approach advocated in scientific musicology.

Core Values of Empirical Music Research

Empirical music research can be summarised with three core values, *empirical*, *systematic*, and *objective*.

Empirical – Knowledge from Factual Evidence

Empirical simply means that the knowledge is derived from factual evidence. This evidence is usually taken from observations and converted to data through a series of steps. The data is then interpreted, which can take many forms and directions. An example from music theory which could be familiar to every student of musical techniques is that of parallel motion in perfect consonances (P5, P8) being forbidden in species counterpoint (Fux, 1725). Why are these motions deemed to be so important in vocal polyphony of the 17th century that they are strictly forbidden? Moreover, what is the evidence that suggests violating this hallowed rule will be detrimental to our appreciation or perception of music? Also, did composers utilising species counterpoint follow the rule? One possibility is that the beauty of complex polyphony can only be fully appreciated when the listener can hear that there are all these distinct voices in the music. Parallel fifths and octaves tend to sound like they are just a single voice, since they have the tendency to be perceptually fused, which will lose the identity of at least one voice and therefore diminish the overall aim of the composition. If the aesthetics of the genre dictate that the four parts should always be perceptible, then avoiding unisons, octaves, fifths, and motion within these intervals is essential. In a simple empirical experiment, David Huron (1989) demonstrated that listeners actually have great difficulty tracking separate voices if there are more than three concurrent voices. Empirical evidence from one non-Western culture has also demonstrated that perfect fourths, fifths, and octaves are perceived as fused by members of the Tsimane tribe living in the Bolivian rainforest (McPherson et al., 2020). The Tsimane, however, did not prefer these consonant intervals over other intervals, which is in stark contrast to Western culture. In other words, the basic rule of species counterpoint can be explained by the need to maximise the identity of separate voices (to avoid fusion), and there is some empirical support for this claim. Of course, it would also be possible to collect empirical data on how frequently parallel movements in perfect fifths and octaves are avoided or present in different genres of music to probe the idea a little further, but let us leave that to the discussion of the second core principle of empirical music research.

Systematic – Knowledge from Organised and Rich Data

Systematic refers to the preference to operate using a data-rich approach to music as opposed to a data-poor approach. This dichotomy can arise from the nature of

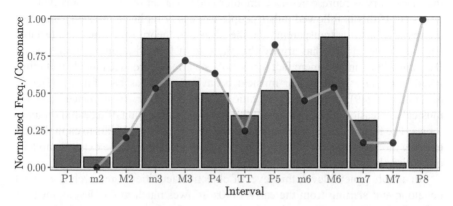

Figure 3.1 Frequency of intervals in Bach sinfonias (bars) and ratings of the consonance of
the intervals (lines, from Bowling, Purves, & Gill, 2018). Interval frequencies
recreated from Huron (2001).

the field of study, where there is either a large amount of data available or very little
data available and no hope of new data emerging from somewhere no matter how
many resources are thrown at the problem (think of Dufay's Requiem or one of the
earliest known collections of polyphonic Western music, a collection known as *The
Winchester Troper*). The data should be set up and collected in a logical, organised
fashion that directly addresses the question posed without any intervening issues
or variables. If we retain here the same example of how the motions of certain
intervals are avoided in species counterpoint, we could look at the actual music and
seek to dispel or corroborate the idea that the perfect fifth and fourth intervals mask
the identity of the independent voices and are therefore largely missing in species
counterpoint. A systematic interval count of all J. S. Bach's three-part sinfonias,
as shown in Figure 3.1, reveal that Bach treated perfect fourths, fifths, and octaves
differently in his compositions (Huron, 1991). To be more precise, intervals tend
to be used as a function of their consonance. The higher the consonance, the more
frequently the intervals occur in all pieces, which is compatible with the second
rule of species counterpoint, which suggests that simultaneous voices should 'go
together'. However, the maximally consonant intervals – octave, unison, fifths, and
fourths – do not actually fit this pattern, since they are significantly less common
than their consonance values suggest. This could be interpreted as supporting the
claim that parallel movements for the most consonant intervals are avoided because
those would violate perceptual clarity.

Objective – Knowledge Through Replicable Steps

When we talk about the objective, we refer to our ability to formalise and reproduce the analysis and all the steps that make up the research. In empirical music
research, all claims can be checked to verify their correctness. This often means

that the theory is represented as computer code or a set of clear axioms that can be tested. If this is followed, other people can easily replicate the study findings, the research itself is transparent, and the ideas and theories presented are testable and falsifiable. Honing has argued that the role of formalisation has been pivotal (Honing, 2006) and the mere fact that scholars started to produce models that mimicked different aspects of our musical behaviours such as beat finding (Desain & Honing, 1989), musical segmentation (Bod, 2002), or performance rules for musical expression (Friberg et al., 2000) led to a proliferation of research on these topics. The formalisation of research models allowed other scholars to capitalise on existing models either by building other research relying on these existing models, or by directly improving or challenging them.

On a more general level, this level of objective activities in research is a recent development; starting from the early 1990s, it owes much to the development of technology and computational tools. Once this development started and gained momentum in the first decade of the 21st century, the number of tools and available data started to accumulate rapidly. In terms of technology, it has become possible to capture various aspects of performance (e.g., the key presses in a piano, the movements of musicians, or the anatomical movements of the vocal folds and vocal tract) with detail and accuracy. Sound waves can be analysed in ever more detail to describe the physical properties of sounds, and more importantly for music, the physical properties of the sounds can be converted into psychoacoustically relevant transformations that capture the way our auditory system handles the information. The markers of a human body that performs or experiences music, such as perspiration, pulse, respiration, or brain states (electric or hemodynamic activities) can be recorded and decomposed into meaningful markers related to arousal, attention, and many other states. Some of these techniques require specialist laboratory facilities only affordable for a few institutions, but perhaps the most influential tools are the ones offered by the music information retrieval community, who have developed user-friendly software such as *music21* and *Sonic Visualiser* to deliver answers to the questions that can be answered with empirical data (see Chapters 9 and 10). In this book, I will attempt to show how some skills in programming and an understanding of the research designs involved in experiments or corpus analyses, combined with open source tools (free and available without commercial licenses), can be levied against numerous topics of great interest for humanistic musicology.

Politics and Empirical Music Research

The values of scholarship are not isolated statements as they are part of the scholarship politics of each time and place, created and upheld by institutions, disciplines, and individuals sharing these politics. However, these processes have the tendency to suffer from lack of diversity at the level of individuals in terms of their gender, race, geographical origin, or language, which will in turn keep the focus of research topics and approaches narrow. In this section, I want to address how empirical music research relates to institutional and disciplinary traditions and what these concerns about diversity are.

Institutional and Disciplinary Traditions

This may also prompt the question of why we cannot combine the best elements of the two paradigms. Before too much optimism is attached to the possibility of bridging the gap between scientific and humanistic musicology, it must be said that institutions, disciplines, departments, chairs, posts, and training is partly unwittingly and partly by choice designed to maintain and deepen such divisions. This is simply how the academic structures (university structures, conferences, scholarships, and grant councils) tend to be organised, which are meant to be helpful and focussed structures for nurturing training and research in a given area that is no larger than a cluster of few related disciplines (i.e., the core of music departments is usually music history, music theory and analysis, and music per-formance and composition). It is normal that any academic training starts with a strong sense of core disciplinary values, methods, and approaches. For this reason, one of the main challenges in bridging the gap between paradigms (humanities, social sciences, and natural sciences) is the unwieldy and unrealistic requirements of the substantial training involved in mastering the concepts and values of each paradigm. From this perspective, it would be rather foolish or impractical to define music scholarship using the broadest possible umbrella term and attempt to cover both humanistic and scientific musicology. However, it would be helpful to both students and scholars to learn and appreciate the roadmap of the territory covered by the two paradigms. Understanding where the common research topics are in terms of paradigms and disciplines would allow students to build a stronger appre-ciation of the areas and methods they study in music theory, history, or psycho-acoustics. More importantly, such a bird's-eye perspective could lead them to think about where their own thinking is headed. A slightly better position for the training of future musicologists would be to equip them with at least one scientific music-ology approach (e.g., corpus analysis or how to organise and analyse empirical behavioural experiments, both of which can be used to probe questions arising from music theory or performance) alongside the humanistic musicology training, in order to create situations where the best of both worlds could be achieved. Also, there are rich possibilities for collaborative opportunities that would bring these two paradigms together through joint PhD projects or other initiatives.

In the previous sections, I have emphasised the new elements and opportunities that empirical music research may provide towards understanding music when the values, approaches, and methods have been adapted from the sciences. However, it is only fair to add to the picture the two fundamental ways in which humanistic musicology has influenced the values and approaches of empirical music research; (1) by promoting the importance of the human subjective experience, and (2) by describing the myriad of ways in which familiarity, tradition, and ultimately cul-ture shape our interactions and processes that have to do with music. The first may be documented and observed from the inside using the so-called first-person perspective, which focusses on the phenomenology of the experience as the centre of research attention. It is rare to marry a full-blown *phenomenological approach* to empirical music research, but Eric Clarke has probably come closest to doing so in his work about ways of listening and meaning in music (2005), where he emphasises the importance of the direct information and action sound itself offers to us through the meaning it encapsulates. The zygonic theory of Adam Ockelford (2013) is another example of bringing science and humanities together on the topic of musical meaning. The second contribution has yet to be fully embraced by empirical music research, but it is the significance of culture and tradition. It has always been recognised at some level, but gradually empirical music research began to doubt the basic elements of musical processes as being immutable, as they had been defined mainly by Western music through cross-cultural comparisons in recent years (Stevens, 2012; Trehub et al., 2015). Studies involving non-Western musical traditions have highlighted the importance of putting meaning and significant cultural variation at the top of the research agenda for empirical music research, as these two issues play a fundamental role in how we perceive and process music. This already introduces the slow but steady move towards a more diverse range of research topics in empirical music research, but there is an equally important discussion to be had regarding diversity of researchers and scholarship opportunities.

Diversity of Empirical Music Research

The academic world has not been very successful so far in providing equal opportunities for people of different socioeconomic backgrounds and gender. The overall numbers do not make pleasant reading whether it is the proportion of women having tenured professorships or people representing black, Asian, minority ethnic (BAME) in academia. For example, the numbers in the UK in 2020 in the Higher Education category of 'Music, dance, drama & performing arts' show that 42.5% of academic staff are women, but only 25.4% of professors are women. And only 3.6% of staff members represent BAME in UK universities, whereas 13.9% of the population of the UK represent this broad ethnic category[1]. Clearly, there are societal and institutional barriers and blocks that have skewed these distributions towards white males. Many of the societal flaws are amplified in academia. There are several filtering systems that need to be dismantled and systematic support from society and institutions is needed to diversify both students and staff in universities. The academic environment has not yet taken sufficient steps to remove barriers from under-represented groups. For instance, many leadership opportunities have been rarer for women because of the stereotypes related to leadership styles, women have fewer role models in academia, and the UK has a problematic socioeconomic filter (high tuition fees embedded in a class society, compounded with a diverse range in the quality of schools relating to the area of living that prevents efficient widening of participation).

In the field of music psychology and music cognition, there has been a strong presence and leadership from women since the 1980s; *Helga de la Motte-Haber* cofounded the German Society of Music Psychology in 1983. *Diana Deutsch* cofounded the Society of International Conference on Music Perception and Cognition (ICMPC) in 1989 and the Society for Music Perception and Cognition in 1990. Her scholarly work pioneered many of the studies involving musical illusions (including the tritone paradox) and absolute pitch. *Carol Krumhansl* bridged the gap between music theory and cognitive sciences in her work detailing the cognitive structures of music. *Irène Deliège* founded the European Society for the Cognitive Sciences of Music (ESCOM) in 1991, developed an influential theory of cue abstraction, and tested the major theories of music theory. The editors of the main journals have recently been mainly women (Kate Stevens for *Music Perception*, Jane Ginsborg for *Musicae Scientiae*, and Alexandra Lamont for *Psychology of Music*), including the presidents of the leading societies (Renee Timmers for ESCOM, Jessica Grahn for SMPC, previously held by Elizabeth Hellmuth Margulis) so there is no shortage of excellent role models for women in this area.

It is important to stress here that while the starting point for empirical music research is more diverse than in many other disciplines and research areas, the situation could be much better in terms of scholarship opportunities and contributions outside the Anglo-American cultural region. Also, women are in the minority in technically oriented sub-disciplines such as music technology, music information retrieval, psychoacoustics, and music computing. Some actions towards increasing diversity in empirical music research are discussed in Chapter 12.

Coda

Multiple terms have been used to characterise the broad area of empirical music research; systematic musicology, music and science, scientific musicology, and cognitive musicology to summarise the main terms. This chapter has explained the background and traditions behind the different terms and argued for a broader term of *empirical music research*. This paradigm was compared to humanistic musicology, and the differences were highlighted in terms of approaches, methods, and values.

Discussion Points

1. Musicology is an established discipline in the humanities, and *empirical music research* reminds us that a part of musicology also subscribes to this scientific approach. Do you think that the labels scientific and humanistic musicology communicate the distinction well? And what could be done to create a productive and fruitful discussion about the values and approaches of these two divisions?

2. *Reductionism* was explained as something that eliminates unnecessary factors or elements from the research object and process. It is not a term often appreciated by scholars engaged in humanistic musicology, but can you think of examples where they commonly engage in reductionism? What kind of reductionism seems to be uncontroversial?

3. One of the dividing lines between scientific and humanistic approaches is the theme of *falsification*. Can musicological theories be falsified? Is the idea of being able to falsify a theory something that is relevant for understanding music?

4. Can you think of an assertion about music theory or history and whether you have been presented with empirical evidence about it? What kind of evidence was used to argue the case?

5. Sometimes in music scholarship, there are not many data to start with. Is there a danger that such topics are not valued in empirical music research because they simply cannot sustain research that utilises data-rich ideology?

6. The idea of other people being able to replicate research holds a high value for objectivity and transparency in empirical music research. Can you think of examples and areas where transparency is already established in humanistic musicology?

Note

1 Annual Population Survey, UK, www.ons.gov.uk

Further Reading

Clarke, E. F., & Cook, N. (2004). *Empirical musicology: Aims, methods, prospects*. Oxford University Press.

Huron, D. (1999). *The new empiricism: Systematic musicology in a postmodern age*. University of California.

Ockelford, A. (2013). *Applied musicology: Using zygonic theory to inform music education, therapy, and psychology research*. Oxford University Press.

References

Becker, J. (2009). Crossing boundaries: An introductory essay. *Empirical Musicology Review*, 4(2), 45–48.

Bod, R. (2002). Memory-based models of melodic analysis: Challenging the Gestalt principles. *Journal of New Music Research, 31*, 27–37.

Bowling, D. L., Purves, D., & Gill, K. Z. (2018). Vocal similarity predicts the relative attraction of musical chords. *Proceedings of the National Academy of Sciences, 115*(1), 216–221.

Clarke, E. (2005). *Ways of listening: An ecological approach to the perception of musical meaning.* Oxford University Press.

Clarke, E. F., & Cook, N. (2004). *Empirical musicology: Aims, methods, prospects.* Oxford University Press.

Desain, P., & Honing, H. (1989). The quantization of musical time: A connectionist approach. *Computer Music Journal, 13*(3), 56–66.

Fodor, J. A. (1983). *The modularity of mind: An essay on faculty psychology.* MIT Press.

Friberg, L., Colombo, V., Frydén, L., & Sundberg, J. (2000). Generating musical performances with Director Musices. *Computer Music Journal, 24*(3), 23–29.

Fux, J. J. (1725). *Gradus ad Parnassum.* Johan Peter van Ghelen.

Grey, J. M. (1977). Multidimensional perceptual scaling of musical timbres. *The Journal of the Acoustical Society of America, 61*(5), 1270–1277.

Grey, J. M., & Gordon, J. W. (1978). Perceptual effects of spectral modifications on musical timbres. *The Journal of the Acoustical Society of America, 65*(6), 149–150.

Honing, H. (2006). On the growing role of observation, formalization and experimental method in musicology. *Empirical Musicology Review, 1*(1), 2–6. https://doi.org/https://doi.org/10.18061/1811/21901

Huovinen, E. (2009). Varieties of musicological empiricism. *Empirical Musicology Review, 4*(2), 12–27.

Huron, D. (1989). Voice denumerability in polyphonic music of homogeneous timbres. *Music Perception, 6*(4), 361–382.

Huron, D. (1991). Tonal consonance versus tonal fusion in polyphonic sonorities. *Music Perception: An Interdisciplinary Journal, 9*(2), 135–154.

Huron, D. (1999). *The new empiricism: Systematic musicology in a postmodern age.* www.music-cog.ohio-state.edu/Music220/Bloch.lectures/3.Methodology.html

Huron, D. (2001). Tone and voice: A derivation of the rules of voice-leading from perceptual principles. *Music Perception, 19*(1), 1–64.

Kendall, R. A., & Carterette, E. C. (1993). Verbal attributes of simultaneous wind instrument timbres: II. Adjectives induced from piston's orchestration. *Music Perception, 10*(4), 469–502.

Kuhn, T. S. (1962). *The structure of scientific revolutions.* University of Chicago Press.

Lashley, K. S. (1950). In search of the engram. In *Society of Experimental Biology Symposium No. 4: Psychological Mechanisms in Animal Behaviour* (pp. 478–505). Cambridge University Press.

Leman, M. (2003). Foundations of musicology as content processing science. *Journal of Music and Meaning, 1*(1).

McPherson, M. J., Dolan, S. E., Durango, A., Ossandon, T., Valdés, J., Undurraga, E. A., Jacoby, N., Godoy, R. A., & McDermott, J. H. (2020). Perceptual fusion of musical notes by native Amazonians suggests universal representations of musical intervals. *Nature Communications, 11*(1), 2786. https://doi.org/https://doi.org/10.1038/s41467-020-16448-6

Ockelford, A. (2013). *Applied musicology: Using zygonic theory to inform music education, therapy, and psychology research.* Oxford University Press.

Ockelford, A., & Welch, G. (2020). *New approaches to analysis in music psychology and education research using zygonic theory: A common framework for music education and psychology research.* Routledge.

Parncutt, R. (2007). Systematic musicology and the history and future of western musical scholarship. *Journal of Interdisciplinary Studies of Music, 1*(1), 1–32.

Peretz, I., & Coltheart, M. (2003). Modularity of music processing. *Nature Neuroscience*, *6*(7), 688–691.

Rahn, J. (1983). *A theory for all music: Problems and solutions in the analysis of non-western forms*. Toronto University Press.

Röhle, B. R. T. (2012). Digital methods: Five challenges. In D. M. Berry (Ed.) *Understanding Digital Humanities* (pp. 67–84). Palgrave Macmillan.

Schneider, A. (1993). Systematische musikwissenschaft: Traditionen, ansätze, aufgaben. *Systematische Musikwissenschaft*, *1*(2), 145–180.

Snow, C. P. (1959). *The two cultures and the scientific revolution*. Cambridge University Press.

Stevens, K. (2012). Music perception and cognition: A review of recent cross-cultural research. *Topics in Cognitive Science*, *4*, 653–667.

Trehub, S. E., Becker, J., & Morley, I. (2015). Cross-cultural perspectives on music and musicality. *Philosophical Transactions of the Royal Society B: Biological Sciences*, *370*(1664), 20140096.

Van Dijck, J. (2003). After the "two cultures" toward a "(multi) cultural" practice of science communication. *Science Communication*, *25*(2), 177–190.

Van Noorden, R. et al. (2015). Interdisciplinary research by the numbers. *Nature*, *525*(7569), 306–307.

Wallmark, Z. (2019). A corpus analysis of timbre semantics in orchestration treatises. *Psychology of Music*, *47*(4), 585–605.

Wessel, D. L. (1979). Timbre space as a musical control structure. *Computer Music Journal*, *3*(2), 45–52.

Williamon, A., Ginsborg, J., Perkins, R., & Waddell, G. (2021). Performing music research: Methods in music education, psychology, and performance science. Oxford University Press.

4 Methods and Research Design

We have established that empirical music research tends to utilise methods from the natural sciences and social sciences. The purpose of these methods is to provide standards for obtaining systematic and reliable information about the phenomenon being measured. Methods are chosen to fit research questions to gather information that will deliver potential for interpretation with the possibility of gaining new insight and knowledge. If the question is whether J.S. Bach followed the rule of avoiding parallel fifths and octaves, the methodological arsenal would relate to corpus analysis, but if the question is about whether violating these rules makes the music sound more or less satisfying, the methods would relate to behavioural experiments. In both cases, there are similar steps to choosing the appropriate methods and approaches, which include defining the design and sample, collecting observations, transferring them into data, and making inferences about that data. All these steps fall into methods and are typically well regulated in terms of how to use them appropriately.

The arsenal of possible methods is bewildering for a novice, and there are some appealing ones that lure researchers into using them even if they are not the optimal one for the research question. Sometimes a method becomes popular just because it is easy to perform (e.g., counting pitch-classes in scores, extracting timbral descriptors of a performance, or capturing body movements of musicians) or because it promises to deliver an objective and direct index of the desired property, such as the *Galvanic Skin Response* (GSR) that taps into stress and arousal levels, or *priming* that can deliver a measure of automatic processing or implicit memory. Of course, the methods themselves should never control or lead the research questions; rather, they are chosen to provide critical evidence for the chosen research question. It is not uncommon in this field to exploit multiple methods to address the same question. For certain topic areas such as music and emotions, this is not only common but a necessity; the object of research is a multifaceted phenomenon and the evidence from one method alone cannot give sufficient information. For example, to understand how music induces emotions, it is useful to measure autonomic responses such as the GSR, which is sensitive to subtle changes in arousal levels (through increased perspiration, detectable within a few seconds on the skin of the hand). However, significant increases in GSR

DOI: 10.4324/9781003293804-4

levels when listening to music do not tell us whether the participant is getting anxious, scared, or very happy, all of which could drive up the levels of perspiration as an index of higher arousal. The best way to find out what the participant is actually experiencing in this situation is to ask them to report their emotional experience, which is typically done using a previously validated instrument, a set of scales characterising the potential emotions (e.g., 'How happy do you feel at this moment? Please answer using a scale between 1 and 7, where 1 is not at all and 7 is maximal happiness'). This is an example of a typical scheme where an objective measure is coupled with a subjective measure to aid the researchers' interpretation arising from the objective measures. Sometimes the emphasis is the opposite, and the main findings concern the results about a subjective measure, and the objective measures serve to corroborate and support the interpretation obtained from the subjective measures. It is also possible to add more measures to the same research paradigm (e.g., following the emotion example, automatic detection of emotions from facial expressions could be used as an objective verification of the emotion experienced, or the participants might be asked to complete a task that indirectly measures their mood).

In the following sections, many of the common methods and measures will be presented and explained. Despite the variety and perhaps complexity surrounding methods in general, the good news is that these methods are very prescriptive. Each method comes with a tradition and guidance on how they work, and on how the data is collected and analysed. Reporting practices usually refer to standard tools or ways of dealing with measures and approaches, along with analysis operations. It pays off to be conservative about the methods and rely on the accumulated knowledge of scholars on how to measure and report something in a reliable manner and leave the innovation to the actual research questions.

Research Process

In empirical music research, there are distinct stages of the research process, as in any scholarly research process. This process is summarised in Figure 4.1, where a researcher starts with an idea and usually after some thinking and reading about past research around the topic, the idea is formulated as a *research question*. The question or series of questions guides what kind of answers are appropriate for the question, and this is where the *research design* comes into play. The design is a crucial step that dictates what kind of answer you can provide to the research question. If the research is open and explorative, you are going to get answers that give some further hints as to how the research question operates, but you are not going to get a definitive answer. Where one aspect is the reason behind a central issue, you need a *causal research design* to do that, or if there is a pattern of relations between multiple variables, their relationships can be explored with *correlational research design*. We will cover the different research designs with examples in the section Research Designs.

After deciding on the research design, you need to make a choice about the data collection methods – and more precise measures within the methods – that you are

Figure 4.1 The seven stages of the research process.

going to use. To make a wise decision, you need to assess whether your chosen method and measure can provide answers to the question within the scope of the design. Once these steps have been defined, and any empirical parts have been set up and piloted, it is time to *collect the observations* (also known as the raw data), which are then subjected to quality control and eventually transformed into the actual data through a series of decisions. The *data analysis* follows the research design, where you may explore the links between the measures as in the correlational design, or test the hypothesis set up as in the causal design. In addition, the relevant analytical operations that will deliver the answers to the question will need to be defined. After the analysis comes the exciting part, *interpretation*, which also contextualises the findings within past research, the research design, methods, sample and type, and the limitations involved in all these elements. Finally, this interpretation is transformed into insight and knowledge. In most cases, the newly obtained knowledge is communicated through reporting, which warrants its own description in Chapter 8. To close the loop, the incremental research processes tend to feed the newly gained insights back into the research questions, and the cycle can be done again with better ideas, improved scope, better measures, new tests, revised assumptions, and enhanced analyses.

There are situations in research where you do not get to plan all the steps of the research process. You might stumble upon an existing dataset (terabytes of videos, spreadsheets detailing millions of onsets in a musical corpus, hundreds of survey responses, stacks of interview transcriptions, folders of field observation notes, or gigabytes of functional Magnetic Resonance Imaging data matrices). A central challenge then is to devise an analysis strategy that can latch onto relevant aspects of the data in a way that tackles a meaningful research question. In this sense, most of the data is usually raw data, just observations, and only when you have carefully defined what the question and scope of the study are going to be, can you turn the observations into actual data. Needless to say, it is better to have this process formulated before obtaining the observations, because only the research question can tell you what kind of data is needed, what the relevant design is and what analyses will provide answers. But the world of research tends to offer opportunities for tapping into interesting sets of observations, so it is not completely unheard of to start in the middle of the research process and try to pedal back to the question. Additionally, there is a research design that purposefully locks most parts of the research process to corroborate or challenge past work. This type of research, called a *replication study*, is extremely useful and is an important part of empirical research that has increased the quality of research in recent years. Replication studies hold the potential to weed out anomalous, unusual studies, or those with unlikely results. We will return to this topic briefly in the research transparency section, since replicability is one of the best ways to increase the transparency of research steps.

Research Conduct and Ethics

Society regulates research through legislation and various agreements and agreements that bind scholars working at the universities and research institutions. These agreements typically state that universities are committed to maintaining the highest standards of rigour and integrity in all aspects of research, and these standards are laid out in a series of Codes of Practices and Toolkits. These in turn assume that all researchers are made aware of the research integrity requirements and are trained appropriately. For students at different levels, institutions have different policies concerning ethics, but generally the same rules apply, although the supervisor of the student is assumed to be responsible for research integrity.

Empirical research involving other people is always subject to ethical approvals and ethical considerations. All universities will have local ethics regulators that govern ethics approvals (e.g., *Institutional Review Boards* in the US and *University Research Ethics Committees* in the UK). The forms and instructions tend to vary across the boards and committees in universities and countries, but the broad principles are similar: do not cause harm, do not lie or deceive, be honest, tell participants what the study is about, and give them full information about the study in order to allow them to volunteer for the study with their full informed consent. There are numerous restrictions that deal with data protection and privacy that stem from legislation, and some research designs and methods are subject to specialist boards or professional boards of regulators, such as medical ethics, clinical psychology, or working with vulnerable participants. Reading the guidelines and seeking examples of what can be done under the guidelines are the first steps to take when tackling ethics approvals.

Ethics do not stop with collecting observations. They also dictate how the observations are stored, processed, and retained, who can access them, and in what contexts the data can be used and with what restrictions. Providing anonymity to participants is often high in the priorities of ethics protocols, and working with vulnerable participants or sensitive topics requires special attention and processes. Further stages of research, analysis, and reporting are also subject to research integrity requirements that mainly concern honesty and trustworthiness of research. Many of these issues can be handled by being open and transparent about the research data, methods, and interpretations. How this is accomplished warrants a separate section because it is particularly important for any high quality research project.

Research Transparency

In addition to research integrity requirements, contemporary research is putting extra emphasis on holding scholars accountable for their work. The early 2010s have witnessed a crisis in terms of reliability, transparency, and actual robustness of the results in empirical research that has damaged the reputation of psychology, biology, and especially social psychology (Baker, 2016). Many studies in these fields have failed when another research group has attempted to replicate the study. *Replication* means that one reruns the whole study in a new setting, with identical design and technical setup, using the same measures and analyses as in the original study, but, of course, with new participants. The failure to replicate many pivotal studies has cast a shadow over the methods, theories, and interpretations. For example, about 50% of the studies failed to be replicated in the so-called *Many Labs 2* project (Klein et al., 2018) that set out to replicate 28 classic published findings. When the journal *Nature* asked more than 1,500 scholars (Baker, 2016), most of them reported that they do not trust published results due to the lack of transparency. About 70% of the scholars surveyed had tried to replicate the work of another scientist and failed to establish the original results. It has often been the case that published research cannot even be replicated since crucial study details (instructions, or detailed information about the methods and analyses) have not been documented sufficiently. Another reason for the poor replication track record is the pressure to publish and specifically to publish positive results, which leads to selective reporting and other questionable practices that lead to studies being published that were originally entirely different experiments. For all these reasons, major initiatives in the empirical sciences have been launched to address the crisis. These ideas to improve reproducibility were first formulated within the computer sciences, but later spread to biosciences and then to social sciences (Asendorpf et al., 2013; Tomasello & Call, 2011).

Reproducible research initiatives have taken many forms, but *Open Data*, *Open Materials*, and *Registered Reports*, and accessible, permanent repositories for the data, materials, and preregistrations such as in the Open Science Framework are the major elements that currently enable the change. Open Data and Open Materials mean that all data and the steps taken to collect and analyse the data are published in an open access format in one of the accepted, reliable open repositories. Open repositories such as Open Science Framework, Harvard Dataverse, UK Data Service, Zenodo, FigShare, or Data Dryad are much better than institutional repositories, individual homepages, or cloud services linked to commercial solutions. Open repositories are transparent in the way they handle all materials; they log details of the uploads, and keep track of versions and updates, and they conform to the publisher and funder requirements for the preservation and availability of the data, while also logging usage, ensuring long-term sustainability, and offering permanent links. The materials in these repositories are also citable, easy to find, and they can be linked to the unique researcher identifier, which is an alphanumeric code known as *ORCID*, Open Researcher and Contributor ID.

It is worth mentioning here that the academic community is not only offering tools and repositories, but many funders require that you release all collected data as open data for the research they have funded. In addition, an increasing number of journals have begun to require open data and open material data. The Center for Open Science has created a series of badges to give compliant research more visibility and to raise awareness of these issues. If we relate transparency to the research process (see Figure 4.1), much of the process is actually covered by these transparency initiatives (design and methods in *preregistrations*, *open data* for observations, and *open materials* for analysis). This movement was preceded by the Open Access initiative, which covers the final parts of the process and advocates for communicating research online for free.

Open Data and Open Materials

In empirical music research, transparency works well in tandem with the core principles of being objective and systematic, where either the central elements of the model are formalised as explicit computational models or the full workflow of the empirical research is done in a transparent fashion using Open Data and Open Materials. Furthermore, the idea of replication has been acknowledged for some years already and may be seen as part of the self-correction process in scientific work. The specialist journals in this field do advocate replication studies and have published special issues dedicated to replication studies (*Musicae Scientiae* vol. 17 in 2013, Frieler et al., 2013) or Open Science in Musicology (e.g., *Empirical Musicology Review* vol. 16 in 2021, see Moss & Neuwirth, 2021). There are also other benefits to operating transparently and following the reproducible research paradigm. Reproducible research facilitates collaboration and is helpful in detecting errors, as well as in encouraging learning and trying new things (Sandve et al., 2013). Transparency forces you to think harder about your research, since preregistration, for example, puts emphasis on detailed design, method, and analysis plans and decisions in advance. This often elevates the quality of research since you double check whether all elements line up (i.e., whether the research question, the methods, the specific analysis options, and the inference that can be drawn from these still provide the desired evidence about the question and whether there is an alternative explanation that needs to be addressed within the design, and so on). There is also some evidence that transparency and sharing details openly also help add visibility to research (Piwowar et al., 2007).

In my own work I have found reproducible research principles to be useful in supervisions and collaborations. It has been something that I have been doing intuitively at some level since 2003 when releasing the first computational toolbox online (Eerola & Toiviainen, 2003). Over the last decade, I have routinely released all datasets that I have collected, using either Harvard Dataverse, Open Science Framework (OSF) or GitHub.

More importantly, I have taken advantage of the datasets and computer codes that colleagues have released. To give you a practical example, in the late 2000s,

I wanted to explore how well the computational models that utilise audio information could predict the emotions that music expresses. By 2009, there had been a moderate number of studies – about 40 – that had collected ratings of emotions expressed by music from real, commercially released tracks of music. So, I contacted every first author of those studies published in the preceding ten years and asked if they could share the anonymised mean ratings of the expressed emotions (not the raw data) and specify the specific timings of the tracks so I could purchase and extract the acoustic features of these tracks myself. With some consternation, I discovered that only about a quarter of the authors I contacted were able to share the data. In many cases the audio and the ratings were lost (due to changes of laboratories or institutions, or the research assistants, postdocs or collaborators who had done the work were no longer available or active, and so on). I was lucky to get data from 13 different studies representing different genres of music, which I used in a rather damning evaluation of the audio-based emotion recognition modelling (Eerola, 2011). To this day I am grateful to the colleagues who shared their materials since they allowed me to leapfrog the data collection at the time, but the process also alerted me to the fact that the work we do is based on vulnerable and fragmentary practices. Reproducibility initiatives have come to address many of these issues that previously prevented the field from building knowledge in a steady manner.

To promote transparent practices, I require reproducible research from my postgraduate students. I also run replication studies as part of empirical lab work in undergraduate teaching. Replicating a published study is a great way to learn to do high-quality research, since most aspects of published studies are well thought out, explained, argued, and analysed, so you learn from good examples (Quintana, 2021). Still, there is a sense of discovery and excitement in getting the same or different results as the published study. In some cases, students come up with really insightful ideas to slightly expand the scope of an existing study, and the act of reading carefully in order to replicate all steps of a study does change their perspective for how they read and understand published studies.

Although empirical music research is well equipped to deal with recent initiatives and requirements of research transparency, this will need to be supported by instilling a significant change in the way we teach and train students to carry out research.

Preregistration

Preregistration refers to the procedure in which you submit a complete study plan with all the details (question, hypothesis, methods, data collection techniques, analysis methods, and outcome variables) to a journal or to a repository. If this submitted document is treated as a preregistration report, it can be reviewed and potentially accepted for publication prior to gathering the evidence and obtaining the results, and you receive a second round of reviews after completing the study. Some journals publish preregistration reports as they are (after a quality check).

It is also possible to deposit the preregistration plan in an open data repository as evidence of your hypotheses, outcome measures, and analysis strategies and use this light-touch approach as a supplementary file when submitting the actual study to a journal.

The purpose of the preregistration is to curb scholars from taking planned studies into other directions, perhaps rescuing a failed study by changing the angle and focussing on other variables or subsets of the data. Preregistration also helps to pin down the sample size and other details and, therefore, acts as a guard against some of the unsanctioned behaviours (p-hacking, selective reporting, or hypothesising after the results) which will be harder to follow with these controls. In case you want to know more about these operations, p-hacking refers to any activity where you manipulate the data, even seemingly innocently such as running the analysis with different subsets, covariates, or outlier detection principles, and once your *p*-values are below the accepted thresholds, you then decide that this is the analysis strategy (Simmons et al., 2011). Some social scientists think that this behaviour is caused entirely by relying on arbitrary *p*-values, and a more probabilistic (Bayesian) approach would remove the desperate hunt for *p*-values smaller than 0.05. *Hypothesising after the results have been known* ('HARKing') is estimated to be widely practised (Kerr, 1998). While there is value in being able to come up with a new solution for unexpected results, and writing guidance sometimes even advocates this type of strategy (Berm, 1987), the problem with HARKing lies in distortion of the scholarship and the potential for other problems such as advancing poor hypotheses and theories, bending statistical rules, and devaluing the worth of truly openly explorative research.

Preregistration also helps to assess the robustness of the results in a field, since preregistrations also function as a null result if no publication is found even years after the study was planned (Nosek & Lakens, 2014). Previously, the lack of evidence from these file drawer studies – and we all have a few of these – biases the evidence base when scholars only published positive results. This will slowly change as preregistration becomes more common, but there is still a long way to go and many still feel that there is a strong pressure to publish positive results since they make better news stories in journals. My own preregistration experiences are positive with both preregistrations (Eerola & Lahdelma, 2022) and registered reports (Armitage & Eerola, 2022; Lahdelma & Eerola, 2024). I feel that adhering to research integrity principles, possessing and upholding a good reputation, and documenting all details about the planned research using Open Data and other initiatives are usually sufficient precautions to keep myself from veering into any of the fishy practices. When you are forced to articulate the details of your research into the preregistration report before the data collection, it does add precision and clarity to the planning of the research. The level of detail required is like writing the full paper and therefore much more detailed than a generic research plan or proposal. Preregistration can certainly improve the research process and force you to decide aspects that you normally would not try to describe in advance (such as quality control operations, data elimination, main analyses, and auxiliary analyses).

It also has the added benefit of registering the unique research idea with the authors even if data collection takes a long time.

Restricted Materials

In music, we are often dealing with commercially released and copyrighted materials (recordings, videos, or scores) or music performances where the performers have not granted the whole world full access to their art. Sometimes, research materials come from clinical, educational, or other sensitive contexts that prevent adherence to transparency principles. However, in my experience, copyright restrictions are the most severe limitation for research aiming to discover the links between acoustic content and any semantic and subjective content (emotions). Because copyright laws prevent sharing the audio digitally or otherwise, music information research (MIR) has come up with workarounds such as using audio preview services (e.g., *7digital*) where one can access a massive (81 million tracks in the catalogue in 2020) amount of audio previews (this is usually 30 seconds of the most prominent part of the track) using a specific *application programming interface* (API). In Chapter 11, I will explain the use of API with an example analysis. Another solution is to rely on specific audio features originally calculated by an MIR company *Echo Nest*, although the features are now accessible within the Spotify API. As useful as these features are, they do not fully comply with transparency initiatives, since not all details have been released. Another workaround involves using an impressive sample of music called the Million Song Dataset (Bertin-Mahieux et al., 2011), which contains audio features and meta-data of 1,000,000 popular music tracks. Although actual audio files cannot be made available, full details of all features, genres, artists, similarities, lyrics, and other interesting information are available. A great deal of excellent research has come out of using Echo Nest features (Carlson et al., 2017; Herremans et al., 2014) and the Million Song Dataset (Mauch et al., 2015; Serrà et al., 2012). More and more relevant musical data (audio and annotations) are being released in research-friendly open-source format such as the mirdata extension for Python (we will look at these in Chapter 11).

When engaging in performance or any music research with production tasks (singing, tapping, or proper music performance), the possibilities of sharing all data are typically limited as the performers (whether they are experienced artists, children, or adult non-musicians) normally do not want all of their performances to be fully available. There are exceptions (such as the *University of Rochester Multi-Modal Music Performance Dataset*, Li et al., 2018), and it is also possible to share only a part of the dataset, for example, just the audio, but not the video, or just the annotation, but not the videos or the audio (Clayton et al., 2021). The videos can also be rendered with only postural information, which does not reveal the identities of the participants. When sharing any data involving creative practice, the principles of sharing should be documented and made clear to the musicians or participants in advance and the dignity and the rights of all involved should be retained. These discussions and guidelines are part of the ethics processes that we covered earlier.

Research Designs

The aims of research projects vary tremendously. Research design is the first and most important element to be chosen to serve the purpose of research. There is a broad menu of five research designs, which each give different emphasis to the research. In the first option, *descriptive research design*, you approach a new topic that is pristine and without much prior information, often because the topic has only recently emerged (e.g., how recommendation systems in streaming services influence music consumption). In this design, the purpose of the research is to describe what the main issues and themes that seem to be relevant under the topic are, in general, which is valuable in any early work on a new topic. In the second, *correlational research design*, you might already have definite ideas of what the main issues from the past research are, but the actual question relates to the vital associations between relevant concepts (e.g., do people who experience chills also have specific personality traits?). This type of *correlational research design* can identify new links between existing topics and diagnose contingencies that would otherwise remain undiscovered.

These two types of research, *descriptive* and *correlational* research, are both vital in many phases of research and capable of revealing novel insights into the topics. The main limitation they both have is that they cannot tell us what is causing the associations and the phenomena in the first place. This needs a separate research design, an experiment with specific manipulation to determine the cause, here labelled *causal research design*. These three research designs cover most research, but there are at least two additional, special types of research design that are important: *theoretical* and *meta-analytical*. These can be understood to be a blend of experimental and descriptive research approaches. Theoretical research aims to formulate a coherent analysis of concepts or to propose a completely new theory based on the evidence available. Meta-analysis is a special form of rigorous analysis of a particular topic using all available empirical studies as its fuel. Let us look at these five types of research design with concrete examples from empirical music research.

Descriptive Research Design

The fundamental purpose of research is to gain a better understanding of a topic. Without having the right concepts at the start, or without narrowing the scope of the study, it is difficult to comprehend the observations around the topic or articulate questions that are important. In the past centuries, there have been plenty of examples where downright wrong concepts led the research in the wrong direction (think of phrenology, the 19th century idea developed by Joseph Gall in which the contours and shape of the skull could inform us of a person's personality and mental faculties, or a musically relevant case where collectors of 19th century folk songs in

Scandinavia forced the music into major and minor modes and standardised metres even though many folk songs were modal with irregular rhythmic structures). Perhaps the danger is not really about misconstructed concepts leading you astray but just failing to diagnose the essential elements in the topic. Often these types of study can define the fundamentals of the topic, and therefore these types of research designs can be remarkably valuable.

Descriptive studies can be carried out in different ways. It is possible to do observational studies where you observe behaviours in their normal context. Interesting examples of these types of studies are observations of children's behaviour in a music classroom (Karlsson & Juslin, 2008). Another common way to obtain rich information about a specific topic is by conducting interviews. Such an approach provides you with plenty of qualitative descriptions which can be analysed further and assembled into useful themes and categories (see Chapter 6). Certain types of activities (composition or improvisation) may be quite difficult to pin down in other research settings, so explorative and descriptive approaches with interviews, observations, and variants of these techniques can be very informative. Case studies are also insightful descriptive studies, which introduce a new phenomenon. A famous example comes from neuroscience, where Isabelle Peretz described a case of acquired amusia (Peretz et al., 1998).

Case Example #1: What are chills induced by music?

An example of a personal interest would be music-induced chills. Chills are assumed to be a rare phenomenon where music seems to cause a real sensation of chills, goosebumps, tingles, shivers, or similar physical sensations. These are usually strong and distinct experiences which can reoccur when listening to the same music again. Although the topic has received some attention over the last decade, Scott Bannister, a talented PhD student who I had the good fortune to supervise, decided after his literature review that it is better to start with descriptive research. Past descriptions of chills had not been systematic and the music consumption habits of people have also altered fairly significantly over the last 10 to 15 years. Scott designed a survey charting many possible aspects of these elusive experiences. For instance, he asked what do the experiences feel like? In what kind of social and situational context do chills occur? What specific music is associated with chills? Are there any actual musical triggers that set off the chills? In this way, descriptive research design can offer critical and valuable information that enables us to pose further questions about the phenomenon. This survey study (Bannister, 2020) identified the central markers of chills and allowed Scott to assemble a sizable list of music from a variety of musical genres that can potentially induce chills in multiple people, which we thought would be a crucial element for any follow-up study.

Correlational Research Design

Correlational study design seeks to identify association between two or more concepts. For example, does the number of chills experienced during music listening relate to the personality traits (e.g., open to experiences, extraversion) people possess? To put this in the language of correlation, do number of chills and personality traits correlate? When two measurable concepts are interrelated, correlation is the quantified index of this relation. The concepts can be any measurable construct (e.g., is there an association between the level of musical expertise and the number of chills experienced?). In mathematical terms, the correlation coefficient (abbreviated in statistics as r) can be expressed between two numerical variables as a coefficient ranging from -1.00 to +1.00, where r=0.00 suggests no correlation, and numbers further away from zero suggest correlation where the sign tells you the direction of the association. The negative correlation indicates that the link between the two concepts is negative (e.g., the amount of musical practice per week and the number of errors in music performance) whereas the positive correlation coefficient tells you that both concepts move in the same way (e.g., the amount of musical practice per week and your overall motivation to perform music). The sign itself does not matter; however, the crucial issue here is the distance from 0, which indicates no correlation (zero correlation) so any number approaching +1.00 or -1.00 is a strong correlation (more about the actual size of the correlation coefficients and the associated statistics in the section titled the Relationships Between Continuous Variables).

Correlational study design can be very productive in many research topics. There are plenty of existing data that lend themselves to correlational study design (entrance exams, school performance grades, music training scores, measures of musical ability and other abilities, demographic information, data on choices and behaviours related to music, and so on). A more advanced version of a correlation study design is one where several variables are mapped into one (technically this would fall under *linear regression*, to be detailed later), which is a variant of correlation coefficients but allows several explanations to be combined to account for one central variable of interest. Another variant of the correlation study design is to identify factors underlying multiple items/concepts (*factor analysis*) such as identifying underlying emotion structures based on individual ratings of a palette of emotion terms (e.g., Eerola & Peltola, 2016) or facets of musical sophistication based on several individual statements about musical training and interest (e.g., Müllensiefen et al., 2014).

The main shortcoming in the design of the correlation study is that, in the end, the correlation cannot support any causal explanation between the concepts. In other words, the identified association cannot be claimed to be the cause of the other concept. There could always be something else (another variable) that could explain the correlation between the variables. For instance, if the number of chills experienced correlates positively with musical expertise, we cannot conclude that musical expertise is causing people to experience more chills since the association could be entirely there because of another explanation that was not measured (e.g., a personality trait such as openness to experience or perhaps musical preferences). Or perhaps the importance of music to those people that have high levels of musical expertise has contributed to the fact that they are extra sensitive to the physiological effects of music. Certainly, correlational analysis and design can be insightful, but this central limitation needs to be kept in mind.

There is a wonderful online resource, spurious correlations, where you can explore completely random but very high correlations between real-world variables (the correlation between maths doctorates awarded in the US and uranium stored at US nuclear power plants is 0.952). My own favourite example is the high correlation between the number of people that drown and the amount of ice cream sold during the different months of the year (which is 0.65 in Finland, where about 100 Finns drown each year). No one would claim that eating ice cream *causes* people to drown, but of course the real variable driving the association is the sun, or warm weather, which influences people to be more likely to be eating ice cream and involved in outdoor activities in the lakes and the sea. If we look at the published studies involving music and correlations, there is a peculiar example, where the title of the study, 'The Effect of Country Music on Suicide', spells out a strange and alarming high and positive link between airtime devoted to country music and incidence of suicides by white citizens (Stack & Gundlach, 1992). However, this study was later argued to have ignored the warnings about correlation not equating to causality by other scholars (Snipes & Maguire, 1995). This reminds us that even experienced scholars are sometimes prone to get carried away with what their research design is able to claim.

Case Example #2: Are chills induced by music linked to specific personality traits?

To give you an empirical example of a useful correlation design, let us look again at the chills induced by music. Some years ago, a curious link between the self-reported chill experience and specific personality traits was reported (Maruskin et al., 2012). Figure 4.2 shows four graphs, each of which captures a correlation between two concepts from the study by Maruskin and her colleagues. The actual observations are mere simulations since the original data is not available, but they display identical correlations as reported in the paper. Maruskin argued that there are two types of chills, *coldshivers*, and *goosetingles*, both of which are similar to overall chills (Panel A), and they also correlate to a certain degree with each other but are not identical (Panel B). However, Panel C suggests that participants who score highly for a trait titled negative emotionality which refers to a tendency to experience sadness, anger, disgust, contempt, guilt, shame, shyness, and hostility frequently (Izard et al., 1993). Finally, there is no correlation whatsoever between goosetingles and neuroticism (Panel D). Here the study does not conclude that the chills are caused by any of these personality traits, but by teasing apart the correlations between the variables, it was able to demonstrate that goosetingles, coldshivers and overall chills are part of the same process; i.e., they operate similarly. They also discussed the weak but interesting potential link between chills (coldshivers) and a stable personality trait (negative emotionality). Other studies of chills with music have been found to correlate mainly with openness to experience (Colver & El-Alayli, 2016; Nusbaum & Silvia, 2011), another personality trait that often goes hand in hand with the experience of chills.

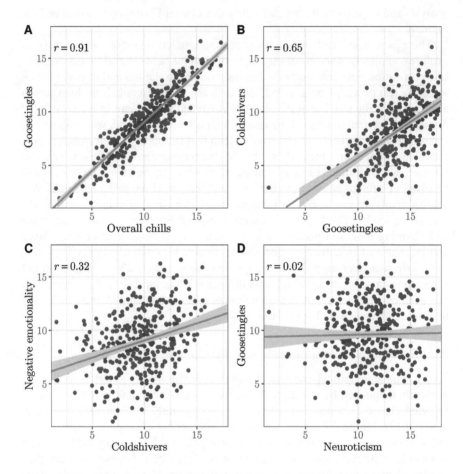

Figure 4.2 Correlations between self-reported chills and personality traits adapted from a study by Maruskin et al. (2012).

Causal Research Design

When research aims to pin down an explanation or a set of explanations of the phenomenon in question, the strongest approach is to formulate an experiment focused on the question. An experiment almost always tests a specific hypothesis which arises from the theory. To make sure that it is the specific explanation, you manipulate the given explanation (then called the *independent variable*, or IV) and hold potential explanations (individual variables, or then these are called *control variables*) constant while you investigate what the effect of the independent variable on your main interest is. To properly measure this, you have implemented the objective of the study as a *dependent variable* (DV), something that can be *measured*. To put this in concrete terms, if you want to know what it is in music

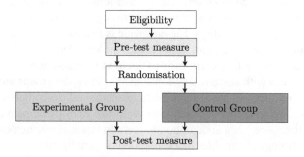

Figure 4.3 A minimal causal study design.

that actually causes chills in listeners, you will manipulate *specific elements of music* (IV) to see whether the amplifying or taking out some musical devices or elements actually leads to an increased or decreased *amount of chills* (DV) in the participants. Such research would also try to control the participant in terms of their predisposition to chills (control variable). Causal research design is the only way to establish the reasons behind the phenomena and for this reason it is valued a great deal as a research design.

Figure 4.3 shows the causal research design as a flow chart, which serves well to highlight some additional important elements. Eligibility refers to the notion which we discuss in a later section where it is assumed that initially all participants are equal and suitable for the study. Next, we randomly assign the participants into two groups, *Experimental Group* and *Control Group*. Experimental Group is the group that receives the manipulation and Control Group is the control group (they do not receive anything). Before we implement the manipulation, we want to measure the dependent variable, say the frequency of chills experienced by the participants. After establishing the initial levels in the task, also called the *baseline measure*, it is time to administer the manipulation; Experimental Group will receive a new training element aimed to enhance the experience of chills through focus on visual imagery, while Control Group will receive nothing (a control condition). After this manipulation has taken place, the performance of both groups is measured again using the same measures as before. If the members of Experimental Group receive consistently better results in terms of the frequency of experienced chills than the control group, manipulation can be the only reason for this difference since there is no other systematic difference available. And manipulation itself is the key explanation targeted in the study.

In the minimal causal study example, each participant belongs to one group. This is called *between-subjects design*. Such designs are common in medical studies, but often in social sciences it is economic and even desirable to have the participants take part in all manipulations. The reason why this is economic is that in this *within-subjects design* the fact that every participant has a different starting baseline or different level of reactivity is accounted for; each participant will act as their own baseline and therefore this allows the manipulation to measure the change within each person. This can be more efficient in situations where the baseline is widely different between people (such as in many physiological variables such as skin conductance or heart rate variability). The downside is that there are manipulations that reveal too much to the participant, which causes the knowledge, or the physiological effects related to the task to carry over to the next manipulation. It is always safe to organise studies with designs between subjects, since the groups are completely independent, but then you need more participants overall to complete your study. The within-subjects type of design allows us to use each participant as their own control, and therefore it is a good option for certain types of research context where you have physiological variables or a rare group of participants.

Case Example #3: Do musical features trigger chills?

If we turn our attention again to the topic of chills induced by music, a causal research design would attempt to go beyond the descriptions and associations outlined in the previous sections. Scott Bannister and I wanted to know whether the actual musical contents are really that important in generating the chills, given that so many different pieces have been implicated in past research, although no consistent musical explanations of these experiences have been offered. Links with the structure, timbre, and increased loudness had been proposed to be associated with the chills, but we wanted to know whether we would be able to eliminate or suppress the chills if we took out crucial sections of the music (Bannister & Eerola, 2018). In other words, we went for the causal link between music and chills. We had three pieces (*Glósóli* by Sigur Rós, *Jupiter* by Gustav Holst, and *Ancestral* by Steven Wilson) indicated to have the potential to elicit chills in listeners in the previous survey. We created a version of each piece, where we removed the section of the music most participants had described as leading to chills by clever audio editing. We recruited participants who had experienced musical chills before. We measured the skin conductance of the participants and allowed them to make continuous judgements of the chills with a slider while the music played. In this design, we did not divide the participants into two groups and have the one group listen to the altered versions and the other group listen to the original versions, since we wanted to capitalise on the fact that the participants can operate as their own controls. Our design was something called a within-subject design, where the same participants are subjected to manipulation, which is particularly useful in situations where there is considerable variation between participants. So, each participant heard the pieces under both conditions in randomised order, and we assumed that the manipulated versions of the pieces would lead to lower self-reports of chills, as well as muted skin conductance responses. This is more or less how the results turned out, and it is worth pointing out that the manipulation actually did not damage the emotional experience of the pieces, just suppressed the chills.

Causal Research Designs with Repeated Observations

The simplest causal design painted in Figure 4.3 is all very good when the data comes from a single observation (one before, one after manipulation). However, as the previous example demonstrated, participants were tested with three pieces of music. It is advantageous to ask participants to provide assessments of multiple items or ask them to complete multiple tasks under the same conditions (as shown in Figure 4.4). Such expansion of the basic design still has the advantage of the original design, but the fact that we are collecting multiple observations under the same conditions is usually a considerable statistical strength. In formal terms, these types of designs are called *repeated measures designs* or *within-subject designs*. Combined with the basic grouping into two or more groups with different participants, the combination of repeated measures (multiple observations within the condition) and between subjects (the group design factor) makes this type of design into a *mixed design*. This type of design carries the advantages of strong causal research and capitalises on the extra statistical power gained from having several measures from the participants. Furthermore, participants themselves act as their own controls, making some measures, such as physiological and neural measures, more sensitive, as each participant may have a different baseline and this design allows the change from each participant's baseline to be traced.

Complex Causal Research Designs

Let us take a more complex causal design where we have three manipulations and three interventions. We also want to know how durable the effects of the interventions are, so we repeat the outcome measures a second time, say three months later. In principle, this is just elaborating on the theme of the simple causal design but adding separate manipulations with new groups and adding temporal dimensions to these measures (Figure 4.4).

Case Example #4: Does music help to combat anxiety and depression in breast cancer patients?

One of the most common forms of cancer for women is breast cancer. Treatment is usually effective, but diagnosis and treatment are usually accompanied by a lot of distress, anxiety, and depression. This mental stress may also influence the way the individual copes with the disease. To examine whether music therapy could be used to alleviate these negative mental effects, Chen et al. (2018) studied 60 women undergoing chemotherapy for breast cancer. They randomly divided women into three groups; one group received a group music intervention, where trained group therapists led small group sessions that involved relaxation, listening to music, and sharing experiences. The second group, called the self-directed music intervention, received the same music CDs used in the group music therapy group, but were asked to listen to music at home at regular intervals (at least an hour each day). Finally, a control group received standard care consisting of getting information about breast cancer and consulting in the outpatient clinic. As an outcome measure, they had two standardised measures for anxiety and depression (Hospital Anxiety and Depression Scale) and a self-report instrument that captures the cognitive adjustment to cancer. These measures were taken a week before the intervention, immediately after the eight-week intervention had been completed, and

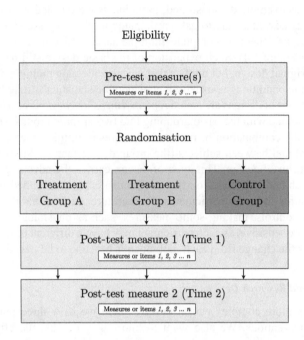

Figure 4.4 A complex causal study design with two treatment groups and one control group and pre- and post-test measures with an additional follow-up test (post-test measure 2).

Note that the measures also indicate multiple items that the same participants are assessing in addition to repeating the conditions (pre-test, post-test 1 and 2).

three months later (this design is similar to the design illustrated in Figure 4.4). The results did not show significant differences between baseline and measures right after the eight-week intervention period in any measures, but three months afterwards, participants who participated in group music therapy had greater reductions in anxiety and depression, as well as in some measures of cognitive adjustment for cancer. Although this was a small-scale study, the results are in line with the notion that music therapy may assist in reframing the problems (Kerr et al., 2001) and consistent with the meta-analyses involving the effectiveness of active music therapy for some situations (Li et al., 2020).

Theoretical Studies

Every field of study needs to theorise and articulate ideas into concepts and frameworks, spelling out the implications of these and forming testable hypotheses. Theoretical studies are a vital part of the researcher's toolkit and are needed to create tools to understand and organise reality before and after empirical experiments. These tools can be called theories or models, and they fundamentally shape the way we can articulate a topic, predict new cases, and grasp the concepts of a phenomenon. One typical opportunity for theoretical studies comes from observed discrepancies in an empirical study, which tell you that there is something amiss, something else that is affecting this phenomenon, or perhaps that the fundamental assumptions are wrong. Many of the most cited studies are theoretical proposals that set a new framework for subsequent studies. A good example of this would be the emotion-induction mechanisms proposed by Patrik Juslin and Daniel Västfjäll (2008) that have generated an active research programme soon after its launch.

Another use of theoretical studies is to adopt a theory from a different field/ domain to music and first carry out a scoping exercise of how this might be a better way to explain a phenomenon before committing to empirical corroboration or checking. For example, David Huron's prolactin conjecture that enjoying sad music (Huron, 2011) might be related to the effects of prolactin, which in turn is a biological adaptation, although this explanation has turned out differently in empirical experiments (Eerola et al., 2021).

Case Example #5: What is the underlying cause of chills?

To keep the theme of these examples consistent with the preceding sections, I offer David Huron's theory of music-induced frisson (Huron, 2006). The idea is that a sharp contrast in affect content may be the key to a special type of experiences, chills, or frissons as Huron prefers to call them. Affects that are negatively valenced such as fear, when encountered in a positive context, heighten the positive experience (and temper the negative one). This is the basic material for any practical prank where the target is first horrified at being subjected to something, but then uplifted when the prank is revealed. The Huron study drew from the physiological fear response in humans, which includes the pilomotor response (hair standing up on the back of your neck) and theories of laughter (Ramachandran, 1998), which have these same elements that initially something alarming happens and then this is soon assessed to be of no consequence. In sum, musical chills occur after music triggers some form of fear reaction, which is subsequently inhibited and appraised cognitively to be non-harmful, which leads to a positive experience. The possible auditory triggers are not yet well understood, but Huron cites loud, approaching sounds, and scream-like timbres.

Theoretical studies can transform the field and shape empirical efforts in new directions. Scholarship is about ideas and how the world operates, and theories are the substance of ideas that allow us to formulate ideas in a way that they can be empirically explored.

Meta-analytical Research Design

One of the most powerful types of research design is *meta-analytical design*. The word meta refers here to studies of studies, and these have been developed in the medical and epidemiological field to assess previous studies on a particular theme rigorously and systematically on a particular research theme using a well-defined body of research. Meta-analysis compiles the quantitative evidence from all the studies under focus, and deciding the actual search criteria, which studies to include, and which databases to use is an important part of the meta-analysis research design. One of the central objectives is to convert a diverse range of outcome measures and statistics utilised in the studies into a uniform statistical metric (e.g., standardised mean difference). A uniform metric will allow comparison of all the studies in terms of the overall strength of the findings in a more robust way than any of the individual studies could do. Meta-analysis also examines the variability of the results and typically focusses on the sources of variability. In summary, meta-analysis is the best known way to put together a summary of a complex and conflicting body of studies on a topic that has been studied numerous times. Often, meta-analytical studies also attempt to evaluate the publication bias, which means that the studies which have ended up in published journals are all reporting positive results, but one would assume that there are studies with limited success that have not been published because the authors or journal editors felt that the results were not worth publishing.

Case Example #6: Does music training lead to increases in cognitive abilities?

In discussions among parents and teachers, it is common to observe links between music as a hobby and academic excellence. There have been studies demonstrating correlations between academic achievement and participation in music (e.g., Gouzouasis et al., 2007), although these kinds of correlational studies do not of course imply that music training would lead to transfer effects into academic subjects, cognitive abilities, or IQ. In the mid 2000s, researchers began to explore this potential link with causal research designs. For instance, Glenn Schellenberg (Schellenberg, 2004) assigned 144 six-year-olds randomly into different groups that received different training (keyboard, vocal music, drama, or no lessons at all) for one year. All participants were tested on their cognitive skills (an IQ test, the Wechsler intelligence scale for children). The results after training suggested that the music training groups (keyboard and voice) showed markedly high improvements in the IQ compared to the two control groups, although the resulting difference was small (less than three IQ points, which is less than the average variation in a person if tested separately several times). A few years later, a similar design with a shorter duration of the intervention (Mehr et al., 2013) suggested that there is no measurable benefit from music training to IQ. Since then, there have been numerous studies that have addressed the topic in one way or another. Recently, these studies about the effects of music training on cognitive measures in schoolchildren found their way into a meta-analysis (Cooper, 2020). This analysis initially identified 52 potential studies that tackled the same broad question, and after checking the quality of each of these studies (design, sufficient reporting, group allocation, control measures), 21 studies were taken into a detailed analysis. This analysis consisted of a total of 5,612 participants in 105 experiments and concluded that music training showed small to moderate main effects of training on cognitive measures, which are significantly influenced by the type of setting

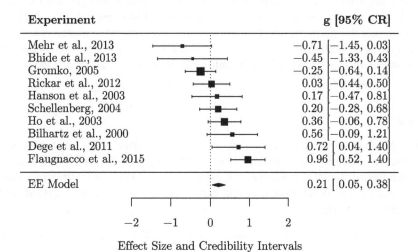

Experiment		g [95% CR]
Mehr et al., 2013		−0.71 [−1.45, 0.03]
Bhide et al., 2013		−0.45 [−1.33, 0.43]
Gromko, 2005		−0.25 [−0.64, 0.14]
Rickar et al., 2012		0.03 [−0.44, 0.50]
Hanson et al., 2003		0.17 [−0.47, 0.81]
Schellenberg, 2004		0.20 [−0.28, 0.68]
Ho et al., 2003		0.36 [−0.06, 0.78]
Bilhartz et al., 2000		0.56 [−0.09, 1.21]
Dege et al., 2011		0.72 [0.04, 1.40]
Flaugnacco et al., 2015		0.96 [0.52, 1.40]
EE Model		0.21 [0.05, 0.38]

Effect Size and Credibility Intervals

Figure 4.5 Demonstration of meta-analysis effect sizes for a subset (N=10) of experiments (N=105) analysed by Cooper (2020).

and type of music training. Settings where individual achievement is emphasised are more efficient, and private music lessons tend to be more efficient towards this direction than group-based lessons. Figure 4.5 illustrates the variability between the studies analysed by showing the overall effect size (g) for a selection of ten experiments out of the 105 analysed by Cooper. When the effect size is greater than 0 and the credibility interval does not cross 0, the results are considered to support the idea that music training contributes to cognitive measures. Overall, only a minority of studies demonstrate unequivocally positive results (see Degé et al., 2011, Flaugnacco et al., 2015) but most studies do not offer such evidence. The overall effect size is positive but small (0.21 in the sample portrayed in the figure) and the conclusions drawn from the meta-analysis state that musical training is not superior to other cognitive interventions.

Postlude

In a research project of almost any scale, there might be a possibility to combine several research designs and gather evidence using different methods (called mixed-method research) and involving different designs. For instance, before launching into a controlled experiment, it is not rare to explore whether the concepts and scales that are planned to be used in the experiment will function properly by carrying out interviews, case studies, and a small-scale survey before even piloting the experiment. These studies can examine the potential missed topics or the suitability of the measures for the planned participants or questions. Such studies are often kept relatively small and exploratory, but can be crucial and fundamentally shape the next set of studies. And occasionally they escalate into studies of their own.

The important message here is to realise that research designs are building blocks that need to be wielded toward the needs of the research topic and the actual research questions, which in turn dictate what type of evidence is needed. It is usually advantageous to approach a particular topic using multiple research approaches and designs in order to be able to focus on the key issues and the underlying explanations.

Coda

This section has covered the research process and, more specifically, given examples of research designs. The examples have highlighted how the same topic can be studied from different perspectives that extract different kinds of information about the topic, such as descriptive research, correlational, causal, meta-analytical, and theoretical research.

Discussion Points

1. When you encounter research in music, is it always easy to decipher what the underpinning research design is?
2. What kind of research design do you find appealing or insightful? Why do you find these research designs attractive?
3. Do you think the terms used in causal research (e.g., intervention, baseline, and outcome measures) are well suited to describing the research of musical behaviours?
4. When the chapter talks about transparency and open access materials, do you think scholars are using other people's data and checking the materials or is it more of a commitment to be open just in case someone wants to check? Do these kinds of activity make you trust research more?

Further Reading

Simmons, J. P., Nelson, L. D., & Simonsohn, U. (2011). False-positive psychology: Undisclosed flexibility in data collection and analysis allows presenting anything as significant. *Psychological Science, 22*(11), 1359–1366.
Nosek, B. A., Ebersole, C. R., DeHaven, A. C., & Mellor, D. T. (2018). The preregistration revolution. *Proceedings of the National Academy of Sciences, 115*(11), 2600–2606.
Sproull, N. L. (2002). *Handbook of research methods: A guide for practitioners and students in the social sciences.* Scarecrow press.

References

Armitage, J., & Eerola, T. (2022). Cross-modal transfer of valence or arousal from music to word targets in affective priming? *Auditory Perception & Cognition, 5*(3–4), 192–210. https://doi.org/https://doi.org/10.1080/25742442.2022.2087451

Asendorpf, J. B., Conner, M., De Fruyt, F., De Houwer, J., Denissen, J. J., Fiedler, K., Fiedler, S., Funder, D. C., Kliegl, R., Nosek, B. A., et al. (2013). Recommendations for increasing replicability in psychology. *European Journal of Personality*, *27*(2), 108–119.

Baker, M. (2016). 1,500 scientists lift the lid on reproducibility. *Nature*, *533*(7604), 452–454.

Bannister, S. (2020). A survey into the experience of musically induced chills: Emotions, situations and music. *Psychology of Music*, *48*(2), 297–314. https://doi.org/https://doi.org/10.1177/0305735618798024

Bannister, S., & Eerola, T. (2018). Suppressing the chills: Effects of musical manipulation on the chills response. *Frontiers in Psychology*, *9*, 2046. https://doi.org/10.3389/fpsyg.2018.02046

Berm, D. J. (1987). The complete academic: A practical guide for the beginning social scientist. In M. Zanna & J. Darley (Eds.), *The complete academic: A practical guide for the beginning social scientist* (pp. 171–201). Random House.

Bertin-Mahieux, T., Ellis, D. P. W., Whitman, B., & Lamere, P. (2011). The million song dataset. *Proceedings of the 12th International Conference on Music Information Retrieval (ISMIR 2011)*.

Carlson, E., Saari, P., Burger, B., & Toiviainen, P. (2017). Personality and musical preference using social-tagging in excerpt-selection. *Psychomusicology: Music, Mind, and Brain*, *27*(3), 203–212.

Chen, S.-C., Chou, C.-C., Chang, H.-J., & Lin, M.-F. (2018). Comparison of group vs self-directed music interventions to reduce chemotherapy-related distress and cognitive appraisal: An exploratory study. *Supportive Care in Cancer*, *26*(2), 461–469.

Clayton, M., Tarsitani, S., Jankowsky, R., Jure, L., Leante, L., Polak, R., Poole, A., Rocamora, M., Alborno, P., Camurri, A., Eerola, T., Jacoby, N., & Jakubowski, K. (2021). The interpersonal entrainment in music performance data collection. *Empirical Musicology Review*, *16*(1), 65–84. https://doi.org/http://dx.doi.org/10.18061/emr.v16i1.7555

Colver, M. C., & El-Alayli, A. (2016). Getting aesthetic chills from music: The connection between openness to experience and frisson. *Psychology of Music*, *44*(3), 413–427.

Cooper, P. K. (2020). It's all in your head: A meta-analysis on the effects of music training on cognitive measures in schoolchildren. *International Journal of Music Education*, *38*(3), 321–336.

Degé, F., Kubicek, C., & Schwarzer, G. (2011). Music lessons and intelligence: A relation mediated by executive functions. *Music Perception*, *29*(2), 195–201.

Eerola, T. (2011). Are the emotions expressed in music genre-specific? An audio-based evaluation of datasets spanning classical, film, pop and mixed genres. *Journal of New Music Research*, *40*(4), 349–366.

Eerola, T., & Lahdelma, I. (2022). Register impacts perceptual consonance through roughness and sharpness. *Psychonomic Bulletin and Review*, *29*, 800–808. https://doi.org/https://doi.org/10.3758/s13423-021-02033-5

Eerola, T., & Peltola, H.-R. (2016). Memorable experiences with sad music – Reasons, reactions and mechanisms of three types of experiences. *PloS ONE*, *11*(6), e0157444. https://doi.org/http://dx.doi.org/10.1371/journal.pone.0157444

Eerola, T., & Toiviainen, P. (2003). *MIDI toolbox: MATLAB tools for music research*. University of Jyväskylä.

Eerola, T., Vuoskoski, J. K., Kautiainen, H., Peltola, H.-R., Putkinen, V., & Schäfer, K. (2021). Being moved by listening to unfamiliar sad music induces reward-related hormonal changes in empathic listeners. *Annals of the New York Academy of Sciences*, *1502*, 121–131. https://doi.org/DOI:10.1111/nyas.14660

Flaugnacco, E., Lopez, L., Terribili, C., Montico, M., Zoia, S., & Schön, D. (2015). Music training increases phonological awareness and reading skills in developmental dyslexia: A randomized control trial. *PloS ONE, 10*(9), e0138715.

Frieler, K., Müllensiefen, D., Fischinger, T., Schlemmer, K., Jakubowski, K., & Lothwesen, K. (2013). Replication in music psychology. *Musicae Scientiae, 17*(3), 265–276.

Gouzouasis, P., Guhn, M., & Kishor, N. (2007). The predictive relationship between achievement and participation in music and achievement in core grade 12 academic subjects. *Music Education Research, 9*(1), 81–92. https://doi.org/https://doi.org/10.1080/14613800601127569

Herremans, D., Martens, D., & Sörensen, K. (2014). Dance hit song prediction. *Journal of New Music Research, 43*(3), 291–302.

Huron, D. (2006). *Sweet anticipation*. MIT Press.

Huron, D. (2011). Why is sad music pleasurable? A possible role for prolactin. *Musicae Scientiae, 15*(2), 146–158.

Izard, C. E., Libero, D. Z., Putnam, P., & Haynes, O. M. (1993). Stability of emotion experiences and their relations to traits of personality. *Journal of Personality and Social Psychology, 64*(5), 847.

Juslin, P. N., & Västfjäll, D. (2008). Emotional responses to music: The need to consider underlying mechanisms. *Behavioral and Brain Sciences, 31*(5), 559–575.

Karlsson, J., & Juslin, P. N. (2008). Musical expression: An observational study of instrumental teaching. *Psychology of Music, 36*(3), 309–334.

Kerr, N. L. (1998). HARKing: Hypothesizing after the results are known. *Personality and Social Psychology Review, 2*(3), 196–217.

Kerr, T., Walsh, J., & Marshall, A. (2001). Emotional change processes in music-assisted reframing. *Journal of Music Therapy, 38*(3), 193–211.

Klein, R. A., Vianello, M., Hasselman, F., Adams, B. G., Adams Jr, R. B., Alper, S., Aveyard, M., Axt, J. R., Babalola, M. T., Bahník, Š., et al. (2018). Many labs 2: Investigating variation in replicability across samples and settings. *Advances in Methods and Practices in Psychological Science, 1*(4), 443–490.

Lahdelma, I., & Eerola, T. (2024). Registered report – Valenced priming with acquired affective concepts in music: automatic reactions to common tonal chords. *Music Perception, 41*(3), 161–175.

Li, B., Liu, X., Dinesh, K., Duan, Z., & Sharma, G. (2018). Creating a multitrack classical music performance dataset for multimodal music analysis: Challenges, insights, and applications. *IEEE Transactions on Multimedia, 21*(2), 522–535.

Li, Y., Xing, X., Shi, X., Yan, P., Chen, Y., Li, M., Zhang, W., Li, X., & Yang, K. (2020). The effectiveness of music therapy for patients with cancer: A systematic review and meta-analysis. *Journal of Advanced Nursing, 76*(5), 1111–1123.

Maruskin, L. A., Thrash, T. M., & Elliot, A. J. (2012). The chills as a psychological construct: Content universe, factor structure, affective composition, elicitors, trait antecedents, and consequences. *Journal of Personality and Social Psychology, 103*(1), 135–157.

Mauch, M., MacCallum, R. M., Levy, M., & Leroi, A. M. (2015). The evolution of popular music: USA 1960–2010. *Royal Society Open Science, 2*(5), 150081.

Mehr, S. A., Schachner, A., Katz, R. C., & Spelke, E. S. (2013). Two randomized trials provide no consistent evidence for nonmusical cognitive benefits of brief preschool music enrichment. *PloS ONE, 8*(12), e82007.

Moss, F. C., & Neuwirth, M. (2021). FAIR, open, linked: Introducing the special issue on open science in musicology. *Empirical Musicology Review, 16*(1), 1–4. https://doi.org/https://doi.org/10.18061/emr.v16i1.8246

Müllensiefen, D., Gingras, B., Musil, J., & Stewart, L. (2014). The musicality of non-musicians: An index for assessing musical sophistication in the general population. *PloS ONE*, *9*(2), e89642.

Nosek, B. A., & Lakens, D. (2014). Registered reports: A method to increase the credibility of published results. *Social Psychology*, *45*(3), 137–141. https://doi.org/http://dx.doi.org/10.1027/1864-9335/a000192

Nusbaum, E. C., & Silvia, P. J. (2011). Shivers and timbres: Personality and the experience of chills from music. *Social Psychological and Personality Science*, *2*(2), 199–204.

Peretz, I., Gagnon, L., & Bouchard, B. (1998). Music and emotion: Perceptual determinants, immediacy, and isolation after brain damage. *Cognition*, *68*(2), 111–141.

Piwowar, H. A., Day, R. S., & Fridsma, D. B. (2007). Sharing detailed research data is associated with increased citation rate. *PloS ONE*, *2*(3), e308.

Quintana, D. S. (2021). Replication studies for undergraduate theses to improve science and education. *Nature Human Behaviour*, *5*, 1117–1118. https://doi.org/10.1038/s41562-021-01192-8

Ramachandran, V. S. (1998). The neurology and evolution of humor, laughter, and smiling: The false alarm theory. *Medical Hypotheses*, *51*(4), 351–354.

Sandve, G. K., Nekrutenko, A., Taylor, J., & Hovig, E. (2013). Ten simple rules for reproducible computational research. *PloS Computational Biology*, *9*(10), e1003285.

Schellenberg, E. G. (2004). Music lessons enhance IQ. *Psychological Science*, *15*(8), 511–514.

Serrà, J., Corral, Á., Boguñá, M., Haro, M., & Arcos, J. L. (2012). Measuring the evolution of contemporary Western popular music. *Scientific Reports*, *2*(1), 1–6.

Simmons, J. P., Nelson, L. D., & Simonsohn, U. (2011). False-positive psychology: Undisclosed flexibility in data collection and analysis allows presenting anything as significant. *Psychological Science*, *22*(11), 1359–1366.

Snipes, J. B., & Maguire, E. R. (1995). Country music, suicide, and spuriousness. *Social Forces*, *74*(1), 327–329.

Stack, S., & Gundlach, J. (1992). The effect of country music on suicide. *Social Forces*, *71*(1), 211–218.

Tomasello, M., & Call, J. (2011). Methodological challenges in the study of primate cognition. *Science*, *334*(6060), 1227–1228.

5   Sources of Information

There are numerous sources of information that can be harnessed to uncover interesting musical phenomena or behaviours. We will give extra emphasis to music in later chapters, but here we focus on self-reports, behaviours, and physiology as broad sources of information. The breakdown into music, self-reports, behaviours, and physiology given in Table 5.1 is not exhaustive, but it gives an overview of the rich menu of choices available. Figure 5.1 outlines the focus of attention in this chapter in terms of *what* the source of information is, *how* the observations are collected, *where* the research is conducted and *who* the participants are.

Music itself is a rich source of information, and whether this is best taken as the recorded sound of a performance or notation in any convention or representation really depends on the type of research question posed. We will cover the analysis of audio and symbolic music information in Chapters 9 and 10. Beyond the scores and the audio signal itself, the most common source of information is simply any behaviour related to music, and these can be anything from tapping one's foot to the beat, to looking at other performers, or singing, or playing an instrument, or clapping along to the music at a gig. Behaviours also cover specific tasks designed to probe a particular behaviour, concept, or theory (e.g., do people actually possess some kind of absolute pitch even if they are not able to name the notes but can sing the notes or, how does the applause from the audience members entrain to a common beat). The third category of responses is formed by specific self-reports, where people give their assessment of some aspect of music or its impact or a related aspect of it (for example, how much do you like this music?).

It is possible to divide the sources of data into low-level and medium-to-high-level in terms of their abstraction. For instance, acoustic features describing the physical signal are considered low-level in this abstraction, as are other signals coming straight from physiology (skin conductance, or electric responses from the scalp) or from the movement of the performers. Self-reports of complex concepts such as melancholia, awe, or performer movement gestures, are on the opposite side of this spectrum as they are very high-level concepts, complex, and have undergone abstraction already. However, any level of data could potentially be used to provide evidence for a question posed at another level, so I have not followed the hierarchical distinction here.

DOI: 10.4324/9781003293804-5

Table 5.1 Example sources of information in empirical music research.

Domain	Sources of information
Music (direct)	Actual music (score, performance, recording)
Music (indirect)	Attributes of music (annotation, usage, review)
Observations	Observing behaviours related to music, interviews
Self-reports (direct)	Ratings, evaluations, attitudes, values
Self-reports (indirect)	Covert tasks (reaction time, non-verbal)
Behavioural (listening)	Actions (swaying, attending, looking)
Behavioural (performing)	Actions (sound-inducing/ancillary movements)
Behavioural (indirect)	Context of music use, production tasks, improvisation
Physiological (peripheral)	Cardiovascular, respiratory, electrodermal
Physiological (chemical)	Neuroendocrine markers (stress, reward), genetic markers
Physiological (neural)	Electric, magnetic, hemodynamic

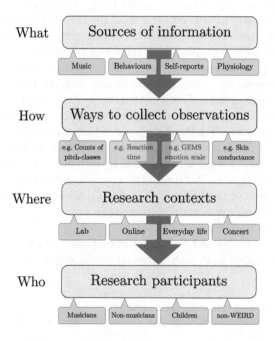

Figure 5.1 Sources of information, measures, context, and samples.

Music

Music as a source of information will be focussed on in three separate chapters. These will focus on empirical analysis of music, on annotation and computational analysis of scores (Chapter 9), on analysis of performance and audio (Chapter 10), and on music corpus studies (Chapter 11). The focus is on exploring what listeners consider to be meaningful in music – structural or conceptual properties – covered in the annotation section of Chapter 9 or what the actual musical contents can tell us about musical processes and how we can extract meaningful information from scores (Chapter 9), performances, and recordings (Chapter 10). It is useful here to distinguish the notions of *close* and *distant readings* of an object (Moretti, 2005). Close reading looks at single objects, performances, and musical works to discover and understand how they work. Distant reading is something that takes a birds-eye view of the musical materials, such as using a very specific corpus of music (Joubert, 2022), such as analysing the expressive performance characteristics in Bach's solos for violin (Fabian, 2015). In this perspective, the specific corpus offers too many examples for a feasible analysis by hand, so a computational analysis is the approach taken instead. Second, distant reading of music is often a valuable way to understand and contextualise individual works, their peculiarities, and exceptions to the norm.

When I explain music as a source of information, it is useful to separate distinct objects of analysis. I have summarised the typical objects and representation of the analysis in Table 5.2, where we also have a comment about the availability of data for empirical music research. Music is a source of semantic descriptions of music and conventional musical scores. The availability of these types of information is usually very good. Another vital source of information are the data related to the performance. These can comprise technically encoded events from the performance of music such as MIDI information and the recorded sound. The caveat here is that when I talk about typical, I mean studies of the past ten years that have mainly focussed on Western art music, but I will address the issue of lack of diversity separately in each analysis topic. All these objects of analysis are relevant to the analysis of music corpora (Chapter 11). Each technique and domain offer challenges and specialist techniques for the analyst that need to be considered and mastered. I will cover examples from most of these objects of analysis and look at some of the topics through a corpus of music or musical performances.

Let's look at an example of *Khyal* performance by Sudokshina Chatterjee (vocal), Kaviraj Singh (harmonium) and Gurdain Rayatt (tabla), recorded in Durham, UK. All the materials (videos, audio, annotations of different kinds)

Table 5.2 Music analysis objects, representations, and availability.

Object	Representation	Availability
Meanings and concepts	Annotation (text, number)	Scarce, created only for research purposes
Performance instructions	Digital score of any kind	Good for Western classical music, variable for other traditions
Performance traces	MIDI or sensor data	Mostly rare, created for research purposes, but exceptions exist (e.g., MAESTRO)
Recording	Audio and video data	Excellent but not exhaustive

mentioned are available in the Open Science Framework as a collection of rich data on interpersonal entrainment in music performance published by Clayton et al. (2019)[1]. Khyal is a virtuoso tradition in Hindustani classical music that affords the performer great freedom to elaborate and ornament the rāga framework. Rāga provides the characteristic sets of pitches and melodic motifs that convey a particular time of day or aesthetic ideal. If we focus on this single performance from the collection, an interesting exchange between the performers starts at five minutes into the performance of *Rag Miyan Malhar*, which is within a 12-beat *vilambit ektal* section.

Figure 5.2 shows four different types of data from this 40-second extract. The topmost panel displays manual annotations (the darker areas with dashed lines around them) and the underlying images are from the video, which has zoomed in on the singer. The annotations, made by experts, describe the moments in time when clear interactions occur between the singer and the other musicians. For example, between 5:19 and 5:21 there is a 'Mutual smile and look and head movement' according to the annotations. This type of annotation data is useful for identifying what happens in the music when musicians are visibly coordinating their performances. The second panel shows the melodic line sung by the singer (in technical terms, the plot displays the F_0 in Hz extracted using a monophonic pitch tracker based on a deep convolutional neural network (Kim et al., 2018)). The extracted melodic line is an interesting object of analysis, but here also shows where the singing stops and where the phrase beginnings are. The third panel shows the waveform of the music. This can be a useful raw representation for analyses of onsets or just to illustrate dynamic changes in the music. The bottom panel displays the vertical head position of the singer by showing the Y coordinate extracted from the video using a computer vision algorithm, see Jakubowski et al. (2017). From this short excerpt, we can already see that the phrase endings and beginnings in the music (e.g., at 5:03 and 5:19) are marked by short bouts of movement, and during the section where the vocalist does not sing (5:20–5:35), she gives encouraging nods and smiles to the other musicians (especially to the tabla player, who is not visible in the extracted video strip).

From these relatively simple basic descriptors (annotations, vocal line, and indicator of the movements) we can analyse how musical structure and performance movements are coordinated between the members in the ensemble. These representations have been used to explore how movements communicate the metrical and cadential structure in this music (Clayton et al., 2018) and how movements between performers can also indicate how they coordinate their actions through interactive segments in music (Eerola et al., 2018).

A similar analysis can be applied to almost any performance with audio and video, be it historical (e.g., Glenn Gould's performance of Bach's *Goldberg Variations* or recordings of Björk's live concerts) or pedagogical, such as looking at the rehearsal sessions of musicians (Williamon & Davidson, 2002) or focussing on the interactions between performers and audience members (Leante, 2016).

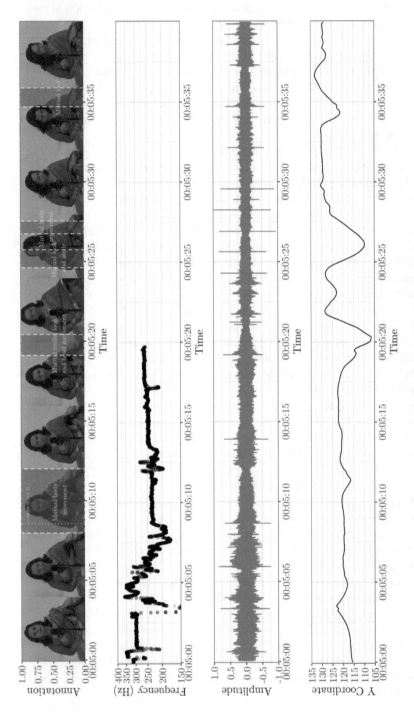

Figure 5.2 Extract from the performance of *Rag Miyan Malhar* by Sudokshina Chatterjee.

The top panel shows video and annotations, the second panel from the top displays the fundamental frequency of the vocal, the third panel the amplitude, and the bottom panel the vertical coordinate of the head. Full documentation of the performance data is available in the OSF repository https://osf.io/ ks325/.

Music Annotation

The idea that music contains shared meanings is an old one and has been much talked about in music research and musicology (Cook, 2001; Kramer, 2003; Scruton, 1997). Here, I want to take this notion into an empirical direction and capture these meanings in relation to music from a pool of people. The purpose is not to try to understand what meanings might be for a *single person*, music analyst, or a casual listener but rather what are the common underlying themes that listeners associate with sonic events. This group of listeners may represent a subculture and specialist expertise (e.g., 'Finnish sound engineers') if we wish. Being aware that meanings in music are not inherently universal and shared by all people is important and does not mean that revealing what a group of people in a culture thinks about certain properties of music would not be interesting and important. On the contrary, tackling the idea that music itself can represent ideas, concepts, affects, and goals is fundamentally important for any music research. For instance, if we think music can express national identity or patriotism, we could ask people to rate several pieces in terms of this rather elusive property. We could then proceed to analyse whether patriotism is linked to the specific piece of melody and harmony, whether it is carried by the lyrics and instrumentation, or whether it requires all three. Or, if we think that certain passages of music are particularly tense, we could ask people to rate specific pieces of music chosen for their levels of tension, or maybe ask people to pinpoint where the tension happens in the music. There are several ways to make such annotations. We talked about the most obvious one, self-reports, in an earlier section (9.1), but annotations of music can also come from existing data (such as comments and tags given by listeners to online services such as *SoundCloud, YouTube* or *Last.fm*) or they can be annotated including labelling of intricate details from the signal itself.

To analyse the contents of the music, we typically need to know what we as listeners consider to be the meaningful content of a piece of music, passage or segment. Interpreting these moments can range from broad expressive emotional content (this passage sounds 'majestic' or 'dignified') to music analytic (the 'surprising key change') or labelling of instrumentation ('saxophone') or identifying structural units of music ('verse' and 'chorus'). Annotation can also indicate to what extent a listener likes a segment of music or wants to dance to it. All these descriptions can serve as vital building blocks for empirical research of music. Annotation is a broad tool to help understand how listeners would label and describe elements of music if given the possibility to do so. Annotations serve as the benchmark against which to evaluate computational models of music perception, or they may form the underlying data for empirical descriptions of musical behaviours and concepts without any computational activities.

I will divide the palette of annotations into *event-based*, *segment-based*, and *inferred* annotations which have different purposes in research and entirely different ways of being obtained.

Figure 5.3 shows the waveform of the first 32 seconds of *Help!* by The Beatles. On top of the waveform, event-based annotations about structure, beats, and chords

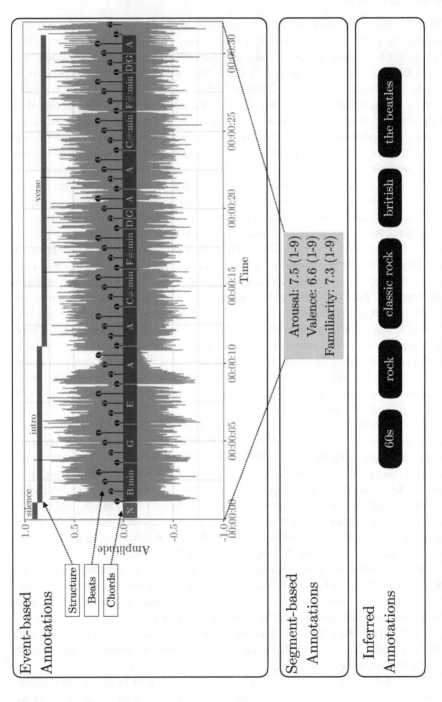

Figure 5.3 Examples of three types of annotations to an extract of *Help!* by The Beatles.

have been imposed. These annotations have been made by Chris Harte (2010) and a team of scholars at Queen Mary University of London, who have also annotated the full catalogue of tracks by The Beatles and a host of other popular music tracks as well. The annotations are all available as easily readable csv files and as *Sonic Visualiser* compatible files[2]. The structure shows the intro and verse, the beats show the timing of the beats (separate identities of four beats in each bar), and the chords show the timing and the content of the chords. One could drill even deeper into the events to isolate the guitar, bass, drums, and the melodic line of singing (see Bittner et al., 2016 for precise annotations of instruments and melody as F_0s in a mixture of genres). The segment-based annotations refer to the whole 32-second excerpt of *Help!* where one frequently finds excerpts to be rated in terms of their expressed arousal (how energetic the excerpt sounds on a scale of 1–9), and valence (how positive or negative the excerpt sounds on a similar scale), or how familiar this track is to the listener (rated also on a 9-point scale). These annotations can be useful broad summaries of the music and are very commonly used in empirical research to control and select musical examples for empirical experiments. The final category of annotations, inferred annotations, refers to labels that have been obtained through aggregation of input from tens or hundreds of thousands of music listeners. In many services, users can label the music they listen to using tags or keywords. When a large number of people agree on these labels, services offer these as the tags, which may describe the genre, era, instrument, and the geographical region represented by the track.

How to coordinate and manage these annotation processes across many individuals in a transparent manner? Scholars from Switzerland and Austria (Hentschel et al., 2021) have proposed a detailed annotation workflow that relies on clear analytical criteria, distributed version control, and aspiration towards consensual annotation solutions through discussion between annotators, reviewers, and curators[3]. Such a process can be applied to event- and segment-based annotations.

Event-based Annotations

While *music information research* aims to develop automatic methods for detecting and recognising properties of music (e.g., fundamental frequency, onsets, instruments, chords, or structure), event-based annotations provide the best way to make the units of analysis visible. These units can be onsets, instruments, segments, chords, or structures of the music. The units are labelled with precise timing of the audio signal and described with an agreed system (functional harmony, instrument families, playing styles, etc.). Annotations such as these are often carried out by experts using tools such as *Sonic Visualiser* that allow the music to be slowed down and to visualise the spectrogram and the envelope of the waveform for accurate placement of the labels. Ontologies and vocabularies for describing the contents are not yet harmonised, but for most key concepts in music theory, noteworthy, annotated datasets do exist. For instance, structure, chords, key, and beats in all songs by The Beatles are available (Harte, 2010), as are many other details of folk music (F_0s, onsets and segment annotations in traditional Georgian vocal music by Rosenzweig et al. (2020)), onsets and metric cycles in a variety of traditions including Cuban son and salsa, North Indian classical music, Malian jembe, and Tunisian stambeli (Clayton et al., 2021) or in Western classical music (Weiß et al., 2017). Some annotations can also be multimodal and contain videos or motion capture data of the performances (Li et al., 2018). As event-based annotations are time-consuming to create and require careful manual craftsmanship, only a relatively small number of music tracks have been described in this level of detail. However, by using machine-learning techniques it is possible to apply the models trained with the annotated data to extract similar information from previously non-annotated data (Kim et al., 2018). The typical use of rich annotations is to develop automatic methods for detecting and recognising onsets, instruments, chords, or structures in music. When a collection of music has been labelled, it is easy to inspect the acoustic qualities that distinguish these events from others using statistical paradigms. Some existing collections of annotations such as the *Real World Computing* dataset (Goto et al., 2002) and various datasets prepared by the Fraunhofer Institute for Digital Media Technology (multiple IDMT-SMT datasets[4]), or the SALAMI datasets for structural analysis of music (Smith et al., 2011) have been pivotal. The ISMIR dataset page currently has links to over 200 datasets[5] so a wealth of information about musical semantics is readily available.

Segment-based Annotations

Annotations of music excerpts typically consist of 15-second, 30-second, or one-minute excerpts and tend to be broad descriptions of musical content such as the emotions expressed, tempo, or genre. These annotations can also capture the popularity, preferences, or familiarity of the excerpts. The reason why these are typically relatively short segments of music is that the purpose is to capture the stable characteristics of the music, and often the character of interest may change if the excerpt duration is longer. The length of this stable segment depends on the concept. For instance, emotions expressed throughout the piece may require shorter clips to capture a well-defined expression compared to genre, which is likely to be more uniform across the piece.

Segment-based annotations are the most common form of annotation and are used extensively in empirical music research. Having annotation data about genres or expressed emotions is often crucial for any empirical work (building a model with acoustic features or using the clips in behavioural experiments), as these properties encapsulate so many different values and acoustic changes in music that keeping them under control is often desirable. It is common to select excerpts for experiments to represent specific music genres and affective contents (e.g., picking music examples from different quadrants of the affective circumplex), or to avoid pieces of music that are overly familiar. Collecting segment-based annotations is simpler than event-based annotations, which require specific expertise and software. Short clips of music can be rated easily by almost anyone and such operations can also be done in online experiments. Of course, the idea of specific expertise may be relevant for segment-based annotations if the research question under investigation requires special expertise. Having participants assess the qualities of music excerpts using well-defined scales (e.g., valence and arousal on a nine-point scale with clearly labelled minimum and maximum points) is relatively easy and offers rich and nuanced data, but sometimes the very definition of the annotation categories may require extensive instruction and some training. To provide some historical context to segment-based annotations, a good example of an annotation system requiring training was the system called 'Cantometrics' proposed by Alan Lomax (1968). This systematic annotation scheme set out to capture the qualities of all the music in the world by proposing a set of 36 assertions that were expressed in terms of a graded scale that could be chosen to denote an aspect of the music. For instance, you could ask whether the music is created by a vocal group or whether it relies on one singer (and few steps between these). Although this scheme was criticised at the time, mainly on the grounds of how the system was used to make inferences about social structures and cultures, the annotation scheme itself was shown to have acceptable reliability when experts familiar with the system used it. Patrick Savage and his colleagues offered an improved version of Cantometrics (Savage et al., 2012) that also integrates some of the instrument features from an influential instrument classification scheme by Hornbostel and Sachs (Hornbostel & Sachs, 1914). This revised Cantometrics scheme has been used to annotate and explore new sets of recordings from various locations around the world (Savage et al., 2015).

An example of a contemporary, large, and good-quality dataset that covers genres, tags, play counts, and many acoustical features for 106,574 tracks is *Free Music Archive: A Dataset for Music Analysis*[6] (Defferrard et al., 2016). What is particularly noteworthy about this dataset is that it offers all audio in a Creative Commons licenced format, allowing everyone to access high-quality, full-length music tracks. The annotated data are rich, well organised, and provided with tools that help with utilising the data (e.g., Python notebooks). For example, the information about genres in the *Free Music Archive* contains a hierarchical system that consists of 163 genres. This kind of dataset allows us to build models for genre recognition, but also allows us to explore the qualities of the music associated with the tags describing the music (more about these in the Corpus Analysis Examples).

There are numerous datasets for labelling emotions induced by music, such as *Emotify*[7] that contains 400 tracks annotated with the GEMS scale (Zentner et al., 2008) or *film soundtracks*[8] that contain 110 and 360 tracks annotated with basic emotions and three affect dimensions (Eerola & Vuoskoski, 2011), just to a name a few. These datasets allow us to build music emotion recognition models, but they are also a good source of musical materials for experiments that probe various aspects of emotions. To give you one more example of segment-based annotations, the *Cross-Composer Dataset*[9] (Weiß, 2017) contains 1,100 tracks from 11 different composers (Bach, Beethoven, Brahms, Dvořák, Handel, Haydn, Mendelssohn, Mozart, Rameau, Schubert, and Shostakovich), and the annotations detail the musical forms, keys, and tempi of these pieces. Such a dataset is useful for understanding not only musical form and tonality, but also differences in compositional devices between eras and composers. Some of the datasets contain an interesting variant of segment-based annotations, in which the annotators have assessed the music they hear on a continuous basis. These continuous annotations often relate to emotions, such as the DEAM dataset (Aljanaki et al., 2017) that contains continuous ratings of valence and arousal for 1,802 tracks covering a diverse range of genres, and in this case, the music is also available under Creative Commons licence.

There are numerous other datasets with rich annotations that cover different styles of music from different cultures, and with different focusses. For instance, annotations exist for beatboxing, cover song identification, choral singing, fla-menco, guitar excerpts, piano excerpts, sheet music, Schenker analyses, texture in string quartets, and many more[10]. The common theme here is that scholars have made the data available and written papers that address a specific problem where the annotated data helps to provide answers. However, utilising these resources does require some computational skills.

Inferred Annotations

The time invested in making event- and segment-based annotations is consider-able. For this reason, inferred annotations have become popular, as they allow the size of datasets to be scaled up. Inferred annotations are a special category of data which typically arises from the data that utilises crowdsourcing or existing label-ling or information about music that has not initially been created for scholarly annotation uses. Users of services such as *Last.fm* or *Jamendo* have 'tagged' the music they listen to. In other words, they have used keywords of their own choice to describe the music (Figure 5.3 displays the top 5 tags from *Last.fm* for the track *Help!* by The Beatles in the bottom panel). The beauty and challenge of such *tags* is that scholars have not imposed the labels or the scheme of annotation on the users, so they represent a raw and rich window into the vocabulary and semantics that can be used to describe music. When you get millions of users describing music, very specific and robust labels and semantic structures emerge (Eck et al., 2007) and these can be used as inferred annotations about genres, emotions, instruments, and many other properties of music. For instance, the *MTG-Jamendo Dataset*[11] (Bogdanov et al., 2019) has 55,000 tracks with tags representing genres, emotions, and instruments. The *Magnatagatune*[12] dataset (Law et al., 2009) contains 25,863 annotated excerpts in terms of genres, but also contains indicators of similarities between the tracks. Several research groups have built so-called 'autotaggers' that allow appropriate tags to be constructed from audio information. This in turn expands the potential scope of annotation to any recording provided that the initial models and tags cover the desired properties of music sufficiently. Other inferred annotations may come from other sources such as social media; the *Million Musical Tweets Dataset* (Hauger et al., 2013) offers listening histories from tweets, and contains the spatial and temporal data that can be used to explore where cultural hotspots in music consumption are. A more extensive and direct exploration of listening activities has been combined from the *Music Streaming Sessions Dataset (MSSD)* (Brost et al., 2019), which contains 160 million Spotify listening sessions.

This data can be used for many purposes and to give you a previously completely inaccessible research question to be answered confidently, a Danish research group has used this dataset to demonstrate diurnal fluctuations in musical choices around the globe (Heggli et al., 2021)[13].

Challenges with Annotations

Although we have seen rapid growth in the number of annotated music datasets, the crucial questions for all of these relate to the *reliability* and *validity* of the data. For reliability, the question is how much agreement there is about a specific label for a segment or an event in the music. This obviously depends on the content of annotation and some contents are notoriously difficult to pin down (what is groove, valence, or even genre for that matter?) while others really depend on the exposure to the music in question (annotations of preference and familiarity). Different datasets come with their own evaluation metrics such as inter-rater reliability that should give you an idea of how reliable and consistent the annotations are. Often, the number of annotators is a good index for this (more is better). But, as we know what the methods are, high reliability does not mean that the annotated concepts are necessarily valid. There may be concepts that are relatively easy to annotate but have little to do with the meaningful contents of the music in question. To give you a trivial but real example, rating the emotional expression of happiness of dance music tracks might give you some data, but does it capture the emotional expression of the music? Probably not – such a description fails to capture an essential element about the expression in this music.

This brings in the culture-specificity of any annotation and the cultural competence and musical expertise of the annotators. For some questions, expertise in the specific genre of music will matter a great deal (what is 'groove' in hip hop or Renaissance music or 'swing' in folk music or jazz?) and certainly for some forms of annotations that cultural expertise is of less importance (for example, annotations of familiarity, which in itself is a measure of how well the listener knows a specific piece of music). To take this idea further for modelling music emotion recognition, Gómez-Cañón et al. (2021) suggested that the annotations should include information about the annotator (cultural background, geographical area, musical expertise, age, gender, and even musical preferences). Only this extra information, often called individual differences information, would allow us to improve current models and to understand the differences in annotations, as well as developing subtle nuances within the annotations.

Annotations are useful and are fundamental building blocks of empirical music research and a powerful resource for musicology. They can address fundamental issues in how we describe music and allow us to test and explore questions that would be impossible to articulate in other ways. The growth of increased technical sophistication and sharing conventions outline a future where empirical research can be constructed with the help of annotations, while new discoveries can be made by expanding the realm of annotations beyond the topics and cultures covered currently.

Observations and Interviews

Observations

Using observations of people as the main source of data comes from anthropology. Over the course of more than a hundred years, anthropologists have perfected the method of *ethnography,* the focus of which was originally to understand the cultural practices of an isolated community. Since then, it has been applied to all kinds of situations and cultural contexts, from sounds and music in football matches (Graakjær, 2022) to practices involved in aerobics classes and listening to music during long-distance flights (DeNora, 2000). Ethnography is the documentation and analysis of culture or subculture and is based on participant observation, which results in an account that describes the cultural practices. It is an excellent way to get an insight into the daily life of members of a subculture and can expose economic, social, and political influences in the daily life of people. Tia DeNora (2000) has explored how music is being used to construct self, or how the act of listening is a construction of the self in an aesthetic sense. She also talks about how diseases like Parkinson's can be interpreted by sufferers as making them 'unmusicked' as their sense of rhythm and initiative are damaged, but at the same time, music itself can partially bring back these damaged properties.

Observation is the simplest way to collect qualitative and quantitative data. Simple does not mean that it would be simple to collect, analyse, or report. Even the act of observation is demanding as it requires us to document and observe details in a much more refined and systematic way than what we would do in our ordinary daily observations. Observation is focussed on identifying key patterns of behaviours but also aims to pinpoint meaningful violations of these. The observers themselves have a set of biases and are influenced by their prior experiences, so being aware of such drawbacks is a part of astute observation. The act of observing is typically done with field notes and photographs and possibly capturing audio and video (if it is meaningful to the study and accepted by the participants). In the analysis phase, these notes are annotated and coded for certain behaviours, or the spoken comments produced by the participants will be turned into text and analysed separately.

Interviews

Interviews are a classic way to get detailed and rich information on a topic. Interviews can be done with individuals, but there is also a variant that uses focus groups. The advantage of an interview is that it offers an open framework where one can get more nuanced information about a topic by allowing people to respond entirely in their own words, even if the topic is shaped through a set of predefined themes. This approach allows us to ask clarifications and follow-up questions that might arise from the answers given. Interviews are great for exploring the views, motivations, experiences, and beliefs of individuals on specific issues. In interviews, questions can be structured, which means that the researcher has defined them beforehand and goes through them all to provide a similar coverage of questions for all people interviewed. In some cases, there is just not sufficient information available about the topic to form a tight thematic structure for the interview, and in those cases the interviews are either semistructured (you have at least a semblance of a starting theme and some loose themes to mention) or unstructured, although the last one is rare beyond some early piloting or informal discussion with some people. When interviews are conducted for a specific group of people, this is often called the *focus group* method. Such focus groups could be, for instance, those who regularly experience chills or choir singers who possess absolute pitch.

Self-reports

The idea of self-reports is simple: a participant indicates her own subjective evaluation of the concept in question. It can be the emotion that music expresses or what kind of emotional experiences the music induces in the individual. Or a self-report can report on how focussed the individual is on a task right now, how bright they think the music example sounds, or how confident they are that this actual moment in time in music contains a clear segment boundary (break, phrasing, or cadence), or how willing they would be to purchase the music they are currently hearing. The variety of these questions is truly huge, and because self-reports can be customised to address almost any aspect of conscious evaluation of music, musical behaviour, or attitude, they tend to be the most common way to obtain information about a phenomenon in this field. Most common does not, of course, mean best, since self-reports do have some limitations, but let us look at the different types of self-reports first before addressing the concerns and limitations.

Direct

Direct self-reports are easy to use. It is typical to offer participants the means to evaluate a concept using a Likert scale. This scale was developed in the 1930s to measure attitudes, opinions, and other subjective states. The scale consists of statements on which participants are asked to indicate their agreement on a scale ordered along the concept of interest such as strongly agree, agree, neither agree nor disagree, disagree, or strongly disagree. Sometimes these categories are replaced with numeric values and only the extremes of the scale are labelled: a scale from 1 to 5 where '1 = strongly agree' and '5 = strongly disagree'. The number of scale steps may also vary (7-point scale, 9-point scale, etc.). There are many standardised instruments that reliably tap into a particular phenomenon, for example for emotions (Zentner et al., 2008), musical sophistication (Zhang & Schubert, 2019), mood regulation (Saarikallio, 2008), or music preferences (Rentfrow et al., 2011). Most self-reports are very easy to collect, and in many cases, they can be collected without complex instructions and training for the participants and often the experimenter does not need to be present, which is advantageous if the anonymity of participants is deemed to be important. Many self-report instruments scale up so that data from many participants can be collected relatively easily, unless the sheer

Goldsmiths Musical Sophistication Index (Gold-MSI)						
Completely Disagree	Strongly Disagree	Disagree	Neither Agree nor Disagree	Agree	Strongly Agree	Completely Agree
1. I spend a lot of my free time doing music-related activities. O	O	O	O	O	O	O
2. I sometimes choose music that can trigger shivers down my spine. O	O	O	O	O	O	O
3.						

Geneva Emotional Music Scale (GEMS)				
Not at all				Very much
Moved 1	2	3	4	5
Filled with wonder 1	2	3	4	5
... ...				

Phenomenology of Consciousness Inventory (PCI)							
I was forever distracted and unable to concentrate on anything. 0	1	2	3	4	5	6	I was able to concentrate quite well and was not distracted.
Time seemed to greatly speed up or slow down. 0	1	2	3	4	5	6	Time was experienced with no changes in its rate of passage.
... ...							...

Figure 5.4 Example questions and scales of three well-known self-report instruments, the *Goldsmiths Musical Sophistication Index* (Müllensiefen et al., 2014), the *Geneva Emotion Musical Scale* (Zentner et al., 2008), and the *Phenomenology of Consciousness Inventory* (Pekala, 1991).

number of items is large and completing all items in an instrument takes a long time from each participant.

Figure 5.4 shows excerpts from three self-report instruments. In the first example, *Goldsmiths Musical Sophistication Index* (Müllensiefen et al., 2014), which has 31 questions divided into five facets, the scale is a 7-point Likert scale. Some of the questions are worded in reverse fashion and the aggregation of the facets is simply adding the scores together (after reversing the items worded in reverse fashion). The *Geneva Emotional Music Scale* (Zentner et al., 2008) has 5 steps, which are defined by the extremes (not at all, very much) whereas the *Phenomenology of Consciousness Inventory* defines a continuum between two descriptors using a 7-point scale. Note that the options used for selecting a choice (empty spaces or the actual numbers from 0 to 6 or from 2 to 5) do not really matter, but if an equally distanced continuum is suggested (interval scale), integer numbers will communicate this clearly to participants. It is also useful to note here that these kinds of well-known scales are often referred to by their acronyms such as Gold-MSI, GEMS, and PCI, to give the abbreviations of the three scales just mentioned.

Self-reports also have significant limitations; they are subject to biases and sometimes give hints about the research question which may influence responses, and they might also disrupt the whole music listening experience if asked to be provided during or immediately after hearing music. Self-reports cannot provide responses to issues that participants cannot easily articulate or access. The response form itself does not allow nuanced information to be captured (gestures, non-verbal behaviour). In some situations, self-reports might be influenced by what the participant thinks the researcher is studying (*demand characteristics*) and this may lead to responses that are more in line with the hypothesis. However, it is normal to disguise the actual purpose of the research to minimise this bias. Other pitfalls include using illogical scales ('how would you rate this music in terms of familiarity and disliking?'), or simply asking participants to respond to questions or statements that are not easy to understand or too demanding and fatiguing to do after a while. Another demanding aspect of self-reports is the attention required when used *retrospectively* – after the event of interest. Such responses are subject to further interpretation and memory errors. For many of these issues, self-reports are a valuable way of collecting relevant data despite being subject to a number of biases and limitations (Paulhus & Varize, 2007).

Finally, I want to clarify one misconception about self-reports that concerns their subjectivity. If the topic in question is something where subjectivity is really at the heart of the issue, such as in emotions and preferences, self-reports do provide essential information about the topic, and there is not necessarily a more objective or reliable version that can be obtained elsewhere (from neuroscience or physiology). A similar realisation was made years ago in the study of pain, where it is acknowledged that the best measure and the gold standard for pain is nothing other than the self-reported level of subjective pain (Hjermstad et al., 2011). When the topic is inherently subjective, these measures should be acknowledged as the best known indicators. This does not mean that alternative measures, such as indirect or physiological measures, should not be used to build a comprehensive picture about a topic that is subjective. Similarly, if the phenomena can be captured with an objective response (e.g., how much performers move during the performance or look at the eyes of other performers), then self-reports are an inadequate way of obtaining reliable information.

Indirect

Indirect self-reports or covert measures are alternative ways of collecting observations from people, which provide a quantitative estimate of a concept while not specifying what is being actually measured. In other words, the object of interest may be something other than the response itself, an incidental quality of the response that has been measured, such as reaction time or affective bias of the response. The participant may be aware of the experimental design, but not what is actually being measured. Semantic priming is an example of such a method: a participant is asked to categorise a target stimulus, for example, to decide as quickly as possible whether a presented word such as 'sunshine' is a negative or positive word. When the presentation of the word is preceded by a sound which can be either negative (diminished chord) or positive (major chord), this can impact the simple task of categorising the words as negative or positive; the decision is faster if the sound is congruent with the word (e.g., positive-sounding chord, i.e., a major chord), and the decision will take longer if the sound is incongruent with the target word (e.g., if a dissonant chord is paired with a positive word, see Lahdelma et al., 2022). The decision is made faster because the person has a mental representation in which the two concepts are associated and the delay is caused by the juxtaposition of two opposite concepts. This method gives an index of how valenced (positive or negative) sounds or music are, for instance, and participants cannot really alter their reaction times consciously, so it does provide an unfiltered estimate of these qualities of the stimuli.

Indirect measures are sometimes used to probe emotions, since affective states are often accompanied by changes in information processing and behaviours (Russell, 2003). For instance, induced affective states may lead to affect-congruent judgement biases, meaning that if the participant is really happy, when presented with some ambiguous objects, that participant tends to see more happiness in these objects than a person who is in an emotionally neutral state. An alternative way to probe the emotion is to have the participants recall objects from memory, and the affective state biases the type of objects recalled. Vuoskoski & Eerola (2012) used these two measures (memory task and rating ambiguous facial expressions) to explore whether self-selected sad music can lead to cognitive biases in the same way as happens when the participants had undergone an emotion induction using an autobiographical task. In the autobiographical task they recall a very sad event of their life in detail.

In addition to emotions and affective processing, indirect and implicit measures have been used regularly to probe social judgements and behaviour (Greenwald & Lai, 2020) such as explicit racial preferences and self-esteem. Indirect measures are nearly free from demand characteristics, and are not affected by the participants' conscious interpretations of their own internal processes. Also, most of these indirect measures rely on minimal verbalisations, so it could be argued that these are more reliable and objective than verbal self-report measures, although there are response methodologies that are designed to be fully non-verbal. It should also be noted that there are disadvantages to the indirect measures as they can be noisy and tricky to set up in a way that captures the intended purpose.

Behavioural Measures

The menu of behavioural measures is also almost as wide as the self-reports; there are plenty of non-verbal measures, a plethora of passive behaviours that can be taken as measures of musical behaviour, and researchers have designed all sorts of active tasks that are able to probe a specific issue, behaviour, or topic. And simply playing and performing music in any form lends itself to a behavioural measure when a specific aspect of the performance (expression, movement, interpretation, communication) is selected as the focus of the study.

Passive

Passive behaviours form the simplest behavioural data that can be captured by observation. This can be achieved by merely looking at how many types of events there are. These may be events in the real world (how many audience members nod their heads in concerts) or something captured in music itself (how many false cadences there are in Bach chorales or pull-offs in Van Halen solos). Sometimes, a good indicator of whether people like some type of music is simply recording how long they listen to the specific type of music when given various options (North & Hargreaves, 2000). In music and consumer behaviour studies, recording the time spent in an area of a shop when a specific background music has been on is a direct measure of this, as is the rather more exotic number of bites per minute, which has been used to measure arousal linked to music (Milliman, 1986). The emotions and attention of listeners and audience members may be captured by tracking their gaze (Ansani et al., 2020) or by analysing their facial expressions using dedicated software (Kayser, 2017). Technical solutions to subtle social cues can be useful indicators of musical aspects that are also unobtrusive and ecologically valid.

Active

Active behavioural tasks are non-verbal or action-orientated (such as playing or tapping) tasks which the experimenter has planned with research questions in mind. These can be non-verbal, production tasks, or performance-related tasks.

Non-verbal responses are a broad category of behavioural tasks that range from similarity rating tasks to all sorts of behavioural tasks, which all strive to avoid verbal labelling or using verbal cues in the task in one way or another. The motivation is to avoid the pitfalls related to language, specifically the semantic and conceptual effects different words and terms have for different people. There are numerous non-verbal response methods, but one of the most fundamental ways of collecting non-verbal responses is to ask people how *similar* two things are that are presented to them. This is, of course, a verbally given task, but the way people do it does not have to be along any verbally or semantically articulated dimension. In this task, an array of items (e.g., short music examples or timbres) is presented in paired fashion to the participant who only needs to say how similar the two items are (say, on a scale of 1 to 7, where 1 is maximally dissimilar and 7 is maximally similar). After evaluating all the pairings of items, these similarity ratings will offer a neat way to construct the semantic mapping of these items based on a clever algorithm that uncovers the underlying similarity configuration (multidimensional scaling). This configuration reveals the defining features of similarity, which are the essence and outcome of this type of data collection. In music, the perceptual foundation of timbre (Shepard, 1962) has been established using this method and similarity ratings have also been used to probe how emotions (Bigand et al., 2005) and melodies (Eerola & Bregman, 2007) are represented.

Another example of an informative non-verbal response task is to utilise the so-called 'jigsaw puzzle' task. In this task, music has been chopped into small chunks (phrases) and participants are asked to reorder the clips in a musically coherent order. The idea is to look at how a long-term structure such as the sonata form is recovered from individual clips (Granot & Jacoby, 2011). A simpler but still non-verbal task is to explore musical imagery by asking participants to compare the pitches of the two separate locations in a song marked by lyrics and to indicate which location has the higher pitch (Halpern, 1988). This reveals the mental play-back speed of music as the participants mentally 'scan' or hear the music in the mind to be able to compare the pitches. Another example would be to tap along with the tempo of an involuntarily imagined piece of music (also known as an *earworm*). As these experiences usually do not occur in a lab, Kelly Jakubowski has collected this information unobtrusively via a smart watch that every participant wore for a study period (Jakubowski et al., 2015).

Music Performance and Creation

Music performance tasks are a rich behavioural measure that can be taken in all kinds of direction, from a full performance to something simplified such as playing small segments of music from memory. Performers can be asked to play excerpts from music with a list of specific emotion expressions, and this allows researchers to establish which acoustic and musical cues they are consistently using to create these expressions (Laukka et al., 2013). Performance can also focus on the actual movements of the performers to see what the expressive movements are, what the movements that coordinate performance with co-performers are, and which movements are just related to the actual playing (called ancillary movements). To probe any of these, it is typical to design the task in a way that manipulates the focus of interest in some way; for instance, the role of movement in expression was famously studied by Jane Davidson by asking performers to play a music example with *normal expression, exaggerated expression,* and *no expression* and their movements were captured (Davidson, 1993). We learnt from that study that movement is a major part of expression. Sometimes, the focus of a performance is on the actual performer and not the music. For instance, how anxious or confident the performer is when performing in front of an important panel of experts (Oudejans & Pijpers, 2009).

Improvisation and composition provide a unique window into the ways in which performers and composers create musical patterns within the confines of style and convention. These can also be viewed as tasks that reveal different aspects of the musical process. For instance, both tasks have been used to study the musical cues utilised by composers (Thompson & Robitaille, 1992) or performers (Laukka et al., 2013) to express emotions. Some theorists have been using evidence from how the mind works and how compositions are created to exploit the ways we remember, parse structure together, and ascribe meaning to music (Lerdahl, 2019).

Music production tasks can be anything from simply tapping with a rhythm or with another person, or a simulated person in some cases, which allows researchers to alter the synchronisation parameters accurately and sometimes quite sneakily (see Keller, 2008). Performance can also be a simple musical reproduction task such as mimicking a rhythm, which is a neat way of tracing the small variations to the rhythm that each participant will bring to their reproduction of the rhythm. When reproductions are passed from one participant to another, this process will eventually converge into stereotypical representations of rhythms (Jacoby & McDermott, 2017). It is also possible to add learning to production tasks, where participants are given different amounts of exposure or different kinds of representations as the learning materials. For instance, Selchenkova and her colleagues (2014) examined how temporal regularity of the presentation of artificial pitch grammar would impact learning the grammar, which they tested implicitly, via a tapping task.

Production tasks can also be singing or humming, continuation of a melody by singing, or producing just a note the listeners expect after hearing an opening fragment (called melodic cloze task, see Fogel et al. (2015)), or reproducing famous tunes from memory (Levitin, 1994). Performing music is a great way of probing where the mistakes occur in performance or how the memory for specific parts of the music is subject to change when attempting to play excerpts after brief exposure. Such tasks are designed to provide information about the stable parts of recall of music (is it the contour, the tonal structure, the intervals, or the rhythm that is central for the memory and production) and the production errors are informative of the kinds of representations and biases that people have (Palmer & Drake, 1997). It is also possible to allow participants to manipulate existing music in terms of how it sounds (timbre, tempo, articulation, etc.) to make it express certain emotions, for instance. This so-called *analysis-by-synthesis* paradigm has been used to expand the possibilities of traditional experiments identifying how musical cues contribute to the emotions expressed in music (Bresin & Friberg, 2011; Micallef Grimaud & Eerola, 2021). In summary, music production tasks offer interesting perspectives on musical processes, and most of these tasks can be framed as engaging music games or tasks that resemble the way music is taught by mimicking and reproducing.

Physiological Measures

Peripheral

Peripheral measures consist of cardiovascular, electrodermal, and respiratory measures, which are typical indicators of stress and relaxation. It is not uncommon to find these measures in studies of anxiety about music performance, emotional reactions to music, or chills related to music. Each physiological measure is collected and analysed differently. Cardiovascular indicators may be measured from an ECG signal (electrocardiogram) that can be collected through two electrodes in the chest area or alternatively from the wrist using a smart watch (which actually relies on photoplethysmography, an optical measure of peripheral changes in blood circulation), if the fidelity is sacrificed to keep the measure less invasive. From the raw ECG signal one can extract the peaks of heart beats (or more technically, the *R wave* that characterises the activity of the heart) and the variation of these peaks over time called *heart rate variability*, which is a collection of measures that capture the variation in different diagnostic ways. In general, heart rate variability measures are known to be sensitive and reliable indicators of stress and relaxation, but are not without problems (Quintana et al., 2016). The electrodermal signal is simply a measure of moisture, or more accurately the increased skin conductance due to repeated sudomotor nerve bursts that secrete sweat to the top of the skin. This activity can be measured from the palmar side of the finger or from other surfaces of the skin. The signal itself can be divided into *tonic* and *phasic* parts, which are indicators of arousal that occurs rapidly after the onset of any stressor or excitement. It is a sensitive and surprisingly fast process, visible within a second of the unexpected event. Respiration is typically measured through a flexible strap across the chest and respiration cycles are connected to heart rate, but the pace and depth of respiration are often taken as an index of relaxation or stress.

To use physiological measures to qualify the experience or emotions, a study design needs to contain a *baseline measurement* – or several baseline measurements if it is a long experiment – to establish the normal level for the individual before intervention or experimental manipulation. The actual objective levels of these measures vary greatly across people, so the absolute levels are not that meaningful, but the change from each individual's baselines is valid when these types of measures are used.

Figure 5.5 illustrates the nature of three typical physiological signals, electrocardiogram (ECG), respiration (RSP), and electrodermal activity (EDA). The ECG signal shows a typical heart rate (75 beats per minute) with a distinctive shape of each heartbeat containing a positive peak (called the R-peak, which indicates the largest contraction of the ventricles) and a smaller positive peak (the T-peak, which is related to repolarisation of the ventricles). Respiration resembles a sinusoidal signal, although it has subtle differences from a pure sine wave, and the example shows a typical pace of respiration (15 cycles per minute). The respiration amplitude, period, and the local pauses of inhales and exhales are the calculated indicators from this measure. Electrodermal activity (EDA) shown here has two impulse-shaped peaks that represent major *phasic* reactions to external events (stress or surprise). An illustrative example of how the phasic components of the EDA reflect the build-up and the drop in EDM music is given in Solberg & Dibben (2019). All such physiological signals require good recording conditions and signal processing techniques to eliminate noise and artefacts from the signal, but the tools for these purposes are well developed (e.g., Figure 5.5 was made with *NeuroKit2*, a free Python-based analysis package for all physiological signals (Makowski et al., 2021)).

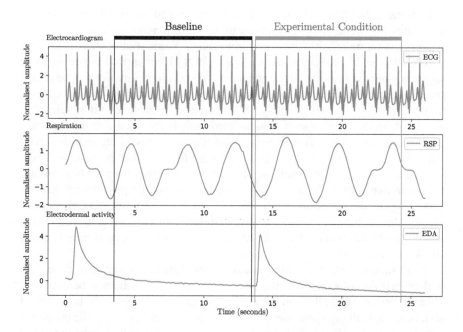

Figure 5.5 A short extract of the raw ECG (electrocardiogram), respiration, and electrodermal activity signals highlighting the need for baseline and experimental conditions.

Chemical

Chemical markers, also known as neuroendocrine markers, are various indicators of stress and reward, and examples range from oxytocin to prolactin or cortisol. Markers of stress, such as cortisol, which can be measured from a saliva sample, albeit not very accurately, are sometimes used as an objective measure of stress in studying music performance anxiety (Guyon et al., 2020), or the relaxing effects of music (Khalfa et al., 2003). The benefit of measuring a stress-related biomarker such as cortisol (CORT) from saliva is that it is relatively easy to obtain samples during the experiment, although the baseline control condition must also be collected for every participant. The downside is that the measure is not a particularly accurate measure of stress because the underlying driver, the hypothalamus-pituitary-adrenal axis (HPAA), is related to a variety of indicators such as corticotropin releasing factor (CRF), and arginine vasopressin (AVP), or adrenocorticotropic hormone (ACTH), which can be measured more directly from blood. Drawing blood samples will not make a study about music performance anxiety or relaxation with music any easier, so researchers may accept the loss of accuracy in terms of the underlying driver to keep data collection feasible.

In some other biomarkers, such as oxytocin and prolactin, there are no substitutes for blood samples because these neurotransmitters and many other markers cannot be reliably measured from saliva. Some studies such as Ladinig et al. (2019) and Eerola, Vuoskoski, et al. (2021) have carried out research in hospitals where volunteers have agreed that several blood samples will be drawn under different experimental conditions. These studies tested the theory of David Huron (2011) about whether enjoyment of sadness in music could be related to release of prolactin. Prolactin is associated with homeostasis, in other words, maintaining psychological well-being, and Huron suggested an appealing idea that music can trigger this system by inducing feelings that emulate real loss, and, in the absence of the actual loss, the overall experience from the homeostatic correction that uses prolactin is positive and enjoyable. Empirical work has not found support for prolactin theory, but our study found fascinating changes in oxytocin levels between those who enjoyed the feeling of being moved during listening to music compared to those who did not derive such experiences (Eerola, Vuoskoski, et al., 2021).

Blood samples are in comparison easy biomarkers if you compare them with markers that do not even cross the blood-brain barrier, which must be measured within the brain. While the non-invasive neuroscience measures will be reviewed next, here I am talking about measuring a specific biomarker within the brain. For example, dopamine (DA), the neurotransmitter widely associated with reward and pleasure (but which also has facilitating functions) can be traced in the brain if it is labelled with a mildly radioactive substance (^{11}C-Raclopride) that is known to bind with dopamine. In effect, participants are administered the tracer through a vein in the arm, and the binding of the tracer and dopamine is captured with Positron Emission Tomography (PET). The timescale of this process is not particularly good, but it has offered insights into the neural locations and functional connectivities in the brain related to intense pleasure induced by listening to one's favourite music (Salimpoor et al., 2011).

Genetic

Genetic markers have also sometimes been explored as potential causal reasons for observing differences in areas of music perception such as absolute pitch perception (AP) (Tan et al., 2014). For example, one project mapped variations in genomes in musical families and controlled who underwent extensive tests on musical aptitude and creativity (Ukkola-Vuoti et al., 2013). They found differences in the variation of genomes in specific markers related to cognitive functions. In another large-scale study, a group of scholars (Theusch & Gitschier, 2011) focused on identical (monozygotic) and non-identical (dizygotic) twins, and a broader picture emerged from AP holders and their siblings that allowed the researchers to estimate the role of genes in absolute pitch ability. Absolute pitch ability was present in nearly all cases of identical twins, whereas non-identical twins had a lower probability of both possessing the ability, suggesting genetic factors strongly influence but do not fully determine this ability. A similar pattern has been reported in another twin study concerning the ability to detect distorted tunes (Drayna et al., 2001).

Neural

Neural signals are based on measuring neural activity via electric impulses (EEG, as in electroencephalography), magnetic impulses (MEG for magnetic encephalography), or hemodynamic responses. One can even record the electrical activity directly from exposed neural tissue and neurons with so-called clamp recordings and single-unit recordings, which have been informative in understanding how brain cells fire. These are typically animal studies, but there are music-related studies with humans undergoing surgery of some kind (such as corrective treatment of epilepsy), which allow the recording of brain responses from a very specific part of the brain. For example, Diana Omigie and her colleagues explored electric responses to dissonant and consonant sounds from very specific cortical locations using depth electrodes placed during presurgical evaluation (Omigie et al., 2015). However, it is more common to carry out EEG research in a non-invasive fashion, where one records responses from a large and quite unspecified neuronal group that can be captured from the scalp via multiple electrodes, from 16 to 256, placed in a cap the participant is wearing. The temporal resolution of the EEG is excellent, down to several milliseconds, although the potential to pinpoint activity within brain areas is fairly limited. This act of localisation can be done to some degree by fitting models that would generate similar electrical patterns that are measurable from the scalp, but such models are a rough estimate at best. Magnetoencephalograpy (MEG) is a technique related to EEG, but in general it is more sensitive and records the weak changes in the magnetic field that any electrical impulse generates. It has the benefit of being temporally as accurate as EEG but having much better spatial resolution. The actual device is costly and less used in clinical work, so hospitals and clinical research settings are more likely to use MRI and fMRI devices than the MEG (Huettel et al., 2004). Figure 5.6 summarises the temporal and spatial accuracy of common methods in neuroscience to capture neuronal activity.

As EEG and MEG have excellent temporal precision, they are often used to probe the brain's responses to specific events. This requires numerous (tens, sometimes even hundreds of) repetitions of the trials that contain the activity of interest. Since responses to any one event are very noisy and idiosyncratic, it is typical to average the responses to these events (e.g., an event can be a musical note or chord onset) over all trials and for participants to estimate the *Event-Related Potentials* (ERPs). ERPs have characteristic interpretations and components defined by the time from the event (aka 'post-stimulus onset'), signal polarity, and amplitude of the signal. For instance, an ERP component called *P3* or sometimes *P300* refers to a positive peak 300 ms after the event, whereas *N2* or *N200* refers to a component that takes place approximately 200 ms after the event and is negative in

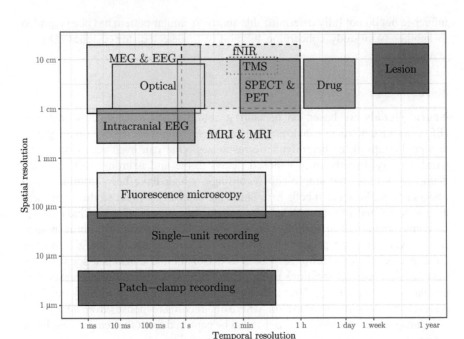

Figure 5.6 Neuroscience methods displayed in terms of temporal and spatial accuracy.

polarity. Various components such as these have been connected in numerous ERP studies to different aspects of early processing, such as hearing a chord or other meaningful stimuli (*N400*, see Steinbeis & Koelsch, 2008) or orienting attention towards a novel auditory event (*P300*, especially a variant called *P3a*, Näätänen et al., 2001).

Figure 5.7 shows the electrical voltage responses to a critical note in 48 melodies from one participant. This is drawn from an open dataset by Shuqing Zhao and Ben Godde (2019). The participant heard 48 melodies, half of them in major and half in minor, and the idea here was to explore how the brain processes the critical note (third scale degree) that defines the melody either as major or minor. In the figure, the critical note occurs at 0 ms. The upper plot shows the activation of all 36 electrodes in 96 trials, without regard to mode. This is to show the overall pattern of activation and how different areas of the scalp receive wildly different voltages (some are positive, some are negative in the same instance). In the lower panel of the figure, I have taken the mean of two electrodes (*P3* and *P7*) representing the left parietal area and calculated the mean for the trials representing the critical notes for major and minor. Overall, there seems to be a large peak around 200 ms (which is labelled as *N2* or as negative *N200*[14]) as well as a small *P1* (positive component around 100 ms), which suggest some type of systematic response to this specific change. To see whether the changes

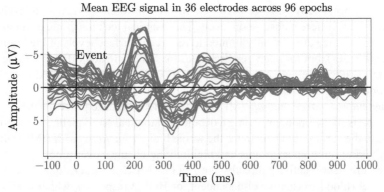

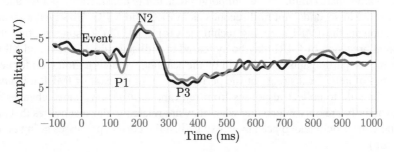

Figure 5.7 Electrode voltages to critical notes in 48 melodies in one participant from the dataset published by Zhao & Godde (2019).

in mode create specific neural responses, one can statistically compare the two. Even in this cursory view, which is now based on the recording of just one participant in 96 melodies presentations, the minor mode seems to evoke a stronger response *P1* and *N2*, the latter linked to the brain's automatic process to detect changes in auditory stimuli. The full analysis of course requires the analysis of all participants (59 in total) and factoring in the crucial differences between the participants such as whether the participants were musicians or non-musicians and spoke either tonal-languages or intonation-languages. These expertise and language differences have previously been shown to lead to differentiated ERP responses in auditory tasks, see Bidelman et al. (2011). The full report and data from this experiment are available as a preprint at *PsyArXiv* and *OSF* (Zhao & Godde, 2019).

There are also other measures that are getting closer to the temporal precision of EEG/MEG such as optical brain imaging techniques (*diffuse optical imaging*, DOI and *near-infrared spectroscopy*, NIRS). These measures are based on exposing the brain to near-infrared light, and the absorption of light in the brain is used as an index of brain activity, since haemoglobin with different oxygenation levels is known to have different absorption levels. These optical techniques are developing fast, although they are currently limited to relatively surface levels of the brain (a few centimetres), but for many research questions, they already offer an affordable and non-invasive alternative neural measure to EEG, which is also picking up the activations from the scalp.

Magnetic resonance imaging (MRI) uses magnetic fields to probe the density of various parts of the brain, providing a detailed anatomical 'still' picture. This is not limited to the surface, but penetrates the whole brain. *Functional MRI* (fMRI) does this by taking multiple snapshots and highlighting changes over time. fMRI does not measure neural activity directly like EEG or MEG but tracks blood oxygenation level (blood-oxygen-level-dependent, or BOLD response), which is related to neural activity, as oxygen must be delivered to locations where electric/neural activity has been high. The spatial accuracy of fMRI is very good, as it can map areas smaller than 1 mm, but its temporal precision is considerably poorer and it is measured in seconds, not milliseconds as in EEG and MEG. However, a recent innovation in the fMRI scanning technique (Toi et al., 2022) suggests that the temporal precision of fMRI may be increased to milliseconds. In fMRI and MEG experiments, participants must lie still on the scanner, which is a limitation for certain types of active tasks (e.g., music performance). In the case of fMRI, it is vital also to be able to collect responses from relevant *control tasks,* since changes in neural activity are only interesting when they are related to those activities that are beyond what would take place anyway (e.g., just the normal processes going on in the brain).

fMRI scanning is particularly insightful when we attempt to connect the processing of musical phenomena or experience to broader functional mechanisms identified in the brain. If we take the example of music-induced chills, we now have ideas about triggers, personality traits, and a few possible mechanisms for chills. fMRI can help to disentangle competing theories by identifying the brain areas involved, which then in turn will help to eliminate or corroborate theories. This assumes, of course, that the competing theories utilise different functional areas of the brain, which is not an easy assumption to be fulfilled.

Let's look at the recent exploration of chills by Klepzig et al. (2020). They used fMRI scanning where participants listened to pleasant music examples known for their ability to elicit chills (e.g., classical music such as Albinoni's or Barber's *Adagio*) which kept intact the original chill-inducing segments or replaced them with harsh and unpleasant sounds (styrofoam rubbing or a fork scraping on porcelain). As they heard the pieces in the scanner, they also gave ratings of intensity of the chills. The researchers analysed the BOLD responses of the sections where participants indicated that they had experienced pleasant chills and used the preceding five seconds as a local baseline. Certain areas of the brain were chosen for a precise analysis based on a previous analysis that had estimated the likelihood of areas for various processes (Koelsch, 2014) and this analysis brought up areas such as the hippocampus, amygdala, thalamus, and primary auditory cortex being active during chills. Klepzig compared brain activation during pleasant chills with neutral baseline sections and found no differences in auditory areas, but there were notable changes in areas such as bilateral anterior insula, putamen, and caudate nucleus. When they contrasted pleasant segments with unpleasant segments, the differences in these areas grew larger despite the rather opposite in the valence of the stimulus. They interpreted these findings from activated areas to be related to prediction of events (caudate), affect processing (thalamus), and sensory processing (anterior insula). Figure 5.8 shows the areas brought out by the contrast between positive chills minus the non-chilling positive sounds using the open access data that the authors offer[15].

Physiological measures provide numerous objective indicators of participant processes related to information processing, emotional reactions, and attention. The key issue with all these measures is the research design that allows one to capture insights from these physiological processes in a way that can be clearly seen

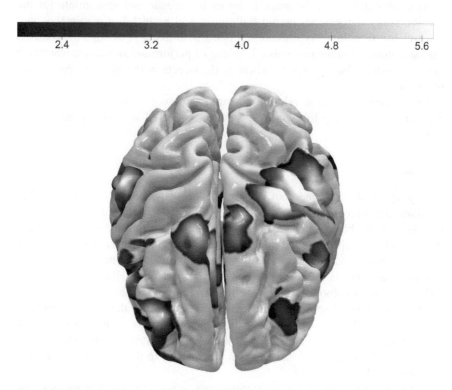

Figure 5.8 Neural areas activated during the listening of pleasant chills-inducing sections in comparison with non-chills-inducing sections (created from the data by Klepzig et al., 2020).

to provide answers to meaningful and controlled research questions. Physiological measures are not suitable for exploratory research as they require repetitions, definition of the baseline, and proof of manipulation checks, and in general they all require a significant commitment and investment of both researcher's and participant's time.

Research Contexts

Responses to music and other tasks related to musical behaviours can be collected in different situations and contexts. Traditionally, many empirical experiments are designed and executed in the safe confines of a laboratory. These tend to be small, soundproof rooms hidden in the middle of university campuses. This is very good for control of the environment such as sound quality, digital display, and uninterrupted time to focus on the task. But these rooms might not be as great for capturing genuine responses nor for attracting participants who do not tend to be near university campuses. Some topics such as strong experiences with music might not really occur easily in such artificial settings, although, of course, laboratories can be made to be more realistic and appropriate for the specific study if resources permit building a real nightclub, for instance, as a research location. In many situations, it is worth thinking of whether the research can be conducted in the real music listening or performing situations, whether it is in concerts, at home, or somewhere in the streets in the case of street music festivals.

Let's survey the most relevant research contexts, including the lab, field experiments, everyday life contexts, studies conducted at concerts, and online studies.

Laboratory

A well-equipped and soundproof laboratory represents the best option for studies involving sensitive measurement devices (psychophysiology, neural responses) or high-fidelity playback (psychoacoustics) or some other physical aspect of the study that needs to be well controlled (monitor with an accurate display of visual stimuli, or seeing another participant, etc.). Labs are traditionally the heart and soul of a research group, and in fortunate situations they are not only well equipped in music technology, sound proofing, and relevant software, but they also come with a lab engineer or technical specialist who knows every aspect of the place, equipment, and software, who listens and who understands the needs of the research. Such a person can be more valuable than all the equipment stored within the walls of the lab, and I will devote a later section (Chapter 8) to the principles of a well-functioning lab.

Labs are well-suited for collecting data involving psychoacoustics and physiological measures since these types require sound-isolated rooms and critical listening is of utmost importance. The second aspect of labs is the ability to control the space. Labs make it easy to welcome participants and debrief them outside the actual data collection situation if needed. The actual research rooms can be changed to suit different designs, sets, and purposes. Laboratory equipment comes with many research devices and equipment. If we keep the truly expensive specialised machinery out of the equation (such as fMRIs, MEGs, and Motion Capture devices that are housed in specialist buildings with research centres), most of the typical equipment for generic music and science research is fairly affordable and not that exotic; computers and different interfaces for them, from button boxes to drum pads and microphones, displays, and, naturally, loudspeakers, mixers, and headphones – these are all normal staples of these facilities. Eye tracking devices and sensors to measure electrodermal responses and heart rate are common devices, although they already require specialist expertise to be used effectively.

One downside of a lab is the price tag these types of facility have with soundproofing, wiring, and specialised equipment and software, which naturally puts a pressure on investment. It is not uncommon that lab leaders need to keep the grants coming just to keep the lab functional. This pressure can, of course, be very positive and feed more research, but it is also a reminder that labs have significant running costs after their initial establishment. The other drawback is that labs tend to easily attract people from the nearest community, students, and well-educated locals who all are likely to be Western, Educated, Industrialised, Rich, and Democratic (WEIRD, see Source of Information) members of society, but efforts can be made to expand the recruit beyond these qualities.

Field

It is possible to collect interesting and highly ecologically relevant data concerning musical behaviours in what could be called field conditions, the actual musical event wherever it takes place (a street corner, a temple, a school etc.). Sometimes it is even almost possible to run a controlled experiment in real musical situations. Two fascinating studies that tackle different aspects of synchronisation offer good examples of field experiments. Glaura Lucas and her colleagues observed the way conga groups entrain to each other during a Congado festival in Brazil (Lucas et al., 2011). Different types of drum group (Congo, Candombe, Moçambique) participate in the festival where they perform while walking on the city streets. All groups have their own rhythms (patterns and tempi) and the fascinating phenomenon is observing how the groups maintain their own tempo, rhythm, and therefore identity when they pass another drum group with a competing tempo and rhythmic pattern. When two groups are playing different patterns in different tempi, say one at 82 BPM and the other 106 BPM, there is a tendency for the tempi to become more synchronised as the groups come in close proximity to each other. This is natural because the members of the group may involuntarily adjust the tempo of their performance in small steps to keep cohesion within the group, and maintaining their own original tempo is not an easy feat during these immersive and somewhat chaotic encounters between the groups. Analysis of recordings of these encounters suggests that the groups can resist the pull toward entraining to the same tempo only with difficulty, but resisting is more likely to happen if their initial tempo and the patterns are dissimilar. Studying such a real musical event with clearly defined theoretical ideas is an example of a study design occurring in a real musical situation, in a field. One could design a similar lab study with simple finger tapping (and in fact, this has been done, see Repp & Keller, 2008), but observing drum groups in the street is a fascinating, albeit technically challenging, way to tackle the question of entrainment *in situ* (Latin for 'on site').

Another blend between the real world and lab experiments is offered by the technique known as *silent disco*. In this setup that has been popularised by market forces, everyone in a confined space – such as a regular night club – gets special headphones that are under the control of the event organiser. The beauty of the silent disco is that researchers can control the audio content of each set of headphones while every individual is listening and dancing to the music, so it allows one to split the behaviours and music in ways that are not possible normally. It is also a very natural situation, just dancing along with others, that occurs without the research angle due to the low noise footprint the silent disco can sustain. This technique has been used to test the claimed positive effects of synchronisation, such as increased social closeness and pain tolerance. In one such study carried out by Bronwyn Tarr and her colleagues (Tarr et al., 2016), they had some participants dance in a synchronised fashion (to the same music) whereas the other dancers in the control condition were exposed to the same situation but dancing in non-synchronised fashion (either in partial synchrony or no synchrony at all, arranged by playing different music between them). The results demonstrated clear increases in many of the predicted social benefits of synchronisation (social bonding, increased pain threshold) although the groups did not show any differences in collaborative measures. The silent disco set-up has also been used to demonstrate that people learn and remember more details about the individuals who dance with the same tempo of music as them (Woolhouse et al., 2016). Overall, these kinds of experiments are fun to organise and participate in, they feel appropriate as far as musical behaviours go but still allow neat and subtle causal manipulation of the crucial elements related to musical behaviours.

Everyday Life

Moving from the special situations offered by field experiments to even more realistic situations in everyday life. As everyone now has a smartphone with access to tens of millions of music tracks, most music listening occurs at home and during commuting, and wherever people have free time at their disposal. By this token, empirical music research should really try to capture the prevalent listening situations and what happens socially, musically, emotionally, and physically in them. One of the great ways to obtain such information is the *Experience Sampling*

Method (ESM). In this method, participants volunteer to give a few weeks of their life to be under scrutiny, where they will be probed (nowadays via smartphone but previously through SMS messages) by predefined randomly timed prompts from the researcher. These prompts will ask questions about where the participants are, what they are doing now, whether there is there music present, who chose the music, what the music is, what their mood is at the moment, etc. Coupled with information about their playlists and other variables that their smartphone can have (location, movement, etc.), this type of research can paint a sensible picture of what people actually do and think in their everyday life, how much music is involved, and what role it has in these situations. After the pioneering studies of everyday life and music by Adrian North (e.g., North et al., 2004), the capabilities of smartphones have overtaken this field. Will Randall has spearheaded the development of the *mobile Experience Sampling Method* (m-ESM) (Randall et al., 2014) and offered a range of interesting insights about how people regulate their moods with their music listening choices. For example, Randall & Rickard (2017) collected such data from over 300 participants to find patterns between the decision to listen to music and the under-lying emotions (before and after listening). For example, they established that the reason for listening to music was often emotional when the listener was in a nega-tive mood. Often, this type of listening was consistent with emotion regulation strat-egies called coping and distraction, where the listener is actively trying to manage their negative mood by taking the attention off the irksome feeling (distraction).

Another example involving listening to music and emotional reactions comes from a compelling comparison of listening to music in a lab and at home by Tervaniemi et al. (2021). They collected physiological measures (electrocardio-gram, skin conductance, and measures of stress from saliva samples) and self-reports of emotions. The participants listened to their favourite music and neutral music of their own choice and this setup was carried out both in the lab and at home. The results showed clear differences in physiology and self-reports between the laboratory and the home (stress indicators were lower at home), although no clear link with the type of music and location was established. This is an example of how studies that used to be exclusively carried out inside the lab have the poten-tial to be run anywhere with the help of mobile devices (such as your smartwatch).

Concerts

Concerts and all other music listening or participation events (festivals, soirees) provide a challenging but rich opportunity to understand what happens to us when we listen to music. These are settings where people often experience strong emotions, they are willing to pay considerable amounts of money to be able to participate in an event, and there is the excitement of the live situation itself, and the influence of other concert goers. Often the venues are inspiring and visually thrilling environments as well. Although events themselves may constitute a small proportion of actual music listening episodes in anyone's life, they can be signifi-cant, deeply emotional, memorable, and even life-changing for many individuals.

Gabrielsson's (2011) book on strong experiences with music contains numerous wonderful and inspiring descriptions of these types of experiences.

Some studies of strong emotional experiences of music have demonstrated the special nature of live concert experiences eloquently. Alex Lamont (2011) had about 50 students give free written reports of their most intense experiences of music listening. These texts were qualitatively analysed and interpreted within the framework of positive psychology. Live events dominated (~80%) the accounts of the experiences, ranging from festivals and pop concerts to weddings and funerals. The experiences were mostly described as positive (intense, exciting, thrilling, fantastic, 'the most beautiful moment of your life') and Lamont arranged these into hedonic responses, flow-type states, and (search for) meaning and connection between the performer and the audience. It is worth noting that these latter themes have been explored in more detail recently; Rafał Lawendowski and Tomasz Besta (2020) surveyed a large number (800+) of attendees of music festivals to elaborate on how these links between feeling united with the artists or other members of the audience operate and whether these are related to possible self-growth and notions of self-construction. Their fascinating set of findings suggest that the importance of the social connection between audience members and the artist is stronger for those who hold a more collective view of the self. This collective vs non-collective view was also connected to feelings of self-growth and emotions in these experiences.

Another example of studying concerts is the Hauke Egermann project (2020), which collected a rich set of self-reports and physiological responses during actual contemporary music concerts. The researchers also manipulated the information the audience members received before the concert, with one group receiving a typical preconcert talk aimed at enhancing the experience by offering insight and information about the music, and another group received a talk unrelated to music. The results showed that the two talks really did not cause differences between the groups in their emotional reactions, but the reactions were different in terms of the underlying dimensions of the experience. Although the size of the groups was modest (41 and 53) in terms of studying full concert halls of listeners, they were able to measure the peripheral nervous system (skin conductance and heart rate) of these participants at the same time in the live concert situation. Although some links between self-reports and physiology were established (analytical processes were linked to decreased skin conductance response scores, and higher semantic values were linked to reduced heart rate variability), it is clear that physiology alone is not sufficient to tell the researcher what a listener experiences, and, in this case, the context of this particular concert with its emphasis on contemporary music was perhaps not the most conducive to leading to intense emotional experiences.

Online

For as long as we have had the internet, surveys have been conducted online. However, studies that go beyond surveys asking questions about music and musical behaviours and present music and require more sophisticated response measures such as production tasks (tapping, singing) or timed responses have only been possible since the development of sufficiently advanced web-based data collection software and increased capacity of computers and browsers during the last five years. Research in the cognitive sciences, social sciences, economics, and AI is steadily turning more and more to online studies that use recruitment services (sometimes called crowdsourcing platforms) to efficiently funnel participants into the study (Buhrmester et al., 2018; Stewart et al., 2017). The term crowdsourcing refers to the notion of distributing work to many users, and it has been hailed as transformative for certain types of research tasks within cognitive and data sciences (Stewart et al., 2017). In studies involving topics within music and science, online studies with recruitment services have only recently been hesitantly taken up since there have been limitations involved in presenting high-quality audio or collecting accurate timings in online studies, but these are largely solved in contemporary online solutions (Eerola, Armitage, et al., 2021). In addition, ethical and regulatory issues for both online platforms and the use of recruitment services are being discussed in this field. With the availability of several recruitment platforms such as Amazon's *Mechanical Turk, Prolific, Clickworker* or *Appen*, these opportunities are driving forward certain types of research questions and designs that can be run in 'virtual laboratories' (Henrich et al., 2010). These online studies differ from laboratory studies by imposing *quality controls* in a more specific fashion than in traditional lab experiments. The controls range from questions about the content or attention checks to control tasks about whether the participant is using headphones (Woods et al., 2017). For a more detailed technical and ethical guide on online studies in music, see a recent summary article by Eerola, Armitage, Lavan, & Knight (2021).

The main benefit of using recruitment services and online platforms for research is that the samples can be more representative of the population than the usual lab or survey samples, and with respect to survey studies, the participants in crowdsourced studies tend to be more reliable and attentive than typical online surveys or lab participants (Hauser & Schwarz, 2016). In addition to the possibility of capturing a more diverse set of participants, it may also help to connect specialist samples such as the speakers of specific languages (Turner et al., 2012) or participants suffering from amusia, or tinnitus. In our studies involving reaction time responses to sounds that are different in terms of the positive and negative emotional connotations, we have found that participant attrition and prevalence of outliers in crowdsourced samples are almost identical to laboratory data and vastly superior to traditional web data that has been recruited through convenience samples (Armitage & Eerola, 2020). The recent pandemic has made the online approach to studies more pressing, and numerous labs have moved some of their studies online. In addition, there has been more interest shown towards studies that utilise a gamification approach, where the tasks involve game-like elements with finer graphics, visual feedback, competition among the participants, and other ploys to make it engaging for the participants.

Samples and Participants

Who do we study in empirical research? We study individuals who represent a larger group of people, since we want to be able to generalise our findings. This representation is the tricky issue in empirical research, since opportunities to access just the right people in the right quantity are not guaranteed. Most of the studies published in our field have been carried out with Anglo-American students, who can be described with a fun acronym (WEIRD), which stands for Western, Educated, Industrialised, Rich, and Democratic. Since this is not the full spectrum of humanity (Henrich et al., 2010), this is considered limited, sometimes misleading, or downright suspicious. However, we often cannot easily deviate from many of these limited characteristics in our research, as our ability to go beyond Western samples is limited. But we can do a lot of relevant studies that involve Western and even educated participants. This merely serves as a reminder to think about these issues. Next, we will break down the typical ways of focussing the sample to certain particularities and then talk about the ways of *sampling* this chosen group in a specific fashion.

Sampling Key Differences

The three most common ways to sample specific groups of people are based on their (i) cultural/political/historical/geographical/socioeconomic characteristics, (ii) expertise, and (iii) individual differences.

The first way, cultural, political, historical, geographical, or socioeconomic characteristics, covers a range of often interrelated factors. For example, political and cultural situations may have impacted the education levels of the participants, which in turn may have an impact on how they think, and on how they make and enjoy music. The differences might influence their musical processes or concepts, their knowledge of repertoire, their choice of timbres, lyrics, keys, and so on, depending on how dependent the phenomenon is to the culture (e.g., hearing thresholds are not dependent on culture, music preferences are mostly about culture). If your aim is to find out how a specific cultural competence influences a musical process such as anticipation of melodic continuations, finding the downbeat in music, or what the emotional parts or cues of the music are, you need to vary this cultural background – while keeping other aspects such as musical expertise, level of education, and age comparable. This kind of comparison between distinct cultures is called *cross-cultural research*, which is a discipline of its own where a lot of emphasis is put on how to actually compare something that might at first even be comparable in terms of the existence of the same concepts in both cultures or of the relevant words in both languages. While the options for finding cultures that are fully distinct and maybe not influenced by Western music have become a difficult challenge despite some fascinating music and emotion studies among Mafa tribes in Cameroon (Fritz et al., 2009), Kho tribes in Pakistan (Athanasopoulos et al., 2021), and people in Papua New

Guinea (Smit et al., 2022), we can think about subcultures in any given culture in this way, too. A typical listener to death metal is going to be quite different to a typical listener of jazz, both in terms of what kind of energy, lyrics, and performance they will expect from their favourite music, and also in the functional ways in which they engage with their music (Thompson et al., 2019). It is necessary to understand how knowledge acquisition influences musical processes, so there is much room for discovery here.

Musical training Perhaps the most common samples in empirical music research involve musicians trained and musicians untrained. Musical training is, of course, expected to make a difference to many questions related to perception, skills, and attitudes toward music. Intuitively, we do seem to know the difference between a musically trained person and a person without musical training, but it is not a trivially easy question for research. Is someone who played trombone for four years between the ages of 12 and 16 musically trained, or is someone who likes to play the drums occasionally and sings in a choir regularly musically untrained? Where do we draw the line between those who have usual exposure to music training through school or maybe some additional years of training as a child and those who actively play and perform music? The dividing line used to be something like four or six years of instrument training, but self-learnt musicians tend to drop out of this definition. Fortunately, there are now several well-established instruments that capture musical expertise, e.g., the *Goldsmiths Musical Sophistication Index* (Müllensiefen et al., 2014) and the *Ollen Musical Sophistication Index* (Zhang & Schubert, 2019), which capture different aspects of training and experience and can be used flexibly.

Individual differences Sometimes research questions lend themselves to focus on a specific aspect of people that calls for a specific sample characteristic, such as gender, age, specific personality traits, or political attitudes. For example, several research questions about music and emotions have observed links between emotions experienced and empathy. To really maximise this distinction, I recruited those who scored high and low in a standard measure of empathy (Eerola et al., 2016). This was done using a large representative sample (n=1,500) and asking participants to complete a survey that contained items from an instrument called the *Interpersonal Reactivity Index* (Davis, 1983). For the actual study, we then recruited from the lower and higher ends of the empathy measure, creating two samples that were otherwise identical but different in terms of their empathy. In other cases, native language might be the variable of interest, as has been the case in some studies concerning absolute pitch (Deutsch, 2002) where participants speaking one of the tonal languages (Mandarin or Vietnamese) have an advantage in pitch memory tasks. Another example would be to explore gender differences related to something that is already suspected to be a heavily gendered topic, such as the choice of musical instrument (Hallam et al., 2008). In this case, children in Western countries have associations that high-pitched, smaller instruments such as the flute or violin are more typically played by girls than boys and instruments such as drums, the trombone, and the trumpet have strong masculine associations.

It seems that these associations have not changed during the last 20 years (Delzell & Leppla, 1992; Wrape et al., 2016).

Sample Characteristics

The decision to sample a specific type of characteristic as defined by culture, expertise, or individual differences must be separate from the need to exclude some types of participants or to collect the necessary information about people in a study. Your sample might comprise non-musicians and while your research question does not pose or require the participants to be of a specific age or gender, you typically collect the basic characteristics (age, gender, musical expertise) about the sample to describe them. You may also want to check that your main questions and variables are not impacted by the backgrounds of the participants. In certain cases, you want to exclude participants with specific characteristics, such as people over or under a certain age (especially with time-dependent tasks or tasks that require maturation) or left-handed people in questions related to neural processing (to avoid complications of having to reverse the assumptions about which side is more important for processing), or perhaps you want to be sure that respondents have sufficient language capacity and competence in the language utilised in the study.

Sample Recruitment

Before talking about the practical issues of how to approach and recruit people, I want to clarify an important principle about how people chosen for the study relate to the population. Volunteers are common to be recruited for one's experiment, recruited by means of posters, email lists, or social media. This type of *volunteer sampling* (also known as *convenience sampling*) is good for getting people to participate but the weakness is that all those recruited may have similar qualities (e.g., they are likely to be more interested in music than an average citizen if they are recruited from your social media contacts) that make this kind of sampling unrepresentative and biased. A variant of this is known as *opportunity sampling*, where one employer (or university college) or an event (a concert or a festival) is used to recruit participants, which is an easy, convenient, and affordable method of recruitment, and may get a more varied set of participants for the study than volunteer sampling. Opportunity sampling still has the same weakness as volunteer sampling, where participants are not likely to be a particularly representative of the actual target population, but the bias can be less dramatic than in volunteer sampling. For a nice example of an opportunity sampling, Annemieke van den Tol and her colleagues studied the potential of music as a mood regulation to control emotional eating by recruiting 800 participants from a university campus in the UK (Tol et al., 2020).

In a *random sampling,* each member of the target population has an equal chance of being recruited, although this is typically quite difficult to organise if the target population is large. However, if successful and done with the help of a government census office or an organisation that holds the critical information for

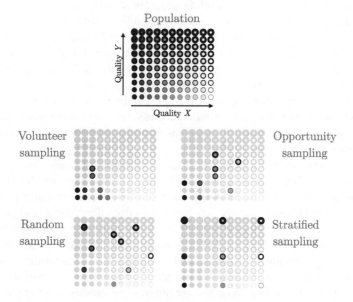

Figure 5.9 An illustration of four sampling strategies.

the population in question (e.g., musicians in orchestras or teachers at schools), the advantage is that the sample then represents the population of interest. A powerful variant of this sampling technique chooses participants according to some system (e.g., every fifth member of the population under interest). This *stratified sampling* balances various demographic characteristics in the sampling. Each section (or stratum) of the population characteristic is sampled according to the same proportion that exists in the whole population (typically age, gender, and education, and often also geographical distribution). In other words, if you know these properties about the population, say from the national statistics that offer open data and great summaries of this type of information, you can define your stratified sampling strategy to reflect these properties so that, in these characteristics, your sample is indistinguishable from the population as a whole.

Figure 5.9 illustrates the differences between the four different sampling strategies described. The dots in the upper rectangle represent the population that has two notable differences, the 'hue' and the 'width' organised in gradual changes across the X and Y axes. In the volunteer sampling strategy, we recruit participants from our contacts or from social networks or from the proximity of our lab and typically get participants who are similar to us or specific to the area or the social media bubble. The figure illustrates how this sample (represented by nine dots) is seemingly random but covers a rather small variation in the key dimensions of the population without us knowing about it. Opportunity sampling captures the population somewhat better than volunteer sampling by introducing a more natural variation in the two qualities, but we have failed to sample some quadrants of the sampling space altogether. Random sampling provides a diverse selection of the population, although it might suffer from sampling similar qualities several times (several dots are from the same rows and columns). For the rectangle representing stratified sampling, the sampling operation is done with the two critical differences in mind, represented by the X and Y dimensions, which are sampled evenly, creating a good coverage of the population for these specific properties.

There are also situations where you have a good sampling strategy in place, but the actual sample you draw turns out to be biased in a way that you did not expect. Say you are studying professional classical musicians who play orchestral instruments and you are interested in how performance anxiety might impact or might have impacted their professional lives. You have obtained a register of musicians from the Association of British Orchestras and know the demographics (age, gender, and education) and instrument distribution of this sample of musicians. You then proceed to recruit a workable sample (say 300 musicians) from the register, and you recruit the musicians by balancing the demographics and instruments so that they reflect the population from which you initially drew them. However, your topic might cause some respondents that have had real difficulties with performance anxiety not to answer as it is a sensitive or painful topic for them, but you will have no idea whether this is happening since you are progressing steadily in getting the data for the survey where the characteristics are kept in check. This is called non-response bias and is a systematic bias where participants drop out of a study. There are ways to examine this bias, especially when you have a recruitment strategy in place, and you get an unusually large number of non-returns from certain types of people. You could interview a few people who did not want to commit to the study, or if there is already information on the prevalence of music performance anxiety, you could check if you are getting the same prevalence in your sample to estimate whether a specific participant loss related to anxiety might have occurred. It is also common to check the demographics of those who decided not to respond and the sampling criteria just in case your study questions or topic have created a situation where some segments of the sample drop out and disengage.

It is rare to be able to utilise the less biased sampling strategies in studies of music and science, but the crucial idea about sampling is to be aware of the limitations and probable biases that are created by the decision of how to sample. Most studies in music and science use some form of convenience and volunteer samples, typically utilising undergraduate university students from psychology or music. This is fine as long as those studies do not make sweeping statements about how the results speak about the whole of humanity as these are very much limited to Western, young, privileged, and educated people, which brings us back to the problematic WEIRD samples (Henrich et al., 2010). There are not too many representative samples used in music and science research, two notable exceptions being some of my studies (Eerola et al., 2016; Eerola & Peltola, 2016) and the study by Patrik Juslin (Juslin et al., 2011), although there are some exceptionally large studies such as the one defining musical sophistication carried out by the team led by Daniel Müllensiefen (Müllensiefen et al., 2014). However, the key issue in sampling is to understand what kind of conclusions you can draw about the topic based on the qualities you sampled. With convenience samples, you will not be able to characterise all the biases and lack of representativeness, so it is important to remember these constraints when writing the conclusions.

Coda

This chapter has covered the *sources of information* for empirical music research, including a wide variety of self-reports, various behavioural methods, and physiological measures ranging from peripheral to neural measures. In addition, different research *contexts* have been summarised and, in the final section, the way data are obtained using *samples* and *participants* has been explained.

Discussion Points

1. What kind of self-reports have you come across in your daily life (political polls, government surveys, student evaluations, etc.) and how does answering them make you feel? Are you paying attention to the wording and what kind of questions tend to infuriate you?
2. Can you think of an example where an indirect measure is better than a direct measure and explain why this is so?
3. What kind of music performance or music production tasks can non-musicians be asked to do and why would it be insightful to be able to capture such responses?
4. Have you monitored your physiological responses (e.g., heart rate and its derivatives) with a smartwatch? How do you see music being linked to applications such as these?
5. How much do your own music-related behaviours and experiences change depending on the location (home, concert, etc.) and social context (alone, with friends, with relatives)? Which locations and social settings have the biggest emotional impact on you?

Notes

1 https://osf.io/zatn8/
2 http://isophonics.net/content/reference-annotations-beatles
3 https://dcmlab.github.io/standards/build/html/index.html
4 www.idmt.fraunhofer.de/en/publications/datasets.html
5 www.ismir.net/resources/datasets/
6 https://github.com/mdeff/fma
7 www2.projects.science.uu.nl/memotion/emotifydata/
8 https://osf.io/p6vkg/
9 www.audiolabs-erlangen.de/resources/MIR/cross-comp
10 https://ismir.net/resources/datasets/

11 https://mtg.github.io/mtg-jamendo-dataset/
12 https://mirg.city.ac.uk/codeapps/the-magnatagatune-dataset
13 https://github.com/OleAd/DiurnalSpotify
14 You notice that EEG research has adopted a scheme where negative is plotted above zero.
15 https://neurovault.org/images/305503/

Further Reading

Daniel, J. (2011). *Sampling essentials: Practical guidelines for making sampling choices.* Sage Publications.

Granot, R. (2017). Music, pleasure, and social affiliation: Hormones and neurotransmitters. In R. Ashley & R. Timmers (Eds.), *The Routledge companion to music cognition* (pp. 101–111). Routledge.

Koelsch, S. (2012). *Brain and music.* John Wiley & Sons.

Paulhus, D. L., & Vazire, S. (2007). The self-report method. In R. W. Robins, R. C. Fraley, & R. F. Krueger (Eds.), *Handbook of research methods in personality psychology* (pp. 224–239). The Guilford Press.

References

Aljanaki, A., Yang, Y.-H., & Soleymani, M. (2017). Developing a benchmark for emotional analysis of music. *PloS ONE, 12*(3), e0173392.

Alluri, V., Toiviainen, P., Jääskeläinen, I. P., Glerean, E., Sams, M., & Brattico, E. (2012). Large-scale brain networks emerge from dynamic processing of musical timbre, key and rhythm. *Neuroimage, 59*(4), 3677–3689.

Ansani, A., Marini, M., D'Errico, F., & Poggi, I. (2020). How soundtracks shape what we see: Analyzing the influence of music on visual scenes through self-assessment, eye tracking, and pupillometry. *Frontiers in Psychology, 11*, 2242.

Armitage, J., & Eerola, T. (2020). Reaction time data in music cognition: A comparison of pilot data sets from lab, crowdsourced and convenience web samples. *Frontiers in Psychology, 10*. https://doi.org/https://doi.org/10.3389/fpsyg.2019.02883

Athanasopoulos, G., Eerola, T., Lahdelma, I., & Kaliakatsos-Papakostas, M. (2021). Harmonic organisation conveys both universal and culture-specific cues for emotional expression in music. *PloS ONE, 16*(1), e0244964. https://doi.org/https://doi.org/10.1371/journal.pone.0244964

Bidelman, G. M., Gandour, J. T., & Krishnan, A. (2011). Musicians and tone-language speakers share enhanced brainstem encoding but not perceptual benefits for musical pitch. *Brain and Cognition, 77*(1), 1–10.

Bigand, E., Vieillard, S., Madurell, F., Marozeau, J., & Dacquet, A. (2005). Multidimensional scaling of emotional responses to music: The effect of musical expertise and of the duration of the excerpts. *Cognition & Emotion, 19*(8), 1113–1139.

Bittner, R., Wilkins, J., Yip, H., & Bello, J. (2016). MedleyDB 2.0: New data and a system for sustainable data collection. In J. Devaney, M. I. Mandel, D. Turnbull, & G. Tzanetaki (Eds.), International Conference on Music Information Retrieval (ISMIR-16) (pp. 1–3). New York City, USA.

Bogdanov, D., Won, M., Tovstogan, P., Porter, A., & Serra, X. (2019). *The MTG-Jamendo Dataset for automatic music tagging.* http://hdl.handle.net/10230/42015

Bresin, R., & Friberg, A. (2011). Emotion rendering in music: Range and characteristic values of seven musical variables. *Cortex, 47*(9), 1068–1081.

Brost, B., Mehrotra, R., & Jehan, T. (2019). *The music streaming sessions dataset.* arXiv. https://doi.org/https://doi.org/10.48550/ARXIV.1901.09851

Buhrmester, M. D., Talaifar, S., & Gosling, S. D. (2018). An evaluation of Amazon's Mechanical Turk, its rapid rise, and its effective use. *Perspectives on Psychological Science, 13*(2), 149–154.

Clayton, M., Jakubowski, K., & Eerola, T. (2018). Interpersonal entrainment in Indian instrumental music performance: Synchronization and movement coordination relate to tempo, dynamics, metrical and cadential structure. *Musicae Scientiae, 23*, 304–331. https://doi.org/https://doi.org/10.1177/1029864919844809

Clayton, M., Leante, L., & Tarsitani, S. (2019). *IEMP North Indian Raga performance.* https://doi.org/https://doi.org/10.17605/OSF.IO/KS325

Clayton, M., Tarsitani, S., Jankowsky, R., Jure, L., Leante, L., Polak, R., Poole, A., Rocamora, M., Alborno, P., Camurri, A., Eerola, T., Jacoby, N., & Jakubowski, K. (2021). The interpersonal entrainment in music performance data collection. *Empirical Musicology Review, 16*(1), 65–84. https://doi.org/http://dx.doi.org/10.18061/emr. v16i1.7555

Cook, N. (2001). Theorizing musical meaning. *Music Theory Spectrum, 23*(2), 170–195.

Davidson, J. W. (1993). Visual perception of performance manner in the movements of solo musicians. *Psychology of Music, 21*(2), 103–113.

Davis, M. H. (1983). Measuring individual differences in empathy: Evidence for a multidimensional approach. *Journal of Personality and Social Psychology, 44*(1), 113–126.

Defferrard, M., Benzi, K., Vandergheynst, P., & Bresson, X. (2016). *FMA: A dataset for music analysis.* arXiv. https://doi.org/https://doi.org/10.48550/ARXIV.1612.01840

Delzell, J. K., & Leppla, D. A. (1992). Gender association of musical instruments and preferences of fourth-grade students for selected instruments. *Journal of Research in Music Education, 40*(2), 93–103.

DeNora, T. (2000). *Music in everyday life.* Cambridge University Press.

Deutsch, D. (2002). The puzzle of absolute pitch. *Current Directions in Psychological Science, 11*(6), 200–204.

Drayna, D., Manichaikul, A., Lange, M. de, Snieder, H., & Spector, T. (2001). Genetic correlates of musical pitch recognition in humans. *Science, 291*(5510), 1969–1972.

Eck, D., Lamere, P., Bertin-Mahieux, T., & Green, S. (2007). Automatic generation of social tags for music recommendation. In J. Platt, D. Koller, Y. Singer, & S. Roweis (Eds.), *Advances in Neural Information Processing Systems,* pp. 385–392.

Eerola, T., Armitage, J., Lavan, N., & Knight, S. (2021). Online data collection in auditory perception and cognition research: Recruitment, testing, data quality and ethical consider-ations. *Auditory Perception & Cognition, 4*(3–4), 251–280. https://doi.org/https://doi.org/ 10.1080/25742442.2021.2007718

Eerola, T., & Bregman, M. (2007). Melodic and contextual similarity of folk song phrases. *Musicae Scientiae, Discussion Forum 4A-2007,* 211–233.

Eerola, T., Jakubowski, K., Moran, N., Keller, P., & Clayton, M. (2018). Shared periodic performer movements coordinate interactions in duo improvisations. *Royal Society Open Science, 5,* 171520. https://doi.org/http://dx.doi.org/10.1098/rsos.171520

Eerola, T., & Peltola, H.-R. (2016). Memorable experiences with sad music – Reasons, reactions and mechanisms of three types of experiences. *PloS ONE, 11*(6), e0157444. https://doi.org/http://dx.doi.org/10.1371/journal.pone.0157444

Eerola, T., & Vuoskoski, J. K. (2011). A comparison of the discrete and dimensional models of emotion in music. *Psychology of Music, 39*(1), 18–49.

Eerola, T., Vuoskoski, J. K., & Kautiainen, H. (2016). Being moved by unfamiliar sad music is associated with high empathy. *Frontiers in Psychology*, *7*, 1176. https://doi.org/https://doi.org/10.3389/fpsyg.2016.01176

Eerola, T., Vuoskoski, J. K., Kautiainen, H., Peltola, H.-R., Putkinen, V., & Schäfer, K. (2021). Being moved by listening to unfamiliar sad music induces reward-related hormonal changes in empathic listeners. *Annals of the New York Academy of Sciences*, *1502*, 121–131. https://doi.org/DOI:10.1111/nyas.14660

Egermann, H., & Reuben, F. (2020). "Beauty is how you feel inside": Aesthetic judgments are related to emotional responses to contemporary music. *Frontiers in Psychology*, *11*, 2959.

Fabian, D. (2015). A musicology of performance: Theory and method based on Bach's solos for violin. Open Book Publishers.

Fogel, A. R., Rosenberg, J. C., Lehman, F. M., Kuperberg, G. R., & Patel, A. D. (2015). Studying musical and linguistic prediction in comparable ways: The melodic cloze probability method. *Frontiers in Psychology*, *6*, 1718.

Fritz, T., Jentschke, S., Gosselin, N., Sammler, D., Peretz, I., Turner, R., Friederici, A. D., & Koelsch, S. (2009). Universal recognition of three basic emotions in music. *Current Biology*, *19*(7), 573–576.

Gabrielsson, A. (2011). *Strong experiences with music: Music is much more than just music*. Oxford University Press.

Gómez-Cañón, J. S., Cano, E., Eerola, T., Herrera, P., Hu, X., Yang, Y.-H., & Gómez, E. (2021). Music emotion recognition: Toward new, robust standards in personalized and context-sensitive applications. *IEEE Signal Processing Magazine*, *38*(6), 106–114.

Goto, M., Hashiguchi, H., Nishimura, T., & Oka, R. (2002). RWC music database: Popular, classical and jazz music databases. *ISMIR*, *2*, 287–288.

Graakjær, N. J. (2022). *The sounds of spectators at football*. Bloomsbury.

Granot, R. Y., & Jacoby, N. (2011). Musically puzzling: Sensitivity to overall structure in the sonata form? *Musicae Scientiae*, *15*(3), 365–386.

Greenwald, A. G., & Lai, C. K. (2020). Implicit social cognition. *Annual Review of Psychology*, *71*, 419–445.

Guyon, A. J., Studer, R. K., Hildebrandt, H., Horsch, A., Nater, U. M., & Gomez, P. (2020). Music performance anxiety from the challenge and threat perspective: Psychophysiological and performance outcomes. *BMC Psychology*, *8*(1), 1–13.

Hallam, S., Rogers, L., & Creech, A. (2008). Gender differences in musical instrument choice. *International Journal of Music Education*, *26*(1), 7–19.

Halpern, A. R. (1988). Mental scanning in auditory imagery for songs. *Journal of Experimental Psychology: Learning, Memory, and Cognition*, *14*(3), 434–443.

Harte, C. (2010). *Towards automatic extraction of harmony information from music signals* [PhD thesis]. Queen Mary, University of London.

Hauger, D., Schedl, M., Košir, A., & Tkalcic, M. (2013). The million musical tweets dataset: What can we learn from microblogs. In A. D. S. Britto, F. Goyon, & S. Dixon (Eds.), 14th International Society for Music Information Retrieval Conference (pp. 189–194), Curitiba, Brazil.

Hauser, D. J., & Schwarz, N. (2016). Attentive turkers: MTurk participants perform better on online attention checks than do subject pool participants. *Behavior Research Methods*, *48*(1), 400–407.

Heggli, O. A., Stupacher, J., & Vuust, P. (2021). Diurnal fluctuations in musical preference. *Royal Society Open Science*, *8*(11), 210885. https://doi.org/https://doi.org/10.1098/rsos.210885

Henrich, J., Heine, S. J., & Norenzayan, A. (2010). Beyond WEIRD: Towards a broad-based behavioral science. *Behavioral and Brain Sciences*, *33*(2–3), 111–135.

Hentschel, J., Moss, F. C., Neuwirth, M., & Rohrmeier, M. (2021). A semi-automated workflow paradigm for the distributed creation and curation of expert annotations. In J. H. Lee, A. Lerch, Z Duan, J. Nam, P. Rao, P. Van Kranenburg, A. Srinivasamurthy (Eds.), *Proceedings of the 22nd International Society for Music Information Retrieval Conference*, online, 7–12 November 2021.

Hjermstad, M. J., Fayers, P. M., Haugen, D. F., Caraceni, A., Hanks, G. W., Loge, J. H., Fainsinger, R., Aass, N., Kaasa, S., et al. (2011). Studies comparing numerical rating scales, verbal rating scales, and visual analogue scales for assessment of pain intensity in adults: A systematic literature review. *Journal of Pain and Symptom Management*, *41*(6), 1073–1093.

Hornbostel, E. M., & Sachs, C. (1914). Systematik der musikinstrumente. *Zeitschrift Für Ethnologie*, *46*, 55–90.

Huettel, S. A., Song, A. W., McCarthy, G., et al. (2004). *Functional magnetic resonance imaging* (Vol. 1). Sinauer Associates.

Huron, D. (2011). Why is sad music pleasurable? A possible role for prolactin. *Musicae Scientiae*, *15*(2), 146–158.

Jacoby, N., & McDermott, J. H. (2017). Integer ratio priors on musical rhythm revealed cross-culturally by iterated reproduction. *Current Biology*, *27*(3), 359–370.

Jakubowski, K., Eerola, T., Alborno, P., Volpe, G., Camurri, A., & Clayton, M. (2017). Extracting coarse body movements from video in music performance: A comparison of automated computer vision techniques with motion capture data. *Frontiers in Digital Humanities*, *4*(9). https://doi.org/10.3389/fdigh.2017.00009

Jakubowski, K., Farrugia, N., Halpern, A. R., Sankarpandi, S. K., & Stewart, L. (2015). The speed of our mental soundtracks: Tracking the tempo of involuntary musical imagery in everyday life. *Memory & Cognition*, *43*(8), 1229–1242.

Joubert, E. (2022). 'Distant reading' in French music criticism. *Nineteenth-Century Music Review*, *19*(2), 291–315.

Juslin, P. N., Liljeström, S., Laukka, P., Västfjäll, D., & Lundqvist, L.-O. (2011). Emotional reactions to music in a nationally representative sample of Swedish adults prevalence and causal influences. *Musicae Scientiae*, *15*(2), 174–207.

Kayser, D. (2017). Using facial expressions of emotion as a means for studying music-induced emotions. *Psychomusicology: Music, Mind, and Brain*, *27*(3), 219–222.

Keller, P. E. (2008). Joint action in music performance. In F. Morganti, A. Carassa, & G. Riva (Eds.), *Enacting intersubjectivity: A cognitive and social perspective on the study of interactions* (pp. 205–221). IOS press.

Khalfa, S., Bella, S. D., Roy, M., Peretz, I., & Lupien, S. J. (2003). Effects of relaxing music on salivary cortisol level after psychological stress. *Annals of the New York Academy of Sciences*, *999*(1), 374–376.

Kim, J. W., Salamon, J., Li, P., & Bello, J. P. (2018). CREPE: A convolutional representation for pitch estimation. *2018 IEEE International Conference on Acoustics, Speech, and Signal Processing, ICASSP 2018 – Proceedings*, 161–165. https://doi.org/https://doi.org/10.48550/ARXIV.1802.06182

Klepzig, K., Horn, U., König, J., Holtz, K., Wendt, J., Hamm, A., & Lotze, M. (2020). Brain imaging of chill reactions to pleasant and unpleasant sounds. *Behavioural Brain Research*, *380*, 112417.

Koelsch, S. (2014). Brain correlates of music-evoked emotions. *Nature Reviews Neuroscience*, *15*(3), 170–180.

Kramer, L. (2003). Musicology and meaning. *The Musical Times*, *144*(1883), 6–12.

Ladinig, O., Brooks, C., Hansen, N. C., Horn, K., & Huron, D. (2019). Enjoying sad music: A test of the prolactin theory. *Musicae Scientiae*, *25*(4). https://doi.org/10.1177/1029864919890900

Lahdelma, I., Armitage, J., & Eerola, T. (2022). Affective priming with musical chords is influenced by pitch numerosity. *Musicae Scientiae*, *26*(1), 208–217. https://doi.org/10.1177/1029864920911127

Lamont, A. (2011). University students' strong experiences of music: Pleasure, engagement, and meaning. *Musicae Scientiae*, *15*(2), 229–249.

Laukka, P., Eerola, T., Thingujam, N. S., Yamasaki, T., & Beller, G. (2013). Universal and culture-specific factors in the recognition and performance of musical emotions. *Emotion*, *13*(3), 434–449.

Law, E., West, K., Mandel, M. I., Bay, M., & Downie, J. S. (2009). Evaluation of algorithms using games: The case of music tagging. In K. Hirata, G. Tzanetakis, & K. Yoshii (Eds.), Proceedings of the 10th International Society for Music Information Retrieval Conference, ISMIR 2009, (pp. 387–392), Kobe International Conference Center, Kobe, Japan, 26–30 October 2009. International Society for Music Information Retrieval.

Lawendowski, R., & Besta, T. (2020). Is participation in music festivals a self-expansion opportunity? Identity, self-perception, and the importance of music's functions. *Musicae Scientiae*, *24*(2), 206–226. https://doi.org/10.1177/1029864918792593

Leante, L. (2016). Observing musicians/audience interaction in North Indian classical music performance. In I. Tsioulakis, & E. Hytönen-Ng (Eds.), *Musicians and their audiences* (pp. 50–65). Routledge.

Lerdahl, F. (2019). *Composition and cognition: Reflections on contemporary music and the musical mind*. University of California Press.

Levitin, D. J. (1994). Absolute memory for musical pitch: Evidence from the production of learned melodies. *Perception & Psychophysics*, *56*(4), 414–423.

Li, B., Liu, X., Dinesh, K., Duan, Z., & Sharma, G. (2018). Creating a multitrack classical music performance dataset for multimodal music analysis: Challenges, insights, and applications. *IEEE Transactions on Multimedia*, *21*(2), 522–535.

Lomax, A. (1968). *Folk song style and culture*. Routledge.

Lucas, G., Clayton, M., & Leante, L. (2011). Inter-group entrainment in Afro-Brazilian Congado ritual. *Empirical Musicology Review*, *6*(2), 75–102.

Makowski, D., Pham, T., Lau, Z. J., Brammer, J. C., Lespinasse, F., Pham, H., Schölzel, C., & Chen, S. H. A. (2021). NeuroKit2: A python toolbox for neurophysiological signal processing. *Behavior Research Methods*, *53*(4), 1689–1696. https://doi.org/https://doi.org/10.3758/s13428-020-01516-y

Micallef Grimaud, A., & Eerola, T. (2021). EmoteControl: An interactive system for real-time control of emotional expression in music. *Personal and Ubiquitous Computing*, *25*, 677–689. https://doi.org/10.1007/s00779-020-01390-7

Milliman, R. E. (1986). The influence of background music on the behavior of restaurant patrons. *Journal of Consumer Research*, *13*(2), 286–289.

Moretti, F. (2005). *Graphs, maps, trees: Abstract models for a literary history*. Verso.

Müllensiefen, D., Gingras, B., Musil, J., & Stewart, L. (2014). The musicality of non-musicians: An index for assessing musical sophistication in the general population. *PloS ONE*, *9*(2), e89642.

Näätänen, R., Tervaniemi, M., Sussman, E., Paavilainen, P., & Winkler, I. (2001). 'Primitive intelligence' in the auditory cortex. *Trends in Neurosciences*, *24*(5), 283–288.

North, A. C., & Hargreaves, D. J. (2000). Musical preferences during and after relaxation and exercise. *American Journal of Psychology, 113*(1), 43–68.

North, A. C., Hargreaves, D. J., & Hargreaves, J. J. (2004). Uses of music in everyday life. *Music Perception, 22*(1), 41–77.

Omigie, D., Dellacherie, D., Hasboun, D., Clément, S., Baulac, M., Adam, C., & Samson, S. (2015). Intracranial markers of emotional valence processing and judgments in music. *Cognitive Neuroscience, 6*(1), 16–23.

Oudejans, R. R., & Pijpers, J. R. (2009). Training with anxiety has a positive effect on expert perceptual-motor performance under pressure. *Quarterly Journal of Experimental Psychology, 62*(8), 1631–1647.

Palmer, C., & Drake, C. (1997). Monitoring and planning capacities in the acquisition of music performance skills. *Canadian Journal of Experimental Psychology, 51*(4), 369–384.

Paulhus, D. L., & Vazire, S. (2007). The self-report method. In R. W. Robins, R. C. Fraley, & R. F. Krueger (Eds.), *Handbook of research methods in personality psychology* (pp. 224–239). Guilford Press.

Pekala, R. J. (1991). The phenomenology of consciousness inventory. In R. J. Pekala (Ed.), *Quantifying Consciousness: An Empirical Approach* (pp. 127–143). Springer.

Quintana, D., Alvares, G. A., & Heathers, J. (2016). Guidelines for reporting articles on psychiatry and heart rate variability (GRAPH): Recommendations to advance research communication. *Translational Psychiatry, 6*(5), e803.

Randall, W. M., & Rickard, N. S. (2017). Reasons for personal music listening: A mobile experience sampling study of emotional outcomes. *Psychology of Music, 45*(4), 479–495.

Randall, W. M., Rickard, N. S., & Vella-Brodrick, D. A. (2014). Emotional outcomes of regulation strategies used during personal music listening: A mobile experience sampling study. *Musicae Scientiae, 18*(3), 275–291.

Rentfrow, P. J., Goldberg, L. R., & Levitin, D. J. (2011). The structure of musical preferences: A five-factor model. *Journal of Personality and Social Psychology, 100*(6), 1139–1157.

Repp, B. H., & Keller, P. E. (2008). Sensorimotor synchronization with adaptively timed sequences. *Human Movement Science, 27*(3), 423–456.

Rosenzweig, S., Scherbaum, F., Shugliashvili, D., Arifi-Müller, V., & Müller, M. (2020). Erkomaishvili dataset: A curated corpus of traditional Georgian vocal music for computational musicology. *Transactions of the International Society for Music Information Retrieval, 3*(1), 31–41.

Russell, J. A. (2003). Core affect and the psychological construction of emotion. *Psychological Review, 110*(1), 145–172.

Saarikallio, S. H. (2008). Music in mood regulation: Initial scale development. *Musicae Scientiae, 12*(2), 291–309.

Salimpoor, V. N., Benovoy, M., Larcher, K., Dagher, A., & Zatorre, R. J. (2011). Anatomically distinct dopamine release during anticipation and experience of peak emotion to music. *Nature Neuroscience, 14*(2), 257–262.

Savage, P. E., Brown, S., Sakai, E., & Currie, T. E. (2015). Statistical universals reveal the structures and functions of human music. *Proceedings of the National Academy of Sciences, 112*(29), 8987–8992.

Savage, P. E., Merritt, E., Rzeszutek, T., & Brown, S. (2012). CantoCore: A new cross-cultural song classification scheme. *Analytical Approaches to World Music, 2*(1), 87–137.

Scruton, R. (1997). *The aesthetics of music.* Oxford University Press.

Selchenkova, T., Jones, M. R., & Tillmann, B. (2014). The influence of temporal regularities on the implicit learning of pitch structures. *Quarterly Journal of Experimental Psychology, 67*(12), 2360–2380.

Shepard, R. N. (1962). The analysis of proximities: Multidimensional scaling with an unknown distance function. *Psychometrika, 27*(2), 125–140.

Smit, E. A., Milne, A. J., Sarvasy, H. S., & Dean, R. T. (2022). Emotional responses in Papua New Guinea show negligible evidence for a universal effect of major versus minor music. *PloS ONE, 17*(6), e0269597.

Smith, J. B. L., Burgoyne, J. A., Fujinaga, I., De Roure, D., & Downie, J. S. (2011). Design and creation of a large-scale database of structural annotations. *ISMIR, 11*, 555–560.

Solberg, R. T., & Dibben, N. (2019). Peak experiences with electronic dance music: Subjective experiences, physiological responses, and musical characteristics of the break routine. *Music Perception: An Interdisciplinary Journal, 36*(4), 371–389.

Steinbeis, N., & Koelsch, S. (2008). Comparing the processing of music and language meaning using EEG and fMRI provides evidence for similar and distinct neural representations. *PloS ONE, 3*(5), e2226.

Stevens, C. J., Keller, P. E., & Tyler, M. D. (2013). Tonal language background and detecting pitch contour in spoken and musical items. *Psychology of Music, 41*(1), 59–74.

Stewart, N., Chandler, J., & Paolacci, G. (2017). Crowdsourcing samples in cognitive science. *Trends in Cognitive Sciences, 21*(10), 736–748.

Tan, Y. T., McPherson, G. E., Peretz, I., Berkovic, S. F., & Wilson, S. J. (2014). The genetic basis of music ability. *Frontiers in Psychology, 5*, 658.

Tarr, B., Launay, J., & Dunbar, R. I. (2016). Silent disco: Dancing in synchrony leads to elevated pain thresholds and social closeness. *Evolution and Human Behavior, 37*(5), 343–349.

Tervaniemi, M., Makkonen, T., & Nie, P. (2021). Psychological and physiological signatures of music listening in different listening environments – An exploratory study. *Brain Sciences, 11*(5), 593. https://doi.org/https://doi.org/10.3390/brainsci11050593

Theusch, E., & Gitschier, J. (2011). Absolute pitch twin study and segregation analysis. *Twin Research and Human Genetics, 14*(2), 173–178.

Thompson, W. F., Geeves, A. M., & Olsen, K. N. (2019). Who enjoys listening to violent music and why? *Psychology of Popular Media Culture, 8*(3), 218–232.

Thompson, W. F., & Robitaille, B. (1992). Can composers express emotions through music? *Empirical Studies of the Arts, 10*, 79–89.

Toi, P. T., Jang, H. J., Min, K., Kim, S. P., Lee, S. K., Lee, J., ... & Park, J. Y. (2022). In vivo direct imaging of neuronal activity at high temporospatial resolution. *Science, 378*(6616), 160–168.

Tol, A. J. M. van den, Coulthard, H., & Hanser, W. E. (2020). Music listening as a potential aid in reducing emotional eating: An exploratory study. *Musicae Scientiae, 24*(1), 78–95.

Turner, A. M., Kirchhoff, K., & Capurro, D. (2012). Using crowdsourcing technology for testing multilingual public health promotion materials. *Journal of Medical Internet Research, 14*(3), e79.

Ukkola-Vuoti, L., Kanduri, C., Oikkonen, J., Buck, G., Blancher, C., Raijas, P., Karma, K., Lähdesmäki, H., & Järvelä, I. (2013). Genome-wide copy number variation analysis in extended families and unrelated individuals characterized for musical aptitude and creativity in music. *PloS ONE, 8*(2), e56356.

Upham, F., & McAdams, S. (2018). Activity analysis and coordination in continuous responses to music. *Music Perception: An Interdisciplinary Journal, 35*(3), 253–294.

Vuoskoski, J. K., & Eerola, T. (2012). Can sad music really make you sad? Indirect measures of affective states induced by music and autobiographical memories. *Psychology of Aesthetics, Creativity, and the Arts*, 6(3), 204–213.

Weiß, C. (2017). *Computational methods for tonality-based style analysis of classical music audio recordings* [PhD thesis]. Ilmenau University of Technology.

Williamon, A., & Davidson, J. W. (2002). Exploring co-performer communication. *Musicae Scientiae*, 6(1), 53–72.

Woods, K. J., Siegel, M. H., Traer, J., & McDermott, J. H. (2017). Headphone screening to facilitate web-based auditory experiments. *Attention, Perception, & Psychophysics*, 79(7), 2064–2072.

Woolhouse, M. H., Tidhar, D., & Cross, I. (2016). Effects on inter-personal memory of dancing in time with others. *Frontiers in Psychology*, 7, 167.

Wrape, E. R., Dittloff, A. L., & Callahan, J. L. (2016). Gender and musical instrument stereotypes in middle school children: Have trends changed? *Update: Applications of Research in Music Education*, 34(3), 40–47.

Zentner, M., Grandjean, D., & Scherer, K. (2008). Emotions evoked by the sound of music: Characterization, classification, and measurement. *Emotion*, 8(4), 494–521.

Zhang, J. D., & Schubert, E. (2019). A single item measure for identifying musician and nonmusician categories based on measures of musical sophistication. *Music Perception*, 36(5), 457–467.

Zhao, S., & Godde, B. (2019). *Mode processing influenced by music training and language experience – An ERP study*. PsyArXiv. https://doi.org/10.31234/osf.io/3nu7j

6 Organising and Summarising Data

In most studies in music and science, you cannot avoid quantifying. Dealing with numbers is not difficult, although there are probably many readers of this book who were drawn to music, arts, and humanities at school and dropped the maths and science subjects and perhaps still feel intimidated by numbers. All new approaches require learning, and statistics and computing numerical descriptors can be mastered quite quickly. In my experience, most students in the humanities have not obtained training in quantitative methods. Why? One might be tempted to answer that quantitative methods tend not to be used in the humanities, but that would be too simple an answer. An answer rooted in recent historical developments would say that the tendency is rooted in the anti-positivist movement that reached its peak in the 1960s and 1970s. That is, several generations of teachers ago, but the reluctance to handle numerical data is part of the culture of humanities and part of the wider gap between the 'two cultures', sciences and humanities, which have split into two different entities in the Western world (Snow, 1959). This characterisation of the widening mutual incomprehension between literary intellectuals and natural scientists has not become obsolete during the last 60 years; on the contrary, this chasm is at the heart of contemporary debates (Pinker, 2013). A great deal of quantification is present in many disciplines of the humanities. History is usually the prime example of how numeric information can be used to delineate economic, political, and regional histories (see Lemercier & Zalc, 2019), but literature and linguistics were using sophisticated quantification years before the term digital humanities was invented.

In traditional music scholarship, quantification in music analysis and music history is often found in descriptions and expressions such as 'almost every instance', 'the majority of cases' or 'this technique is so common in music of the mid-eighteenth century'. Let me cite a few examples: 'Hepokoski and Darcy plot the various outcomes and solutions of each sonata along a series of default options that are proportionate with their frequency of usage. Frequency is a key component of their theory' (Ludwig, 2012, p. 4). 'A particularly common type of disrupted ending arises …' (Burstein, 2014, p. 218). These types of descriptions, which seem to capture prevalence and frequency without delving deeper into them, are common. There are also more explicit studies where quantification has been used

DOI: 10.4324/9781003293804-6

to study music, from classifying British-American folk songs (Bronson, 1949), to attempt to verify the authenticity of compositions (Mendel, 1976), to trace the sonata form in symphonies (Cannon, 2017), and to write a big data history of music (Rose et al., 2015).

Although this book might be preaching to those already converted, I strongly advocate students and teachers in humanities to adopt all approaches to research that are able to provide answers to legitimate research questions despite the historical or philosophical burdens of these approaches. I know that I am not alone in this plea (Bryman, 2006, p. 124). Several scholars have advocated for this approach and have made significant resources available to facilitate this. John Canning's *Statistics for the Humanities* (Canning, 2014), Taylor Arnold and Lauren Tilton's *Humanities Data in R* (Arnold & Tilton, 2015), Matthew Jockers' *Text Analysis with R for Students of Literature* (Jockers & Thalken, 2020), and *Computational Historical Thinking* (Mullen, 2018) are examples of hands-on guides on how to carry out quantitative and computational analyses on relevant data in humanities.

Understanding the basics of statistical thinking makes you a better citizen since you are able to understand news items that contain polls, summaries, comparisons, and inferences, all usually numerical with confidence and error marginals associated with them. Decision-making principles that involve hypothesis testing are also part of basic literacy skills and provide important tools for understanding how the world works and what is offered to us in the findings of scientific research. To put this point in words, the lack of these skills inhibits the 'ability to both critique the ideological misuse of statistics and participate in broader cultural and public policy debates' (Deacon, 2008, p. 103).

Transparent Analysis Tools

A large part of the value of computation and statistics comes from the realisation that the steps of research should be *reproducible* so that other scholars can access and understand and replicate your data and analyses, even if they would disagree with your interpretations. As a practical solution, I have chosen R as the tool for the analyses presented here, although of course other statistical software could also be used. However, there are several good arguments to support R or Python as a better choice than, say, *Matlab* or *SPSS*. They are both powerful software packages, but R has several advantages over these. R is the most accessible software; it is free and open source, available for all operating systems, and does not require much of the computer. R is also completely programming-driven (thus fully transparent). Matlab is equally so, but since it is essentially a MATrix LABoratory, it is very good for numerical analyses. R is more versatile for strings and data structures that are most commonly used in statistics and empirical experiments. SPSS also has a syntax option, but it is much more cryptic and unwieldy than R and Matlab. A clear syntax makes the analyses easily human-readable, which is important for collaborations and for the longevity of the analyses. To sing the praises of R even more, it has an excellent coverage of statistical modelling tools. Thousands of R packages exist for any state-of-the-art statistical technique (Bayesian, structural equation modelling, rare regression analytics, most machine learning algorithms with effective implementations, and so on) and these can be conveniently loaded from within R without too much hassle. Finally, I would argue (and I'm not the only one) that R is rational and even pedagogical in many of its functionalities and combined with necessary libraries such as tidyverse including ggplot2, and knitr when it becomes an excellent reporting tool as well. It can even be used to build interactive websites and produce analyses and reports in the same document (R Markdown or Quarto).

In this book, I will not be duplicating basic tutorials beyond an introduction on how to use R, but instead I will point to the excellent guidebooks (e.g., Field et al., 2012) and online sites (https://education.rstudio.com/) that deliver these in style. However, I will still talk about the organisation of data analysis to be suitable for empirical research in music and science, and I will also give the R code that provides the figures in this book as examples of what can be done with R.

There are many tools available for data analysis and statistics. I will only consider those that are open source and free to use as this is the only way to guarantee that people can access the tools. Sadly, some fine tools, such as SPSS, JMP, Minitab, SAS, or Stata, do not fulfil these principles. R and RStudio, JASP, Jamovi, and Python (made better with libraries such as SciPy) and some others are free and open-source software that have become common research tools in empirical sciences. In addition to being free and easily available, they have excellent capacities to share the analysis workflows, and some have tools to ensure replicability over years and different versions. I will focus on R in the statistical analysis and explain why I think this is a good option for empirical data analysis (see box).

Why use R? R is a versatile environment for analysing any data. It is interactive and well suited for casual exploration of data that come in many different forms (numbers, text strings) and different shapes (long and wide data). What is even more important in R is that it is fundamentally based on scripts that serve as a blueprint for the analysis you have done and allow you, or anyone else, to replicate your analyses simply by running the same script. Other benefits of R include the following:

1. It is free and open source.
2. It works well on all operating systems: Windows, Mac OS, UNIX/Linux.
3. The community of R users is broad and active, and for this reason the resources for learning and asking questions are impressive and well-developed (see online repository links).
4. It already has some music-specific tools (e.g., incon, gm, humdrumR, and hrep libraries) and datasets (MusicScienceData).

Most of the arguments about using R could be made to support Python, which has gained support in data analysis and music research. In later sections, we will be using Python for specific music analytical tasks. I have created separate online tutorial for using R, which goes through the nuts and bolts of this tool.

See Chapter6.1 code at https://tuomaseerola.github.io/emr/

Organisation of the Analysis Workflow

Before the actual analysis that will be covered in Chapter 7, it is useful to think about the workflow for analysis of quantitative data. Here, we assume that there are some raw observations coming from an empirical experiment. To create a clear workflow for the analysis, it is useful to adhere to certain structures and conventions. Here, I propose a structure (see box) where the main operations are clearly separated into folders. I have expanded this in Chapter6.2 at https://tuomaseerola.github.io/emr/.

- /data Data in read-only format (preferably CSV or TSV format).
- /munge All operations to pre-process, recode, or trim data.
- /scr All actual scripts used in the analysis.
- /figures Outputs from the scripts
- /docs Outputs from the reports

In this structure, a single notebook or script (e.g., contents.R) will be needed to reproduce the analysis. It contains an example of how the different stages, structures, and processes in the analysis can be executed in a coherent order and manner (i.e., loading, transforming, and screening the data, and then visualising, applying statistical analyses, creating figures and tables). This is designed as a small tutorial for reproducible research from the perspective of our needs in music and science. report.Rmd will create the report that incorporates comments and actual analyses and produces either an html or a pdf file (report.html, report.pdf) in the docs folder.

Pre-processing and Quality Control

All data are messy and very possibly in a format that is not convenient for analysis. Quite often, the main challenge is to apply the necessary data carpentry skills to wrangle the data into a format that will be easy for the analysis. The raw numbers may have to be aggregated into a standardised measure such as a *musical sophistication index* or a *personality trait*. Let us first see what the usual organisation of the data is.

A common assumption in most analysis software suites is that columns relate to variables and rows relate to observations. R is no exception, and this is a good way to organise and share the data. Code 6.1 at Chapter6.3 shows an example of the normal organisation of the data, where the first line labels the variables (subj, age, gender) and each row represents the values for one participant for all variables. This is not to say that all data will always be in the same format, but this is quite a typical structure of the data.

```
# Code 6.1
print(MusicScienceData::sadness[1:4,1:7])
## # A tibble: 4 × 7
##    subj  age       gender listen   expert listensad ASM1
##    <fct> <fct>     <fct>  <fct>    <chr>  <fct>     <int>
## 1 1      35 to 44 Female d        MusicL Sometimes     6
## 2 2      45 to 54 Female mult./d  MusicL Often         2
## 3 3      18 to 24 Female d        NM     Sometimes     6
## 4 4      25 to 34 Male   d        Amat.  Sometimes     5
```

Sometimes, the data have a more complicated design. It might be that the data include multiple observations from multiple participants, and this type of structure is called *long format*. In long format, rows have multiple observations, while the columns still represent the variables. Code 6.2 shows the first rows of a dataset, where each participant has reacted to numerous musical examples in a priming study. You can see how the first line now keeps repeating the same participant number ('1') but the values in the RT (reaction time) column change in response to different conditions (each row is still an observation, but there are repeated observations from each participant). There are also variants of this structure where the variables are expanded in the columns, and this is called a *wide format*.

```
# Code 6.2
print(MusicScienceData::priming[1:3,1:6])
## # A tibble: 3 × 6
##   Participant Prime_V  Target_V    RT Correct  Age
##   <fct>       <fct>    <fct>    <int> <fct>   <int>
## 1 1                    Positive Negative   444 Correct    24
## 2 1                    Positive Negative   437 Correct    24
## 3 1                    Negative Negative   453 Correct    24
```

Getting to know your data by understanding the organisation variables and observations and having seen the distribution of the numbers is a vital part of quality control. In online studies, you often have cryptic output formats and a lot of partial data from participants for a variety of reasons. Some became bored with your survey or were cut out due to network issues. In lab studies, there might be technical glitches that cause strange observations in your data, and missing observations can be due to simple errors. In simple counts of behaviours from the real world, or in any manual coding of the data, one typo might ruin a perfectly respectable set of data. Without exploring these types of issues, you really risk misunderstanding the data.

Post-processing and Open Data

Now I am deliberately skipping over the analysis and reporting sections and talking about the way the data is shared in repositories. Although it might feel premature before we have even talked about the analysis, it is important to understand the steps involved in preparing and sharing the data before the data analysis. These steps include prescreening, logical naming and storing of the variables, quality control, and the structural conventions of the data. Good conventions and transparency about these decisions are not just for the analyst and the small cadre of collaborators. The analysis workflow itself should be thought of as part of the data report and that comes with long-term storage and dissemination of the data (see box). If you follow the kind of structured approach I advocated earlier, your data are already in compatible format and you can communicate this clearly, but it is useful to know the recommendations for data sharing. And sharing is not just something you do for posterity, but is more often the way you share your workflow with a supervisor, colleague, or collaborator. In many cases, it might even be you when you return to the topic after a long break.

---

1. Make all resources human-readable text-files (preferably in UTF-8 format that preserves special characters and line breaks).
2. Avoid proprietary formats such as Microsoft's *doc*, *rtf*, or *xls*.
3. Use simple formats such as *csv* (comma-separated values) or *markdown* rather than *xls*, *json*, or *xml*.
4. Use open-source and free software like R or Python instead of SPSS or Matlab to increase the audiences for the research and the accessibility of the data files.
5. Offer the resources as an archived directory (single zip file) that can be deposited in a repository (see Research Transparency on the repositories).

Datasets organised in this way are easy to share in data repositories such as the *Open Science Framework*, *Zenodo*, *GitHub*, or *Harvard Dataverse*. I already presented these in more detail earlier in the Chapter 4 section titled *Research Transparency*.

Diagnostic Visualisations and Descriptives

Numerous books have been written about visualising data. In the next sections, I will follow good conventions promoted by several authors on data visualisation (Cleveland & McGill, 1984; Kelly et al., 2005; Tufte, 2016). The main rule in creating a great visualisation is to allow the data to speak for themselves and offer the reader all necessary information (but not more) about the graph (e.g., label the axes clearly). A graph should have clearly labelled axes with appropriate units, sufficiently large and legible text legends, and in the case of central tendencies, indicators for the error margins (or confidence intervals) and a title. What is not needed in any graph is 'chartjunk' such as 3D effects, complex shading, or background colours or icons.

All analyses and visualisations can be found separately in the digital materials. The basic plots are illustrated with the full R code. The data are available as an R library called MusicScienceData that can be installed from https://github.com/tuomaseerola/MusicScienceData following the instructions. You can run and edit the code in a browser window if you follow the 'Open in Colab' links in the repository. This allows you to explore all the operations shown without the necessary software or data.

Distributions: Histograms and Boxplots

The histogram is a useful first step in visualising the pattern of responses. It will show the count of each possible response and can diagnose several issues in the data. The distribution might have impossible values, weird gaps in the middle of the scale, or all responses are located at the lower or higher end of the scale, which might reflect the so-called 'floor or ceiling effects' that are problematic if the instrument used to collect the data cannot capture the full range of responses.

Let us look at some example data. This is taken from a study on music and sadness (Eerola & Peltola, 2016), and the full data are available online at *Harvard Dataverse* https://doi.org/10.7910/DVN/GLSIXB, and here, in this R script (Code 6.3) it is read directly from within R. We focus on one set of questions related to attitudes towards sad music that was part of the study. Let us look at item 20 that contains the responses to the statement 'Listening to sad music uplifts me'. The participants rated the statement from 1 to 7, where 1 was 'strongly disagree' and 7 'strongly agree' with the statement.

See R code in Chapter6.3 at https://tuomaseerola.github.io/emr/

```
# Code 6.3
library(MusicScienceData)
library(ggplot2)
library(tidyverse)
sadness <- MusicScienceData::sadness
g1 <- sadness %>%
  drop_na(ASM25) %>%    # drop missing values
  ggplot(aes(x = ASM25))+
  geom_histogram(bins=7,fill="grey50", colour='black')+
  scale_x_continuous(breaks = seq(1,7,by=1))+
  ylab('Count')+
  xlab('1 = Strongly disagree, 7 = Strongly agree')+
  theme_MusicScience()
g1
```

In this item, Figure 6.1 shows a distribution of ratings, which are centred around 6 and generally the majority of the participants agree with the statement, although there are a small number of people who strongly disagree with it as well. The next example draws a more varied range of responses, since they come from reaction times related to a decision. This allows us to explore the importance of the way the X axis is organised into 'bins' in a histogram, which is the most important organisational aspect of a histogram. In the previous example, the bins were equal to the seven response options, but if we have a wider range of response options, the width of these bins will dictate the way the histogram looks. And this is not strictly about accuracy; often broader binning is useful to clearly demonstrate underlying trends without getting too many details that distract from the communication.

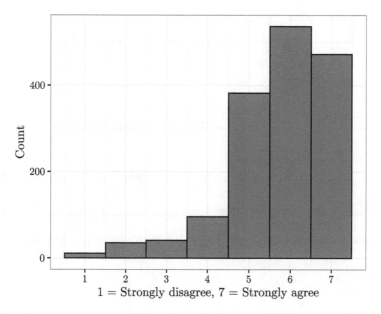

1 = Strongly disagree, 7 = Strongly agree

Figure 6.1 A histogram showing the distribution of responses to a particular question (no. 25) in the Attitudes towards Sad Music (ASM) instrument.

The four graphs shown in Figure 6.2, created by Code 6.4, show the distribution of reaction times to a question of whether a word displayed on the computer screen is negative or positive. It is a simple task, and people can make this decision in half a second after seeing the word appear. However, when exposed to an emotional sound at the same time (here we have used negative or positive music examples from a collection of film soundtracks), the responses of the participants will be faster or slower depending on the congruence or incongruence of the musical valence (positive or negative) with the word. If they hear positive music and see a negative word, it takes them more time to respond, as the combination is conceptually jarring and the listener unconsciously works out the decision about the word despite the opposite association delivered through sound. If the word and the music are congruent, participants tend to be faster and more accurate than in incongruent pairings. This paradigm, called priming, is often used to explore whether concepts, sounds, or images are perceived as negative or positive. These data come from Armitage & Eerola (2020).

The interesting part of this approach is that these types of responses are automatic and impossible to consciously manipulate, in contrast to self-reports (where the participant may try to please the researcher or to answer in a way that is most typical). The top left panel shows the distribution of reaction times in 100 ms bins, and the top right has the same data divided into 10 ms categories. The two panels emphasise slightly different aspects of the data; the peak is more distinct in the

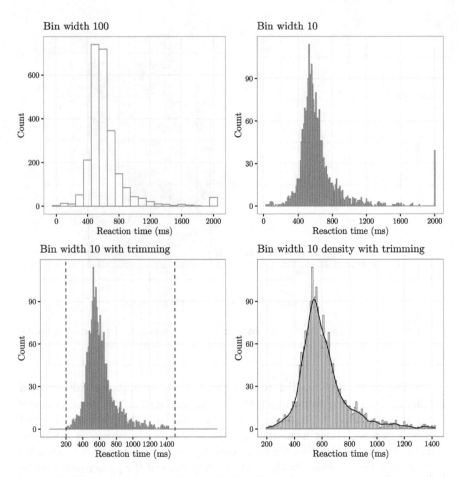

Figure 6.2 Histograms showing the distribution of reaction time responses in a musical priming task using different options.

shorter binning, but the accuracy itself brings some noise to the figure as well. Both graphs show an odd peak around 2 s, which relates to the slowest allowed response time, so these are actually responses that came too late. In the lower panels, the responses that are too fast (faster than 150 ms) or too slow to be meaningful (slower than 1,500 ms) to be meaningful have been trimmed away (shown as the dashed lines in the lower left panel) as this is one of the common ways to remove noise from such data (see section Outliers, Missing Data and Other Problems). Finally, the lower right panel illustrates another common way of displaying distributions based on the estimated density of the underlying distribution (the black line drawing the clear outline of the distribution).

ASM25: I easily empathize with the sad atmosphere or narrative conveyed by sad music

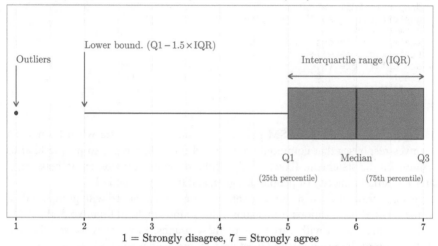

Figure 6.3 Explanation of the boxplot showing responses to ASM instrument question no. 25.

Instead of looking at the whole distribution, we are often keen to know the central tendencies of the distributions and especially what the means of the data look like. Before calculating the mean, it is a good habit to explore how reliable the mean is as a descriptor of the central tendency. Boxplots are handy for this purpose as they offer an easy visualisation of the median value (the line in the middle), and the middle 50% of the observations (the boxed area, which is the area above the 25th percentile, technically called Q1 and below the 75th percentile, Q3), and the minimum and the maximum. This middle part of the data is called the *interquartile range* (IQR, from Q1 to Q3) and gives a rough account of where most of the observations are. Boxplots often show *outliers* as small markers in the extremes, and these are observations that are far away from the interquartile range. To be precise, these are 1.5 times smaller than Q1 or larger than Q3 and refer to rare extremes in the observations. Outliers can be problematic for many statistical operations, and we will deal with them in a later section.

Figure 6.3 shows the boxplot of responses to ASM question 25 with a detailed explanation of the key properties of boxplots (median, interquartile range, outliers). This code is also available as Code 6.4.

It is common to organise boxplots vertically instead of the horizontal layout used in the previous example.

```
# Code 6.5
g5 <- sadness %>%
  drop_na(ASM25) %>%    # drop missing values
  ggplot(aes(y = ASM25,fill=gender))+
  geom_boxplot()+
  scale_y_continuous(breaks = seq(1,7,by=1))+
  scale_x_discrete()+
  scale_fill_grey(start = .4,end = .8,name='Gender')+
  ylab('1 = Strongly disagree, 7 = Strongly agree')+
  theme_MusicScience()
print(g5)
```

In Figure 6.4 we see that ASM item 23 ('I listen to sad music when I am sad') receives responses that commonly are around 6 (median is 6), so people tend to agree with the statement. Exactly 50% of the responses by women lie between 5 and 7. A small minority of people disagree, and the minimum is 1.

Visualisation of the distributions can, of course, be enriched with grouping data or the original observations if this adds value to the graph. In Figure 6.5, the ASM questions are shown with variations of these graphs. In panel A we see that the distribution of the responses to Question 1 by men and women are quite different; women tend to agree with the statement that they listen to sad music only in a certain state of mind. Note that a minority of all participants choose the middle option on the scale. In panel B questions 1 to 4 have been displayed in a single graph, and

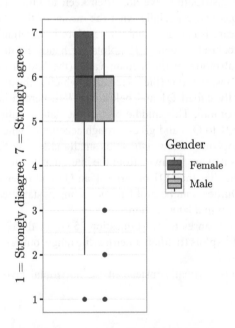

Figure 6.4 A boxplot showing the distribution of responses to a particular question (no. 23) in the Attitudes towards Sad Music (ASM), instrument split across gender.

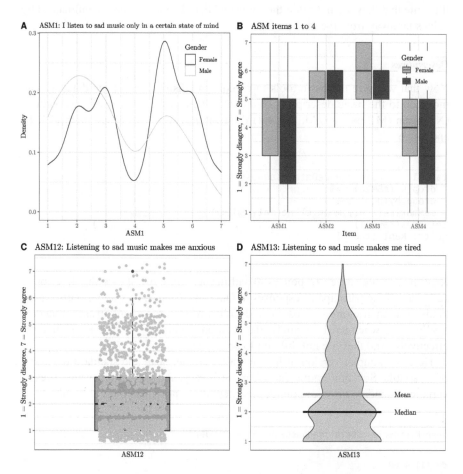

Figure 6.5 Alternative visualisations of data. A: density plot across gender, B: multiple boxplots, C: boxplot overlaid with original data, D: violin plot with mean and median overlaid.

the boxplots have additionally been divided according to gender to identify other questions where gender might play a role. ASM4 seems to be one such question ('Sad music intensifies my own negative feeling') where a prominent gender difference is shown. Panel C shows a boxplot of ASM question 12 overlaid with raw responses. Notice how the boxplot displays the value of 7 as an outlier (an exceedingly rare occurrence) but if you look at the raw responses, there are about ten or so, which is still exceedingly rare considering that the data have 1,570 observations (10 is 0.637%). These plots can be recreated with script Code 6.4 extra.

The final panel, D, introduces an alternative visualisation of the distribution, called the *violin plot*. This highlights the density of the values at each point in the distribution. I have added the mean (2.6) and median (2.0) to the violin plot just to illustrate that they are not often the same and that the mean is easily influenced by values far away from the mean.

Descriptives

Now that we have the basic tools to explore the distribution of the data, we can move on to the basic descriptors of the data such as the number of observations (N), mean (M), median (Md), standard deviation (SD), confidence interval (CI), and range.

```
# Code 6.7
table1 <- MusicScienceData::sadness %>%
  drop_na(ASM20) %>%   # drop missing values
  group_by(age) %>%
  summarise(n=n(),mean_cl_normal(ASM20))
colnames(table1) <- c('Age','N','M','95% CI LL','95% CI UL')
knitr::kable(table1,digits = 2, format='simple',
  caption = 'The means of the ASM question 20 across the age.')
```

Returning to the survey responses to sad music, Table 6.1 shows the descriptive summary of the participant responses to Question 20 in the six age groups. These kinds of summaries are very useful in deciding what to report and in assessing data quality, and, when used sparingly, they can communicate the pattern of findings effectively. And they are not difficult to obtain either.

Here is a simpler version of how to calculate the mean and standard deviation of a variable. Substituting median for mean is easy, and getting other measures of variation (standard error, or confidence intervals) is not much more difficult.

```
# Code 6.8
mean(MusicScienceData::sadness$ASM20, na.rm=TRUE) # Mean (ignore missing
values)

## [1] 4.68

sd(MusicScienceData::sadness$ASM20,na.rm=TRUE)  # Standard Deviation

## [1] 1.35
```

Table 6.1 The means of the responses to ASM question 20 by age.

Age	N	M	95% CI LL	95% CI UL
18 to 24	355	4.51	4.38	4.64
25 to 34	497	4.64	4.52	4.76
35 to 44	329	4.74	4.60	4.88
45 to 54	213	4.75	4.55	4.95
55 to 64	136	5.00	4.77	5.23
65 to 74	40	4.92	4.50	5.35

In Code 6.8 we also ignore all missing values in the data. This is a perfectly normal and common operation, which does not cause concern. It might be prudent to let the reader know initially how frequent the missing values are and it is not unusual to have 1–3% of the data missing for various reasons. The missing values might cause some problems for certain analyses and disrupt balanced group comparisons, but most of the analyses can deal with some missing observations. I will briefly address this issue in more detail in a later section on outliers and missing data.

Central Tendencies: Bar Charts and Error Bars

When we are about to compare groups, it is helpful to visualise the means of the variables based on different ways of grouping them. It is easy to calculate the means or median and show these, but this is only half the information as we want to know how solid the means are. For this reason, error bars play an important role in any graph displaying the means as it is really the variation that tells us whether the means are quite similar, slightly overlapping, or very different. In the inferential statistics in Chapter 7 we will of course see how such a difference will work out in statistical terms, but a good graph goes a long way in communicating this to the reader.

```
# Code 6.9
g6 <- sadness %>%
    drop_na(ASM20) %>%     # drop missing values
    group_by(gender) %>%
    summarise(mean= mean(ASM20),ci = mean_cl_normal(ASM20)) %>%
    ggplot(aes(x = gender,y = mean,fill=gender))+
    geom_col(colour='black',show.legend = FALSE)+
    geom_errorbar(aes(ymin=ci$ymin,ymax=ci$ymax),width=0.5)+
    scale_y_continuous(breaks = seq(1,7,by=1), expand = c(0,0))+
    scale_fill_grey(start=.25,end=.75)+
    coord_cartesian(ylim = c(1, 7)) +
    ylab('Mean ± 95% CI')+
    xlab('Gender')+
    theme_MusicScience()
print(g6)
```

In Figure 6.6 we see that ASM question 20 ('Listening to sad music uplifts me') receives slightly different mean responses from men and women. The difference does not seem large; for women, the mean (M) is 4.59 and the 95% confidence interval (CI) of this mean is from 4.51 to 4.67, and for men, M=4.96, 95% CI 4.84–5.08). As you can see, the confidence intervals do not overlap. This would suggest that the difference is significant, at least statistically speaking. Why there is a difference between men and women in this question cannot be derived from this data alone but would be best targeted with focussed interview and survey designs. Some recent studies of this kind have suggested that young women do indeed experience elevated levels of depressive mood after listening to sad music (Bogt et al., 2021) and women tend to rate negative emotions higher in energy and fear (Fuentes-Sánchez et al., 2021), which has also been observed in other stimuli such as affective pictures (Carretié et al., 2019).

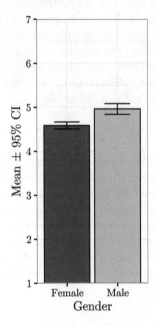

Figure 6.6 A bar graph showing the means of responses to question no. 20 in the Attitudes towards Sad Music (ASM) instrument across gender.

In a slightly more elaborate example, we plot the means and confidence intervals of another ASM question across different levels of musical expertise. Here, the musical expertise has been simply coded by the participant's own self-nomination into one of five broad categories (non-musicians, music lovers, amateur musicians, semiprofessional musicians and professional musicians), which has been derived from a one-question version of the *Ollen Musical Sophistication Index* (Zhang & Schubert, 2019). There are of course much more nuanced tools for capturing musical sophistication (Müllensiefen et al., 2014) but the simple self-nomination captured by the one-question version of the OMSI measure is a surprisingly good predictor of levels of musical identity. However, Figure 6.7, created with Code 6.10, shows how lyrics are an essential part of the sadness expressed by music. Generally, the participants agree with this statement, but perhaps musicians (especially instrumentalists, not singers) express lower agreement to this because their experiences of expressing sadness are not necessarily dictated by lyrics. We don't know why semiprofessional and professional musicians tend to de-emphasise lyrics compared to others, but it is also worth noting that the variation is much larger for two subgroups of experts than for the other groups, reflecting the smaller

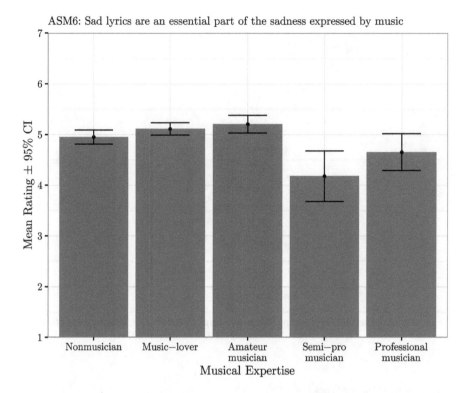

ASM6: Sad lyrics are an essential part of the sadness expressed by music

Figure 6.7 A bar graph showing the means of responses to question no. 6 in the Attitudes towards Sad Music (ASM) instrument across musical expertise.

number of participants belonging to these expert groups and the divided opinions within them.

This plot can be recreated with script Code 6.10. We will explore the differences evident in the responses across musical expertise spectrum later in the inferential statistics (Chapter 7).

Patterns Between Variables: Scatter Plots

When the interest is in exploring the relationships between two continuous variables, visualising them in different axes can be informative. This type of graph, called a scatterplot, can demonstrate a pattern of correlation, direction, and magnitude of association between variables.

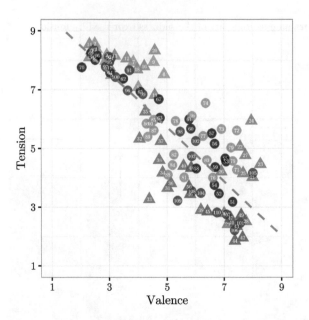

Figure 6.8 A scatterplot showing the means of ratings to 110 film soundtrack excerpts using scales of tension and valence in Eerola & Vuoskoski (2011).

```
# Code 6.11
g9 <- ggplot(soundtrack) +
  aes(x = Valence, y = Tension, colour = TARGET_EMOTION,
      label=Number,
      shape= TARGET_FRAMEWORK) +
  geom_point(size=4,alpha=0.80,show.legend=FALSE) +
  coord_fixed(ratio = 1)+
  geom_smooth(aes(shape = NULL,colour=NULL),method="lm",
              formula='y ~x',se=FALSE, fullrange=TRUE,
              level=0.95, colour='grey50', # adds trendline
              linetype='dashed',show.legend = FALSE)+
  geom_text(show.legend=FALSE,color='white',size=1.7,
            family="CMU Serif")+ # labels
  scale_colour_grey(name='Emotion',start = .6,end = 0)+
  scale_shape(name='Framework')+
  scale_x_continuous(breaks=seq(1,9,by=2),limits=c(1,9))+
  scale_y_continuous(breaks=seq(1,9,by=2),limits=c(1,9))+
  theme_MusicScience()
print(g9)
```

Figure 6.8 displays the mean tension and valence ratings of a selection of clips extracted from film soundtracks (Eerola & Vuoskoski, 2011). Both concepts were rated on a scale of 1 to 9 which in the case of tension, was labelled as 1 = relaxed/calm/at rest and 9 = tense/clutched up/jittery. For valence, 1 was defined as unpleasant/bad/negative, while 9 was pleasant/good/positive. The mean ratings have been labelled with numbers referring to the individual tracks, and the shape of the markers relate to the emotion framework from which the clips were selected (basic emotions or dimensional framework of emotions). There is a strong negative correlation between tension and valence, and this trend, although not shown as a correlation coefficient here, is drawn in the plot with a dashed line (also known as the *trend line*, obtained by calculating a least-squares fit with the data points). The graph says that when music examples are rated as very tense, they tend to be rated as negative or unpleasant. When film music examples are rated as pleasant and positive, they also tend to be rated as relaxed or having low tension. We will cal-culate the correlation coefficient and the related probability value in the Chapter 7.

Outliers, Missing Data, and Other Problems

It is not uncommon to obtain data that have some missing observations, perhaps even some nearly impossible values, and skewed distributions. There are remedies and procedures to diagnose and address these types of issues in statistics, some easy, some more tricky and controversial. This text will not be deeply involved in the analysis of these issues, but I will present the basics. It is worth saying here that sometimes these problems may lead to insurmountable challenges for the analysis, but more often there are simple techniques that can mitigate the problems. The key in all these operations is that you are transparent in what you do and explain why an operation was done to the data and what the operation was.

Outliers

An unusually high or low value in the data may have a catastrophic impact on descriptive and inferential statistics. The source of the unusual value, which we call an *outlier*, could have been caused by a typo in the data, or a conversion error (mis-takenly replacing the comma with the full stop as the decimal separator or some-thing else), or sometimes in a large sample, extreme values just appear in the data. Outliers will cause problems for traditional analysis operations such as calculating the means, performing t-tests, correlations, and regressions, as these calculations usually assume a normal distribution of values and an extreme value will likely violate this assumption. The practical reason for treating outliers in the first place is that they may render these calculations misleading, as the extremes wield a high leverage on otherwise relatively stable values that tend to centre around a mean.

Imagine one simple typo in the valence ratings for the film soundtracks described in the previous section where the mean ratings of one track have been converted erroneously without the decimal separator. In this fictious case, a rating of 4.00 appears as 400. This single typo would raise the mean of the valence ratings from 5.3 to 8.9, which is close to the maximum of the scale (9) and quite implausible as a mean. Note that the median of the valence ratings would be largely unaffected by this outlier (the original median is 5.3, but with the typo included, the median is 5.4). And often potential outliers in the data are not as easily apparent as this one, but even this extremely blatant outlier might remain hidden if the analyst proceeds from obtaining observations directly to statistical descriptions and inferential statistics, as the means and inferential tests might not immediately reveal that there is something quite suspicious in the data. Fortunately, we do not have to wish that the data are free of outliers, as there are ways to diagnose and deal with them.

The first diagnostic action towards finding out the potential outliers is to visualise the data. If you plot the histograms or boxplots of your variables or scatterplots between two variables, the outliers are usually quite easily visible in these visualisations (see Figure 6.3 for an example). It is a sensible idea to always get a feel for the distribution of the data by plotting the values in a meaningful fashion (boxplots are always a good starting point). The shape of the distribution might reveal other unwanted issues such as all values being clustered near one end of a scale (called a *ceiling effect* or a *floor effect* where the measurement scale is attenuated because it is not sensitive enough or it is oversensitive, scoring only few values at the positive extreme of the scale). Or visualisation between two variables might reveal that the relationship between the two variables is not a linear one but still clear and regular but in a polynomial relation (e.g., a U-shaped or inverted U-shaped pattern). It is possible to diagnose the potential outliers using several quantitative techniques, but before mentioning two options, let me warn that there is no definite recommendation on what is classified as an outlier, as different types of data, distributions, and disciplinary orientations might have slightly different practices for dealing with these offending values. One of the most used measures already introduced in relation to boxplots is to use the *interquartile range* (IQR) to define the range of acceptable values (outliers are above 75% quantile plus $1.5 \times$ IQR or below 25% quantile minus $1.5 \times$ IQR).

Let us look at two examples from the data that we have already seen in this chapter. The first boxplot example, shown in Figure 6.3 concerning the attitudes towards sad music question 25, showed the ratings of 1 diagnosed as outliers (indicated by the dot at the value of 1) by the boxplot routine. The median of that distribution is 6 and the lower end of the IQR is 5 and the interquartile range is 2, so the lower threshold for the outliers is $2 (5 - 2 \times 1.5)$ and therefore the few values of 1 are singled out as potential outliers. The second example comes from the priming study and the reaction time responses (see Figure 6.2). The mean response time was 632 ms; the upper threshold for outliers using the IQR-based technique is 930 ms, and the lower threshold is 254 ms, so any value below 254 ms or above 930 ms could be considered as a potential outlier. To be fair, reaction times are not even supposed to be normally distributed and they have a strong right-skewed shape caused by the participants' tendency to respond asymmetrically (more responses towards the slow end of the response than the fast). There is a specific way to eliminate overly fast reactions (<200 ms) or slow reactions (>1,500 ms) (Brysbaert & Stevens, 2018), and even after this, analysis of reaction time data will use a statistical operation that is suited to the specific distribution of the data (e.g., GLMM with shifted log-normal distribution) or apply a log transformation of the data. But, as we can see from Figure 6.2, eliminating over 40 timed-out responses (>2,000 ms) does make the data much cleaner.

If the IQR-based method is the first way to diagnose outliers, the other common way to diagnose outliers is to convert the variables into *z scores,* where the mean is

0 and the standard deviation is 1. A z score of -4 would mean that it is four standard deviations from the mean. One rule of thumb suggests that observations ±3 standard deviations from the mean are potential outliers. Besides these two simple metrics, there are more sophisticated ways to identify outliers, such as using a normal distribution (Grubb's method) or a distance measure (the Mahalanobis method) but ultimately the standard for making decisions based on any technique is subjective and must be clearly explained and motivated.

Dealing with Outliers

After diagnosing that there are outliers in the data, you need to decide what to do with them. It is possible to keep the outliers in the data if the analysis can work with outliers and not be disruptively influenced by them. For instance, if the analysis operations can be done with non-parametric inferential statistics that rely on ranks (the order of the values) – not the actual distances – between the observations, this can avoid the detrimental effect of the outliers to statistical inferences (see Chapter 7). There are also variant techniques to perform correlation and regression analyses that are designed to work with data that partially violate assumptions of normality (e.g., *rank correlations, robust regression,* and *lasso regression*). Similar operations exist for comparing means, ranging from non-parametric variants of the t-test (*Mann-Whitney U test*) and ANOVA (*Kruskal-Wallis test*) to generalised linear mixed models (GLMMs), where one can change the underlying assumptions of the distribution from normal distribution to something else that better reflects the underlying data.

A simpler option is either to eliminate the outliers or replace them with the nearest plausible data (sometimes called *Winsorising*) where you trim the values to the edge of the definition of the outliers. The decision of what is an appropriate way to deal with the problematic observations depends on many issues, but the idea of trimming them to the edge of the outliers is to preserve the observations in the data, but just to remove their leverage (the distance from the mean) by moving them to the acceptable range. Again, there is no hard guidance on what the best practice for dealing with outliers is, as sometimes data are extremely rare and throwing parts of them away can handicap the analysis. In any case, reporting the diagnosis (what diagnosis operation was used and how many outliers were detected) and treatment of the outliers is always necessary.

Missing Data

Sometimes there are missing observations in the data and the reasons for these might be as varied as the reasons for outliers. Also, you might have created more missing data if you decide to eliminate outliers, which could mean that those offending extreme observations are considered missing. If the missing data are in the original observations, it is worth considering the reason for the missing data before deciding what to do with them; it might tell you that a survey question was badly formed or related to a private issue that many people did not want to respond to, they skipped a question, or perhaps the experiment data had an erroneous coding for a trial. When the missing observations are clearly linked to such a data collection issue, it might be best to report this as is. When the amount of missing data is low and not clearly linked to any known issue, there are several ways to deal with them. One is to allow them to be missing, and most of the analysis operations are competent statistical software suites that can deal with the omissions. These missing observations, if they are coded properly in the statistical software (e.g., NA in R) and not as values of any kind (coding missing values as zeros is downright dangerous as further calculations will then start to treat them as actual values). For instance, in the examples above, I have dropped missing observations when constructing plots (line 3 in Code 6.5) and tables (Table 6.1) and calculating means (the example just below the table above).

In most cases, reporting how many missing observations there are and whether they are specifically affecting the study design is sufficient to press on with the analysis with keeping the data as it is (with the missing observations in the data frame if they are properly coded as missing). More advanced ways of dealing with the missing observations is to infer the missing values from the other variables (*imputation*) or to *interpolate* the missing observations from the other data (Howell, 2008), but the prudent use of either of these techniques requires sophisticated data analysis skills and I would not recommend following the route of filling in the gaps in the data with educated guesses, unless this is absolutely necessary and you know exactly what you are doing.

Non-normal Distributions

The final issue of data quality relates to distribution of the data. Most of the operations I have talked about – and will be talking about in Chapter 7 – assume that the observations fall into the *normal distribution*, which is symmetric and governed by mean and variance of a specific kind (σ^2). When the observations have wildly different distribution from this one, skewed in one direction (asymmetrical), or *heteroscedastic* (where the variation is uneven across the range of a variable), one might need to revert to statistical operations designed to handle non-normal distributions (non-parametric operations) or to try to *transform* the observations into something closer to normal distribution. There is nothing suspicious or problematic in the act of transforming a variable if it makes the analysis and interpretation easier, but again one must report and justify such operations with caution.

We have already come across one common transformation that is often applied to reaction time data, namely the logarithmic transform. Other transformations for data that have positive skew include the square-root transformation. There is also a technique called power transformation which attempts to find the best transformation that creates the closest match to the normal distribution (also known as the *Box-Cox* technique). A statistical software package comes with routines that can identify violations from normality such as *Kolmogorov-Smirnov* or *Shapiro-Wilk* tests. Rather than blindly attempting to use a neat transformation to rescue a problematic variable, I would recommend a common-sense approach where the underlying reason for the non-normality of the distribution is considered. If it is something that typically happens with the measurements (such as reaction time data) and not just a poorly designed measure with ceiling or floor effects, the transformation is easy to motivate and apply. In other cases, it is probably wise to take a deep breath and consult an advanced statistics guide, for example Howell (2016), or see recommendations at the end of the book.

Qualitative Analysis

Much of the qualitative data in empirical music research comes from interviews and sometimes observations. Analysing open-text responses in surveys or interview texts or some other qualitative comments is not a single method or technique but comes in a variety of traditions and purposes. Some of the analytical options will start from a blank canvas (e.g., grounded theory), others seek to explain the meanings found in a text through themes highlighted by existing theory, or to understand the experiences themselves via text (e.g., *Interpretative Phenomenological Analysis*). Qualitative analysis begins by assembling the text into logical themes (thematic content analysis) and does not aim to dig deep into the underlying experiences but is more systematic in its coverage of all the themes. Those closest to the quantified analysis technique are the ones where text is subjected to simple coding (such as *Linguistic Inquiry and Word Counts*) where categories of words (affective processes, cognitive processes, pronouns and to whom they relate, negations, relations, physical states) are tallied together.

In all these analytical traditions and techniques, qualitative analysis is something that is built in iterations of interpretations and reflection, so flexibility and sensitivity toward the aims of the research are central elements in this approach.

I will briefly cover three main techniques that offer alternative ways of analysing qualitative data.

Interpretative Phenomenological Analysis

Interpretative Phenomenological Analysis (IPA) is a well-established qualitative analysis method (Alase, 2017). The purpose of IPA is to understand how participants make sense of the world, including their social and personal meanings and interpretations. The meanings are drawn from experiences and events, and from the mental states of the participants. In this framework, there is no objective statement of the object or the event itself, only an individual's interpretation of it. These interpretations must consider the cognitive, linguistic, and affective aspects of the speaker. In other words, why the person might be expressing this notion, how they are able to convey it through language, and what emotional drivers might be associated with their experiences. These are similar to the assumptions about human thinking that are held in mainstream cognitive psychology.

IPA analysis is well suited to small samples and case studies. Collecting data and performing a proper IPA analysis is time-consuming, so it is normal to have only a small handful of participants/responders (3, 5, 8 …). The idea is to discover insights about a phenomenon and not whether it can be generalised. A success measure in an IPA is how well it reports the richness of the topic, and of course what insights it can generate about the topic.

The most common way to collect data for IPA is to employ semi structured interviews. As covered earlier, these types of interviews are flexible and allow the researcher to ask additional questions when the need arises. A good interviewer allows the respondent to talk freely, without interfering or leading too much, although there is a clear plan of the main themes and overall focus of the interview. Once the interviews have been carried out, they are transcribed, usually just by typing the spoken words and ignoring incomplete expressions and pauses in the verbal output. The text is then annotated by marking those sections and expressions that are thought to be significant and meaningful. This typically requires several read-throughs of one text from one respondent, and the process is repeated for other respondents. After reading and annotating each text from each respondent in this way, the analysis can compile a list of themes that reoccur and stand out. This is not purely calculating the frequency of occurrence, but determining and deciding which themes are important. After this, the findings can be summarised by explaining what these themes covered. It is of course important to link the themes to the literature about the phenomenon in the summary.

There are dedicated tools such as *NVivo* or *ATLAS.ti* that facilitate coding and summary of textual data. Small-scale analysis can also be done in Excel and using word processing software. IPA has been used in empirical studies of music to identify the core elements of live music festival experiences (Moss et al., 2020), the underlying reasons for anxiety about music performance (Clearman, 2020), and the experiences of carers when using personalised music with people with dementia living at home (Kulibert et al., 2019). The IPA method is able to highlight and focus on meaningful aspects of these phenomena and can be vital in identifying key issues to be considered and examined in follow-up studies.

Thematic Content Analysis

Thematic Content Analysis is a method for 'identifying, analysing, and reporting patterns (themes) within data' (Clarke & Braun, 2014). It is the primary qualitative method, which is essential for conducting qualitative analysis. This kind of analysis should be systematic and can be done on paper or using computer software such as NVivo. It is also important to note that the analyst acknowledges the decisions, since no themes will magically emerge from the transcripts.

In thematic content analysis, the decisions of what themes are meaningful and how they are chosen shape the process. How frequent do the themes need to be? Generally, flexibility is thought to be important. For instance, the raw frequency can be a useful aid, but more important is to determine whether the theme captures something essential about the overall research topic. In the analysis, it is customary and necessary to move back and forward between the data, the coded extracts of data, and the overall analysis you are producing. Writing the actual report based on the analysis themes is also a crucial part of the process.

Once the coding has been done, the question arises of how reliable the codings are. Is the annotator putting his own themes there, and would other people be able to come up with the same themes? One operation that can be used to overcome the problem is to use double coding and estimate the coder reliability using *Inter-Coder Agreement* (ICA). This simply means that a second coder annotates the text and the agreement between the classification of the themes ascribed to the sections by the original coder and the new annotator is calculated. Usually, the second coder only annotates a portion of the original data, 10–20% depending on the amount of material. The second coder is also given the themes and just applies them to the materials. The agreement can be calculated by counting the percentage of agreed cases or by using a measure of consistency for classes. A good example of thematic analysis is offered in the study by Williamson et al. (2014). Their survey on earworms (music that you hear in your mind's ear involuntarily) contains an open question where participants could describe their experiences and how they tend to eliminate them. Key themes in the texts were identified through analysis of thematic content and the themes and cases were also independently verified.

Event or Word Coding and Counting

The bigger the dataset and the less deeply we may want to analyse it – or the fewer nuances the text contains, which is often true in online surveys that allow for open responses that yield brief responses as compared to the kind of rich text that one gets from any interview – the shallower, but more automatic means of organising qualitative data we need. Instead of human interpretation, one can ask a computer to count specific aspects of the text. This may sound limited, but there are situations where such methods can be potent. You might have a massive text corpus, or you may be interested in the type of distinctions that exist at the level of word choices. In these cases, you may want to use specialised software such as *Linguistic Inquiry and Word Count* (LIWC) (Tausczik & Pennebaker, 2010), *SentiWordNet* (Baccianella et al., 2010), or *Affective Norms for English Words* (Bradley & Lang, 1999). Such tools provide the researcher with automated and objective methods for extracting insights about the attentional focus reflected through language. They operate by splitting the words into basic units (tokens) and count the different categories of the words based on established dictionaries. These dictionaries can score the affective terms, the use of first, second, and third person accounts, and reveal other linguistic categories (content categories such as drives, personal concerns, perceptual processes but also function word categories such as pronouns, conjunction, and negations) and abstractions that give the analyst a summary description of the linguistic content. In many cases such quantitative summaries are analysed and compared with inferential statistical analyses. It is worth noting that while these tools have been developed for the English language, LIWC supports multiple languages (e.g., Dutch, Brazilian Portuguese, and Romanian) although there is still much work to be done before the approach operates at equivalence between the dictionaries (Dudău & Sava, 2021).

Yinger & Springer (2022) used this method to understand the emotional experiences of autobiographical memories related to music. They coded positive and negative emotions, as well as pronouns, and vocabulary-related causal thinking from texts written by nearly 100 US students. They compared the indicators using LIWC with the positive/negative emotion ratings the participants had given for these experiences. The experiences were not actually separated by positivity/negativity, but the essential content revolved around social experiences and achievements.

Coda

This chapter has presented an overview of the ways to describe different qualities of the data, mainly by presenting summaries of central tendencies and distributions. Being able to visualise the raw data in different ways is important for understanding how the data behave, and suitable techniques such boxplots, histograms, and scatterplots were introduced. Identifying anomalies in the data, such as outliers and missing observations, and how they should be treated was also discussed. The end of the chapter also summarised some qualitative analysis techniques, such as interpretative phenomenological analysis, thematic content analysis, and word coding and counting, as these can be seen as summaries of textual data.

Discussion Points

1. At the beginning, I mentioned how quantitative data analysis is not taught or regarded as valuable in many discussions of curricula in the humanities. Why is this thinking problematic?
2. Most of the operations covered in this chapter have to do with visualising the observations. What kinds of aspect of the data are easily missed if the analyst proceeds directly to statistical testing without plotting the data?
3. Qualitative analysis methods are powerful tools to discover the meaningful aspects of musical phenomena, attitudes, or behaviours. How is the reliability of these methods often demonstrated?

Further Reading

Field, A., Miles, J., & Field, Z. (2012). *Discovering statistics using R*. Sage.
Clarke, V., & Braun, V. (2014). Thematic analysis. In T. Teo (Ed.), *Encyclopedia of Critical Psychology* (pp. 1947–1952). Springer.

References

Alase, A. (2017). The interpretative phenomenological analysis (IPA): A guide to a good qualitative research approach. *International Journal of Education and Literacy Studies*, 5(2), 9–19.

Armitage, J., & Eerola, T. (2020). Reaction time data in music cognition: A comparison of pilot data sets from lab, crowdsourced and convenience web samples. *Frontiers in Psychology, 10.* https://doi.org/https://doi.org/10.3389/fpsyg.2019.02883

Arnold, T., & Tilton, L. (2015). Humanities data in R: Exploring networks, geospatial data, images, and text. In *Exploring networks, geospatial data, images, and text* (1st ed.). Springer. https://doi.org/10.1007/978-3-319-20702-5

Baccianella, S., Esuli, A., & Sebastiani, F. (2010). SentiWordNet 3.0: An enhanced lexical resource for sentiment analysis and opinion mining. *Lrec, 10,* 2200–2204.

Bogt, T., Canale, N., Lenzi, M., Vieno, A., & Eijnden, R. van den. (2021). Sad music depresses sad adolescents: A listener's profile. *Psychology of Music, 49*(2), 257–272.

Bradley, M. M., & Lang, P. J. (1999). *Affective norms for English words (ANEW): Instruction manual and affective ratings.* The Center for Research in Psychophysiology.

Bronson, B. H. (1949). Mechanical help in the study of folk song. *The Journal of American Folklore, 62*(244), 81–86.

Bryman, A. (2006). Paradigm peace and the implications for quality. *International Journal of Social Research Methodology, 9*(2), 111–126.

Brysbaert, M., & Stevens, M. (2018). Power analysis and effect size in mixed effects models: A tutorial. *Journal of Cognition, 1*(1), 1–20. https://doi.org/http://doi.org/10.5334/joc.10

Burstein, P. L. (2014). The half cadence and other such slippery events. *Music Theory Spectrum, 36*(2), 203–227.

Canning, J. (2014). *Statistics for the humanities.* Brighton University. http://statisticsforhumanities.net/book/

Cannon, S. C. (2017). Sonata form in the nineteenth-century symphony. *Empirical Musicology Review, 11*(2), 204–224.

Carretié, L., Tapia, M., López-Martín, S., & Albert, J. (2019). EmoMadrid: An emotional pictures database for affect research. *Motivation and Emotion, 43*(6), 929–939.

Clarke, V., & Braun, V. (2014). Thematic analysis. In T. Teo (Ed.), *Encyclopedia of critical psychology* (pp. 1947–1952). Springer.

Clearman, J. A. (2020). Experiences in music performance anxiety: Exploration of pedagogical instruction among professional musicians. In S.-H. Lee, M. L. Morris, & S. V. Nicosia (Eds.), *Perspectives in performing arts medicine practice: A multidisciplinary approach* (pp. 241–255). Springer International Publishing. https://doi.org/https://doi.org/10.1007/978-3-030-37480-8_14

Cleveland, W. S., & McGill, R. (1984). Graphical perception: Theory, experimentation, and application to the development of graphical methods. *Journal of the American Statistical Association, 79*(387), 531–554.

Deacon, D. (2008). Research methods for cultural studies. In M. Pickering (Ed.), *Research methods for cultural studies.* Edinburgh University Press.

Dudău, D. P., & Sava, F. A. (2021). Performing multilingual analysis with linguistic inquiry and word count 2015 (LIWC2015). An equivalence study of four languages. *Frontiers in Psychology, 12,* 2860.

Eerola, T., & Peltola, H.-R. (2016). Memorable experiences with sad music – Reasons, reactions and mechanisms of three types of experiences. *PloS ONE, 11*(6), e0157444. https://doi.org/http://dx.doi.org/10.1371/journal.pone.0157444

Eerola, T., & Vuoskoski, J. K. (2011). A comparison of the discrete and dimensional models of emotion in music. *Psychology of Music, 39*(1), 18–49.

Field, A., Miles, J., & Field, Z. (2012). *Discovering statistics using R.* Sage.

Fuentes-Sánchez, N., Pastor, M. C., Eerola, T., & Pastor, R. (2021). Individual differences in music reward sensitivity influence the perception of emotions represented by music. *Musicae Scientiae*. https://doi.org/https://doi.org/10.1177/10298649211060028

Howell, D. C. (2008). The analysis of missing data. In W. Outhwaite, & S. Turner (Eds.), *Handbook of social science methodology* (pp. 208–224).

Howell, D. C. (2016). *Fundamental statistics for the behavioral sciences*. Cengage Learning.

Jockers, M. L., & Thalken, R. (2020). *Text analysis with R*. Springer.

Kelly, D., Jasperse, J., & Westbrooke, I. (2005). Designing science graphs for data analysis and presentation. In *Department of Conservation Technical Series*. New Zealand Department of Conservation.

Kulibert, D., Ebert, A., Preman, S., & McFadden, S. H. (2019). In-home use of personalized music for persons with dementia. *Dementia, 18*(7–8), 2971–2984.

Lemercier, C., & Zalc, C. (2019). *Quantitative methods in the humanities: An introduction*. University of Virginia Press.

Ludwig, A. (2012). Hepokoski and Darcy's Haydn. *HAYDN, 2*(2), 5.

Mendel, A. (1976). Towards objective criteria for establishing chronology and authenticity: What help can the computer give? In E. E. Lowinsky & B. J. Blackburn (Eds.), *Josquin des Prez. Proceedings of the International Josquin Festival Conference* (pp. 297–308). Renaissance Society of America.

Moss, J., Whalley, P. A., & Elsmore, I. (2020). Phenomenological psychology & descriptive experience sampling: A new approach to exploring music festival experience. *Journal of Policy Research in Tourism, Leisure and Events, 12*(3), 382–400. https://doi.org/https://doi.org/10.1080/19407963.2019.1702627

Mullen, L. A. (2018). *Computational historical thinking: With applications in R*. https://dh-r.lincolnmullen.com.

Müllensiefen, D., Gingras, B., Musil, J., & Stewart, L. (2014). The musicality of non-musicians: An index for assessing musical sophistication in the general population. *PloS ONE, 9*(2), e89642.

Pinker, S. (2013). Science is not your enemy. *New Republic, 244*(13), 28–33.

Pinker, S., & Wieseltier, L. (2013). Science vs. The humanities, round III. *New Republic, 26*.

Rose, S., Tuppen, S., & Drosopoulou, L. (2015). Writing a big data history of music. *Early Music, 43*(4), 649–660.

Snow, C. P. (1959). *The two cultures and the scientific revolution*. Cambridge University Press.

Tausczik, Y. R., & Pennebaker, J. W. (2010). The psychological meaning of words: LIWC and computerized text analysis methods. *Journal of Language and Social Psychology, 29*(1), 24–54.

Tufte, E. (2016). The visual display of quantitative information (1983). In J. Wöpking, C. Ernst, & B. Schneider (Eds.), *Diagrammatik-Reader: Grundlegende Texte Aus Theorie Und Geschichte* (pp. 219–230). De Gruyter.

Williamson, V. J., Liikkanen, L. A., Jakubowski, K., & Stewart, L. (2014). Sticky tunes: How do people react to involuntary musical imagery? *PloS ONE, 9*(1), e86170.

Yinger, O. S., & Springer, D. G. (2022). Using psycholinguistic inquiry and content analysis to investigate emotions in memories of musical experiences. *Musicae Scientiae, 26*(2), 227–242. https://doi.org/10.1177/1029864920939603

Zhang, J. D., & Schubert, E. (2019). A single item measure for identifying musician and nonmusician categories based on measures of musical sophistication. *Music Perception, 36*(5), 457–467.

7 Statistical Analysis

It is valuable to be able to describe data distributions, to summarise means across the groups, and to illustrate associations between separate measures. However, these descriptions do not provide a way to judge whether the patterns that you might see on the graphs are mere random variation or a reflection of some true difference in the data. To do this, one needs to turn to inferential statistics. As the term implies, the purpose is to infer whether the data support or contradict the hypothesis you have formulated. This statistical testing is all about providing an answer to a hypothesis and coming to a reliable conclusion based on the data. There is no single inferential statistical operation as different types of design and forms of data require specific types of tests. But there is a common terminology and a set of assumptions behind inferential statistics that describe the steps and elements of the process. I will next introduce the main terms and describe this process before moving onto examples drawn from music studies.

Inferential Statistics

The goal of inferential statistics is to make a decision about a research hypothesis. A hypothesis in this context is statement that something is true. A hypothesis test is concerned with two competing statements, one called *null hypothesis* (H_0) which stands for the hypothesis to be tested, and the *alternative hypothesis* (H_A). Taking an example from the previous chapter, in Figure 6.6 we saw that men and women tend to answer the question 'Listening to sad music uplifts me' slightly differently (the means were 4.59 for women and 4.96 for men). In the language of hypothesis testing, our null hypothesis (H_0) is that there is no gender difference, and the alternative hypothesis (H_A) is that there is a gender difference in this question. Although we see a small difference in these means, we do not know the reliability and consistency of this difference. Inferential testing calculates the risk of the decision error when we reject the null hypothesis. The rationale in inferential statistics is that every time you measure something, the numbers will differ from the population mean, but whether the difference is just random variation or an indicator of a true underlying difference requires some kind of metric about this property. This inferential testing gives you a measure of risk that your decision to

DOI: 10.4324/9781003293804-7

reject the null hypothesis is wrong. This is commonly talked in terms of probabilities and therefore inferential statistics offers probabilities of errors when making
decisions about hypotheses. In a common *frequentist inference*, testing proceeds by
choosing the test statistic appropriate for the distribution and makes the inference
based on relating the observations to the underlying distribution. The outcomes of
the process are (1) the test statistic, and (2) probability values (often abbreviated as
p-values, or just *p*) that gives you the probability of getting a random sample that
is as inconsistent with the null hypothesis as the random sample you have. This
p-value ranges from extremely small (say 0.001) to 1 and it can be interpreted as
the probability that our decision is wrong if we reject the null hypothesis. We don't
like to make inferences that are likely to be wrong, so we accept low *p*-values when
rejecting a null hypothesis. A *p*-value of 0.001 means that there is 0.1% probability
of rejecting the null hypothesis erroneously and a *p*-value of 0.05 puts this risk at
5% and 0.40 suggests 40% risk. The discipline of psychology has agreed to work
with arbitrary thresholds such as 5% (*p*-value ≤ 0.05) when making inferences
about hypotheses, although the threshold should not be used blindly and alternative ways to assess the reliability of hypotheses exist. In sum, *p*-values do not tell
the whole story of whether the finding is significant or whether the hypothesis is
true, as the *p*-values themselves need to be interpreted in the context of the research
question, sample size, and expected effect size (how large we are expecting the
differences to be).

Hypothesis Testing and p-values

In the frequentist paradigm, when the analysis produces a small *p*-value, which
indicates stronger likelihood of rejecting the null hypothesis, we are basically saying
that yes, we have something here which differs significantly from the assumption
that everything is similar or unrelated (null hypothesis) and we have evidence to
support the alternative, actual research hypothesis. The smaller the *p*-values, the
stronger the evidence against the null hypothesis and in support of the defined
hypothesis that you set out to test with your inferential statistic in the first place.
The *p*-values are usually interpreted within a few arbitrarily defined thresholds
under which the tests are thought to be significantly different; a *p*-value of 0.05 is
the magical threshold, which is traditionally used as the first cut-off between significant and non-significant. It simply says that this result may crop up randomly
5% of the time (1 in 20), which is relatively low probability, but if you think about
it, it does turn up every 20th time with data consisting of random numbers. In fact
this is one of the most abused arbitrary thresholds in statistics[1]. Lower thresholds
for *p*-values such as a *p*-value of 0.01 or 0.001, are used as more robust thresholds
to indicate higher significance and less likely occurrence by chance. All these
thresholds can sometimes be substituted by symbols such as $*p<0.05$, $**p<0.01$,
and $***p<0.001$, which is a particularly useful convention in tables. Note that some
formatting conventions do omit the leading zero from the *p*-values (e.g., $p<.05$).

One remedy for many of these problematic issues about arbitrary thresholds
comes from the *Bayesian statistical approach*, which fundamentally alters how

the success of a statistical test is defined by the existing evidence in comparison to how it is defined by any new evidence (McElreath, 2020). This approach is commonly used and elegant, but I have a feeling that for the moment anyone wanting to master empirical research methods in music first needs to master the basics of frequentist (non-Bayesian) statistics before moving onto a more advanced way of thinking about statistics.

Inferential Tests for Different Designs and Variable Types

Most inferential tests examine the relationship between two or more variables. What makes inferential testing complicated is the fact that there are separate statistical tests for different types of designs and different types of data. For example, a comparison of two groups requires a different test from comparing three or more groups. Examining the association between two variables requires a different test than comparing how two variables together relate to a third variable. To make matters more complex, the way the variable is composed, whether it contains categorical values (such as gender), ranked values (such as age ranges), or continuous values (such as obtained from a physiological measure or self-report scale having equal steps), all impact what kind of different inferential test can be used. The most common test is to compare means (and are called *t-test* and *ANOVA*) or measure associations (and are known as correlation, regression, and χ^2 test[2]). In Figure 7.1, I have drawn a menu of options that outlines which tests are plausible given the type of variable and the grouping. All highlighted inferential tests assume that the continuous numerical data are normally distributed (i.e., they are not skewed, see Chapter 6 for normal distribution) and if they violate this assumption, there is a variant for each test that handles such data. These so-called *non-parametric tests* still function in an essentially similar manner to the tests (which are called *parametric tests* in statistical jargon) shown in the diagram. Note that Figure 7.1 does not provide an exhaustive list of all options available to an analyst. Some examples covered in the text may use slightly different terms (e.g., *paired t-test* in the figure is discussed within the text through a broader concept of within-subjects tests, which are essentially paired tests).

When you want to compare means between two groups, the appropriate inferential statistics method is a *two-sample t-test* or simply a *t-test*. There will be examples of this test in a subsequent section. When your variables are both continuous, you can perform a *correlation test* or *linear regression*. If you are dealing with categorical data, basically counts of things, then the menu of options relates to χ^2 testing or its variants. There will be an example of each type of test later.

Reporting Inferential Tests

When inferential tests are reported, you need to tell the reader (1) what inferential test was used, (2) the numeric result of the test in the form of the test statistic (t, F, r, or χ^2 to name the most common ones), (3) how many degrees of freedom there were, and (4) relate this inferential test quantity to the probability, the p-value of

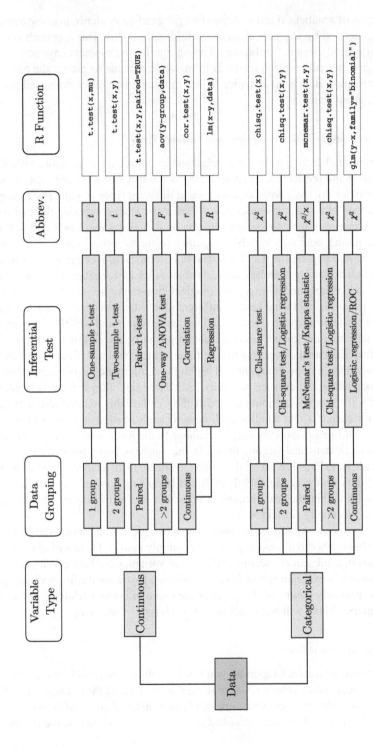

Figure 7.1 A menu of options for inferential tests and their implementation in R.

the test. This is the full report of the result of your inferential test. The degrees of freedom are related to the number of observations you have[3].

In summary, you need to provide three numbers that are reported in a very specific way and you need to be able to explain in plain language what this test really means and how it answers the hypothesis. Usually, the explanations are easier to understand if you mention the means (*M*) and some form of indicators of variations (*standard deviations, standard errors,* or *confidence intervals*) when explaining the results. The section on Diagnostic Visualisation and Descriptives may prove useful here.

Let us look at a typical example of reporting statistics concerning group differences. This example returns to the question of sad music, specifically the statement 'Listening to sad music uplifts me' that was visualised across gender in Chapter 6 (Figure 6.6). Here we pose the null hypothesis (H_0) that there is no gender difference.

A t-test was conducted to test gender differences in attitudes towards sad music (statement 'Listening to sad music uplifts me'). The t-test showed a significant difference between women (M=4.59) and men (M=4.96), $t(1568) = -4.83$, $p < 0.001$), leading to rejecting the null hypothesis and favouring the alternative hypothesis.

The first report explains what the variables are (gender and one statement) and what inferential test was carried out (t-test). The result of the test reports first the value of the *t*-test (-5.05), the degrees of freedom (1,568, which refers to the number of observations we have) and the *p*-value (<0.001). The latter part of the second sentence addresses this hypothesis. This is a typical formula for reporting statistical tests (tell the reader the test statistic, the number of observations, and the *p*-value, and finally interpret and explain).

Group Comparisons

T-test: Comparison of Two Groups

Let's look at the inferential tests for Figure 6.6 which showed a possible difference in gender responses to the claim that 'Listening to sad music uplifts me'. Here, we have a continuous variable (ratings of the statement on a scale of 1 to 7) and a categorical grouping variable (gender). Now we want to know whether this difference shown in Figure 6.6 is statistically significant or only part of normal random variation. As part of the inferential testing, we run a t-test. We also calculate the means and standard deviations just to make reporting easier. The R code from all examples can be run using the online notebook.

See Chapter7 R code at https://tuomaseerola.github.io/emr/

```
# Code 7.1
library(MusicScienceData)                              # Loads library w data
df <- MusicScienceData::sadness                        # define data
t <- t.test(ASM20 ~ gender, data=df, var.equal = TRUE) # t test
print(t$statistic)                                     # show the t value
##     t
## -4.83

print(t$parameter)                                     # print the obs.

##      df

## 1568

print(scales::pvalue(t$p.value))                       # print the p value

## [1] "<0.001"

dplyr::summarise(dplyr::group_by(df, gender), # means and SDs
  M=mean(ASM20,na.rm=TRUE),
  SD=sd(ASM20,na.rm=TRUE))

## # A tibble: 2 × 3
##   gender       M    SD
##   <fct>    <dbl> <dbl>
## 1 Female    4.59  1.37
## 2 Male      4.96  1.24
```

The results of the t-test indicate that the t-value is -5.05 and the *p*-value is lower than 0.001, suggesting that there is a difference between the ratings given by men and women. Using the terms of hypothesis testing, this suggests that we cannot support a null hypothesis, but must side with an alternative hypothesis, according to which there is a statistically significant difference between the ratings of men and women (t=-5.05, p<0.001). The mean rating for men is 4.96 (SD=1.24) whereas women gave this question lower ratings on average (M=4.59, SD=1.37). What this difference tells us about the topic itself is not clear from this analysis and 'statistically significant' does not mean that this would be a significant result in itself. This analysis merely suggests that there is a difference in responses from men and women to this specific question about whether 'Listening to sad music uplifts me'. There could also be differences in this question related to age groups. This idea can be tested using a related inferential test, which will be explored next.

ANOVA: Comparison Between Multiple Groups

Using the same data and question (ASM20 'Listening to sad music uplifts me') as above, we can explore whether the responses to this question draw out differences across another categorical variable in addition to gender. Here we have age, which commonly is a continuous variable, but this data has been collected using six different age groups (18–24, 25–34, 35–44, 45–54, 55–64, and 65–74). The appropriate inferential test is analysis of variance, or ANOVA (ANalysis Of Variance). This is easily done in R with the aov function (see Code 7.2).

```
# Code 7.2
library(MusicScienceData)              # Loads library w data
df <- MusicScienceData::sadness        # define data
model.aov <- aov(ASM20 ~ age, data=df) # run ANOVA
F <- summary(model.aov)                # summarise
print(F)

##                 Df Sum Sq Mean Sq F value Pr(>F)
## age              5     30    5.99    3.32 0.0055 **
## Residuals     1564   2819    1.80
## ---
## Signif. Codes:  0 '***' 0.001 '**' 0.01 '*' 0.05 '.' 0.1 ' ' 1
## 7 observations deleted due to missingness
```

The results are summarised in the output, articulated in the line beginning with age and showing the critical numbers under the headings Df, Sum Sq, Mean Sq, F-value and Pr(>F). From the results we gather that there is a significant difference between the responses given by some of the age groups for this item. The test statistic is F-value, 3.32, and the Df column displays the degrees of freedom, which now has two numbers, 5 (six groups were compared), and 1,564 which is related to the total number of observations minus 1. Finally, the column labelled Pr (>F) refers to probability, the *p*-value, which is 0.0055. The report also tells us some other useful things such as that there were seven missing observations in the data. This analysis *does not* reveal what groups differ from each other at this stage, as the ANOVA merely indicates that there is a difference somewhere between the groups. Finding out the specific group differences will require further testing (using so-called *post-hoc tests*).

Let's carry out one of the most common post-hoc tests, called *Tukey's Honestly Significant Differences*, which guards against multiple comparisons by adjusting the *p*-values so that you are less likely to find significance just because there are multiple comparisons. Adjusting the *p*-values for multiple tests is very much relevant here, as we have 6 groups leading to 15 different combinations of the groups, which already makes the likelihood of us finding a difference in the data by chance uncomfortably high. Remember that a *p*-value of 0.05 means that there is a 1 in 20 chance that a random variable is statistically significant, so running 15 comparisons is not that far from this risk and hence the need to adjust for multiple comparisons. The process of adjusting statistical significance for multiple comparisons using a Tukey (or Bonferroni) operation is common – and usually built into analysis routines – to keep error rates within the same family of tests under control.

```
# Code 7.3
TABLE<-TukeyHSD(model.aov,conf.level = 0.95)
print(knitr::kable(TABLE$age,digits = 3,
                   caption = 'Comparison of age groups
                   for Item 20 in ASM survey.',
                   format = 'simple'))
```

Table 7.1 reveals that most of the differences between age groups are small (see the *diff* column in the output) and only the difference of 0.493 between 55–64-year-olds

Table 7.1 Comparison of the responses given by different age groups for question 20 in the ASM survey.

	diff	Lwr	upr	p adj
25 to 34-18 to 24	0.133	−0.133	0.399	0.713
35 to 44-18 to 24	0.232	−0.062	0.525	0.214
45 to 54-18 to 24	0.244	−0.088	0.576	0.289
55 to 64-18 to 24	0.493	0.107	0.879	0.004
65 to 74-18 to 24	0.418	−0.221	1.057	0.423
35 to 44-25 to 34	0.099	−0.174	0.371	0.906
45 to 54-25 to 34	0.111	−0.202	0.425	0.914
55 to 64-25 to 34	0.360	−0.011	0.731	0.063
65 to 74-25 to 34	0.285	−0.344	0.915	0.789
45 to 54-35 to 44	0.013	−0.324	0.349	1.000
55 to 64-35 to 44	0.261	−0.129	0.652	0.396
65 to 74-35 to 44	0.186	−0.455	0.828	0.962
55 to 64-45 to 54	0.249	−0.172	0.669	0.540
65 to 74-45 to 54	0.174	−0.486	0.834	0.975
65 to 74-55 to 64	−0.075	−0.764	0.614	1.000

and 18–24-year-olds is significantly different, with a *p*-value of 0.004 (which could be reported as $p<0.01$). The rest of the adjusted *p*-values (column labelled *p adj*) – which incorporate the issue of multiple tests and the different number of participants in different age groups – are above the agreed threshold of 0.05.

We might suspect that gender and age work together in some way. In other words, these two background demographics, age and sex, might *interact* in this question, since perhaps young men do not feel that 'Listening to sad music uplifts me' or maybe men over 50 really agree with the statement. One way of finding this out is to put these in the same analysis. Let's run a *two-way ANOVA* (Code 7.4) on the same question to see if there is an interaction between the two factors, age and gender.

```
# Code 7.4
library(MusicScienceData)               # Loads library
df <- MusicScienceData::sadness         # define data
model2.aov <- aov(ASM20 ~ age * gender, data=df)  # run ANOVA
F2 <- summary(model2.aov)
print(F2)

##              Df Sum Sq Mean Sq F value  Pr(>F)
## age           5     30     6.0    3.38  0.0049 **
## gender        1     46    45.7   25.77 4.3e-07 ***
## age:gender    5     12     2.3    1.30  0.2600
## Residuals  1558   2762     1.8
## ---
## Signif. codes:  0 '***' 0.001 '**' 0.01 '*' 0.05 '.' 0.1 ' ' 1
## 7 observations deleted due to missingness
```

The results of this two-way ANOVA show a significant main effect for age and gender. This can be read from lines 8 and 9 in the code output which spells out the key values for age and gender, where age is again significant (F=3.38, p<0.01) and gender also shows statistical differences (F=25.77, p<0.001). When we look at the row that has age:gender at the beginning, which is a shorthand for the interaction between the two, this does not seem to be particularly strong (F=1.40, p=0.26), and the test values suggest that the interaction is not statistically significant. So, it turns out that while this question is impacted by both gender and age, there is no special combination where, say, older men would be likely to answer this question differently from younger men.

These two ANOVA examples tested first separately the effect of two factors using the same data and finally explored what happens when the two are put together. This approach with separate tests was to introduce one operation at a time for pedagogical reasons. In the actual analysis, it would be important to perform only a minimal number of statistical tests. This means that if you are interested in both factors, gender and age and their interaction, you would only carry out the combined analysis reported last (Code 7.4) as this includes the tests for the main effects of gender and age and their interaction. The need for a restricted number of tests relates to the danger of finding some spurious relationships in the data with the accepted p-value levels just because you would be carrying out many tests.

Comparison of Multiple Observations per Participant

Most of the experiments in empirical research of music gather *multiple observations from the same participant*. In the terminology of experiments, most experiments are *within-subjects experiments*, which requires slight adjustment to the basic analysis of t-tests or ANOVAs since each response is not sampled from a group of people but initially from an individual. This is an advantage, since (1) it is economical to collect multiple observations from participants, (2) one can deal with the different variation of the responses that an individual tends to have, and (3) a participant can also function as their own baseline in measures that are known to vary across people (such as the physiological variables like heart rate and skin conductance). At the same time, repeated measurements from the same individual violate the assumption in a t-test and ANOVA that the observations are independent. If a participant gives self-report ratings about their emotional responses to ten different music tracks, or their skin conductance is measured five times during an experiment, the observations are not considered to be independent, as they are likely to be related to that specific participant, which violates the assumptions of independence.

The analysis of repeated measures data can be done in several ways. Probably the most direct way is to perform *repeated measures ANOVA*. There is a more flexible variant analysis technique called *Linear Mixed Models* (LMM), which is described next because it has many advantages over repeated measures ANOVA. LMM will be able to support dependent variables that are ordinals or counts, and has better support for missing data and uneven numbers of repeats compared to repeated measures ANOVA.

Linear Mixed Models fall under the category of *Generalised Linear Mixed Models* (GLLMs), which is the broad term for all models that contain random and fixed effects with a different range of underlying models (non-linear, linear) and data (scale, ordinal, or counts). LMM assumes that the underlying distributions are normal and that we apply linear models. In most cases, these are the right assumptions, but it is possible to expand the analysis into ordinally organised variables or to analyse distributions that are not normal with this mixed models framework. The term mixed comes from the fact that the analysis breaks the variance down into *fixed* and *random effects*. This breakdown relates to the research question and the design, not the technicalities of the variables. *Fixed effects* are variables that we expect to influence the dependent variable. *Random effects* are typically grouping factors which we are trying to control, and for which we know there is a variance but it is not related to the main question of interest[4]. Random effects are always categorical, and there are usually more than five levels of them. We are not interested in random effects as such, but we know that these might influence the results by increasing noise that is not related to the research question. So, in LMM analysis, we incorporate this information into the analysis as a random effect, which allows us to build more accurate models when more variation is accounted for. This is a very powerful framework for analysis and is worth learning (Gelman & Hill, 2006).

Let us demonstrate LMM with an example. In the film soundtrack study (Eerola & Vuoskoski, 2011), a subset (49) of the 116 participants rated 110 film soundtrack excerpts varying in their emotional expression for tension, energy, and valence. For now we focus on the ratings of valence for each excerpt. The excerpts represent different discrete categories of emotions (happiness, anger, fear, tenderness, and sadness) with ten excerpts chosen to represent each category. The first question is whether the rating of valence reflects the emotion categories. The second question, recently suggested by Fuentes-Sánchez et al. (2021), asks whether gender influences the emotion ratings of these excerpts. We clearly have observations that are repeated across participants, but also across excerpts representing the categories (each participant heard 50 excerpts, ten from each emotion category). So, let us ask a question about whether the valence ratings are different across the emotion categories and whether the ratings are influenced by gender. We also think that participants themselves tend to have slightly different ways of responding to these questions (we treat them as a random effect) and that the excerpts have variable efficiency in communicating emotions (another random effect).

Using the R and the lme4 library for LLM analysis, we can build a simple LMM model where we explore whether the valence ratings are affected by the emotion category and the gender and their interaction (Valence ~ Category * Gender in Code 7.5). These two variables are our fixed factors that address our main research question. The important variance in the data, which we want to include in the analysis but effectively eliminate from the variables of interest are the random effects, here participants and tracks (+ (1|id) + (1|Track) in the Code 7.5). To include these two variables (participant and track) as random factors implies that we allow each participant to have their own response style and each excerpt to have its unique properties in communicating emotions, but while we allow this variation to exist, we will be looking at the broader impact on valence ratings created by emotion categories and gender. In this case, we have fitted a so-called *random-intercept model*, where each participant and track have a different intercept. In some cases, this is unrealistic, and some samples/populations come systematically with different assumptions. For instance, some participants may come from certain ensembles/ orchestras or schools, and in these cases we can specify random-slope and random-intercept model, where we allow the intercepts to be influenced by this grouping variable rather than allow everything to be random. However, getting deeper into the intricacies of the LMM approach is beyond the scope of this text (cf. Gelman & Hill, 2006).

```
# Code 7.5
d <- read.csv('raw_ratings.csv') #
d2 <- dplyr::filter(d,Emotion=='Dimensional')  #
d3 <- dplyr::filter(d2, Category=='Anger' |
                    Category=='Fear' |
                    Category=='Happy' |
                    Category=='Sad' |
                    Category=='Tender')
library(lme4)
library(lmerTest)
m1 <- lmer(Valence ~ Category * Gender + (1|id) + (1|Track), data = d3)
s <- summary(m1,corr=FALSE)
S<-s$coefficients; S<-round(S,2); S[,5]<-scales::pvalue(S[,5])
print(knitr::kable(S,format = 'simple',
                   caption = 'LMM results of Valence ratings.'))
```

Table 7.2 shows the statistical results for fixed effects only. It displays the tests for emotions and gender and their interactions. However, it does not show the full breakdown as we do not see anger (as emotion) and women (gender) as these are used as baseline conditions in this analysis and are therefore only implicitly present. Otherwise this table resembles the ANOVA report, except that here the first column reports the estimate (coefficient) and the fourth column is *t*-value instead of *F*-value. The estimate is the coefficient that describes the slope by which the

Table 7.2 LMM results showing the main effects of emotion category and gender and their interactions for valence ratings.

	Estimate	Std. Error	df	t-value	Pr(>|t|)
(Intercept)	3.43	0.25	58.17	13.51	<0.001
CategoryFear	0.07	0.34	47.43	0.19	0.850
CategoryHappy	4.16	0.34	47.43	12.24	<0.001
CategorySad	1.63	0.34	47.43	4.79	<0.001
CategoryTender	3.4	0.34	47.43	10.01	<0.001
GenderMale	−0.09	0.21	110.04	−0.45	0.650
CategoryFear:GenderMale	−0.07	0.19	2348	−0.34	0.730
CategoryHappy:GenderMale	−0.04	0.19	2348	−0.22	0.820
CategorySad:GenderMale	−0.46	0.19	2348	−2.41	0.020
CategoryTender:GenderMale	0	0.19	2348	0.01	0.990

factor is related to the valence. In other words, if we look at examples categorised to express happiness, this receives a statistically significant coefficient of 4.16 ($t[47.4]$=36.15, p<0.001), which is a large positive value and means that happy excerpts tend to score high valence ratings (above 7 to be precise, the coefficient of 4.15 plus the intercept of 3.43, which must be interpreted on a scale of 1 to 9, where 9 is very positive and 1 is very negative). To put this analysis into an equation, with this model you can predict the valence rating by adding the intercept (+3.43) and category in question (+4.16 for tracks representing happiness) so that would give us 7.59 as the model prediction, which is not far from the actual data (7.59 for women and 7.49 for men).

We do not see a significant main effect of gender in the results ($t[110]$=−0.43, p= 0.670), reported in the row labelled GenderMale. However, if we look at one specific combination of emotion and gender interactions, namely CategorySad:GenderMale, which relates to tracks that portray sadness and gender, this seems to suggest a statistically significant interaction ($t[2348]$=−2.14, p<0.05) between the two factors. Looking at the coefficient of this interaction (the Estimate column), we notice that it is negative (−0.46), which suggests that men tend to rate the valence of excerpts representing sadness significantly lower than women.

```
# Code 7.6
S <- d %>%
  filter(Category=='Sad') %>%
  group_by(Category,Gender) %>%
  summarise(M=mean(Valence,na.rm=T),SD=sd(Valence,na.rm=T),
            .groups = 'drop')
print(S)

## # A tibble: 2 × 4
##   Category Gender     M    SD
##   <chr>    <chr>  <dbl> <dbl>
## 1 Sad      Female  5.05  1.69
## 2 Sad      Male    4.5   1.54
```

Indeed, analysis shows that the mean for sadness for men is 4.50 whereas women rate those excerpts higher (5.05) in valence. You can also work this out using the coefficients in the LMM results. For men, this would be 3.43 Intercept + 1.63 CategorySad − 0.09 GenderMale − 0.46 CategorySad:GenderMale = 4.51. The mean calculated from the raw data is 4.50, very close to our how our LMM is characterising the data.

There are more options in the LMM analysis, and one can also carry out comparisons of different groups as post-hoc analyses or specific comparisons that are particularly interesting for the research question (e.g., all positive emotions vs negative emotions, or sadness versus all other emotions, just to give you some examples). LMM analysis is flexible and allows you to analyse almost any combination of repeated measures data, allows you to analyse non-normal distributions, and permits missing observations and non-symmetrical designs.

Compare Counts of Groups (Cross-tabulation)

When the observations are counts of categories (e.g., number of people of different age groups or gender, the type of instrument played, or the counts of pitch-classes from the music), one can *cross-tabulate* the data to explore the relationship between two variables. The appropriate measure of difference between such count profiles is the χ^2 test, which gives you the test value and the probability that two variables are of the same distribution. To give a demonstration, let's explore whether we have comparable numbers of men and women in the six age groups in the music and sadness study. We first pull the age and gender variables into a table as counts (line 3 in Code 7.7) and then run the test to determine whether the two age distributions are identical between men and women (line 5 in Code 7.7). The results show that the χ^2 is high (17) and the associated *p*-value is below 0.01, suggesting that there is a statistically significant difference in the number of men and women in the age groups. To find out where the difference lies, we can look at the table produced by Code 7.7 and work out where the observed and expected frequencies are different.

```
# Code 7.7
library(MusicScienceData)                    # Loads library w data
gender_age_xtab <- table(MusicScienceData::sadness$age,
                          MusicScienceData::sadness$gender)
print(gender_age_xtab)

##
##              Female Male
##   18 to 24     269   87
##   25 to 34     361  137
##   35 to 44     231  101
##   45 to 54     158   55
##   55 to 64     118   19
##   65 to 74      34    7

result <- chisq.test(gender_age_xtab)
print(result)

##
##   Pearson's Chi-squared test
##
## data:  gender_age_xtab
## X-squared = 17, df = 5, p-value = 0.005
```

After the comparison of values or counts between groups, let us move on to deal with two or more continuous variables.

Relationships Between Continuous Variables

Correlation

Correlation measures the association between two variables, where -1.00 is the perfect negative linear relationship, +1.00 is the perfect positive relationship, and values around 0 tend to tell the analyst that there is no association. To be precise, there are several correlation coefficients, the most common being the Pearson correlation coefficient (r), named after Karl Pearson (in the 19th century). The Pearson correlation coefficient is suitable for normally distributed variables (which also assumes that the variables are measured with interval scales). There is a variant measure that is suitable for data that comes from ranked measures or does not really fall under the normal distribution, and this is called the Spearman's rank correlation coefficient (r_s), which also ranges from -1.00 to +1.00 with a similar type of interpretation as the Pearson correlation coefficient.

Let us apply correlation to familiar data from the visualisation section. The pattern shown in Figure 6.8 suggested that there is a strong negative association between valence ratings (which relate to a continuum of emotions that range from negative to positive) and tension (i.e., from relaxed to tense) when participants rated 110 examples of film music using these two concepts. Let us calculate the correlation coefficient and obtain an estimate of the probability that this correlation coefficient is occurring by chance.

```
# Code 7.8
library(MusicScienceData)            # Load library w data
data <- MusicScienceData::soundtrack # define data
r<-cor.test(data$Valence, data$Tension) # calculate correlation
print(r$estimate)                    # print coefficient

##      cor
## -0.827

print(scales::pvalue(r$p.value))     # print pretty p value

## [1] "<0.001"

print(r$parameter)                   # print df

##  df
## 108
```

This correlation analysis would be reported as a significant negative correlation between valence and tension, $r(108)=-0.83$, $p<0.001$. Here -0.827 is the correlation coefficient, the value within the brackets is the degrees of freedom (df). The exact p-value is actually 2e-16, which means that it is 0.0000000000000002 (that's fifteen zeroes), very close to zero. It is good to note that this p-value is reported as $p<0.001$ as in principle, a probability value cannot be zero in statistics.

Regression

Regression analysis is an expansion of correlation, in which you combine multiple variables to predict one variable. It is also related to Linear Mixed Models (LMM) in the way that it builds the equation to account for the observations in the same way, and many of the terms (coefficients, intercepts) are already familiar from the LMM analysis.

Let us take an example. Ratings of perceived valence and tension in film music soundtracks are presented in Figure 6.8. The ratings probably reflect the acoustic and musical properties of the tracks. We can pull out some pre-calculated acoustic descriptors of the tracks to create a model that attempts to explain the tension ratings with acoustic features. The feature extraction will be covered in Chapter 10 about audio analysis, but let us just use existing features that come with MusicScienceData here.

Let us first look at how four acoustic descriptors correlate with energy ratings (Code 7.9). These acoustic features relate to dynamics (RMS) and timbre, such as spectral centroid (sp_centr), spectral roll-off (spec_rolloff), and zero-crossing (spec_zcr). Dynamics are an indicator of how loud the music is, and two of the spectral descriptors, spectral centroid and spectral roll-off, relate to where the energy of the signal falls in the spectrum and both capture semantic concepts that we can call brightness (a dark sound colour has more energy in the lower frequencies, whereas a bright timbre has its dominant part of the spectral energy in the high frequencies). Zero-crossing captures the rate of occurrence of a signal changing from positive to negative and vice versa, and this index does not have a clear perceptual correlate, but complex, noisy, and percussive sounds score highly for zero-crossing.

```
# Code 7.9
library(MusicScienceData)              # Loads library w data
d1 <- MusicScienceData::soundtrack      # get ratings
d2 <- MusicScienceData::soundtrack_features[,c(2:3,5:6)] #
d1[,17:21] <- as.data.frame(scale(d2))  # normalise

tmp <- cor(d1[,c(3,17:20)]) # get correlations
print(round(tmp[2:5,1],2))  # display first line

##            RMS     sp_centr spec_rolloff     spec_zcr
##           0.58         0.36         0.40         0.32
```

The four acoustic features show moderate correlations with the energy ratings in these data. We can already see from the correlation coefficients that the dynamics (RMS) has the highest correlation (r=0.58) with the energy and that this relationship is positive. That is, when a track is loud, it tends to be rated high on energy. However, we learn more about how all four acoustic features contribute *together* to the energy ratings when we run the regression analysis (Code 7.10).

```
# Code 7.10
model.reg <- lm(Energy ~ RMS + sp_centr + spec_rolloff +
                spec_zcr, data = d1)
s <- summary(model.reg) # R2adj = 0.424 (Energy)
print(s)

##
## Call:
## lm(formula = Energy ~ RMS + sp_centr + spec_rolloff + spec_zcr,
##     data = d1)
##
## Residuals:
##    Min     1Q Median     3Q    Max
## -2.472 -1.104 -0.206  0.943  3.450
##
## Coefficients:
##               Estimate Std. Error t value Pr(>|t|)
## (Intercept)      5.486      0.131   41.90  < 2e-16 ***
## RMS              0.907      0.140    6.49  2.9e-09 ***
## sp_centr        -1.907      1.224   -1.56    0.122
## spec_rolloff     1.966      0.950    2.07    0.041 *
## spec_zcr         0.600      0.417    1.44    0.154
## ---
## Signif. codes:  0 '***' 0.001 '**' 0.01 '*' 0.05 '.' 0.1 ' ' 1
##
## Residual standard error: 1.37 on 105 degrees of freedom
## Multiple R-squared:  0.45,   Adjusted R-squared:  0.43
## F-statistic: 21.5 on 4 and 105 DF,  p-value: 5.53e-13
```

The regression analysis shows that energy ratings can be predicted to a moderate degree ($R^2=0.45$) by these four acoustic features. R^2 is interpreted as the variance explained, where 1.0 would be a variance of 100% (a perfect prediction) and 0.0 would be no variance at all (nothing predicted). Here the features explain 45% of variation in the energy ratings. It is not a perfect model, but this one captures some aspect of energy. Regression analysis comes with an overall test statistic, F (here 21.52), degrees of freedom (105, starting from 110 observations minus 5 for 4 variables and a constant), and a p-value (here 5.528e−13, or simply $p<0.001$).

If we look at the regression results more closely, we notice that only two of the four acoustic characteristics contribute to this model. The first column (Estimate) tells us the standardised regression coefficient (aka *beta coefficient* or *beta weight*, or simply as β). This is the coefficient by which the values of the acoustic features need to be multiplied to obtain the best fitting model. For RMS, the standardised beta coefficient is 0.91, and there is a separate test statistic associated with including this characteristic in the regression, namely the t-test (t-value of 41.9) and the associated p-value (2e−16 or <0.001). As the coefficient is positive, it means that the higher the RMS, the higher the energy ratings are, which makes sense (louder excerpts sound more energetic). Another acoustic feature, namely spectral roll-off, also seems to contribute to the model, although its contribution is much weaker than that of the RMS (the beta coefficient is 1.97 and the p-value is 0.041, just barely below the agreed threshold of $p<0.05$). This coefficient also has a positive sign, so it means that excerpts that have high energy ratings also have higher values of spectral roll-off, which relates to how bright the timbre is. This makes sense since many instruments, when played loudly, produce higher spectral roll-off values (and sound brighter).

You can express the regression model as an equation. In this equation, first a constant (b_0, an intercept to make sure the values are in the range predicted), the two predictors (X_{i1}, X_{i2}) that contribute to the model, and an error term (ϵ_i) are included. The model equation is as follows:

$$Y_i = b_0 + b_1 X_{i1} + b_2 X_{i2} + \epsilon_i$$

In this specific case, when filled with the correct weights, the equation is:

$$Y_i = 5.49 + 0.91 \cdot RMS + 1.97 \cdot spec\_rolloff$$

This equation can be used to predict the energy rating in other music examples. Applying the equation to a new example, we would take the RMS value it has and multiply it by 0.91, and add the spec_rolloff value multiplied by 1.97, and add the constant of 5.49 to give the predicted value of energy. To make our model a little neater, we could recalculate the model after omitting the two predictors that did not contribute to the model. Also, we normally report a slightly more conservative measure of fit for the regression than the statistical software will give us, called *R squared adjusted* (R^{2adj}). This value is shown in the original regression results (0.43), and is somewhat lower than the full R^2 value, as the conservative estimate incorporates the number of variables in the model, which tends to increase the model fit.

It is also useful to note that correlation and regression have similar properties. In fact, r and R^2 are related, and if you square the former (r^2), it is identical to the R^2 value from a linear regression with a single predictor. Let us try to check that.

```
# Code 7.11
r <- cor(d1$Energy, d1$RMS)
print( r^2 )     # print the squared correlation

## [1] 0.338

summary(lm(Energy ~ RMS,data=d1))

##
## Call:
## lm(formula = Energy ~ RMS, data = d1)
##
## Residuals:
##    Min     1Q Median     3Q    Max
## -2.664 -1.192 -0.385  1.187  3.330
##
## Coefficients:
##             Estimate Std. Error t value Pr(>|t|)
## (Intercept)    5.486      0.142   38.72  < 2e-16 ***
## RMS            1.057      0.142    7.42  2.8e-11 ***
## ---
## Signif. codes:  0 '***' 0.001 '**' 0.01 '*' 0.05 '.' 0.1 ' ' 1
##
## Residual standard error: 1.49 on 108 degrees of freedom
## Multiple R-squared:  0.338,  Adjusted R-squared:  0.332
## F-statistic: 55.1 on 1 and 108 DF,  p-value: 2.79e-11
```

Multiple regression is a useful analysis that has a very intuitive interpretation. It is sensitive to outliers and violations of normality and linearity, but there are variant versions that can cope with these violations (ridge regression or lasso regression). Regression analysis can also be used to compare a set of predefined elements of a model, and there are ways to diagnose the overall individual contribution of the model components using *semi-partial correlations*. If the amount of data permits, there are useful operations to increase the reliability of the regression. Cross-validation is one such operation that will build the model using only a portion of the data and test with another portion. I will cover this additional reliability operation in Chapter 11 on corpus analysis by introducing cross-validation into the statistical analysis.

Modelling

To complete the analysis chapter, I want to demystify the term *modelling* used frequently in empirical studies and often mentioned in the earlier pages of this book. Modelling and models can be simple, as in linear regression, or complex, as in models that use neural networks or machine learning to simulate human psychoacoustics by emulating the working of the hair cells in the cochlea (see Chapter 10). The common properties of all computational models are that they have some operating principles, pre-defined parameters, and standard inputs and outputs, and that their performance has been assessed with relevant data. Models should also be shared in a transparent and well-documented way so that others can explore, modify, and expand them. However, the term modelling can refer to three notions of models: (1) a specific statistical description of the data, (2) a generalised model that generates predictions, or (3) the broad process of organising, testing, and communicating ideas in empirical research through modelling.

In the first use of the term modelling, models are *descriptions of empirical data*. These models are obtained through statistical or machine-learning analysis of the data, and the model is taken to be a description of what central elements contribute to the outcome, how the elements in the model work, and how successful the model is. Within the context of statistical models, creating such a model is a straightforward process and we have covered this already twice, once when we built the regression model that described the way energy ratings related to acoustic features, and also in the case of the Linear Mixed Model example, where we created a statistical model describing the links between valence ratings and gender and emotion categories in the film soundtrack data. In both cases, the resulting statistical solution is a *model* that accounts for the self-report ratings in these studies. Of course, such statistical models can be created to explain other behaviours and data too (movement, neural patterns, music choices, synchrony, etc.).

In the second use of the term modelling, we are talking about a computational model that can generate predictions from new data. The challenge of any model is how well it predicts observations in other relevant datasets. Separate competing models can also be compared if they have compatible elements, and both are applied to the same data. A model that outlines a new set of principles and perhaps a formulation of these as a computational model can provide us with a generalised function for future studies. Many of the machine-learning models provide this option. For example, the so-called autotagger (Bertin-Mahieux et al., 2008), which is able to populate new descriptive tags to any audio, or CREPE (Kim et al., 2018), which is a data-driven pitch tracking algorithm, are examples of such models. In more cognitive processing of music, the *Information Dynamics of Music* (IDyOM) by Marcus Pearce (2018) is a generalised modelling architecture of musical style based on statistical learning and probabilistic prediction. Another example of a model that was initially a set of empirical observations and later turned into a computational model is the Krumhansl-Schmuckler key-finding algorithm (Krumhansl, 2001) that we will explore in Chapters 9 and 10.

The third meaning of modelling relates to the notion where a *computational model* is used to simulate a musical behaviour/phenomenon more broadly. This use of the term modelling is interesting in its scope, as the model is not just a piece of software capable of transforming a set of observations into other categories, but it also represents a 'cognitive aid' for research (Farrell & Lewandowsky, 2018). In this notion, theoretical ideas need to be explored empirically, and the first task is to convert ideas into components of a model and design it in a way that the problem is situated in the theory. After these steps, the model can be tested and optimised by running it against the estimation of the parameters of the model. In other words, the purpose of the model is to understand the problem and share this understanding among scholars. In this way, models are implementations of theories, and there can be competing theories that may be compared through models. The evaluation of such high-level models is not only quantitative, but also rests on intellectual judgement of the solution (Farrell & Lewandowsky, 2018, p. 6). In empirical studies of music, research on musical consonance and dissonance is focussed on broad conceptual elements such as roughness, harmonicity, and familiarity (Eerola & Lahdelma, 2021), which are in turn implemented and compared with several competing computer models (Harrison & Pearce, 2020). The debate is not so much about which specific model representing an area of consonance and dissonance is the best, but whether understanding of the phenomena needs to be modelled with precise psychoacoustical simulations of the auditory systems or broader heuristics relating to the frequency of simultaneous pitches in the actual music and the physical properties of sounds.

Coda

This chapter has presented a summary of the typical inferential statistical tests that can be encountered in projects involving empirical music research. Although this is not a statistics handbook nor a guidebook on how to use statistical software (see the online resources for further materials on these), the basic principles of hypothesis testing, selecting the appropriate statistical test, and how to interpret the reports obtained have been given. The examples addressed typical research questions that involved comparing groups (t-tests and ANOVA) and comparing variables (correlation and regression). The practical examples of how to analyse data covered only a limited palette of analysis options, but in each case, a complete flow of analysis and reporting was given and explained in detail.

Discussion Points

1. 'Lies, damned lies, and statistics' is a quip attributed to Mark Twain. What kinds of issues have lent credence to this notion, and do you think they can be avoided?
2. Many people think the way questions are posed in inferential statistics is convoluted. The ideas of the null hypothesis and how inferential tests seek to find evidence against the null hypothesis are difficult to grasp. Why do you think these terms have been introduced in this fashion and not in the opposite way (i.e., that we seek to confirm the experimental hypothesis)?
3. The text mentioned that finding statistical significance in an inferential test does not mean that the finding has general significance. Can you think of findings that would be statistically significant but not worthy of attention in the general sense?

Notes

1 See www.nature.com/articles/506150a
2 Pronounced kaɪ skweə(r)
3 The degrees of freedom calculation assumes that the statistical test decreases the number of degrees of freedom your test has by 1 or 2 (or it can be a much more complex issue in advanced tests). If you have 100 observations, and you calculate the correlation coefficient between two variables, the degree of freedom is 98 (100-2, observations minus two parameters).
4 Terminologies tend to vary across techniques; fixed effects and random effects are used in GLLMs but fixed factors and random factors in other analysis of variance contexts, see Gelman & Hill, 2006.

Further Reading

Harris, J. K. (2020). *Statistics with R: Solving problems using real-world data*. Sage.
McElreath, R. (2020). *Statistical rethinking: A Bayesian course with examples in R and Stan*. Chapman & Hall/CRC.
Tabachnick, B. G., Fidell, L. S., & Ullman, J. B. (2013). *Using multivariate statistics*. Boston, MA.

References

Bertin-Mahieux, T., Eck, D., Maillet, F., & Lamere, P. (2008). Autotagger: A model for predicting social tags from acoustic features on large music databases. *Journal of New Music Research, 37*(2), 115–135.

Eerola, T., & Lahdelma, I. (2021). The anatomy of consonance/dissonance: Evaluating acoustic and cultural predictors across multiple datasets with chords. *Music & Science, 4.* https://doi.org/https://doi.org/10.1177/20592043211030471

Eerola, T., & Vuoskoski, J. K. (2011). A comparison of the discrete and dimensional models of emotion in music. *Psychology of Music, 39*(1), 18–49.

Farrell, S., & Lewandowsky, S. (2018). *Computational modeling of cognition and behavior.* Cambridge University Press.

Fuentes-Sánchez, N., Pastor, M. C., Eerola, T., & Pastor, R. (2021). Individual differences in music reward sensitivity influence the perception of emotions represented by music. *Musicae Scientiae.* https://doi.org/https://doi.org/10.1177/10298649211060028

Gelman, A., & Hill, J. (2006). *Data analysis using regression and multilevel/hierarchical models.* Cambridge university press.

Harrison, P., & Pearce, M. (2020). Simultaneous consonance in music perception and composition. *Psychological Review, 127*(2), 216–244. http://dx.doi.org/10.1037/rev 0000169

Kim, J. W., Salamon, J., Li, P., & Bello, J. P. (2018). CREPE: A convolutional representation for pitch estimation. *2018 IEEE International Conference on Acoustics, Speech, and Signal Processing, ICASSP 2018 – Proceedings,* 161–165. https://doi.org/https://doi.org/10.48550/ARXIV.1802.06182

Krumhansl, C. L. (2001). *Cognitive foundations of musical pitch.* Oxford University Press.

McElreath, R. (2020). *Statistical rethinking: A Bayesian course with examples in R and Stan.* Chapman & Hall/CRC.

Pearce, M. T. (2018). Statistical learning and probabilistic prediction in music cognition: Mechanisms of stylistic enculturation. *Annals of the New York Academy of Sciences, 1423*(1), 378–395.

8 Reporting and Craftsmanship

Now that we have covered research design, data, and analysis, let us look at reporting structures and formats, and then review the forms of publication (books and articles) in this field.

If you have been following the principles of transparent and reproducible research mentioned in the Research Transparency section, you will have most of the report already ready by the time your observations are available for analysis. Even if you do not strictly follow these principles, you will have the background, goals, hypotheses, and methods already committed before you have the data. When working within reproducible research, the objectives and hypotheses including the design, methods, measures, and analysis strategy have been defined well in advance of the collection of the observations. It is possible to report the plans as a *Registered Report,* which many journals accept as submissions (see Chapter 4). Such a plan will be reviewed and, if found to be sound with coherent and flawless methodology including the statistical analysis procedure, it will be provisionally accepted (called Stage 1 approval). This means that if you complete the plan, the journal will publish it no matter what the results are, provided that you adhered to the plan described. The intention here is (1) to avoid the bias of only publishing studies with positive results, since null or negative results are equally important for promoting understanding of a topic, (2) to avoid collecting data that have already been collected, and perhaps most importantly, (3) to curb all kinds of bad habits such as HARKing (hypothesising after the results), *p*-hacking (stopping the data collection or analysis when the results are conveniently under conventional *p*-value thresholds), or to mention some additional misbehaviours, cherrypicking (analysing and reporting parts of the data), or just using variables that were not initially thought to be important (Nosek et al., 2018). One can also submit a study *preregistration* to an open repository of preregistrations https://osf.io/prereg/, which would reveal if you resorted to these sorts of dubious and dangerous practices in your research. My initial experiences of the preregistration procedures are positive; the act of writing the preregistration makes you think through the details of the study so much more carefully, and when we went through the submission process to a journal (e.g., Armitage & Eerola, 2022), the reviewers suggested helpful and

DOI: 10.4324/9781003293804-8

constructive improvements, and it felt that they were on our side and wanted to see how the results eventually turned out.

Reporting Structures

Research communication in empirical music research typically has a specific reporting structure that facilitates locating the relevant information easily, and the standardisation helps to communicate many compulsory and repeating aspects of reports. The readers of empirical music research studies expect to discover methods, participants, stimuli, and procedures, and they expect to find very specific details within these short sections. This contrasts with the writing conventions in humanistic musicology, where a good narrative and the topic itself largely dictate the structure of writing, and strict structures are avoided. In empirical music research, it is very much a standard to have the following sections in any report: *introduction, aims, methods, results*, and *conclusions*. Usually, aims are tagged on to the end of the introduction and these are typically articulated in the form of precise questions or even research hypotheses. In addition, the methods are usually broken down into *participants, stimulus materials*, and *procedures,* since these are the common elements of many empirical studies.

Abstract
Introduction
Method
Design
Participants
Materials/Stimuli
Procedure
Results
Discussion/Conclusions
References

The structure itself – listed here – might feel like a rigid template, but within the confines of this structure, one can express ideas eloquently and efficiently. Brevity is a celebrated virtue in this field, and it is typical for articles to have fairly strict word count limits (see the section 'Journal Articles vs Books' in this chapter). Writing concise and succinct reports on a topic is usually more challenging than writing a long, elaborate version of the text because in the more economic and trimmed version, every sentence must count. There cannot be too much redundancy or repetition. These traditions (structure and length) have been influenced by publishing conventions enforced by journals that have strict limits on maximum word counts, but being able to express ideas in a succinct form is a major asset and a celebrated skill in this field.

This suggested structure can be varied and altered based on need, such as omitting participants if it is a corpus study or ignoring design if the design is simply to correlate variables together. You can also split sections into smaller units if you want to separate some of the main elements in the introduction or in the discussion or conclusions. Overall, scholars reading empirical reports expect to find these structures in the reports, and inventing your own ways of communicating the elements of empirical research to the reader is usually not a great idea. Leave the creativity to the original research ideas and interpretations and conform to the tried-and-tested conventions in the structure of scholarly communication.

Let's go through the types of issues that are covered in each section of the manuscript.

Introduction

The introduction is a vitally important part of the report as it needs to pull in and persuade the reader to the topic, present the research question early in the introduction, explain what we already know about the topic (known as a literature review) and what we do not know about it, and why this is so important. It is a common and functional technique to end the introduction with a statement of hypotheses of the study, and these should organically arise from the gaps in the knowledge exposed by the literature review. Within the introduction, you can think of the focus of the ideas as moving from generic to specific as in a funnel. Initially, you start with broad statements about how this subject area is such an important one in general, perhaps even starting with a great quote from a source outside of the research literature. The opening sentence should be a motivating and memorable one and it is worth studying the opening gambits of the articles in your topic area. As you proceed along the introduction, you bring elements and insights from existing studies and narrow down the topic with working definitions, findings, and results. This is not to say that such a summary would be just listing what the findings and studies are, but rather your task is to highlight what is agreed by scholars and what is not and whether the discrepancies or gaps are there because of different definitions, samples, methods, interpretations, or other issues. A chronological summary is a natural way of providing this discursive presentation of past findings, but sometimes a thematic organisation of the ideas can highlight the issues more efficiently. Toward the end of the introduction your operational definitions are crisp, narrow, and clear, and you are able to articulate a very specific set of questions that provide answers that are not yet known, are motivated by the literature and common sense, and are also possible to study. After the introduction, it is time to tell the reader how you designed the study, and which methods and materials were used.

Method

Subheadings within the *Method* section vary across the types of studies, but let me summarise here a typical structure of a behavioural study. The commonly used subheadings are *Design*, *Participants*, *Stimuli*, and *Procedure*. If your study is a corpus study, it is possible to leave sections out; you will have no participants in a corpus study but instead you will have the definition of the corpus. You can also insert new ones to highlight the specific elements related to your study. But let me briefly talk through the issues that the reader expects to find in these common subsections of the method section.

In the *Design* section, you outline whether your work is a case study, corpus study, theoretical study, or meta-analytical study and whether it is descriptive, experimental, correlational, or observational. You also define the variables and the logic of experimental manipulation (if you have one). This is often such a short section that it might not need a separate heading.

In the *Participants* section, you explain how the participants were recruited (where, what criteria if any, what information was conveyed to the participants in the recruitment, etc.), how many there were, and the characteristics of your sample (gender distribution, mean age, and age range). You will typically describe the musical training of the participants and probably other background information as well (education etc.) if these were deemed to be important for the research question. This section can also report how many participants' data were not included (typical in surveys where you may want to discard incomplete answers, or in experiments when some participants failed attention checks or other control criteria, or there can simply sometimes be coding errors and missing observations).

The section titled *Materials* or *Stimuli* explains how the study materials were created, where they were initially obtained, what kinds of operations were done to them, how they were presented, and where they can be found (if possible). When referring to music stimuli, the source can be an existing database of melodies (e.g., the Essen collection by Schaffrath & Huron (1995) or the rock song collection by De Clercq & Temperley (2011)), or alternatively a selection of the specific excerpts should be explained and justified. You should also explain how the specific tunes were selected and how they were rendered into audio files (what instruments were used, what sample library was used, whether there was an expression added that affects the dynamics and microtimings of the notes, and whether the sounds were calibrated, etc.). There is a surprising wealth of details even in the simplest experiments with music examples. If you can share the stimuli with the readers via open repositories, that is very useful, although not always possible due to copyright reasons. Even if you are not able to share all the stimuli, you should think about whether other people can prepare and replicate your experiment based on your description of the stimuli and at least provide audio examples for readers to understand the sounds that you are using. Materials also includes instruments, questionnaires and established measures that the study uses.

The *Procedure* section contains a brief description of what the experimental process entailed for the participants. In a sense, it is a summary of what instructions they were given, how the experiment proceeded, what the tasks were, what scales/questions/existing instruments were used, and how the different sections or blocks of the experiment unfolded (with breaks or without breaks, with feedback or without feedback, with the items presented in counterbalanced manner, randomised, etc.). The procedure section might also mention that an ethics approval was secured from the host institution (and quote the reference) and that the participants first signed an informed consent. It is also common to mention any compensation that participants received after completing the study (even if it was just for a course credit).

A variant of the method subsection may include *statistical methods*, especially if the study uses an unusual set of statistics or if a very specific method of analysis needs to be explained before the results are presented.

Results

The *Results* section states what was analysed and what was found. Although an interpretation of these is necessary, one should not really delve too deeply into interpretations of the results, as there will be a subsequent section about this (*Discussion*). Purely factual statements that describe what was found, and which include the statistical information, are a very typical way of reporting the results. Note that you should report any eliminated or transformed data and explain how these issues were identified, what was done to them, and how many cases we are talking about.

> Ratings of pleasure for each track were positively correlated with mean ISCR for Track 3, Spearman $rho(24)=.42$, $p=.04$ (two-tailed). (Solberg & Dibben, 2019, p. 383, where ISCR stands for integrated skin conductance response.)

Discussion and Conclusions

The purpose of the *Discussion* and *Conclusions* (sometimes only one of these headings is used or, in long texts, they might be separate sections) is to interpret results in the context of your hypotheses and the past literature. A good discussion avoids being a summary of the results, but offers a broader interpretation by linking it to the broader research area. Remember that I mentioned earlier the notion of the funnel when presenting ideas in the introduction? The discussion can be thought to work in reverse order; you start with the specific findings of your study and gradually broaden the scope of the discussion. The final sentence is sometimes as memorable and as broad as the opening sentence and inspires the reader to recommend your report to their friends and supervisors.

The discussion provides an opportunity to evaluate theories and discuss the current results in terms of how similar or different they are to past findings. If your results differ significantly from what previous research has reported and perhaps how the hypotheses operated, you should discuss what the possible reasons for the differences are. There are of course many sources of differences (samples, designs, stimuli, ways of measuring, different analysis techniques) and instead of just listing all possible differences, a good strategy is to focus on the substantial issues and broader trends.

As all research has limitations and caveats, it is important to discuss the *specific* shortcomings of the research. Again, I would not recommend trying to offer a list of things that could have been done differently or better, but focus on limitations that might have bearing on the findings and that could be addressed in future research. It is also prudent to avoid making strong claims such as 'these results prove that ...' as such claims tend to be too strong and easily dismantled by other scholars. Instead, you can express the same idea by saying 'these results are consistent with theory/hypothesis X', which is gentler and emphasises the link between current empirical data and the underlying ideas.

Identifying the next research directions that are suggested by the present findings is a classic move in the last part of the conclusions. These can range from small-scale suggestions for altering the design/stimuli/procedure/participants for future studies to possible ways of plugging the gap mentioned as a shortcoming of the present study or highlighting an interesting way to move forward in the topic. It is also possible to suggest expanding the theories and notions to include other ideas and concepts for future studies. Finally, it is also common to discuss the real-world implications of the findings and end the section with a positive statement about what research in this area can achieve in general.

References and Other Possible Sections

In this section, you simply list the references cited, usually in alphabetical order based on the first author's last name, but there are also citation conventions based on numbering and the order is based on the sequential order of sources cited in the text. No matter which style is chosen, the important thing is to be consistent and follow the style guidelines. Adopt a reference manager (see next section) if you are not keen to edit the references by hand.

You may need to report your original items, measures, full statistics, or other such details in the report. These can sometimes go into *Appendices* (*Appendix 1*, *Appendix 2* and so on) or sometimes journals prefer to call these *Supporting Information* or *Supplementary Information* that will be released online. If the online solution is offered, there are usually no page limits for these types of contribution, so it is possible to include a lot of information in these extra sections if it is meaningful. In some ways, these sections are close to the reproducible research principles and could also be released as part of the data analysis in the research repository (see Section on Research Transparency).

Reporting Conventions

There are several conventions that govern citation and referencing styles and some other details such as how numbers, statistics, tables, and figures are formatted. The first rule is that you need to be *consistent* with all the requirements that the system has. If the reporting requirement states APA (*American Psychological Association*) referencing and American spelling, just follow the guidelines that are available (e.g., https://apastyle.apa.org). APA style is just one example. Many journals have unique conventions and styles that can be seen as variants of APA or other major citation and referencing styles such as the *Chicago Manual of*

Style, the *MLA* (*Modern Languages Association*) style, or the *Harvard* style. These conventions may also relate to the suggested structure of the text such as recommended section headings. Listing the options here is not possible, but typically most reports in empirical music research adhere to APA style (which is currently on its 7th version[1]).

There are technical solutions that make adhering to the numerous reporting conventions a little easier; reference managers, manuscript templates, and a combination of these such as documents that can be created with R Markdown or LaTeX, which can combine styles and references. Many people combine Microsoft Word with a reference manager such as *EndNote, Mendeley,* or *Zotero.* The reference management software is basically a database of references, which users can easily populate from online sources or simply by inserting the necessary bibliographic details of a book or an article. Actually, typing in the details is fairly rare now that scholarly journals provide export options that allow you to insert details of the item easily. Once you have the details in the system, the reference manager can export the bibliography in the desired style or even integrate the references with your word processing software.

I have written this book in R Markdown, which is a simple plain text format based on *markdown* conventions, which have been enhanced to support R code and *RStudio/R* functionalities. I manage references as a *.bib (BibTeX) file using *BibDesk* software, and I bring the references directly into my writing environment (R Markdown), as it can follow almost any required referencing and citation style, which is a lifesaver. You can also capitalise on the fact that your bibliography is a database that can be sorted, annotated, and reorganised, and I have often summarised studies of a certain topic using the details that I have annotated to this database (e.g., 250 music and emotion studies in Eerola & Vuoskoski, 2012 or the 500 references of this book). This system of simple markdown and reference management is convenient and, in my opinion, makes writing less technical than using Word or similar for document creation. Using markdown is also more reliable, lightweight, and flexible than a set of documents created by Microsoft Word or other full text editors. But relying on open-source tools tends to be a personal preference, and mastering such tools does take time, and does not always provide easy solutions for co-writing and publishing, where the default option is typically Word[2].

Posters

In my view, posters may be one of the most potent forms of presenting scholarly ideas in an economic fashion. A good poster allows the reader to assimilate the main points of the study with a few key bullet points and delivers a summary of the results with great graphics without being distracted by trivial details. The presentation of a great poster might only take about two minutes, and then the reader usually has the luxury of asking for clarifying questions of the author in person. This is far more efficient than a presentation, which typically would take 20 minutes, and then there might be about 5 minutes for questions, which allows for about 3 questions. So, from this perspective, posters are of great value for science communication, but this assumes that the poster itself is functional. What is a functional poster?

It should focus on the main message and emphasise the findings. You should be selective and choose only the essential results. The prospective reader of the poster tends to spend less than 60 seconds looking at the poster, so you need to make the title, aims, and results count. For empirical studies, it is common to follow the typical structure of a report (introduction, aim, methods, results, and conclusions). The layout should be clear, and use graphs and images to deliver the main message. Posters can be reused on the lab walls after their presentation. It is also possible to print posters on cloth canvas for easier carrying (and these posters can have other uses as well).

Presentations

Research applying the empirical approach to music does not differ too much from any other presentation except that it is usually a good idea to rely on empirical reporting structures when communicating the results. As with posters, a presentation must be selective and focus only on the main results. There are several very good compact texts about how to make excellent presentations and what the most important design principles in communicating ideas effectively in presentations are. I urge you to consult the recently published 'Ten simple rules' (Naegle, 2021), which, if everyone adhered to them, would make a massive difference to presentations. If you want to read an interesting, data-driven take on why poor presentations often violate perceptual or psychological processes, read Stephen Kosslyn and collaborators' empirical study about eight principles of cognitive communication that can be violated or adhered to (Kosslyn et al., 2012).

Publishing Research

Publishing in empirical music research is aligned to practices in social sciences and departs from conventions in the arts and humanities in certain ways. I will cover the scope of publishing and the collaborative nature of the research that contributes to these publishing conventions and the pace and format of the publishing pipeline.

Journal Articles vs Books

The format of publishing is linked to the community of readers; journals effectively specify the type of community they represent (the 'aims and scope' section of each journal defines these). Books may be more important than articles for some communities, but it can be the other way round for another community. In empirical music research, it is more common to publish articles than to publish monographs. This relates to the incremental and empirical nature of the research process, where articles may present new innovations and insights in a rapidly progressing research topic. Turning these into monographs would be a slow process and would not guarantee the best review processes available. Also, it is typical to have multiple authors contribute to a study as authors, whereas monographs tend to be produced by a single scholar. It is not a coincidence that arts and humanities research has been called the 'lone scholar' model in the past, although this is starting to be an outdated notion, since there are more and more collaborative teams in the humanities, and the value of articles has risen to be equally important as books in the humanities (Clark & Hill, 2019).

The more collaborative nature of research outputs and review processes, the incremental nature of research, and shorter publication turnaround times all favour articles instead of books. Articles, however, are much more restricted in length than monographs. When articles present cutting-edge research, brevity is a positive value. Part of this ideal comes from the heavily structured reporting convention explained earlier, which does not really foster creative freedom around how the text is structured, but facilitates readers finding the information they need economically. This is quite a different story in many articles on music history or music analysis, where the narrative itself contains details of the rationale of the study, and the structure is looser, sometimes to the detriment of finding out easily what the scope, materials, and results of the article were. However, while frequency of publishing tends to favour articles in empirical music research, there is value in publishing books grounded in empirical research as books allow setting out a more comprehensive account of a topic than short articles can ever do. Indeed, there are some excellent and profoundly influential books in empirical music research, for example, Alf Gabrielsson's *Strong Experiences with Music* (2011) and Marc Leman's *Embodied Music Cognition and Mediation Technology* (2007).

Returning to the value of brevity, the goal of research reporting is to communicate effectively, and clarity and brevity are central pillars in this process. As any writer knows, writing a concise text from a longer text is a demanding task and requires hard work and numerous rounds of edits. The notion that reports are heavily structured and the scholar only says what needs to be said avoiding wordiness and redundancy has created a set of expectations for article length in empirical music research, which is about half of the length when compared to humanistic musicology. Journals in humanistic musicology such as *Music and Letters* recommend articles be 8,000 and 15,000 words, and the *Journal of American Musicological Society* has a maximum of 20,000 words. In empirical music research, in contrast, *Psychology of Music* suggests that articles should be 4,000–6,000 words, and articles in *Music & Science* should be 4,000 and 7,500 words. There are even shorter formats in most empirical music research journals, often called *Brief Reports*, that may have a maximum word count of only 1,000, 2,000 or 3,000 words.

Some of the most influential studies in empirical music research have been very short communications in eminent journals; Blood & Zatorre (2001)'s paper on intense emotions is a mere five pages long. This example was published in a journal (*Proceedings of the National Academy of Sciences*) that has very constrained word count allowance but adhering to it makes for punchy statements and works well to communicate the main findings. Details of methods, stimuli, and procedures are often not included in the paper but published as *Supporting Information* or *Supporting Materials* which the publisher releases online.

Prestigious generic journals such as *Nature, Science, Proceedings of the National Academy of Sciences* (PNAS), or *Nature Human Behaviour* rarely publish music-related articles. They have obtained their reputation by existing for a long time, but also because the articles in these journals – for various reasons – tend to get cited a lot. The fact they are cited means that they are influential articles and considered to be central references, although these metrics need to be treated with caution. There is a metric behind the citation of the publication forum (journal) with the steadfast and uncritical assumption that top-tier journals publish top-tier articles, which is not entirely true because the quality of the articles inevitably varies. Journal quality is usually conveyed by the average citations in the journal per year (called journal *Impact Factor*), or the journal h-index, which is the number of articles (h) that have received at least h citations. These metrics are hosted by private companies, such as Elsevier, Thomson Reuters and SCImago, and, in a less structured fashion, by Google Scholar.

Unfortunately, historically these metrics did not have full coverage of all academic journals, and the arts and humanities journals were traditionally less well indexed, but this is no longer the case. Also, citation counts are influenced by matters such as gender, race, name (nationality), and language. In sum, citation counts are elusive indicators of value.

The decision to submit to a specific journal is very likely to be a combination of the speed of the review process, the quality of reviews, the reputation of the journal, and the fit of the journal with the study topic. Furthermore, accessibility of the study after publication is a critical factor as some articles are impossible to access without institutional subscriptions and are hidden behind the publisher's paywall. I describe the issues related to peer review in a later section.

Preprints

Authors can make their work accessible to others before peer review by publishing the manuscript in one of the preprint repositories such as PsyArXiv or arXiv. This has the advantage of disseminating the work immediately, without waiting for two to four months (or longer if you are unlucky or submit to journals with a slow pace). Preprints have also been shown to increase reach and visibility that might be especially important for the crucial early career stage (Serghiou & Ioannidis, 2018). Also, it is one more way to benefit from feedback from a larger community than just reviewers from one journal. On the negative side, analyses of preprints suggest that some of the benefits mentioned earlier are not really realised as authors mainly use the preprints to establish their stake on the claim and – in the worst case – preprints are mainly used for marketing purposes (Anderson, 2020). Despite this criticism, preprints are a very useful way to communicate research and, in my opinion, increase the trust and transparency of research activities. I have several times benefited from reading a good study at a preprint stage that has given me insight into designing an ongoing study slightly differently or at least articulating the study to be more aligned with the most recent studies. I have also shared my own manuscripts at preprint stage for all these reasons.

Authorship

In earlier sections, I outlined that it is common to have multiple authors in articles within empirical music research. The reason for having multiple authors on an article is that each author brings a separate skill set and knowledge background to the study. Interdisciplinary or sub-disciplinary collaborations are often required when tackling topics that combine approaches and methods (e.g., a topic such as chills induced by music that requires knowledge of music theory, psychophysiological indicators, and advanced statistical models). What counts towards being an author in these cases? Sometimes there is an impression that these multi-authored publications will easily land someone an authorship on a minimal contribution and sharing the authorship detracts from the individual contribution of the authors. Well, there is a lot of guidance on authorships being defined, but it tends to be one of the areas where diplomacy and negotiation are needed. Early discussions are crucial in finding out what everyone involved in the project assumes and contributes to the project and the publications. Multi-authored studies are also opportunities for students to collaborate and learn from others. These collaborators may be formal supervisors, informal collaborators, or non-academic collaborators who have contributed intellectually and organisationally to the project.

The main definition of authorship is that you can, and will, be held accountable for the research claims and findings. The APA guidelines stress that 'An author is considered anyone involved with initial research design, data collection and analysis, manuscript drafting, and final approval. However, the following do not necessarily qualify for authorship: providing funding or resources, mentorship, or contributing research but not helping with the publication itself'. These are important definitions, and there certainly are local traditions or beliefs that go against these, unfortunately. Often junior authors (postgraduate students, early career postdocs) are not in a position to challenge a senior scholar's claim of authorship, but it is precisely for these situations that more specific guidelines have been developed. The APA code of ethics states: 'Principal authorship and other publication credits accurately reflect the relative scientific or professional contributions of the individuals involved, regardless of their relative status'[3]. There is even a special comment about student dissertations, where the student is assumed to be the principal author on any work stemming from the dissertation. Another set of guidelines from *Frontiers*[4] outlines four criteria for authorship (see box).

Authorship Criteria (Frontiers)

1. Substantial contributions to the conception or design of the work; or the acquisition, analysis, or interpretation of data for the work;
2. Drafting the work or revising it critically for important intellectual content;
3. Provide approval for publication of the content;

4. Agree to be accountable for all aspects of the work in ensuring that questions related to the accuracy or integrity of any part of the work are appropriately investigated and resolved.

And if there are contributors who do not meet these criteria but have nevertheless made noteworthy contributions to the study and the manuscript, they should be included in the *acknowledgements* section.

There are also schemes that allow us to specify all aspects of contribution. A scheme titled *CRediT (Contributor Roles Taxonomy)* defines 14 different aspects of contribution. All in all, there are great guidelines that are now well established and followed, so deciding authorship is a rational activity in principle.

Authorship discussions should be held at an early stage of any research. There are, of course, complications when the project changes along the way, or the collaboration is with scholars from another discipline where the authorship conventions are slightly different. Problems arise if the authors disagree on who is a contributor, or there are so-called ghost or gift authors, and perhaps an important contributor has been relegated to the acknowledgements. There are mechanisms to handle disputes[5], but it is advisable to avoid such disputes in the first place by clear planning, organisation, and communication.

Peer Review

When a manuscript is complete, it is submitted to a journal (or to a book publisher or to an editor of an edited book). This submission normally undergoes a technical check that the required elements of the manuscript are present and adhered to, and that it fits the aims and scope of the publishing forum. After this initial triage, the manuscript will be reviewed by peers. This is a fundamental principle in scholarship that ensures *quality control*. Peer review is usually organised by experienced scholars acting as editors of a journal or book series. The editor invites two to four subject specialists to evaluate the manuscript and articulate a structured review and textual feedback on the possible shortcomings and implications of the manuscript. It is common but not necessary that the process is double-blind, which means that the author does not get to learn who the reviewers are, nor do the reviewers get to know who the author is. This anonymity serves to keep prestige and reputation out of the review process and protects participants in the process from conflicts outside of the paper being reviewed. The review decisions are arbitrated by the editor, and the process either stops at outright rejection, a request for resubmission with revisions (typically classified either as major or minor) is made, or the manuscript is accepted (usually with some caveats and improvements). The process is iterative when resubmission is concerned; the revised manuscript is reviewed again initially by the editor and sent to the same reviewers with a summary of the changes made. This summary usually takes the form of a detailed response to all the issues raised by the reviewers and pointers of how the manuscript was changed to reflect the feedback. Some journals (such as *Empirical Musicology Review*) publish the whole peer review process to offer full transparency of how the article was reviewed and accepted.

The peer review process is the best system that scholarship has for quality control, but it is far from perfect. In fact, it has several recognised problems. Despite the idea of anonymity, the process is prone to biases relating to author status, gender, and under-represented minorities (Bornmann et al., 2007; Severin et al., 2020). There are some initiatives that allow reviewers to get credits for their efforts (e.g., *Publons*, *Peerage of Science*, or *Reviewer Credits*[6]).

The most dangerous issue with peer review is that it does not always spot deliberate frauds or major errors. Fraudulent data and results are difficult to spot, and every now and then someone in the scholarly community can detect anomalies in the published papers that – after a thorough investigation – turn out to be scientific misconducts or genuine errors, both of which can lead to the paper being redacted from the journal. This is a process where the publisher adds a retraction notice, usually written by the publisher (editor), to explain the reason for the redaction. It is extremely rare in studies related to music (e.g., there were 3 out 1,127 retracted studies in 2021 according to the retraction database[7]). Science is a self-correcting process, and in addition to peer review, there are processes in place by which problematic or erroneous research can be flagged up even years after publication. One of the possible fixes to any troublesome quality control issue is to share the data, protocols, and analysis code (see Section on Research Transparency).

When you are the author responding to the comments of the reviewers or the reviewer evaluating a manuscript, it pays to be courteous, respectful, and brisk with the pace. You should remember as an author that other scholars are trying to help you better communicate your study, and the manuscript will always be better after incorporating most of the suggestions. I said most because you can also decline to follow their recommendations and justify your decision with firm reasons. As a reviewer, you need to focus on the substance, not the personalities or competences of the authors. In the best case, the peer review can be an engaging and rewarding experience for both parties. Writing reviews can be one of the best scholarly training exercises, since it allows you to engage with an interesting topic, and you will also see other reviews of the same manuscript. In essence, this is a form of continued professional development where you will quickly discover whether your values about quality control, novelty, and scientific rigour are in line with those of others in the field.

Craftsmanship

After talking about the basic elements of research methods and publishing, it is also important to discuss why the same elements can lead to different results and how much the quality of the scholarship has to do with overall research impact. What makes researchers succeed in their field and choose to embark on life-long scholarly development? In this section, I have attempted to discuss at least some of these elements, such as attitudes, skill sets, and collaboration, which I think contribute to impact and quality of research. Another side of these valuable elements is equality and diversity, which merits its own section in Chapter 12.

Attitude and Skill Set

'Attitude is everything' proclaims an old adage. In my opinion, having a curious mind is the primary trait that drives all scholarly thinking. Curiosity needs to be coupled with competence and healthy scepticism, and being able to be fascinated with how things work. Curiosity and scepticism will need to be driven by persistence if one wants to do well in academia. Being the one who believes in the idea and has the stamina to see it through planning, data collection, analysis, reporting, revision, and then several additional loops of research iterations does require dogged tenacity. At the same time, willingness to be proven wrong and to review premises, methods, and analyses is a valuable and beneficial trait.

In the set of key competences and skills, intimate knowledge of music, music theory, and music performance is a prerequisite to being able to understand the basics in the field in the first place. I would say that understanding coding comes in handy in empirical research. Not fearing numerical analysis or statistics comes with a knowledge of coding, although one does not need great mathematical skills to do research involving numbers, just basic knowledge of probability calculus will get you far.

Collectives – Labs

Research efforts in empirical music research are often organised in labs. Labs can be helpful communities that facilitate the transfer of knowledge from more experienced members to less experienced members. Labs tend to have a specific identity based on their strengths and focus. They are usually open, have established their own training regime, and have efficient ways of collecting data and analysis routines that can be shared among members. Some research is challenging without the required skill levels and infrastructure, and the purpose of the lab is to enable the individual to capitalise on the resources available in the lab. In short, laboratories can be efficient hubs of scholarship, where knowledge can be transferred, resources are pooled together, and practical data collection is organised in an effective way. If the lab is particularly well supported, it has its own technical resources. A skilled technician has the potential to raise the scientific quality of a lab. A productive lab also needs strategic thinking and experience to steer collective efforts towards targets that are worthy, engaging, and where genuine progress can be made.

Collaboration

Labs are the first unit to share expertise and work towards joint goals. But sometimes the research theme requires a wider network or teams across universities or countries. Collaboration and multi-site studies can be valuable for several reasons; diversity of perspectives will typically generate stronger research, and collaborations across universities and countries offer generally more diversity and may guard against biases that are a product of single culture, language, or an approach favoured by one lab. However, collaboration is a skill that needs to be acquired and honed, like any other skill, as we discussed in the section on authorship issues. Establishing ways of understanding how to talk and transform ideas freely and constructively together requires spending time together talking about the ideas under different formats (e.g., presentations, seminars, and informal chats). Collaborations are also useful to pool methodological and topic competences together; some people are stronger in statistics or have a lot of experience of a certain method (interviews, qualitative analysis), or have language skills and cultural competences that are required. In summary, collaborations offer ways to pursue research that is interdisciplinary and requires expertise from separate disciplines. It can also improve the standards of research by critically exposing the assumptions of studies simply by incorporating another perspective that operates in a different (cultural, disciplinary) environment.

Citizenship

To learn the craft of research in any field of study, it is important to be a responsible and active member of the scholarly community and to carry out normal academic citizenship duties. These not only keep the community active, but they are also useful educational operations that help early career academics get vital experience of central areas of academic citizenship. Here are seven actions that I consider to be essential to develop yourself as a junior member of the community. I have organised these actions from those benefitting undergraduate (1–3) to MA (1–5) students and beyond (1–7).

(1) *Being mentored or supervised* by someone who is generous with their time and attention. Each student and early career scholar will greatly benefit from a person who is willing to support their learning and provide feedback and encouragement.

(2) *Attending talks and events* is the backbone of learning scholarship in general, and there is value in them even if they are not directly related to the topic of your interest. You may learn how to present and engage audiences effectively and you will broaden your general knowledge of research themes and methods.

(3) *Networking and organising events* are incredibly useful experiences for several reasons. Running and organising events allow you to learn effective ways of handling deadlines and communications, and they certainly broaden your networks, but most importantly, they allow you to influence the choice of topics, invited speakers, and the formats of these events.

(4) *Explaining* your research to laypeople offers important opportunities to refine the questions that matter most. These opportunities may come in arts and science festivals, school events, radio shows, podcast opportunities, and

TED talks. There are also written forums such as *The Conversation*, articles in popular science journals, online magazines such as *Psychology Today*, blogs, and other fora. Such exercises will sharpen your ability to nail that simple explanation of why research in your area really matters and why it is so interesting that others want to hear about it too.

(5) *Writing and documenting code and curating data* is a valuable contribution to scholarship as it first offers tools, data, and processes for colleagues to use in empirical music research. But even if you do not have a great deal of coding experience, you can use the tools to describe the processes better and write example analyses, or you can provide a description of the data and how it is best used.

(6) *Supervising* anyone (intern, undergraduate student) is invaluable in the same way as reviewing as it helps you see the issues better from the outside. Sharing good practice will also foster better future team members and collaborators who often emerge from these opportunities.

(7) *Reviewing* is excellent training for research and writing. Early on, you can review for postgraduate conferences, and after obtaining your PhD, for conferences and journals. Giving constructive and helpful feedback will change the way you report and think about your own work. And reviewing continues to be one of the most valuable lessons in any career stage that lets you compare your expertise and quality control against those of one or two experts in the field (because the editor typically shares the feedback from all reviewers), which is precious to you as well.

Coda

This chapter has shown that reporting in empirical music research is typically heavily structured and follows the conventions of empirical sciences. The actual publishing conventions favour journal articles over monographs for a multi-authored work in a fast-paced research landscape where peer review, preprints, and open data all contribute to the idea and practice of incremental scholarship. The remainder of this chapter explained how quality control works in scholarship and what steps could be done to succeed in the field.

Discussion Points

1. Students often refer to 'recent studies' and then quote a book or paper from eight years ago. Why do you think this happens regularly, and where does one draw the line of 'recent' in empirical music research? How is this related to the publishing conventions of different areas of scholarship?
2. Peer review was explained as a fundamental way of carrying out quality control in research. Peer review can also be applied in student projects as part of assessment and learning. What kind of challenges would you

expect to encounter if your work is reviewed by your peers and what type of benefits would you see this form of evaluation having for learning?

3. Empirical music research seems to thrive in small teams and collaborations. What kind of disadvantages do you think such conventions may have for individuals? Can these disadvantages be avoided or mitigated with some actions or principles?

Notes

1 https://apastyle.apa.org
2 Yes, you can convert R Markdown and markdown files into fully functional Word documents using the open-source pandoc converter.
3 www.apa.org/ethics/code/#812b
4 www.frontiersin.org/about/author-guidelines
5 https://publicationethics.org/guidance/Guidelines
6 https://publons.com, www.peerageofscience.org/ or www.reviewercredits.com
7 http://retractiondatabase.org

Further Reading

Falk, A., & Heckman, J. J. (2009). Lab experiments are a major source of knowledge in the social sciences. *Science, 326*(5952), 535–538.
Osbeck, L. M., Nersessian, N. J., Malone, K. R., & Newstetter, W. C. (2010). *Science as psychology: Sense-making and identity in science practice*. Cambridge University Press.
Sternberg, R. J. (2018). *Guide to publishing in psychology journals*. Cambridge University Press.

References

Anderson, K. R. (2020). bioRxiv: Trends and analysis of five years of preprints. *Learned Publishing, 33*(2), 104–109. https://doi.org/https://doi.org/10.1002/leap.1265
Armitage, J., & Eerola, T. (2022). Cross-modal transfer of valence or arousal from music to word targets in affective priming? *Auditory Perception & Cognition, 5*(3–4), 192–210. https://doi.org/https://doi.org/10.1080/25742442.2022.2087451
Blood, A. J., & Zatorre, R. J. (2001). Intensely pleasurable responses to music correlate with activity in brain regions implicated in reward and emotion. *Proceedings of the National Academy of Sciences, 98*(20), 11818–11823.
Bornmann, L., Mutz, R., & Daniel, H. D. (2007). Gender differences in grant peer review: A meta-analysis. *Journal of Informetrics, 1*(3), 226–238.
Clark, D., & Hill, M. (2019). *Researchers' perspectives on the purpose and value of the monograph: Survey results 2019*. Cambridge University Press. https://global.oup.com/academic/pdf/perspectives-on-the-value-and-purpose-of-the-monograph
De Clercq, T., & Temperley, D. (2011). A corpus analysis of rock harmony. *Popular Music, 30*(1), 47–70.

Eerola, T., & Vuoskoski, J. K. (2012). A review of music and emotion studies: Approaches, emotion models and stimuli. *Music Perception, 30*(3), 307–340. https://doi.org/https://doi.org/10.1525/mp.2012.30.3.307

Gabrielsson, A. (2011). *Strong experiences with music: Music is much more than just music.* Oxford University Press.

Kosslyn, S. M., Kievit, R. A., Russell, A. G., & Shephard, J. M. (2012). PowerPoint presentation flaws and failures: A psychological analysis. *Frontiers in Psychology, 3*, 230.

Leman, M. (2007). *Embodied music cognition and mediation technology.* MIT Press.

Naegle, K. M. (2021). Ten simple rules for effective presentation slides. *PloS Computational Biology, 17*(12), e1009554.

Nosek, B. A., Ebersole, C. R., DeHaven, A. C., & Mellor, D. T. (2018). The preregistration revolution. *Proceedings of the National Academy of Sciences, 115*(11), 2600–2606. https://doi.org/10.1073/pnas.1708274114

Schaffrath, H., & Huron, D. (1995). *The Essen folksong collection in the humdrum kern format.* Center for Computer Assisted Research in the Humanities.

Serghiou, S., & Ioannidis, J. P. (2018). Altmetric scores, citations, and publication of studies posted as preprints. *The Journal of the American Medical Association, 319*(4), 402–404.

Severin, A., Martins, J., Heyard, R., Delavy, F., Jorstad, A., & Egger, M. (2020). Gender and other potential biases in peer review: Cross-sectional analysis of 38 250 external peer review reports. *BMJ Open, 10*(8), e035058.

Solberg, R. T., & Dibben, N. (2019). Peak experiences with electronic dance music: Subjective experiences, physiological responses, and musical characteristics of the break routine. *Music Perception: An Interdisciplinary Journal, 36*(4), 371–389.

9 Analysis of Scores and Performances

Let us start the sequence of three music analysis chapters with a focus on annotations and analysis of scores, which are the most typical focus of empirical research. In the following chapter, we will look at performance analysis and analysis of audio. In the third music analysis chapter, the focus will be on collections of music (corpus analysis). I will attempt to use the same piece of music across the different objects of analysis. We will first focus on the original recording of *Help!* by The Beatles to explore annotations (expert identification of the onsets, and non-expert descriptions of the track through tags and non-expert rating of the valence and arousal of the track). In the audio analysis, the track will be subjected to audio-based analyses of onset detection, chord detection, and fundamental frequency estimation. Finally, we look at how to scale such analyses up as corpus studies, and we will contextualise *Help!* and its acoustic descriptors within the music from the same era. The purpose is to demonstrate how separate objects of analysis may well work together and often require and rely on the information provided by another approach.

Analysis of Scores

Traditional Western notation contains a myriad of information for the performer: notes, timing, dynamics, phrasing, expression, and occasional prompts for articulation. This is, of course, valuable information for the analyst as well. But it is important to keep in mind that the score is really a set of instructions for the performers to recreate the music. The debate about what notation should contain to represent music adequately has been going on for a long time in music and science (e.g., von Hornbostel and Seashore) and in ethnomusicology (Bartók, von Hornbostel, Seeger, and Hood) where the sticking point has been the 'disparity between a culturally-determined system of notation and the musical sounds of some other culture it was never intended to represent' (Hood, 1971, p. 89). This raises a question about the nature of music: what is the definitive object of music analysis: is it a performance, recording, or a score, or a representation in the mind of a composer, performer, or listener, or perhaps a musical activity within a cultural context shared by people? These types of questions are useful to ask (Marsden,

DOI: 10.4324/9781003293804-9

2016). In computational analysis of music, we are taking the score as a very concrete starting point for analysis that captures some elements that we are interested in. That is not to say that the score is the only object of music analysis, but the score can be interpreted to illustrate some relevant details of what composers and performers were recreating and prioritising in their minds or with their instruments at the time of composition or performance.

In many cases, a score is sparse and devoid of many details, because the tradition itself contains many assumptions of how the chords and melody should be performed, embellished, and delivered with emphasis and rhythmic swing (*basso continuo* in the Baroque, or the *Fake Books* for jazz repertoire are good examples). Of course, the score does not really have a precise way of describing timbre and texture beyond the choice of instrument, articulation, and dynamics. It is also worth bearing in mind that many other notation systems in addition to the Western notation scheme exist, from non-Western notations to notation systems such as *global music notation* developed to be used across different non-Western musics (Killick, 2020) to contemporary graphical notations. And most of the music in the West and around the world simply is notated in any system, so the analysis of scores is limited to traditions which have been preserved in some sort of notation. Notation may sometimes be the only remaining document about the music tradition, although these traditions and the way they have been recorded on paper often require a great deal of interpretation. A notation is an active reconstruction of the music it attempts to capture, and as such, it offers glimpses into the details that the creator of the notation thought to be important in music. It is worth remembering though that this importance and these details vary across traditions and centuries. Computational score analysis itself is a flexible approach that can be adapted to different notation traditions if there is a systematic way of representing the time and frequency of the sonic events.

The research questions that computer-aided empirical music analysts can ask are numerous. Is a particular theme recurring during the piece, and does it exist in other pieces? What are the common rhythmic or melodic patterns in a specific collection of music? Let us start to explore the basics of computational score analysis with the materials that most Western readers are familiar with, the notated examples of Western classical music. For example, Allen Forte (1983) showed how a specific motif, 'alpha', is the most prominent motif in the Brahms *String Quartet* (Op. 51, No. 1). This motif, which consists of a sequence $C - D - E\flat$, can be represented in semitone intervals as $+2 + 1$. This is called the *prime* form of the motif, which can occur anywhere in the music (any pitch height, register, or instrument). But Forte also considers variants of this pattern, namely the *inversion*, $-2 -1$ (which is flipped upside down), *retrograde inversion* $-1 - 2$ (flipped upside down and left to right), and *retrograde* $+1 +2$ (flipped left to right). Forte's analysis traces the variants of this alpha motif throughout the quartet No. 1. However, David Huron (2001) pointed out that such small stepwise movements are remarkably prevalent in any music, most likely related to motor constraints related to the production of music/sounds (Savage et al., 2017). When Huron applied computational score analysis to this string quartet and two other string quartets by Brahms (nos. 2 and 3) where he simply counted the occurrences of motifs (any variant) in the scores of these three string quartets, he noticed that the alpha motif was, in fact, more common in the String Quartets Nos. 2 and 3 than in the No. 1. This casts doubts on the distinctive nature of this motif. It can be argued that a more subtle analysis could possibly consider additional aspects of these motifs, such as how metrically salient the motifs are, or the fact that the motifs are not violating phrase boundaries, and other aspects that are relevant for our identification of patterns, which a simple interval cataloguing exercise is not able to capture.

There may also be more nuances to the computational analysis. This is an interesting prospect as this approach would carry out the music analysis in a trans- parent manner that allows the analyst to weigh explicitly how much the different aspects are influencing the discovery of the motifs. This in turn can help us focus more sharply on elements that contribute mostly to the discovery of the correct motifs in computational analysis. For instance, in a computational approach to the- matic and motivic analysis that can tackle more nuanced aspects of music percep- tion, the duration of the notes and the metrical position of the notes are an important part of the analysis. It is also possible to represent pitch in a way that allows dia- tonic and chromatic transformations or allows comparison of the contours of mel- odies instead of discrete notes. Olivier Lartillot (2005) applied a pattern matching approach to musical scores that takes diatonic intervals, note durations, and gross melodic contour as the three fundamental elements in pattern matching. His ana- lytical scheme can produce a plausible automatic motivic analysis of a Bach inven- tion, Arabic flute improvisation, and a medieval song. Note that his analyses focus on scales and discrete notes and may not be an appropriate way to approach musical cultures that feature micro-tonal variations as a central part of the music, but this is one possibility where pitch representation is expanded to accommodate finer steps of the scale (Bozkurt et al., 2014).

The computational approach has been taken outside of the Western classical music context and applied to Western popular music (De Clercq & Temperley, 2011) and to non-Western pop such as Japanese popular music (Tsushima et al., 2018). Tsushima and colleagues wanted to establish what the most common chord sequences are in US and Japanese popular music. They took a McGill Billboard corpus (N=468) with annotated chords (Burgoyne, 2012) and a J-pop corpus (N= 3500) and transposed everything to a common key (C), and proceeded to count the frequency of occurrence of chord sequences to create a matrix of chord transition probabilities. What is really fascinating in their approach is that by abstracting the chord choices into variants of *tonic* (in *C*, *Am*), *subdominant* (*F*, *Dm*, *Dm⁷*, *FM⁷*), *dominant* (*G*, *G⁷*, *G_{sus4}*), and others, they could summarise the chord probabilities and transitions of all pop songs using a simple chart that displays the probability of one chord category following another or staying in the category. If we pick just one path from this diagram following the highest probabilities, we will get something like this in the Billboard dataset: *tonic* → 0.38 *submediant* → 0.45 → *subdominant* → 0.54 → *dominant* → 0.82 → *tonic*. This is, of course, the famous 'Doo-wop' progression – I-vi-IV-V in Roman numeral analysis – that was common in the 1950s and 1960s. Dozens of other typical pop chord progressions in both the Billboard and J-pop corpus can be read from such transition probability charts, which also allows comparison of songs based on their syntactic structure. This grammar of chords in specific genres of music is useful information for music theory, but also for applications such as automatic chord recognition from audio.

We can now move on from counting some properties of music to more traditional music analytical operations, and to structural analyses of music. For instance, music theory has a long-standing fascination with the sonata form that permeated much of classical music during the 18th and 19th centuries. Computational identification of elements in sonata form has been attempted most recently by Pierre Allegraud and his colleagues (Allegraud et al., 2019). They approached the question armed with a corpus of annotated sonata forms consisting of a sample of string quartets by Haydn and Mozart. They extracted the underlying tonality, harmony, cadences, and a few other devices (breaks, pedals, and unisons) from the scores, and then applied a sequential prediction model (a hidden Markov model) to the combined features. This model was able to recognise the sonata form in Haydn and Mozart string quartets fairly well (with 76% success of predicting the annotated sonata form boundaries) despite failing to account for many local-level details (e.g., specific devices such as cadences and transitions).

Other research such as Hirata et al. (2016) has implemented the rules governing the *Generative Theory of Tonal Music* (GTTM) by Fred Lerdahl and Ray Jackendoff (1983). To properly apply the rules in GTTM and take care of various analytical decisions depending on the content, perception, and ambiguity, they wrote automatic analysis functions to create plausible timespan tree structures and segmentation from the regularities in the music. They evaluated the automatic and a semiautomatic version of these computer models against expert annotation of 300 monophonic, 8-bar excerpts of music from the Western art music canon and found that their model did a surprisingly good job in predicting the expert annotations; the proportions of correct predictions ranged from 0.49 to 0.90 in different tasks. Adding to the classic structural theories in music analysis literature, Alan Marsden (2010) has offered an example of how a computer could implement a Schenkerian analysis of music, which has inspired a host of research focussed on building grammar and syntax-based computational models for music (Rohrmeier, 2011).

Examples of score analysis from outside of the Western classical repertoire come also from analyses of Western folk music, where focus has been put on analysing the global shape of melodic phrases, which is typically an arch (Huron, 1996) and where variations tend to occur most in folk songs (Janssen et al., 2017). And more Western folk song collections are being created, such as the *Dutch Song Database* (Van Kranenburg et al., 2019) which offers more than just the scores (links to manuscripts, recordings, etc.). For more examples, see Chapter 11.

All these examples of computational analysis of scores have focussed on pitch information of some kind, but of course computational analysis does not need to be restricted to analysis of pitch information; it can also look at the use of dynamics (Hansen & Huron, 2018), timbre (Wallmark, 2019), or timing and metre (Toiviainen & Eerola, 2006). For now, let us explore more carefully how the analysis of a Western classical music score can be done in practice.

Computational Tools and Representations

For music analysis, a score is a rich and accessible representation that allows us to carry out certain types of analyses that either replicate or extend existing analytical questions about music concerning melodies, motifs, rhythms, harmonies, forms, or other parameters. Most Western classical music scores have explicit bar lines and metre, which makes questions about these structural units easy to analyse. However, one needs a suitable conversion of the visual score into a symbolic format that a computer can easily read. The conversion from a physical score to a digital representation is a challenge of its own. The solution for this process, *optical music recognition* (OMR), has improved in accuracy over the standard Western repertoire, but is still far from being perfect as the notation may represent music in many different, often ambiguous ways. Notational conventions from different eras, instruments, practices, and layouts pose serious challenges for the OMR algorithms (Calvo-Zaragoza et al., 2020).

Once the notation is in the digital domain, there are several useful and accessible representations that allow sophisticated analysis operations to be developed. Representations such as *MusicXML*, *abc music notation*, and the *Music Encoding Initiative* (MEI) are representations that allow different notation software packages to represent digital scores, but none of these are really designed for music analysis. In the 1990s, David Huron developed a representation called **kern (2002) that was designed to work with a music analysis toolkit called *Humdrum*. This tool has numerous music-theoretically inspired functions and can carry out a huge variety of operations for many analytical tasks. Humdrum utilises Bash shell commands in an elegant way, but the rather tricky syntax and delicate software installation procedures are probably the main reasons why Humdrum has not made its way into music analysis research or teaching more widely. There is an R package called HumdrumR[1] that brings the power of Humdrum to R and allows us to use the flexible syntax of R to organise analysis workflows in an intuitive fashion. However, as compulsory education in many Anglo-American societies usually includes the rudiments of programming and currently the most widely used language to teach programming is Python, I want to focus on a newer tool titled *music21* that relies on Python. music21 (Cuthbert & Ariza, 2010) makes computational music analysis more accessible and flexible than most previous tools.

music21 is relatively simple to use and has an abundance of useful representations, functions, and conversions for mainstream music-theoretical and analytical purposes. It also comes with a built-in corpus and examples of how to carry out hundreds of different types of analysis. Importantly, this tool is straightforward to set up, the analysis can be shared via functional Python notebooks, and the software can be run in a virtual machine that behaves like a real computer, except that it runs on a cloud server that you seamlessly access via your browser. All this allows the analyst to focus on the actual analysis, not on how to set up the system on a computer. It has excellent support for notation (*MuseScore* and *Lilypond*, both free and open-source libraries), and it can import and export almost any digital music representation invented. Let us look at some examples that will prepare the ground for analyses that are relevant for empirical music research designs.

Analysis of Music-theoretic Concepts in a Bach Chorale

To make computer-based music analysis more specific and familiar to students of music techniques, let us look at an example that takes a Bach chorale and performs harmonic analysis and labels metrical positions.

Case Example #1: Harmonic and Metrical Analysis

See the Python code in Chapter9.1 at https://tuomaseerola.github.io/emr/

```
# Code 9.1
from music21 import *                    # activate library
### 1 Select one example from Bach chorales
bwv30_6 = corpus.parse('bach/bwv30.6.xml')# Take an example
bwv30_6.measures(1, 3).show()            # Display 3 bars
### 2 Harmonic analysis
bChords = bwv30_6.chordify()             # Slice the chords
for c in bChords.recurse().getElementsByClass('Chord'):
    c.closedPosition(forceOctave=4, inPlace=True)
# Run analysis and add Roman numerals as lyrics
for c in bChords.recurse().getElementsByClass('Chord'):
    rn = roman.romanNumeralFromChord(c, key.Key('A'))
    c.addLyric(str(rn.figure))
bChords.measures(0,3).show()             # Display the result
### 3 Metrical analysis
bass = bwv30_6.getElementById('Bass')    # Get the bass part
excerpt = bass.measures(1,3)             # Bar 1 through 3
analysis.metrical.labelBeatDepth(excerpt)# Metrical analysis
excerpt.show()                           # Display the results
```

In this example, we pull in one chorale (BWV 30.6, *Tröstet, tröstet meine Lieben*, from the internal corpus that comes with music21) arranged by J.S. Bach and show the first three bars of it (lines 3–4 in the code). Next, we make a reduction of the four parts into one part where the pitches are voiced in the closed position within an octave (lines 6–8). This is a suitable representation for the analysis of harmony, where we ask the algorithm to label the chords with Roman numerals (lines 10–11) and show them as lyrics under the chords (line 12). Finally, we extract the bass voice from the score (line 13) and analyse the metrical hierarchy to each note (line 15) and display this (line 16). Figure 9.1 shows the output of these three analytical operations. Although this example is not as insightful as a music analysis, it shows how music is stored in a variable (bwv30_6) and how analytical operations such as chordify, romanNumeralFromChord, or getElementbyId can be applied to this variable. I might add here that a human analyst would not label all the chords, as many of them are by-products of passing notes or decoration. The analysis also demonstrates how instances (notes, or chords) can be analysed within a loop (for c in bChords.recurse().getElementsByClass('Chord')) for the variable that stores

Figure 9.1 Score analysis example (Bach Chorale BWV 30.6).

this piece of music. Finally, the code snipped shows the logic of Python programming, where known types of variables have specific functional outputs that can be called (e.g., .measures() is a filter that shows the desired measures, and .show is a display function that usually shows the musical score or the events. Notice that these outputs can be combined (line 5: measures(1,3).show()).

Analysis of Event Frequencies

The next example displays the raw contents of the music using the basic commands in music21. We can summarise the pitch-classes, intervals, and durations used in any piece of music, as demonstrated in the second example.

Case Example #2: Pitch-classes and Other Events in a Bach Chorale

See the Python code Chapter9.2 at https://tuomaseerola.github.io/emr/

```
# Code 9.2
from music21 import *                        # activate library
bwv110_7 = corpus.parse('bach/bwv110.7.xml')# select piece
bwv110_7.plot('histogram', 'pitchclass')    # plot pcs

duration = graph.plot.HistogramQuarterLength(bwv110_7)
duration.run()                              # plot durations
bass = bwv110_7.parts[3]                     # take bass
intervals = analysis.discrete.MelodicIntervalDiversity()
iv = intervals.countMelodicIntervals(bass)  # count intervals
iv_summary = [[i, iv[i][1]] for i in iv]
print(iv_summary)                            # display ivs
```

This code uses the basic commands of music21 to describe the pitch contents of another chorale, BWV 110/7. First, the pitch-class distribution is plotted (line 3), then the duration distribution (lines 5–6), and finally the bass voice is extracted (line 7) and the interval distribution is calculated (line 8). These distributions are shown in Figure 9.2, although this figure includes additional information.

The raw summaries of the distributions have limited usefulness, except to describe the pitch-class profile and the interval distributions broadly. But what do these summaries say about the music itself, are they sensitive to small nuances between different pieces of music? It can be more informative to obtain such counts of the pitch-based properties of music for at least two pieces of music, or to compare them to a reference. For the first operation, we need to make the counts directly comparable by transposing them to the same key (so that they have the same tonic) and show the counts as percentages to keep the different lengths of the pieces from obscuring the comparisons. The script Code 9.3 (not printed in the text) uses a slightly more elaborate sequence of commands using music21 to make such a comparison. This script produces a combined graph where the pitch-class, interval, and duration distribution across all four voices of the two Bach chorales – BWV 110/7 ('Wir Christenleut habn jetzund Freud') and BWV 40/3 ('Wir Christenleut habn jetzund Freud') – are displayed on the same graph (Figure 9.2). As you can see, the chorale texts are the same, but they have been composed separately, and they have different keys and harmonies. In fact, Bach has adapted them from different cantatas, composed for separate occasions. BWV 40/3 is from the cantata 'Dazu ist erschienen der Sohn Gottes' (BWV 40) composed for the second day of Christmas and first performed in 1723. BWV 110/7 is from the cantata 'Unser Mund sei voll Lachens' (BWV 110), composed for the first day of Christmas and first performed two years later (in 1725). I would assume that the simple counts of pitch-classes, intervals, and durations between the two close variants show overwhelming similarities without being identical.

Figure 9.2 shows that the pitch-class distribution is nearly identical between the two chorales. Note that both pieces have been transposed to C minor using automatic key-finding analysis to make the pitch-class distributions comparable. This assumption that the pieces are in a clearly defined major or minor key might not

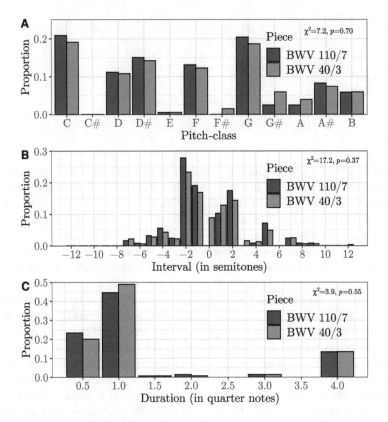

Figure 9.2 Comparison of two Bach chorales in terms of (A) pitch-class, (B) interval, and (C) duration distributions.

always hold, as there can be modulations and tonal structures avoiding the common modes, but in most music from the Western canon this is a reasonable starting point for at least short passages. The interval distribution shows mainly stepwise movement using mainly major and minor seconds, some thirds, a few fourths, and overall very similar profiles for both chorales. The note durations used in both chorales are nearly identical.

This is a very descriptive analysis, and it is difficult to say from this whether the observed differences in the pitch-class profiles suggest substantial differences or just a superficial or natural variation. But we can empirically test the hypothesis of whether the distributions are likely to come from the same underlying distribution using the goodness-of-fit test for counts in categories, which is known as the χ^2 statistic. This comparison between the chorale distributions is printed in the upper-right corner of the graphs. If we look at the short statistical summary for the pitch-class distributions ($\chi^2 = 7.2$, $p=0.70$), we learn that the two distributions are indeed similar, in other words they are likely to represent the same underlying distribution as the *p* value is 0.70. Recalling the way statistical testing works, we would have expected the probability to be low (preferably under 5% or 1%) before we could be confident to proclaim that there is a difference. We see the same pattern for intervals and durations, suggesting that indeed these descriptors do not differentiate these two chorales.

The logical question to ask is whether any other arrangement of a chorale by Bach would have different distribution profiles from our examples, and if not, are we just tapping into very generic descriptors of any Western classical music from the Baroque period, or are these the typical properties of German chorale arrangements of their time with their specific constraints on vocal range and voice-leading? It is fair to remind the reader that not all Bach chorales are clear examples in terms of key or chords, as he sometimes emphasised inessential notes with metrical accents and created intriguing harmonic sequences.

Other Descriptors of Musical Content

The three distributions that were used as an example in the previous section are by no means the only descriptive properties that can be derived from the computational analysis of scores. These are sometimes called zero-order distributions as they encode the counts of the events without any sense of order. We can also calculate the distribution of pitch-class *transitions*, that is, how often a combination of two consecutive pitch-classes occurs, for example, how many times C is followed by C, or C is followed by C♯, or C is followed by D and so on (formally as E_i, E_{i+1}). These can be also called *bigrams*, which are instances of *n-grams*, which capture the probabilities of different sequence lengths. N-grams are often used in linguistic analysis based on sequences of letters or words but can also be applied to pitch-classes, intervals, durations, or even chords. The bigrams are called first-order distributions/statistics and are more specific than zero-order distributions. These first-order distributions have been demonstrated to capture more stylistic patterns in music than zero-order distributions. It is also possible to extend these transitions into three consecutive events (trigrams) – the second-order statistics of pitch-classes ($[E_i, E_{i+1}, E_{i+2}]$). As you can imagine, there is a large space of possible responses (for pitch-classes, there are $12^3 = 1,728$ possible trigrams). For intervals spanning an octave up and down, there are already $25^3 = 15,625$ possible interval trigrams. For this reason, the higher-order statistics summarising music are often described by showing the top-ranked transitions or using other ways to encapsulate the probability of the events such as using the entropy of the distribution (Pearce & Eerola, 2017).

Pieces of music can be described with other summary measures such as melodic ambitus (difference between the highest and lowest pitch), melodic complexity, and many other measures related to harmonies, rhythms, intervals, or a combination of these. In fact, an analysis toolkit for music called *jSymbolic 2.2* lists 229 features that include pitch, melodic intervals, vertical intervals, rhythm, texture, instrumentation, and dynamics (McKay et al., 2018). Many of these measures are derivatives of the distributions that can be obtained from all these representations and these features have been used in deciding the potential origin of unattributed or doubtfully attributed Renaissance Coimbra manuscripts (found in the *Monastery of Santa Cruz* in Portugal) as Franco-Flemish or Iberian (Cuenca-Rodríguez & McKay, 2021).

The features characterising music in this section are such that they are relatively easy to calculate and extract from scores. While many of them are useful in discriminating different pieces of music from each other, they are rarely meant to be representations that we, as listeners, rely on when we perceive, assess, remember, and produce music. Some of the features such as n-grams or melodic complexity are attempts to bring these representations closer to perceived qualities of music, but music cognition specialists have developed entirely different sets of descriptors with music perception in mind.

To make some of the count-based statistics of music analysis such as pitch-class profiles more perceptually plausible, the note events may be weighted by their perceptual salience. This means that instead of simply tallying together the raw number of these events, the analysis should acknowledge and incorporate more weight to events that are known to be more important for us as listeners. In a simple tally carried out in the previous section, every occurrence of a note is counted as one event in the tally, but shouldn't longer notes carry more weight than shorter notes? Also, the notes occurring at the important metrical positions are known to be perceptually more salient than notes at less important metrical positions (Palmer & Krumhansl, 1990). Weighting notes by their position in the metrical hierarchy may also bring the tallies closer to how listeners might perceive and remember them. It is also possible to impose limitations on whether intervals are counted across rests – or even phrase boundaries – to make the patterns more valid perceptually.

Another interesting perspective to note counts (pitch or pitch-class profiles, interval, or duration profiles) is to inspect their information content rather than the actual tallies of the events. The classic measure for the information content is *entropy*, defined by Claude Shannon after World War II (Shannon, 1951), which codes the amount of surprise or unexpectedness of the message in the channel. In the case of a pitch-class profile, this 'channel' has 12 pitch-classes, and one of the most surprising passages, or most difficult to predict, that you could create would have an equal proportion of all 12 pitch-classes. This is basically a 12-tone, which is the best-known technique in which the 12 pitch-classes are used equally frequently. The compositions of Anton Webern and Arnold Schoenberg made good use of 12-tone rows as recipes in some of their music (e.g., Webern's *String Quartet* Op. 28 or Schoenberg's *Piano Pieces* Op. 33a and Op. 33b). The least surprising pitch-class distribution would be one with only one or two pitch-classes being used (e.g., the first part of *One Note Samba*). A more realistic and varied example of a predictable sequence would use the hierarchically important pitch-classes in the Western key profiles. C C G G A A G F F E E D D C a fairly predictable and unsurprising passage as we expect these pitch-classes to be more prevalent than non-diatonic (e.g., $C\sharp$, $F\sharp$, $A\sharp$) pitch-classes in the key of C.

Case Example #3: Tension in a Bach Chorale

Another interesting high-level description of musical content in Western tonal music is *tension*. Tension has been the candidate for creating interest and emotions in music by means of patterns of tension and release (Meyer, 1956), usually achieved with harmonic devices, but rhythms, timbres, and dynamics can also contribute to the ebb and flow of tension. These ideas were initially formalised by Leonard Meyer's student, Fred Lerdahl, who formulated a pioneering model of tension (Lerdahl et al., 2001), which was later empirically explored by him and Carol Krumhansl (2007). There is a fascinating recent model of tension by Herremans and Chew (2016), which uses a three-dimensional model of tonality to assess the tension created by the tonal shifts as changes within the geometric space. As this model is available as a Python package called partitura, let us demonstrate how the tonal space between sets of successive notes (which is called *cloud momentum* in their model) traces the tension in our earlier analytical example of a Bach chorale. I have added the prediction of this tension model under the basic analysis elements extracted by music21 to Figure 9.1, and the calculation of the tension is available in Code 9.4 as a Python script that uses a package called *partitura*[2], which is a tool created by the members of the Institute of Computational Perception at Johannes Kepler University Linz for processing and analysing music in symbolic format. As the chorale shown in Figure 9.1 begins, there is a slight increase in tonal tension in bar 1, which stabilises throughout the second bar with the supertonic to culminate with the dominant chord at the beginning of bar 3, after which the tension drops together with the move from dominant to submediant. Although this snippet of music might not be the most exciting in terms of the creating a strong tension–release pattern, even this cursory analysis with a few lines of code should demonstrate that music analysts have potent tools at their disposal. Coupled with empirical data on how listeners evaluate tension or annotate affects across the passage, it becomes rather easy to see how theories about tension and emotions can be empirically tested and systematically improved.

Case Example #4: Key-finding in a Bach Chorale

Many of the pitch-related features of music (keys, pitch-classes, harmonies) described earlier require a reference to a tonal system. This is of course not always a relevant assumption for all kinds of music, but in most Western music, a hierarchical tonal frame is known to provide such a reference. In the North Hindustani art music tradition, several sets of reference are available at the level of rāgas. In Indian music theory, rāga refers to a type of melody or mode that conveys a specific ethic or devotion. In the Western context, music psychologists have empirically established the hierarchies of pitch-classes in tonal music by posing a question about how stable each pitch-class is in a tonal context. To be more concrete, Carol Krumhansl and Edward Kessler (1982) played participants short chord sequences such as I-IV-V that effectively establish a clear tonal context, and immediately following this sequence, the participants heard an additional tone, called a *probe tone*. This probe was systematically varied to go through all pitch-classes in different trials, and the task of the participants in each trial was to rate how well the probe tone fit with the preceding tonal context. When all pitch-classes were tested using the probe tone method, two profiles that characterise the stability of all pitch-classes emerged, one for major and one for minor keys. For instance, in the context of C major, probe tones C and G fit the context well, while F and A are a moderate fit and F♯ and C♯ are a poor fit with the context. This profile is surprisingly stable across Western listeners, and interestingly, these profiles were also very similar to the profiles obtained from the analyses of Western tonal music by means of counting the notes in the score. This is the operation that we did in the example where we described the proportion of pitch-classes in a Bach chorale (Figure 9.2). Somewhat unexpectedly, the profiles obtained from classical music were later noticed to be highly similar to profiles extracted from notated bebop jazz solos (Järvinen, 1995) and in *Rolling Stone* magazine's list of 500 greatest songs (De Clercq & Temperley, 2011), suggesting that most Western tonal music relies on broadly similar hierarchical structures. The key profiles were also discovered to be a good empirical method for determining the key of a passage. In this method, which is formally known as the Krumhansl-Schmuckler (or Krumhansl-Kessler) key-finding algorithm, a correlation coefficient between 24 key profiles representing 12 major and 12 minor keys and the pitch-class distribution of the passage under investigation is calculated (Krumhansl, 2001). The highest correlating key profile is taken to represent the appropriate key. While there are some shortcomings to this method, key-finding is a useful operation for many other analytical operations and easy to implement in almost any music analytic computer software. For example, this algorithm and its variants are contained within the music21 package for Python.

Let us look at the estimation of the key of the first music example in this section, Bach's *Chorale 30/6* ('Tröstet, tröstet meine Lieben'), the first three bars of which are shown in Figure 9.1. In the code example, Code 9.5, the key-finding algorithm is first applied to the entire chorale (line 5). This will suggest the key of A major, which seems to be correct. However, if we apply the algorithm to short segments, say half a bar at a time, we can learn which key the method would predict on a much more local level. Lines 7 to 10 apply the key-finding to the first three bars of the chorale using two-beat windows (line 10). Lines 17–18 collect the values from the analysis, namely the winning key, the mode (major or minor), and the correlation coefficient of the highest key as a measure of key clarity. The result of this analysis is shown in the bottom panel of Figure 9.1. The algorithm starts on the wrong foot, labelling the first two beats as E major (dominant) with a high correlation (r=0.88) although a human analyst would probably start with a tonic (A major) unless the analyst thinks that the phrase modulates directly to E major as there is no D♮ in the phrase, only D♯. The analyst would of course see the key signature whereas the algorithm only gathers information from pitch-classes. The second half of the first bar is identified as tonic, but the correlation coefficient drops dramatically (r=0.59) due to so many passing notes and the changing between the tonic and supertonic (II). The second bar shows a shift to the dominant (E major) and to the submediant, and again this focus of the algorithm on the local key picks up uncertainties that are shown as a relatively low correlation for F minor (r=0.72) before clearly moving onto the dominant at the beginning of bar 3.

See the code in Chapter9.5 at https://tuomaseerola.github.io/emr/

```
# Code 9.5
from music21 import *                        # activate library
import pandas as pd

bwv30_6 = corpus.parse('bach/bwv30.6.xml')# 30.6
print(bwv30_6.analyze('key.krumhanslkessler'))

bwv30_6_3meas = bwv30_6.measures(1,3)       # 3 measures
KK = analysis.discrete.KrumhanslKessler() # Key analysis
wa = analysis.windowed.WindowedAnalysis(bwv30_6_3meas, KK)
a,b = wa.analyze(2, windowType='noOverlap')

keyclar=[]; mode=[]; key=[]
for x in range(6):
    key.append(a[x][0])
    mode.append(a[x][1])
    keyclar.append(a[x][2])
data=pd.DataFrame({'key':key,'mode':mode,'r':keyclar})
print(data)
```

There are several variant key profiles that have been offered by different scholars to improve the accuracy of the key-finding algorithm. Generally, key-finding algorithms can identify the key highly accurately when compared to their attributed keys from the score (Albrecht & Shanahan, 2013) or to human annotations of segments (Weiß et al., 2020). The reason I bring up key-finding as an important fundamental analysis operation is that it is often a precursor to many other analyses that require a common reference to compare the contents of the pitch information in a meaningful fashion. More broadly, key-finding itself may be too narrow a term, as the focus on key may often hide the historical dimension of *modes*; we only call attention here to major and minor modes, and 24 keys, but the palette of modes is broader as music theorists and historians (e.g., Aldwell et al., 2018; Wiering, 2013) have detailed the emergence of tonality and how several distinct modes were in use before the 18th century in Western classical music. Compelling empirical support for the existence of at least four modes in the Renaissance has recently been offered by Harasim et al. (2021), who clustered a large (13,000) set of Western classical music based on their use of pitch-classes without presuming the existence of any modes. We also need to acknowledge that this discussion is only relevant for Western classical music, but the notion that musical systems organise the palette of pitches in a structured way (as a hierarchy of pitch-classes) allows score analysis to identify and capitalise these regularities in music.

Summary

Some aspects of music analysis can be carried out efficiently with computers, particularly operations that relate to counting or matching events encoded explicitly in the score. Traditional music analytical tasks such as identifying harmony and motifs and form and structure in music are more challenging tasks for computational analysis as they require a high-level abstraction and an ability to transform and tolerate variability. Often there are also built-in decisions in the analysis options about how different elements of music that are not always explicitly formalised and only intuitively applied by human analysts work together. But we saw how some high-level analytical terms such as tension or key clarity can be extracted from the score. Rudimentary analysis of functional harmony is certainly possible, and identifying melodic and rhythmic motifs is also possible with the right kind of computational tools.

It is important to stress here that the point of computational analysis is not simply to attempt to mimic what human analysts are skilful at doing; rather computer-driven analysis makes the process precise and transparent, and therefore easy to replicate and scale up. Once the analytical routines are set up, other scholars can use, evaluate, and improve them, and the models and analytical routines can be applied to any number of examples. This is what we will address in more detail in the dedicated corpus analysis in Chapter 11.

Analysis of the scores does come with notable limitations as well. First, we must remember that the score itself can be a poor proxy of what music actually is in the minds of people. Notational systems have blind spots, and important features of music that are difficult to notate such as microtunings, microtimings, and precise dynamics are not captured by most notational schemes, and timbral nuances are only crudely approximated in the notation.

Computational analysis of scores can also be seen as a new way to create music, or to allow creative interaction with music, or, to facilitate algorithmic composition. Current advances in deep learning have created a wealth of possibilities for generating music given different underlying representations and analyses of music (Carnovalini & Rodà, 2020; Loughran & O'Neill, 2020). Music generation following the deep learning approach is already capable of mimicking any musical style – given a sufficient corpus – to a degree that is promising although the compositions do not exhibit true creativity and lack large-scale forms (Briot & Pachet, 2020).

No matter what the purpose of the analysis is, this way of analysing scores with the help of computational tools will allow researchers to collaborate and build their analyses on top of past research and frameworks, with the hope that the analytical options will incrementally contribute and help to develop better and more precise ways of understanding musical structures, behaviours, and minds.

Analysis of Performances

In this section, I will introduce representations that are not quite as prescriptive as notation but not as close to the sonic information as the actual audio signal. I will call these *event structures* and I will use MIDI as an example representation. The timings of onsets are another set of structured data about musical events that can be subjected to useful analytical operations. The event data could also be more sophisticated data from a performance technology, control information from the sequencer that goes beyond the MIDI information, or other, perhaps analogue performance data such as the timing and pitch information encoded in piano rolls that is the storage medium of music for player pianos (self-playing mechanical pianos that were popular in the late 19th and early 20th centuries).

In the 1980s, a standard called MIDI (Musical Instrument Digital Interface) was developed to enable the first generation of digital instruments to talk to each other. The MIDI standard records the time, velocity, and pitch of the note onsets and offsets. It is a simple scheme, and it was expanded in various ways, such as key signature and certain instrument banks. It has been an extremely popular standard that has permeated music-making since its inception, and it also is often the representation available from measurements of performances obtained with specialist instruments that have sensors to measure the keys (actual key and their timing and velocity). This standard is about to get a major update (MIDI 2.0), which will have higher precision and interoperability between devices. Availability of music in MIDI format is also relatively good, although the quality does vary considerably. There are hundreds of thousands of pieces of music represented in MIDI files, in collections such as *ClassicalArchives* or curated corpora (see Chapter 11); there are also music analytical tools designed with this representation in mind. However, MIDI does not contain explicit analytical information, not even bar lines. Although MIDI is not suitable for operations that rely on information encoded in full scores (dynamics, expressions, phrasing), it does lend itself to analysis of music from the listener's perspective, who must work out these details from the sonic stream using various musical cues that often reveal phrasing and expression. MIDI is also often used to examine the nuances of microtiming in captured performances of music, although audio may also be used for this end, but with some extra challenges since part of the analysis is to discover which notes were performed. In MIDI, this additional challenge is missing, making it an easy object of analysis into how performers create expressive and emotional performances. Let us look at this classic topic in more detail.

Expressive Timing

When a pianist performs on specific pianos such as Yamaha's *Disklavier*, the Bösendorfer's *SE290,* or Steinway's *Spirio*, which can record the movement of the hammers and pedals (their timing, velocity, and pitch) using extremely accurate sensors (timing is less than + / - 10 ms in accuracy and sensors capture over 1,000 levels of dynamic range), the recording of the performance contains every necessary detail to recreate the performance afterwards. From this information one can also inspect interesting aspects of performance. One of the most fascinating possibilities that such information offers is to reveal how performers deviate from the nominal timing represented by the score and how performers adjust the dynamics of each note in systematic ways. Performers take the liberties of distorting time across the notes, bars, and phrases of music, which makes the performance sound natural and expressive and often unique to that performer. If you have ever heard genuinely mechanical performances – such as those rendered by sequencer software – then you will know how lacklustre a performance with the nominal timing of each note is. Now, this assumes that the aesthetics of music are akin to Western art music and not, for example, electropop from the 1980s, as the music by Kraftwerk or Jean-Michel Jarre removed the expressive timing of the performance on purpose as an aesthetic choice and statement in their music. We call the expressive timing *deviations from the normative values encoded in the score*. The patterns underlying expressive performance are not arbitrary; there are specific ways to bend the time (play the notes earlier or later, or longer or shorter) that make the music sound natural. For instance, in much of the Western canonical piano repertoire, it is normal to slow down towards the ends of phrases and highlight large leaps and the highest note in the melodic line by playing these slightly longer in duration and louder than the score would suggest. There are several other generic ways by which many performers try to highlight the structure and interpretation to the listener, and many of these patterns have been fairly successfully modelled by expressive performance models (Cancino-Chacón et al., 2018).

Let us look at an example of expressive timing from pianists. We pick pianists here since their expressive performances have attracted large volumes of research because the actual performance data have been easy to capture with the specialist pianos. For many other instruments, the process of capturing timing is more complicated, as many instruments have more degrees of freedom to adjust the expression by manipulating onsets, timbre, vibration, and so on. But there are great datasets for other instruments and ensembles; see two large ones for string quartets (Li et al., 2018; Marchini et al., 2014) and Brahms' cello sonatas (Llorens, 2021).

Case Example #1: Expressive Timing in Rachmaninoff

Let's grab a recent dataset containing real performances of classical piano repertoire with carefully measured timings of the notes. We will look at a dataset called *Aligned Scores and Performances (ASAP)* (Foscarin et al., 2020)[3], which contains aligned data of the score and MIDI and expressive performances of 1,067 Western classical music piano performances. This dataset is related to a larger dataset called *MIDI and Audio Edited for Synchronous TRacks and Organization (MAESTRO)* (Hawthorne et al., 2019), which is a fantastic resource and builds on top of one of the most impressive performance repositories that contains the raw recordings from the *International Piano-e-Competition* over ten years. In this competition held in Minnesota in the US, pianists perform the competition pieces using Yamaha's *Disklavier* and the database contains highly accurate synchrony of audio and all performance events (pedals, key strike velocities) for more than 170 hours of recordings.

Let us take the beginning of Sergei Rachmaninoff's *Prelude Op. 23 No. 4* that has appeared in the competition programme several times. The ASAP dataset has already provided us with the alignment between score (the nominal note onset times) and performance timings, so we can easily compare how several performers have created their own interpretations of this movement. One of the classic ways to visualise this is to show how much the performers deviate from score-based timing. In this small analysis example, we have data on beats (three beats per bar in 3/4 metre), so we cannot get into more granular timing than the quarter note level, but this should suffice to demonstrate the processes in the overall timing curves. We take three performances from the dataset (by Chen Guang, Yevgeny Morozov, and Elliot Wuu), normalise them to the same length as the score to facilitate direct comparison, and then visualise the deviation of each of their performed beats from the timing in the score. The results of an R code (Chapter9.4) that carries out these operations are shown in Figure 9.3. The horizontal axis shows the time in bars, and the vertical axis displays the deviation from the nominal timing encoded in the score in milliseconds. There are three lines marked with different shapes, referring to each of the performers, and an additional bolder line, which is a smoothed trendline of the common tendency shown by all three pianists. First, we notice there is quite a good overall consistency in how the micro-timing differences from the nominal timing are taken by all three performers; the overall pattern looks very similar, with the peaks and troughs largely in the same places. In the first bar, all three pianists take their time playing the second beat of the bar (Chen Guang has a particularly rubato timing here, playing the note 750 ms later than it would have been played with metronomic timing). They all compensate for the initial slow start by playing the third beat earlier. Then they all slow down towards bar 4, and then repeat the same micro-timing pattern in bar 7. These ritardandi often relate to the phrase boundaries, which we can see in bars 4 and 8 and in a milder way in bar 6.

Recording and analysing the expressive timing curves from actual performances may have multiple uses for empirical music research. It allows us to seek understanding of the emotional expression in a nuanced fashion, how it is being created under different conditions and styles. The expressive variations in timing and dynamics may be used to study the way expression varies across stylistic periods and performers, or how skilled performers have developed their expressive timing strategies. Having reliable data about expressive timings allows us to test models designed to emulate the expressive timing. These models, in turn, can test our understanding of what the crucial elements of expression are. Early on, such models consisted of sets of rules which described the typical changes expression makes to a nominal score (Friberg et al., 2000). The rules cover instances such as slowing down at the end of phrases, or having the melody lead the accompaniment where the notes of a melody are played (20–30 ms) earlier than the accompaniment to allow the melody to stand out to the listener. Also, playing the notes at the melodic peak slightly longer and louder is a typical expressive device. More recent models apply more generic principles that use information-theoretic features that summarise the expectations of listeners in order to implement expressive timing by emphasising certain locations in the music in line with listeners' expectations (Gingras et al., 2016). There are also more complex models that use rule-type basic functions that can be driven from performance data (Grachten & Widmer, 2012). Models such as these with relatively few principles which can be optimised with sets of real performance data tend to produce a remarkably good fit with actual

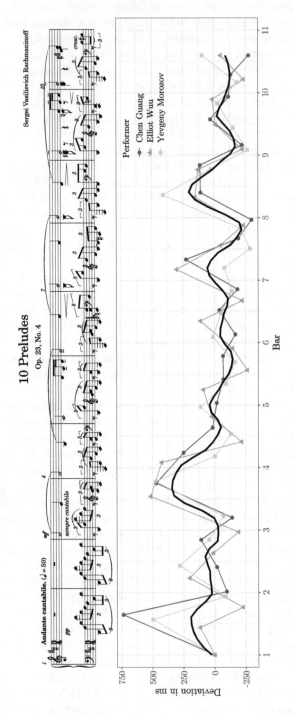

Figure 9.3 Micro-timing in three professional performances of Rachmaninoff's *Prelude* Op. 23 No. 4.

expressive timings and dynamics, although they tend to emulate the idiosyncrasies of those pieces, performers, and genres with which they have been trained. Finally, such models will allow the rendering of more natural sounding performances directly from notation software.

Timing Between Performers

The introduction of expressive timing opened the door to various other issues of timing in music. I mentioned a timing asynchrony of 20–30 ms between accompaniment and melody when pianists want to highlight the melody. But what then is accurate timing between the voices, say when two performers are playing the same notes so that they sound tightly synchronised? Perhaps this does depend on the genre of music, or the instruments played, or the tempo of the music, and naturally the skill level of the musicians? Probably all of these have an influence on timing accuracy, but what kind of timing accuracies are we talking about? An analysis of synchrony can be done from event-based data encoded as MIDI data (if performed with instruments that can store this information) or from onsets extracted from close-up microphones from acoustic instruments, which we will talk about in more detail in the subsequent sections of this chapter.

Past analysis of synchrony has focussed on the timing accuracy of playing together within the range of so-called *sensorimotor synchronisation* (SMS), which refers to the range of periods between 100 and 1,800 ms. Accuracy of synchronisation is related to our ability to tell two sounds apart in time, which is around 20–30 ms (Butterfield, 2010). Laboratory experiments involving tapping have shown that the standard deviation of successive tap intervals tends to be around 15–30 ms, and it has been established that the typical asynchrony in string quartets is around 30–40 ms whereas the mean asynchrony tends to be as low as 13–30 ms in Cuban son and salsa (Clayton et al., 2020), and 13–20 ms in Malian drum ensembles (Polak et al., 2016), but it can also vary depending on the section of music, for example in North Indian rāga performances where the mean asynchrony is 19–54 ms (Clayton et al., 2018).

Case Example #2: Onset Synchrony in Cuban Son

Let us empirically explore how different instruments in a salsa group synchronise their playing with each other. We took an open dataset from the OSF involving a professional Cuban salsa and son group, available at https://osf.io/sfxa2/, collected and curated by Adrian Poole (2013). The instruments in the performances in this corpus have been recorded carefully with separate microphones and multiple video cameras, and, even better, the recordings have been annotated for metric cycles and structures, and the onsets of each instrument have been extracted from the audio files using a combination of algorithmic estimation and manual annotation and checking (Clayton et al., 2021).

We will use an R library called onsetsync available on GitHub[4], designed to analyse onset synchronies in music performances (Eerola & Clayton, 2024). onsetsync has functions for useful operations such as adding isochronous beats based on metrical structure, incorporating annotations to the analysis, calculating classic measures of synchrony between two performers, and visualising synchrony across metrical cycles or any other variable.

We take one example of Son performance that comes with the built-in corpus of onsetsync. This performance is retrieved in line 3 of the code example Chapter9.5. Let us explore the onsets in this piece, called *Palo Santo*, across four instruments. In this piece there are 16 sub-divisions (4 beats each having 4 sub-beats at the level of 16th notes) in a cycle. We can visualise all onsets over time across the beat subdivisions by a simple function, shown in the code in lines 4–8. The results are shown in the upper plot of Figure 9.4. As we can see from the figure, the guitar and tres (a Cuban guitar-like instrument that has three pairs of strings) tend to play constantly at each beat subdivision, whereas the bass plays a pattern of two beats (beats 5 and 7, and 13 and 15) and the clave plays the distinctive son clave pattern (1, 4, 7, 11, and 13). We also note that during the last minute (from 05:00 onwards, see the vertical axis, which refers to the time across the performance), the bass varies the beat structure and plays additional beats. From this visualisation, we notice that all four musicians tend to play at beats 4 and 13, but otherwise the instruments co-occur at different beats. The guitar and tres play the same beats most of the time. But the question is how temporally close – synchronous – are the onsets between different instruments that play on the same beat sub-divisions?

See the R code in Chapter9.5 at https://tuomaseerola.github.io/emr/

```
# Code9.4.R
library(onsetsync)                         # activate library
set.seed(1234)
CSS_Song2 <- onsetsync::CSS_IEMP[[2]] # take song 2
subplot1 <- plot_by_beat(df  = CSS_Song2,
                  instr   = c('Bass','Clave','Guitar','Tres'),
                  beat    = 'SD',
                  virtual = 'Isochronous.SD.Time',
                  pcols   = 2)
inst <- c('Clave','Bass','Guitar','Tres') # define instruments
dn <- sync_execute_pairs(CSS_Song2,inst,100,1,'SD')
subplot2 <- plot_by_pair(dn)
fig <- cowplot::plot_grid(subplot1, subplot2, nrow = 2)
```

We can visualise the asynchronies between the selected instruments by defining the list of instruments we are interested in (code line 9) and then calculate the onset asynchronies between the pairs of instruments (line 10) and plot the ensuing onset asynchronies with so-called violin plots (line 11). These plots are useful for displaying the way the onset synchronies are distributed overall, and we have the mean onset asynchronies marked over the distribution with a vertical line as well as the actual onset asynchronies plotted as dots on top of the distribution. This plot, shown in the lower part of Figure 9.4, suggests that the clave and guitar play incredibly tightly together (the mean asynchrony is <0.4 ms), whereas the bass tends to play before most of the instruments (e.g., the bass plays an average of 15.0 ms before the clave and 17.2 ms ahead of the guitar).

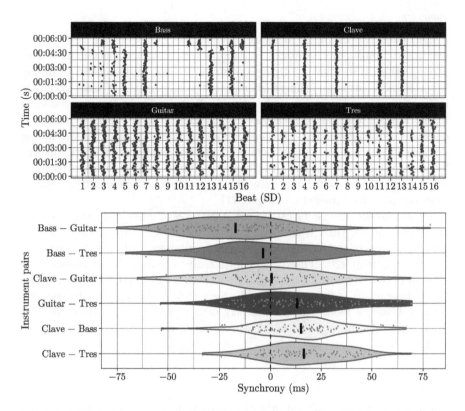

Figure 9.4 Onsets for a son piece (*Palo Santo*) across beat sub-divisions and time (upper panel) and the distribution of synchronies between the instruments (lower panel).

For empirical research on music, we first realise that it is relatively easy to measure the degree of synchrony between multiple musicians when appropriate good quality data are available. The synchrony itself is a good index to questions relating to musical groove, tightness of playing, and skill competency of the musicians. Synchrony has also been used as a proxy for studying how prosocial behaviours are facilitated by synchrony between people via music (Cirelli et al., 2014). There is a lot to be done in terms of understanding how synchrony changes in different musical situations and contexts. Synchrony may also give a clear indication of how the communication and leadership in an ensemble operate, who leads and follows the other musicians, as these relationships are usually evident in the relative timing of the differences between instruments. Synchrony can also be connected to the structures of the music, either to metre or cycles, or to larger spans such as phrases or sections, where synchrony may either tighten or loosen as the tempo changes depending on the aesthetic ideals, performance practices, and genres of the music. We also know that the synchrony tends to fluctuate across the different beat sub-divisions in different genres of music.

Summary

I highlighted two examples of musical event analysis, expressive performance within a performance by a musician, and timing synchrony between four musicians playing different instruments. Being able to delve into the fine details of timing between musicians is something that empirical research of music needs to be able to do in a manner that is clear and replicable. Fortunately, the methods and tools for this topic of research are already available and ready to be applied to a range of questions of timing in music. The same applies to the analysis of expressive timing in music. There is also plenty of data available that comprises real performances by musicians in MIDI standard (see Chapter 11). Onset data has also become more easily available and more can be created by combining annotations and automatic onset detection from audio (see Chapter 11).

Event analysis can also be carried out at the level of musical repertoire or concert programming. There is already a long tradition of counting and summarising the programmes of certain important festivals, institutions, and concert venues. For instance, Glatthorn (2022) used a repertoire analysis to trace the performances of musical theatre in Central Europe in the late 18th century, and Accominotti et al. (2018) have analysed the repertoire of the New York Philharmonic in the late 20th century. Datasets about playlists and play counts in streaming services such as Spotify can also be regarded as high-level music event analysis (Kamehkhosh et al., 2020).

Coda

Music scores can be analysed in a myriad of ways. This chapter has reviewed some computational analysis options for score-based music. Computational tools can identify some traditional indicators of interesting elements in music (chords, metrical hierarchies, tension, key). For a more in-depth look at the analysis of scores, Dave Meredith's *Computational Music Analysis* (2016) is an indispensable resource. In addition, the music21 tutorial and help files contain useful example analyses on a range of topics.

The threshold for committing to a computational analysis is still moderately high. However, it no longer requires superhuman efforts or a computer science degree, as the tools have become more accessible and easier to master. Carrying out computational analyses still requires programming your own analytical operation as a sequence of commands on a script, although AI solutions are allowing plain-language descriptions of the code, which are a great help when learning.

Discussion Points

1. When you see a study that uses computer-aided music analysis of some kind, is it always clear how the study was done? If you were given time, could you find the materials and the code to recreate the same analysis?

2. Annotation was portrayed as an aid in labelling music (events and segments). What kind of annotations are subject to high variance across people, and how could the act of annotation incorporate and benefit from the subjective, cultural, and acquired nature of labelling objects in music?
3. Has the Western preoccupation with pitch (e.g., scales, tonality, pitch-classes, modes) seen also in many computational analyses. Which elements of music would you put more emphasis on?

Notes

1 https://computational-cognitive-musicology-lab.github.io/humdrumR/
2 https://partitura.readthedocs.io
3 https://github.com/fosfrancesco/asap-dataset
4 https://github.com/tuomaseerola/onsetsync

Further Reading

Meredith, D. (2016). *Computational music analysis*. Springer.

References

Accominotti, F., Khan, S. R., & Storer, A. (2018). How cultural capital emerged in gilded age America: Musical purification and cross-class inclusion at the New York Philharmonic. *American Journal of Sociology, 123*(6), 1743–1783.

Albrecht, J. D., & Shanahan, D. (2013). The use of large corpora to train a new type of key-finding algorithm: An improved treatment of the minor mode. *Music Perception: An Interdisciplinary Journal, 31*(1), 59–67.

Aldwell, E., Schachter, C., & Cadwallader, A. (2018). *Harmony and voice leading*. Cengage Learning.

Aljanaki, A., Yang, Y.-H., & Soleymani, M. (2017). Developing a benchmark for emotional analysis of music. *PloS ONE, 12*(3), e0173392.

Allegraud, P., Bigo, L., Feisthauer, L., Giraud, M., Groult, R., Leguy, E., & Levé, F. (2019). Learning sonata form structure on Mozart's string quartets. *Transactions of the International Society for Music Information Retrieval (TISMIR), 2*(1), 82–96.

Bittner, R. M., Wilkins, J., Yip, H., & Bello, J. P. (2016). MedleyDB 2.0: New data and a system for sustainable data collection. *ISMIR Late Breaking and Demo Papers*, 36.

Bogdanov, D., Won, M., Tovstogan, P., Porter, A., & Serra, X. (2019). *The MTG-Jamendo Dataset for automatic music tagging*. http://hdl.handle.net/10230/42015

Bozkurt, B., Ayangil, R., & Holzapfel, A. (2014). Computational analysis of Turkish makam music: Review of state-of-the-art and challenges. *Journal of New Music Research, 43*(1), 3–23.

Briot, J.-P., & Pachet, F. (2020). Deep learning for music generation: Challenges and directions. *Neural Computing and Applications, 32*(4), 981–993.

Brost, B., Mehrotra, R., & Jehan, T. (2019). *The music streaming sessions dataset*. arXiv. https://doi.org/https://doi.org/10.48550/ARXIV.1901.09851

Burgoyne, J. A. (2012). *Stochastic processes and database-driven musicology* [PhD thesis]. Schulich School of Music; McGill University.

Butterfield, M. (2010). Participatory discrepancies and the perception of beats in jazz. *Music Perception, 27*(3), 157–176.

Calvo-Zaragoza, J., Jr, J. H., & Pacha, A. (2020). Understanding optical music recognition. *ACM Computing Surveys (CSUR), 53*(4), 1–35.

Cancino-Chacón, C. E., Grachten, M., Goebl, W., & Widmer, G. (2018). Computational models of expressive music performance: A comprehensive and critical review. *Frontiers in Digital Humanities, 5*, 25.

Carnovalini, F., & Rodà, A. (2020). Computational creativity and music generation systems: An introduction to the state of the art. *Frontiers in Artificial Intelligence, 3*. https://doi.org/https://doi.org/10.3389/frai.2020.00014

Cirelli, L. K., Wan, S. J., & Trainor, L. J. (2014). Fourteen-month-old infants use interpersonal synchrony as a cue to direct helpfulness. *Philosophical Transactions of the Royal Society B: Biological Sciences, 369*(1658), 20130400.

Clayton, M., Jakubowski, K., & Eerola, T. (2018). Interpersonal entrainment in Indian instrumental music performance: Synchronization and movement coordination relate to tempo, dynamics, metrical and cadential structure. *Musicae Scientiae, 23*, 304–331. https://doi.org/https://doi.org/10.1177/1029864919844809

Clayton, M., Jakubowski, K., Eerola, T., Keller, P. E., Camurri, A., Volpe, G., & Alborno, P. (2020). Interpersonal entrainment in music performance: Theory, method, and model. *Music Perception: An Interdisciplinary Journal, 38*(2), 136–194.

Clayton, M., Tarsitani, S., Jankowsky, R., Jure, L., Leante, L., Polak, R., Poole, A., Rocamora, M., Alborno, P., Camurri, A., Eerola, T., Jacoby, N., & Jakubowski, K. (2021). The interpersonal entrainment in music performance data collection. *Empirical Musicology Review, 16*(1), 65–84. https://doi.org/http://dx.doi.org/10.18061/emr.v16i1.7555

Cuenca-Rodríguez, M. E., & McKay, C. (2021). Exploring musical style in the anonymous and doubtfully attributed mass movements of the Coimbra manuscripts: A statistical and machine learning approach. *Journal of New Music Research, 50*(3), 199–219.

Cuthbert, M. S., & Ariza, C. (2010). music21: A toolkit for computer-aided musicology and symbolic music data. In J. S. Downie & R. C. Veltkamp (Eds.), *11th International Society for Music Information Retrieval Conference (ISMIR 2010)* (pp. 637–642). International Society for Music Information Retrieval.

De Clercq, T., & Temperley, D. (2011). A corpus analysis of rock harmony. *Popular Music, 30*(1), 47–70.

Eerola, T., & Clayton, M. (2024). onsetsync: An R package for onset synchrony analysis. *Journal of Open Source Software, 9*(93), 5395. https://doi.org/10.21105/joss.05395

Forte, A. (1983). Motivic design and structural levels in the first movement of Brahms's string quartet in c minor. *The Musical Quarterly, 69*(4), 471–502.

Foscarin, F., McLeod, A., Rigaux, P., Jacquemard, F., & Sakai, M. (2020). ASAP: A dataset of aligned scores and performances for piano transcription. *International Society for Music Information Retrieval Conference (ISMIR)*, 534–541.

Friberg, A., Colombo, V., Frydén, L., & Sundberg, J. (2000). Generating musical performances with Director Musices. *Computer Music Journal, 24*(3), 23–29.

Gingras, B., Pearce, M. T., Goodchild, M., Dean, R. T., Wiggins, G., & McAdams, S. (2016). Linking melodic expectation to expressive performance timing and perceived musical tension. *Journal of Experimental Psychology: Human Perception and Performance, 42*(4), 594–609.

Glatthorn, A. (2022). *Music theatre and the Holy Roman Empire*. Cambridge University Press.

Grachten, M., & Widmer, G. (2012). Linear basis models for prediction and analysis of musical expression. *Journal of New Music Research, 41*(4), 311–322.

Hansen, N. Chr., & Huron, D. (2018). The lone instrument: Musical solos and sadness-related features. *Music Perception, 35*(5), 540–560. https://doi.org/10.1525/mp.2018.35.5.540

Harasim, D., Moss, F. C., Ramirez, M., & Rohrmeier, M. (2021). Exploring the foundations of tonality: Statistical cognitive modeling of modes in the history of western classical music. *Humanities and Social Sciences Communications, 8*(1), 5. https://doi.org/10.1057/s41599-020-00678-6

Hawthorne, C., Stasyuk, A., Roberts, A., Simon, I., Huang, C.-Z. A., Dieleman, S., Elsen, E., Engel, J., & Eck, D. (2019). Enabling factorized piano music modeling and generation with the MAESTRO dataset. *International Conference on Learning Representations*. https://openreview.net/forum?id=r1lYRjC9F7

Herremans, D., & Chew, E. (2016). Tension ribbons: Quantifying and visualising tonal tension. *Second International Conference on Technologies for Music Notation and Representation (TENOR), 2*.

Hirata, K., Tojo, S., & Hamanaka, M. (2016). An algebraic approach to time-span reduction. In D. Meredith (Ed.), *Computational music analysis* (pp. 251–270). Springer.

Hood, M. (1971). *The ethnomusicologist*. McGraw-Hill.

Hornbostel, E. M. von, & Sachs, C. (1914). Classification of musical instruments. *Galpin Society Journal, 14*, 3–29.

Huron, D. (1996). The melodic arch in Western folksongs. *Computing in Musicology, 10*, 3–23.

Huron, D. (2001). What is a musical feature? Forte's analysis of Brahms's Opus 51, No. 1, revisited. *Music Theory Online, 7*(4), 1–12.

Huron, David. (2002). Music information processing using the Humdrum Toolkit: Concepts, examples, and lessons. *Computer Music Journal, 26*(2), 11–26.

Janssen, B., Burgoyne, J. A., & Honing, H. (2017). Predicting variation of folk songs: A corpus analysis study on the memorability of melodies. *Frontiers in Psychology, 8*, 621.

Järvinen, T. (1995). Tonal hierarchies in jazz improvisation. *Music Perception, 12*(4), 415–437.

Kamehkhosh, I., Bonnin, G., & Jannach, D. (2020). Effects of recommendations on the playlist creation behavior of users. *User Modeling and User-Adapted Interaction, 30*(2), 285–322.

Killick, A. (2020). Global notation as a tool for cross-cultural and comparative music analysis. *Analytical Approaches to World Music, 8*(2), 235–279.

Krumhansl, C. L. (2001). *Cognitive foundations of musical pitch*. Oxford University Press.

Krumhansl, C. L., & Kessler, E. J. (1982). Tracing the dynamic changes in perceived tonal organization in a spatial representation of musical keys. *Psychological Review, 89*(4), 334–368.

Lartillot, O. (2005). Multi-dimensional motivic pattern extraction founded on adaptive redundancy filtering. *Journal of New Music Research, 34*(4), 375–393.

Lerdahl, F. et al. (2001). *Tonal pitch space*. Oxford University Press.

Lerdahl, F., & Jackendoff, R. S. (1983). *A generative theory of tonal music*. MIT Press.

Lerdahl, F., & Krumhansl, C. L. (2007). Modeling tonal tension. *Music Perception: An Interdisciplinary Journal, 24*(4), 329–366.

Li, B., Liu, X., Dinesh, K., Duan, Z., & Sharma, G. (2018). Creating a multitrack classical music performance dataset for multimodal music analysis: Challenges, insights, and applications. *IEEE Transactions on Multimedia*, *21*(2), 522–535.

Llorens, A. (2021). The recorded Brahms corpus (RBC): A dataset of performative parameters in recordings of Brahms's cello sonatas. *Empirical Musicology Review*, *16*(1-2), 124–133. https://doi.org/10.18061/emr.v16i1.7612

Loughran, R., & O'Neill, M. (2020). Evolutionary music: Applying evolutionary computation to the art of creating music. *Genetic Programming and Evolvable Machines*, *21*(1), 55–85.

Marchini, M., Ramirez, R., Papiotis, P., & Maestre, E. (2014). The sense of ensemble: A machine learning approach to expressive performance modelling in string quartets. *Journal of New Music Research*, *43*(3), 303–317.

Marsden, A. (2010). Schenkerian analysis by computer: A proof of concept. *Journal of New Music Research*, *39*(3), 269–289.

Marsden, A. (2016). Music analysis by computer: Ontology and epistemology. In D. Meredith (Ed.), *Computational music analysis* (pp. 3–28). Springer.

McKay, C., Cumming, J., & Fujinaga, I. (2018). JSYMBOLIC 2.2: Extracting features from symbolic music for use in musicological and MIR research. *ISMIR*, 348–354.

Meredith, D. (2016). *Computational music analysis*. Springer.

Meyer, L. B. (1956). *Emotion and meaning in music*. Chicago University Press.

Palmer, C., & Krumhansl, C. L. (1990). Mental representations for musical meter. *Journal of Experimental Psychology: Human Perception and Performance*, *16*(4), 728–741.

Parsons, D. (1975). *The directory of tunes and musical themes*. S. Brown.

Pearce, M. T., & Eerola, T. (2017). Music perception in historical audiences: Towards predictive models of music perception in historical audiences. *Journal of Interdisciplinary Studies of Music*, *8*(1–2), 91–120.

Polak, R., London, J., & Jacoby, N. (2016). Both isochronous and non-isochronous metrical subdivision afford precise and stable ensemble entrainment: A corpus study of Malian jembe drumming. *Frontiers in Neuroscience*, *10*, 285.

Poole, A. (2013). *Groove in Cuban dance music: An analysis of son and salsa* [PhD thesis]. The Open University. https://doi.org/https://oro.open.ac.uk/61186/1/680519.pdf

Rohrmeier, M. (2011). Towards a generative syntax of tonal harmony. *Journal of Mathematics and Music*, *5*(1), 35–53.

Savage, P. E., Tierney, A. T., & Patel, A. D. (2017). Global music recordings support the motor constraint hypothesis for human and avian song contour. *Music Perception*, *34*(3), 327–334. https://doi.org/10.1525/mp.2017.34.3.327

Shannon, C. E. (1951). Prediction and entropy of printed English. *Bell System Technical Journal*, *30*(1), 50–64.

Toiviainen, P., & Eerola, T. (2006). Autocorrelation in meter induction: The role of accent structure. *The Journal of the Acoustical Society of America*, *119*(2), 1164–1170.

Tsushima, H., Nakamura, E., Itoyama, K., & Yoshii, K. (2018). Generative statistical models with self-emergent grammar of chord sequences. *Journal of New Music Research*, *47*(3), 226–248.

Van Kranenburg, P., De Bruin, M., & Volk, A. (2019). Documenting a song culture: The Dutch song database as a resource for musicological research. *International Journal on Digital Libraries*, *20*(1), 13–23.

Wallmark, Z. (2019). A corpus analysis of timbre semantics in orchestration treatises. *Psychology of Music*, *47*(4), 585–605.

Weiß, C., Schreiber, H., & Müller, M. (2020). Local key estimation in music recordings: A case study across songs, versions, and annotators. *IEEE/ACM Transactions on Audio, Speech, and Language Processing*, *28*, 2919–2932. https://doi.org/10.1109/TASLP.2020.3030485

Wiering, F. (2013). *The language of the modes: Studies in the history of polyphonic modality*. Routledge.

10 Analysis of Audio

All music – that we can listen to – is sound, and in physics, sound is just movement of molecules in the air or other medium and can be picked up by recording with a microphone. As listeners, we do not operate similarly to a modern microphone, or to a Digital Audio Workstation, as our auditory, perceptual, and cognitive processes filter the signal in profound ways. We utilise our knowledge of the music to dissect relevant aspects of the signal, and we can also actively focus our attention on specific aspects of it. When we take the audio signal as a starting point for our analysis, we must accept that, in order to analyse the signal, a series of transformations are required.

The idea of looking at the details of the sonic signal itself is not new in empirical studies of music. Carl Seashore (1938) wanted to pin down the actual details of singing and succeeded in characterising the dynamics and vibrato of sung examples by using phono-photographic recordings. He also pioneered the study of expressive performance parameters by looking at the precise timing of the notes and how they deviated from the time defined by the score.

Audio Analysis Basics

In this section, I will cover some of the basic representations to guide you through analysis of onsets, fundamental frequency, timbre, and harmony from audio. This will be a rather brief and non-technical rendition of these topics. If you want to dive properly into the specifics of audio analysis and learn more about digital audio representation and how each algorithm works with concrete Python code examples using functional notebooks, I strongly recommend Meinhart Müller's book *Fundamentals of Music Processing* (Müller, 2015) and the associated online sources[1].

This section will cover some of the basic representations that are geared towards analytical operations such as identifying onsets, assessing spectrum and timbre, and estimating pitches, pitch-classes, and key. There are several software solutions for performing audio analysis. Out of the options available, *Sonic Visualiser* is worth mentioning here as a tool that has a great graphical user interface and the ability to also collect and show annotations. Sonic Visualiser also has numerous

DOI: 10.4324/9781003293804-10

algorithms that extract meaningful contents of music (tempo, beats, chromagram, fundamental frequency, and so on). Most of the other analysis tools rely on coding in one of the common programming languages such as Python, which, to be frank, is an easier way to make transparent, replicable, and sophisticated analytical workflows than a solution with a graphical user interface. Tools such as *Essentia* (Bogdanov et al., 2013), *Marsyas* (Tzanetakis & Cook, 2000), and *Librosa* (McFee et al., 2015) utilise Python as the language of choice and are free, open-source software, whereas others, such as *MIR Toolbox* (Lartillot et al., 2008), are open source as such, but to function this one relies on *Matlab*, which is not open source software. To be able to run on open notebooks, online within a browser window, using a cloud computing service (*Google Colaboratory*), I will rely on Librosa as the choice of analysis tool here, as it is open source, and runs on Python, and lends itself to online use easily. Librosa also has a good range of existing analytical functions, and it has become a common tool of choice, albeit not the only one, amongst the MIR and music and science community for analysis of audio.

Figure 10.1 introduces the basic concepts. The upper panel shows a sine wave where the *amplitude, period,* and *phase* are annotated. The amplitude, here 1, is related to loudness (although loudness is a relative measure) and the period is the time between the peaks of the sine waves, here it can be seen to be 0.0025 seconds, or 2.5 ms, and you could fit 400 of these into a second (1 / 0.0025 = 400). The period is conventionally referred to in hertz (Hz), cycles per second. In this case, the sine wave is 400 Hz, and we can see the first 10 ms of this signal. The phase (denoted by ϕ), which is 270 ° as our signal crosses the zero amplitude at 3/4 of its period. The phase is illustrated with a copy of the signal (in grey colour) that has a 90 ° phase delay compared to the original signal and the delayed signal has a phase of 360 ° (which is the same as 0 ° in the cycle). The phase-shifted copy of the signal has otherwise the same properties (same amplitude and period) as the original signal. The next panel down shows a complex tone, which is a summed signal of three sine waves, each having a different period. One sine is again the 400 Hz sine, the second one is 600 Hz and the third one is 1,600 Hz (shown as small figures on the left side of the second panel). Once these signals are summed together, they create a regular pattern that is a little harder to decipher in terms of the periods, but we see a strong peak at the 0.005 s (200 Hz) and smaller peaks of the sine waves at 0.0025 s (400 Hz) and 0.00167 s (600 Hz), to mention some. Why is the 200 Hz wave present there so prominently although it was not in the original frequencies summed together? Well, 200 Hz is the common denominator between all three frequencies, which has been amplified when the sine waves were summed. In fact, our hearing system does something similar when hearing complex tones by inferring the lowest frequency, which we call *virtual pitch*, from complex harmonic tones such as speech and singing (Terhardt, 1979). So we have created a complex tone consisting of three sine waves and we have created this sound to last for 0.5 seconds (the code for creating the signal is available in Chapter10.1).

In the lower two plots of Figure 10.1 we see two common representations of audio, *waveform,* and *envelope* (which describes how the amplitude of the sound changes over time) on the right, and the *spectrum* on the left. Waveform (the grey

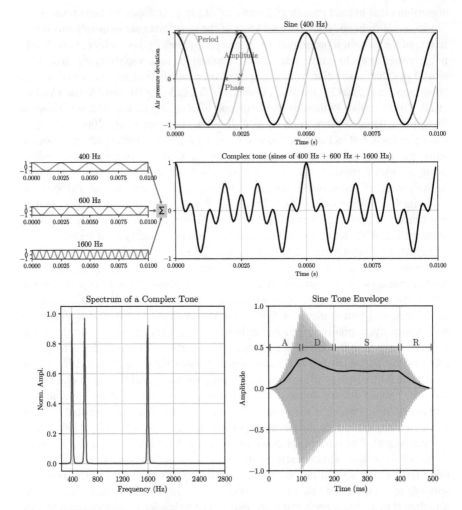

Figure 10.1 Illustration of basic representations and transformations of audio using a 400 Hz sine wave and a complex tone consisting of 400, 600 and 1,600 Hz sine waves.

area in the figure) is familiar from any sequencer and shows the signal amplitude, while the envelope is just tracing the positive part of the amplitude (shown as the black line in the figure). Different parts of the envelope are referred to by different names; here I have annotated the envelope with A, D, S, and R, referring to *attack, decay, sustain,* and *release* of the envelope. These terms were initially part of the vocabulary used in sound synthesis in the 1960s and 1970s, but they are still useful, and often available in synthesiser plugins, allowing us to refer to the parts of the envelope. Attack is the time it takes for the amplitude of the envelope to rise from nothing to peak. Attacks are important when defining the *onset* of sounds. Sustain refs to the period when the amplitude is relatively level, and decay or release refers to the decrease most instruments sounds have after the initial attack and sustain when the envelope amplitude returns to its initial level.

Note that the shape of the envelope is independent of the frequencies in the sound, and in fact I have just created an archetypical envelope shape by just multiplying the amplitude of the summed sine waves in four different parts of the audio. On the left we have the spectrum of this sound as a whole, in other words, collapsed over time, so we only see the frequencies that are extracted from the signal by Fourier analysis. We see that this gives us three neat peaks at 400 Hz, 600 Hz, and 1,600 Hz. These are the basic representation and transformations in a nutshell for a simple artificial sound. But since we tend to analyse actual musical sounds, let us move on to more real instrument sounds and apply the basic representations to one of these examples.

For this, we take one note ($D\sharp_4$, which is 311.1 Hz) played by three instruments: violin, clarinet, and marimba. The sounds have been taken from our previous timbre study (Eerola et al., 2012) where we took the sound excerpts from within the high-quality *Vienna Symphonic Library*. Analysis of the audio of the three instrument sounds is available as Chapter 10.2. In the leftmost panel of Figure 10.2 we see the spectra of each instrument. The fundamental frequency (311 Hz) is evident as the largest peak in each plot, and the partials conveniently fall into the multiples of the fundamental frequency, which are labelled in the X axis up to 3,111 Hz. Violin and clarinet show peaks in the higher partials with the distinct difference that the clarinet emphasises odd partials (1st, 3rd, and 5th), which relates to the cylindrical bore of the instrument. Marimba, in contrast, has most of the energies in the fundamental frequencies and only muted peaks in higher partials. One of these is at 933 Hz and another around 2,000 Hz, which does not line up well with the harmonic series. As a result, the marimba will sound less rich and there is something inharmonic in the sound of marimba. One simple summary descriptor of the spectrum is a *spectral centroid*. This measures the centre of mass of the spectrum and summarises where the energies over the spectrum are located; usually the perceptual interpretation of this is the brightness of the sound. If the spectral centroid is low, listeners rate the timbre as sounding dark, and if the centroid is high, listeners will say that the sound is bright (Grey & Gordon, 1978). The centroid has been added to the plots representing the spectra of the three instruments, showing similar centroids for violin and clarinet (around 1,700 Hz) while the marimba has a lower spectral centroid, 1,155 Hz, and generally a darker timbre than violin or clarinet in this register. The amplitude of the partials is crucial for creating the distinct identity of the sounds. It is one of the defining characteristics of the timbre, but the other key property of timbre is the envelope of the sound.

The panels on the right of Figure 10.2 show the envelope of each instrument sound. The envelope, shown as a black curve, is an approximation from the actual waveform (depicted using a grey colour) that simply traces the energy along the temporal axis. At the top of the envelope, the parts of the envelope are labelled with the letters referring to attack, sustain, and decay. Now, envelopes of these three instruments vary considerably depending on the type of sound generation of

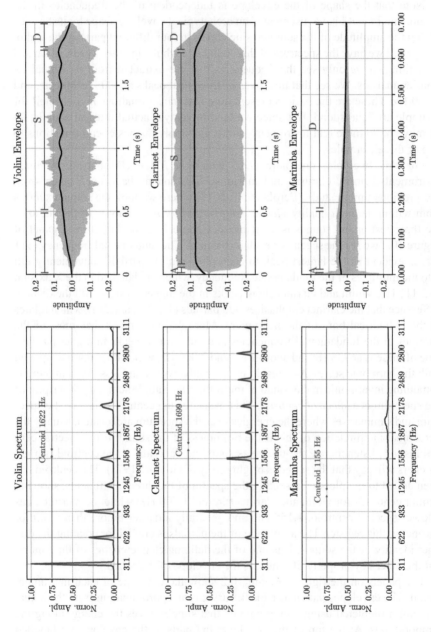

Figure 10.2 The spectrum and envelope of three instruments (violin, clarinet, and marimba).

the instrument (blowing, plucking, bowing, striking) (Hornbostel & Sachs, 1914). Here, our three examples demonstrate this by showing remarkably slow attack by the bowed instrument (violin, which is bowed, not plucked in this example), moderately fast attack by the blown instrument (clarinet), and an instant attack by the plucked instrument (marimba). Beyond the attack shape and duration, the rest of the envelope shows remarkably different shapes; the violin shows vibrato, creating an amplitude modulation of the sound that can be seen as an undulating sustained part of the envelope. The clarinet has a steady sustain and an orderly decay part, whereas the marimba displays a long decay of the initial attack, where it is difficult to denote when sustain turns into decay.

In the real world, analysis of the contents of music from audio is complex, as most music is polyphonic and contains a mixture of instruments that overlap in terms of frequencies and amplitude envelopes. In other words, instruments or singing voices will not have such well-defined beginnings and endings, and many of the higher-level concepts such as tonality or structure require many rough inferences to be made from the signal itself.

Table 10.1 lists five domains of acoustic and musical descriptors and breaks these down into three levels of abstraction. This is a simplification, as the domains and the levels of abstraction cannot always be separated clearly. At the lowest level we have the *physical* level of the signal, then *perceptual* and *semantic* at the highest level. The boundaries between these are not crisp and well defined. Sometimes, the literature refers to low-level, mid-level, and high-level descriptor categories, and occasionally some descriptors occur in the perceptual or semantic levels. However, the idea of the table is to emphasise that there is a continuum of representations from the most rudimentary readings of the physical signal to something that is already a transformation of the raw signal into something that we think is relevant to our perception. The final level contains terms that are familiar from music theory and have been discussed in an earlier section (Chapter 9), but it is worth bearing in mind that inferring these semantic qualities from an audio signal requires multiple transformations and assumptions that are not always so reliable.

The five *domains* are an attempt to separate the principles in calculating the descriptors, from the purely *amplitude domain* that relies on the energy in the signal,

Table 10.1 Examples of acoustic descriptors across different domains and abstraction levels. Acronyms (RMS, STFT, MFCC, CQHC) are explained in the text.

Domain	Physical	Perceptual	Semantic
Amplitude	Zero-crossing, RMS	Loudness	-
Frequency	Time-frequency (STFT)	Pitch, chroma	Melody, chords, key
Cepstral	Auditory models	MFCCs, CQHCs	Instrument
Fluctuation	Spectral flux, onset change	Onsets, beats	Metre, tempo
Multi-feature	-	-	Valence, arousal

to the *frequency domain,* which focusses on the frequency elements of the signal. The *cepstral domain* is a special case of time, amplitude, and frequency combined together that captures a very particular aspect of the signal that is often mostly related to the timbre. The *fluctuation domain* represents the temporal changes in the energy across the signal, building onsets, tempo, and rhythms. Finally, the *multi-feature domain* is a special category that only relates to high-level semantic descriptors, which are constructed from combinations of descriptors from other domains.

Let us ramp up the complexity of the audio analysis and plunge into analysis of an actual recorded performance after these two illustrative toy examples (complex sound and three instrument sounds). I have taken on one of the music examples used in Chapter 9, namely *Help!* by The Beatles. Let us focus on extracting some useful measures of acoustic and musical content from the beginning of this track.

Physical Descriptors

Let us first look at the energy across the audio file of *Help!* and see what can be done with it using Librosa. The full code is available in Chapter10.2.

We see the waveform of this intro in the upper plot of Figure 10.3. The middle panel displays the transformation of the waveform into root mean square (RMS)

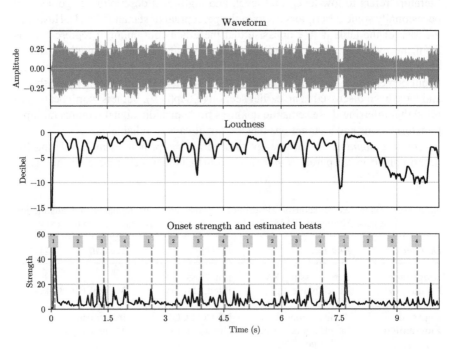

Figure 10.3 Waveform, loudness, and onset strengths (black curve) and estimated beats (dashed lines) of the intro of *Help!* by The Beatles.

values of the sound pressure over a sliding window, which is then converted to a perceptually meaningful unit, namely *decibels* (dB). Note that this measure is relative to a reference point as the actual sound pressure level depends on how close we are when recording or when listening to the playback. The maximum loudness here is defined as 0 and the lower sound pressure is represented as a drop from this reference using a logarithmic scale. So, the decrease in dB at around 7.5 seconds, which is about −11 dB, has nearly ten times less energy than the next full second that hovers around −1 dB. And we can easily detect changes of 3 dB, although the actual loudness is also dependent on the frequency range and the envelope of the sound. What we see here is that loudness mimics the amplitude of the waveform but the scale of the change is different.

The lower panel shows the estimated beats from the audio as dashed vertical lines and the strength of the underlying onsets. These beats are akin to quarter note positions, but do not contain any other information such as the metrical position in the bar, whereas human annotations of the beats could contain those details (annotated beats and metrical positions of the same clip were shown in the annotation section in Chapter 9). The onset strength is based on spectral flux that measures the change in the spectrogram over time. This has been found to be an effective way to detect onsets in instruments that may not have sharp attacks, but a change in pitch or timbre over time. The beats are estimated initially from the peaks of the onset candidates, but then a steady beat is also imposed on the most plausible tempo suggested by the onsets. In this short example, the estimated tempo is 95.7 BPM (beats per minute). Because the algorithm estimates the steady beat and is not only based on onsets but on an inferred steady stream of beats, it is able to suggest beats in places where the onsets are not visibly present (such as in the vicinity of 8.5 and 9 seconds). It is also satisfying to note that the estimated beats align with the manual annotations (depicted as squares with the numbers for the beats added at the top of the bottom panel in Figure 10.3).

This analysis ventured from the pure energy-based descriptors to fluctuation-based descriptors when I calculated the spectral flux. As one more alternative, low-level representation of the signal, I introduce a simulation of the auditory nerves as a method of audio analysis. Figure 10.4 shows neural firing of inner hair cells for our 0.5 second complex tone comprised of three sine waves (400, 600, and 1,600 Hz) illustrated previously in Figure 10.1. This simulation has been done with the brian2hears library for Python, which allows us to simulate various aspects of the auditory system such as inner hair cells or head-related transfer functions, which are important for sound localisation (Goodman & Brette, 2009). In this particular simulation, achieved through Python code Chapter10.4, the sound is first filtered through a bank of gammatone filters that emulate the auditory range and transformation of the frequencies, and this output is then fed into an array of neurons that behave like the actual inner hair cells (Goodman & Brette, 2010). This is the behaviour of these neurons, which is governed by the known refractory period (how often a nerve can fire) and thresholds (how strong the activation needs to be above the noise) of these neural cells. The output shows the triggering of the neurons in different channels that represent frequency as dots in the plot. It is easy to see

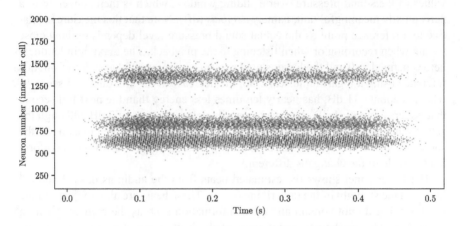

Figure 10.4 Auditory nerve fibre model and inner hair cell spiking for the example of a complex tone consisting of 400 + 600 + 1,600 Hz sine waves.

the frequencies of the three sine waves triggering a constant firing in three broad channels (the channel numbers are centred around 600, 800, and 1,350, which are not in Hz, but these are the neurons that represent frequency bands).

I wanted to bring one low-level transformation of the acoustic signal into another representation to exemplify how many ways computational tools can approach audio analysis. For specific questions of perception, the neural encoding shown above could well be the most persuasive starting point. However, often the question does not require a psychoacoustically realistic representation of the audio signal, but something that offers a convenient way to approximate or estimate the higher-level cognitive, semantic, or emotional descriptors. These are discussed next, but it is important to clarify here that such descriptors rarely start from low-level psychoacoustic descriptors.

One could also argue that several of the representations I outlined earlier in the section are actually perceptual, as they incorporate rather complex perceptual filters and transformations. It is certainly true that the boundaries are blurry; for example, the extraction of beats is a perceptual descriptor that does not really reside in the signal itself. However, I have tried to point this out when discussing the onsets and beats and let us focus on perceptual descriptors next.

Perceptual Descriptors

Let's explore the perceptual descriptors in more detail and visualise the spectrum, the chromagram, and fundamental frequencies as common perceptual starting points for many analytical operations. We will again use the beginning of *Help!* as the analysis example.

In Figure 10.5 we see three representations related to the time-frequency domain for the first ten seconds of *Help!* The upper panel displays the spectrum, which

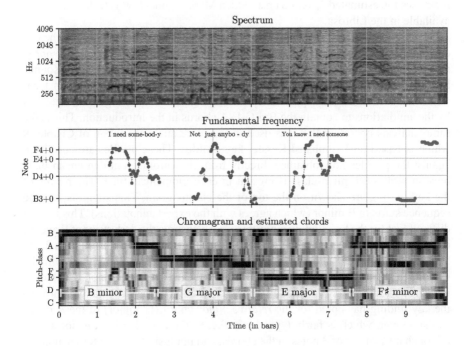

Figure 10.5 Spectrum, estimated fundamental frequency, and chromagram representation of *Help!* by The Beatles.

shows the energies of the frequencies over time. We can see the opening chord in the first 0.5 seconds as a stripe spanning frequencies from 500 Hz to 2,000 Hz, and if we follow the dark pattern discernible around 200–300 Hz, we should be able to follow the approximate melody line with the partials of the voice shown as the additional vertical stripes. Spectrum is a helpful representation for looking at the contents of the audio, but we often want to know the specific pitches that spectrum highlights. In the middle panel, the fundamental frequency (F_0) of the singing voice has been extracted and plotted along the same temporal axis as the other plots, but instead of the frequencies in Hz, the Y axis is labelled with musical notes. This traces the melody of the vocal line (the blues scale from B minor, where 'I need somebody' is E-F♮-D-E-D). The lyrics of the vocal line have been manually added to make the interpretation of the vocal line easier. The extraction of the melody is not a trivial task from a polyphonic mixture. Here, the vocal line was separated from the rest of the signal using a similarity-based technique proposed by Rafii & Pardo (2012), which has been implemented by Brian McFee[2]. After separating the vocals from the rest of the mix, the F_0 was extracted using a well-known YIN algorithm (De Cheveigné & Kawahara, 2002) that uses autocorrelation to determine the most plausible frequency. This was carried out by a more recent variant by Mauch & Dixon (2014), called the probabilistic YIN algorithm (pYIN) that further processes the estimated F_0 based on a hidden Markov model. This technique is also available in the Librosa.

The lowest panel shows the *chromagram*, which refers to the energies in the frequencies that have been collapsed into pitch-classes using a so-called *constant-Q transform* (Brown, 1991). To make the energies stand out, the percussive sounds have been eliminated from the track by a harmonic-percussive separation technique. In addition, I have applied a key-finding algorithm to the segments identified by the annotations to contain the Bm-G-E-A chords in the introduction. This is the same analysis operation that was used in the score analysis section of Chapter 9 which is based on Krumhansl-Kessler key profiles. These profiles are correlated against the profiles now obtained directly from the chromagram that encapsulate how strongly each pitch-class is present in each moment in time. The results of the key-finding are shown on the top of the chromagram. This suggests that the sequence starts in B minor (which agrees with the expert annotations). This is not a difficult feat for the key-finding algorithm, as we observe the dark stripe at B and $F\sharp$ during the first two seconds. The next chord is estimated to be G major (from 2.5 to 5 s), and the following chord is E major (5 to 7.5 s); both estimations agree with the expert annotations of chords. The final chord is estimated as $F\sharp$ minor, which does not agree with the expert's view, as they have labelled this as an A major chord. So the key-finding has opted for the *relative minor* chord ($F\sharp$ minor) of the A major as the winner, which is fairly typical mistake, as the two chords, A major and $F\sharp$ minor share 2 of out of 3 notes in the chords, and in music-theoretic terms, relative keys share the same key signature. This mistake is also compounded by a simple localised application of the key-finding algorithm. Despite the one minor mistake, key-finding offers plausible results even though this is a rather naive way of estimating the chords. There are more sophisticated ways that use chord templates and incorporate the sequential probabilities of the chords (e.g., preferring common sequences such as IV-V-I captured in Markov models) to resolve the issues that we saw with the erroneous $F\sharp$ minor (McVicar et al., 2014).

Concerning chromagrams and estimation of key, chords, and pitches from the audio, reducing everything into 12 equal tempered pitch-classes is not the only option available, as the tuning and intonation systems show a diversity across cultures. For instance, Librosa comes with the possibility of analysing and labelling the octave into just *intonation system* or *svaras* (Koduri et al., 2012), which are North Indian (Hindustani) and South Indian (Carnatic) definitions of intervals in specific rãgas. There are also corpora (Srinivasamurthy et al., 2021) that come with annotations about melodic phrases, tempo, and structure[3]. I have also mentioned two abbreviations in Table 10.1, MFCCs (mel-frequency cepstral coefficients) and CQHCs (constant-Q harmonic coefficients). MFCCs are the product of a transformation of audio signals that uses the mel scale of frequencies, represented typically by 20 mel frequency bands, which are converted into coefficients using log and discrete cosine transforms and taking the lowest coefficients in each frame of analysis. This representation is popular in speech recognition, but it is also sometimes used as a perceptual description of the timbre in music information research. A new technique called constant-Q harmonic coefficients (CQHCs) does a similar reduction of data but operates with logarithmic frequency using a constant-Q transform (Rafii, 2022). This transformation decomposes the spectrum into pitch and spectral components, and the latter forms the representations (harmonic coefficients) that are pitch-independent and more sensitive, at least to Western musical content, than MFCCs.

Semantic Descriptors

Often the aim of the acoustic analysis is to connect the acoustic properties to various high-level semantic descriptors such as liking, valence, arousal, or genre, but here we have an immediate problem. These concepts are not considered to be embedded in the audio signal, nor even directly emerging from it. This challenge is sometimes called the *semantic gap*. However, the semantic descriptors – or concepts – can be, to some extent, inferred from intermediate representations of descriptors, if we have many of them, and if we have the data necessary to model them from a combination of descriptors that may produce the best estimation of the annotated high-level concept such as valence or arousal. However, let us refrain from trying to do this in this section, as we can pursue the idea when looking at multiple examples in Chapter 11. Instead, we could easily pull existing and well-known (and often used) mappings of audio and high-level semantic concepts by getting them from existing analyses and a commercial source, namely from streaming service giant Spotify.

I don't have the intention to endorse the descriptors we can retrieve from Spotify as the most formidable and robust sources of information, but here I want to show that such a source has certain advantages when used in empirical music research. Obtaining descriptors from Spotify capitalises on years of MIR research that has gone into characterising these descriptors. The other consideration is that there are multiple ways of calculating many of the descriptors (e.g., different tempo estimation algorithms). The advantage of Spotify is that it gives identical information for everyone, and the analysis itself can be scaled up easily for hundreds of thousands of excerpts. Also, retrieving musical descriptors using Spotify is easy with respect to the required expertise, and this approach does not force you to download any music tracks and thus violate the copyright. From this perspective, this is an interesting process to learn for empirical research of music, although it has its shortcomings as well (calculation of descriptors is not transparent and the long-term reliability of the data is uncertain). This approach of turning to Spotify to obtain descriptors of music can be especially valuable in research tasks where one needs to characterise the music listened to by the participants or define and select the stimuli according to very specific musical and acoustic parameters for research purposes.

Here we focus on a piece of music that we introduced in the annotation section and used in the audio analysis operations earlier, *Help!* by The Beatles. To understand the range and values of the descriptors that we will extract from the Spotify service that characterise this piece, let us contextualise them within other comparable tracks from the same era using a sample of 500 tracks.

To obtain musical descriptors of tracks from Spotify, we need to use an API (application programming interface) that Spotify offers to developers to build services that use their framework and data. We, as researchers, are such developers in this context. Using the Spotify API is not difficult and it is a well-documented service but comes with certain restrictions about how many queries you can make in a short time span and how you will use the data. These restrictions and policies are enforced by having each developer/researcher use their own *client identity key* when authorising the API to run the queries. This is nothing to be concerned about, just a verification service, and it has no relation to whether you are a Spotify subscriber or not. Once this identification is verified, a bit of programming will open the Spotify data for all sorts of purposes. Tracks, artists, genres, playlists, and audio descriptors as well as high-level concepts such as valence, energy, tempo, speechiness, acousticness, or even popularity can be retrieved for any given track in the service. Valence, energy, and tempo have been explained in previous sections, but the rest of the descriptors are new in our context. The exact algorithms for the descriptors are not available due to the proprietary nature of these descriptors, which is a shame and against the transparency principles advocated, but the reasons relate to the proprietary nature of this information as it forms a part of their intellectual property and business logic. Speechiness refers to how much the signal resembles the characteristics of speech, where a low value (0.0) is obtained by instrumental music and a high value (1.0) by spoken text. Acousticness refers to instrumentation where natural acoustic instrument combinations (guitar, violin, etc.) receive high value and synthetic, non-acoustic instruments (synth pad sounds, electric guitar sounds with distortion, etc.) obtain low values. Popularity ranges from 0 to 100 and is based on how much the track is played on the service, but the direct way the popularity is defined is shrouded in mystery. I would treat popularity as an unpredictable descriptor compared to the acoustic descriptors, which are stable, as popularity should wax and wane as the popularity of a track changes due to external circumstances (a track appearing in a popular movie/TV-series, artist death, associations with a meme, etc.).

Let us retrieve *valence, energy, tempo,* and *acousticness* for *Help!* and *Yesterday* by The Beatles to get a feel for these descriptors. To truly understand these descriptors, it is useful to cast them within the context of similar music. In this case, I will extract the same variables from the top 500 Spotify tracks of the same era and genre. Here, I define the era as any track published between the years 1964 and 1966 as *Help!* and *Yesterday* were both released in 1965. In addition, I will narrow down this search for tracks to two genres, either 'rock' or 'pop' as the minimally relevant musical context. The Python code to retrieve the descriptors for all 500 tracks is available as Chapter10.5.

Once we have retrieved the descriptors, we can plot them and show where *Help!* and *Yesterday* are located within the context of each descriptor from the 500 rock or pop tracks from the mid-1960s. This allows us to think about the descriptors in a more intuitive way. Looking at Figure 10.6, we notice that these two classic tracks occupy opposite ends of the valence and energy descriptors. The scale of these descriptors in Spotify ranges from 0 to 1. Here we see that *Help!* is considered

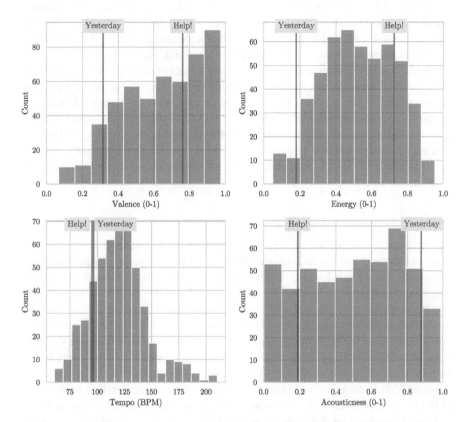

Figure 10.6 Visualisation of the features of two songs (*Help!* and *Yesterday*) by The Beatles within the context of 500 other tracks from 1964 to 1966 using four high-level features retrieved from Spotify.

positively valenced (0.77, above the midpoint of the scale, which is 0.5) and high in energy (0.77) whereas *Yesterday*, rather unsurprisingly, is represented by negative valence (0.33) and low energy (0.22).

We can compare these descriptors with the expert annotations we have for *Help!* In Chapter 9, I presented annotations of valence and arousal (which is interpreted to be similar to energy) by experts for *Help!* (shown in Figure 5.3), which largely agree with Spotify's descriptors, such as valence, which scores 6.6 (which is 0.70 if rescaled to 0–1) and energy, which scores 7.5 (which is 0.81 when rescaled). In terms of tempo, the tracks are similar (95 and 96 BPM), which, by the way, is also consistent with our own audio analysis carried out above when we estimated the tempo of *Help!* to be 95.7 BPM. The last concept, *acousticness*, does divide the two tracks sharply, as *Help!* is low in acousticness whereas *Yesterday* is high (again, not surprisingly, as it features acoustic guitar, violin, viola, and cello along with the singer). Although we do not have the exact acoustic formula for the Spotify descriptors, retrieval of the features suggests that at least in these cases the features are intuitively plausible. While the research community is critical of Spotify descriptors, they are based on a combination of acoustic descriptors that have been optimised through various techniques (annotations and signal processing).

Here the main message is that we can access a number of meaningful, high-level descriptors of music from a massive streaming service such as Spotify. Despite the issues related to transparency, this common source allows for large-scale analysis of music with uniform inputs. These may be used to explore new topics such as how the descriptors reflect consumption habits depending on the time of day – as one recent study explored (Heggli et al., 2021) – or how external interventions such as the COVID-19 pandemic impacted music consumption (Hurwitz & Krumhansl, 2021).

Summary

For empirical research of music, it is important to realise that computational music analysis offers a well-equipped toolbox for the analyst to design analytical operations for recorded sound. Extracting onsets and melody lines is often feasible, and describing the harmonic, timbral, and rhythmic contents of music from the audio file is possible but will require careful application of the appropriate analytical techniques. The good news for researchers is that there are several good software options for performing audio analysis. Some of them integrate the analysis with the possibility of displaying annotations – even collecting some forms of annotations (Sonic Visualiser) – while most (Librosa, Marsyas, Essentia, MIR Toolbox) do not come with a graphical user interface and need basic programming skills to be used effectively. I consider this an advantage for empirical research because implementing the analysis as a code (e.g., a Jupyter notebook or Python scripts) makes the whole analysis process transparent and easy to scrutinise, replicate, and share.

The common uses of audio analysis for empirical music research are to provide a solid description of the music used in empirical research. This might mean that the researcher has used many of the extracted properties of music to select the stimuli such as only music with a specific range of tempi or contrasting brightness levels. Or perhaps the experiment design allows the participants to choose their own favourite music tracks or their own sleep-inducing music selections, and in all of these cases, acoustic analysis is a valuable part of the experiment design or – in the latter two examples – the analysis process.

Being able to describe music through its sonic qualities opens the door to research involving the fundamental properties of music and their relation to experience and semantic contents. For example, a popular question, but a tough one to crack, is how to predict a hit song. We have access to the past 70 years of Western popular music varying in success across different metrics (chart positions, sales, streaming popularity), and we can extract numerous acoustic and musical descriptors out of these. One would assume that a linear regression or its variants would have revealed the key components of the hits already, but it seems that popularity is subject to many other indirect influences (e.g., fashion trends, videos, lyrics, social media discussions, the eminence of the artist to mention a few), and the acoustic or musical contents of the music are not the only possible source of explanation of popularity (Lee & Lee, 2018).

Coda

This chapter has outlined possibilities for the analysis of recordings, beginning with the basics of audio analysis. I outlined a simple division of acoustic descriptors into three abstraction levels (physical, perceptual, and semantic) over several domains (amplitude, frequency, cepstral, fluctuation, multi-feature) which helps to conceptualise the types of operations, representations, and features available. I also acknowledged that there is considerable overlap between levels and domains. For those who wish to get further into signal processing and computation of musical content from audio, I recommend Meinhart Müller's *Fundamentals of Music Processing* (2015) which is an excellent source that – together with online Python notebooks – helps to learn the nuts and bolts of many state-of-the-art musical content processing techniques.

Discussion Points

1. Usually, acoustic analysis can only be done if one has access to the audio files. This can be a practical limitation with respect to the size, availability, and legality of the recordings. What are the ways to analyse recordings that cannot be accessed and how relevant is this data accessibility for music research?
2. Sometimes audio analysis is divided into two approaches: engineering and perceptual. In the former, any descriptor or technique that allows us to tackle the question can be used in the analysis. In the latter, only the representations that either mimic the way listeners hear the signal or use descriptors that have well-established perceptual correlates and validity can be used to understand the audio (Friberg et al., 2014). How would you characterise the differences in results and models that these approaches bring?
3. Spotify and the semantic descriptors available to developers and the research community through it were used as a prominent analysis example. What are the main concerns when relying on this data? Are there ways to circumnavigate these concerns?

Notes

1 www.audiolabs-erlangen.de/fau/professor/mueller/bookFMP

2 https://librosa.org/doc/latest/auto_examples/plot_vocal_separation.html#vocal-sep
aration
3 https://github.com/MTG/saraga

Further Reading

Müller, M. (2015). *Fundamentals of music processing: Audio, analysis, algorithms, applications.* Springer.

References

Bogdanov, D., Wack, N., Gómez, E., Gulati, S., Herrera, P., Mayor, O., Roma, G., Salamon, J., Zapata, J., & Serra, X. (2013). Essentia: An open-source library for sound and music analysis. *Proceedings of the 21st ACM International Conference on Multimedia*, 855–858.

Brown, J. C. (1991). Calculation of a constant Q spectral transform. *The Journal of the Acoustical Society of America*, *89*(1), 425–434.

De Cheveigné, A., & Kawahara, H. (2002). YIN, a fundamental frequency estimator for speech and music. *The Journal of the Acoustical Society of America*, *111*(4), 1917–1930.

Eerola, T., Ferrer, R., & Alluri, V. (2012). Timbre and affect dimensions: Evidence from affect and similarity ratings and acoustic correlates of isolated instrument sounds. *Music Perception*, *30*(1), 49–70. https://doi.org/10.1525/mp.2012.30.1.49

Friberg, A., Schoonderwaldt, E., Hedblad, A., Fabiani, M., & Elowsson, A. (2014). Using listener-based perceptual features as intermediate representations in music information retrieval. *The Journal of the Acoustical Society of America*, *136*(4), 1951–1963.

Goodman, D. F., & Brette, R. (2009). The Brian simulator. *Frontiers in Neuroscience*, *15*, 26. https://doi.org/https://doi.org/10.3389/neuro.01.026.2009

Goodman, D. F., & Brette, R. (2010). Spike-timing-based computation in sound localization. *PloS Computational Biology*, *6*(11), e1000993.

Grey, J. M., & Gordon, J. W. (1978). Perceptual effects of spectral modifications on musical timbres. *The Journal of the Acoustical Society of America*, *65*(6), 149–150.

Heggli, O. A., Stupacher, J., & Vuust, P. (2021). Diurnal fluctuations in musical preference. *Royal Society Open Science*, *8*(11), 210885. https://doi.org/https://doi.org/10.1098/rsos.210885

Hornbostel, E. M. von, & Sachs, C. (1914). Classification of musical instruments. *Galpin Society Journal*, *14*, 3–29.

Hurwitz, E. R., & Krumhansl, C. L. (2021). Shifting listening niches: Effects of the COVID-19 pandemic. *Frontiers in Psychology*, *12*, 648413.

Koduri, G. K., Gulati, S., Rao, P., & Serra, X. (2012). Rāga recognition based on pitch distribution methods. *Journal of New Music Research*, *41*(4), 337–350. https://doi.org/10.1080/09298215.2012.735246

Lartillot, O., Toiviainen, P., & Eerola, T. (2008). A Matlab toolbox for music information retrieval. In C. Preisach, H. Burkhardt, L. Schmidt-Thieme, & R. Decker (Eds.), *Data analysis, machine learning and applications* (pp. 261–268). Springer.

Lee, J., & Lee, J. (2018). Music popularity: Metrics, characteristics, and audio-based prediction. *IEEE Transactions on Multimedia*, *20*(11), 3173–3182. https://doi.org/10.1109/TMM.2018.2820903

Mauch, M., & Dixon, S. (2014). PYIN: A fundamental frequency estimator using probabilistic threshold distributions. *2014 IEEE International Conference on Acoustics, Speech and Signal Processing (ICASSP)*, 659–663.

McFee, B., Raffel, C., Liang, D., Ellis, D. P., McVicar, M., Battenberg, E., & Nieto, O. (2015). Librosa: Audio and music signal analysis in python. *Proceedings of the 14th Python in Science Conference*, *8*, 18–25.

McVicar, M., Santos-Rodríguez, R., Ni, Y., & De Bie, T. (2014). Automatic chord estimation from audio: A review of the state of the art. *IEEE/ACM Transactions on Audio, Speech, and Language Processing*, *22*(2), 556–575.

Müller, M. (2015). *Fundamentals of music processing: Audio, analysis, algorithms, applications*. Springer.

Rafii, Z. (2022). The constant-Q harmonic coefficients: A timbre feature designed for music signals. *IEEE Signal Processing Magazine*, *39(3)*, 90–96.

Rafii, Z., & Pardo, B. (2012). Music/voice separation using the similarity matrix. *ISMIR*, 583–588.

Seashore, C. E. (1938). *Psychology of music*. McGraw-Hill.

Srinivasamurthy, A., Gulati, S., Caro Repetto, R., & Serra, X. (2021). Saraga: Open datasets for research on Indian art music. *Empirical Musicology Review*, *16*(1), 85–98.

Terhardt, E. (1979). Calculating virtual pitch. *Hearing Research*, *1*(2), 155–182.

Tzanetakis, G., & Cook, P. (2000). MARSYAS: A framework for audio analysis. *Organised Sound*, *4*(3), 169–175. https://doi.org/10.1017/S1355771800003071

11 Corpus Studies

Corpus is not a commonly used term in music research, but you might already have used a digital music corpus without paying attention to it. For example, the *International Music Score Library Project* (IMSLP[1]) is a corpus of scores, links, and metadata. *MusicBrainz*[2] is a rich music encyclopaedia that coordinates important recording information across different platforms. Maybe you have used *The Global Jukebox*[3] to listen to folk songs from around the world or have sung along to music from *Spotify* using the lyrics provided by *Musixmatch*. You may also have used some of the summaries provided by Spotify or another streaming service about your preferred genres and listening habits throughout the year. These are all digital music corpora, although those mentioned are less frequently used in academic research and not necessarily curated in the same way we expect academic researchers to build, maintain, and share corpora. In this section, we focus on corpora that are designed to be used in empirical research.

Computational music analysis can look at traditional music-theoretical questions by offering data-rich approaches and making statistical inferences about the likelihood of specific musical devices thought to play an important role in certain styles of music. In essence, corpus studies are a contemporary and data-driven way to conduct style analysis of music, which Leonard Meyer defined as a practice 'to describe the patternings replicated in some group of works, to discover and formulate the rules and strategies that are the basis for such patternings, and to explain in the light of these constraints how the characteristics described are related to one another' (Meyer, 1989, p. 38). Corpus studies can also attempt to discover elements and features of music that transcend styles and traditions. Claims such as that the exposition section in symphonies decreased in length in the early 19th century or that pop music has become louder or faster over time, can be tested if appropriate corpus and analytical tool sets are available. For instance, corpus studies have shown time and time again that small intervals tend to dominate most music cultures (Tierney et al., 2011) and tracing the evolution of popular music recordings shows a steady increase in loudness (compression of the signal) over the last 50 years, which transcends the popular genres (Mauch et al., 2015).

Questions about whether a composer/songwriter has plagiarised someone can also be tackled with a corpus study. A corpus study could allow the date of an

DOI: 10.4324/9781003293804-11

unknown work by comparing its musical 'signature' with other works of the same period or geographical area (Brinkman et al., 2016) or compare stylistic traits of known jazz improvisers (e.g., John Coltrane vs Miles Davis, Frieler, 2020). More psychologically oriented studies about how we perceive music might use corpus studies to define the regular properties of music that we are attuned to or use specific corpora to represent specific musical knowledge for a particular set of specialist listeners. Or a corpus study could be leveraged to questions motivated by applied uses of music, for example, classification of music according to genre, mood, or more refined properties (e.g., what kind of music has the potential to induce relaxation or sleep or exercising with more vigour). Corpus analysis can also expose and mitigate some of the biases that traditional music analysis often has in terms of selection of examples, representativeness of the corpus, and the actual way the analysis is carried out. For instance, analysis of the Western canon has long been focussed on male composers for historical reasons, and corpus studies offer an empirical way to explore the impact of this bias on inferences about musical properties. This assumes that we collectively build more balanced music corpora by focussing especially on women or other previously marginalised composers (or musical genres), and such work has begun in the last decade (Tan, 2021).

The idea of corpus studies is not new. Large-scale analyses of folk song collections were carried out at the end of 19th century Europe, and a computational approach to corpus studies began after World War II using punch-cards to classify British-American folk songs (e.g., Bronson, 1949). Since the 1990s the tools and the representations described in earlier sections have paved the way for corpus studies to become a well-defined strand for the empirical study of music.

Corpus Elements

A *corpus* is a digital collection of music that has been assembled with a general purpose in mind, and consists of real examples of music. *Datasets* are usually more specific, created to answer specific research questions where the context is much more restricted, and they might not contain actual examples of music but information about some aspects of it. However, the distinction is often blurred and a specific corpus may be used for a particular analysis. The actual representation of music can vary according to the origins and purposes of the corpus. Beyond the ones that I mentioned in the beginning of this section, there are significant research corpora of notated Western music, but also a growing number of non-Western corpora as well. A great deal of notated folk music is also available in one digital format or another. Generally, the range of musical materials encoded in corpora is growing and expanding steadily to cover not only more music outside the Western canon, and this expansion brings attention to the representations, features, and questions that are beyond the usual ones about motifs, harmonies, and structures, or about music composed by male composers from Central Europe between the 17th and 20th centuries.

In terms of the elements in the corpora, there is no single authoritative list of what should be included since the purposes and nature of the corpora are diverse, but any music corpus comes with three essential elements: (1) *music*, (2) *metadata*, and (3) *methods of access/documentation*. While we discussed the first element at length in the previous section, it is useful to present all three elements from the perspective of corpus studies.

Music Representations

Music can be represented digitally in different ways (scores, encoded events in the audio, audio, or images of scores). Copyright restrictions may prevent the actual audio or original score from being shared or being part of the corpus. In some of these cases, colleagues have provided solutions that bypass these restrictions, for instance, by not providing the audio but instead offering descriptors extracted from the audio (chromagrams, MFCCs, or other descriptors). These descriptors are useful for scholars exploring the acoustic and musical qualities of the corpus and building models out of the results, as the descriptors themselves are interpreted to be derivatives of the audio that are not subject to copyright. Score representations vary and can be anything from notation software solutions (*Sibelius, MuseScore*), to scanned images of the scores, to digital representations such as MusicXML that can be readily used by computational tools. Scores may also have copyright restrictions, depending on the edition, publisher, and age of the arrangement or score (Towse, 2017). It is also possible that a corpus has other related musical information which is not exactly the representation of music, such as texts (lyrics, writings, social media postings, reviews, newspaper articles, album cover texts, etc.) or real-world usage data (playlists, counts of plays, tallies of shared tracks, the amount of repertoire played in a historical context), but this information forms a vital part of the corpus. In essence, the choice of suitable representation truly depends on the type of research question; to study the pitch structures in music, musical scores provide adequate information, but scores fail to offer any meaningful information about timbre or expressive timing. Also, each representation and data format require different analytical techniques, as we have already discovered in the earlier chapters. In some cases, a corpus has several sources and representations of the data, which brings us to metadata and the importance of its function as an index for linking and describing data.

Metadata

The second element, metadata, is perhaps the most unique and valuable property of many corpora, as this element covers annotations and the crucial information about the exact types and classes that go into them. Sometimes the annotations represent hundreds of hours of manual work by experts (who have, for example, manually labelled each chord, verified the onset times and the instruments, or applied formal structural analysis to different sections of the work, etc.). Metadata also describes the internal structure of the data, how files are labelled, stored, and possibly linked to external sources, and how they are usable by external functions. As the corpora are getting more diverse in terms of what music they represent, but also which formats and standards are used and what type of information is available in the metadata. For instance, some corpora focus on melody (Baker, 2021; Brinkman & Huron, 2018), others on harmony (Albrecht & Huron, 2012; De Clercq & Temperley, 2011; Moss et al., 2019) or structure (Carnovalini et al., 2021; Moss et al., 2020). Another type of corpus provides information about the uses of music (play counts, shared playlists, Bertin-Mahieux et al., 2011), the onsets in the performances (Polak et al., 2016), or the vocabulary used in orchestration treatises (Wallmark, 2019). The requirements of metadata are different depending on the purposes and types of data. I will try to give concrete examples of this diversity in the following sections.

As we have already discussed the annotation issues at length in an earlier section (Chapter 9), let us move to the final and usually underappreciated element of corpora: methods of access and documentation.

Methods of Access and Documentation

Methods of access and the level of documentation offered are themes where the existing corpora show massive differences. At one extreme there are corpora where one needs to compile all the elements together by oneself by downloading various files from the project web pages (often migrated from one location to another) and figure out how the files are linked, labelled, and formatted. At the other extreme, there is a single Python package (e.g., mirdata) that gives you direct and uniform access to several dozen corpora (music files, metadata, documentation) for MIR research. Let's not focus on this diversity as such, but bring in a set of principles that facilitate the transparent research and data management process that goes under the acronym FAIR. The FAIR principles state that datasets/corpora should be *Findable*, *Accessible*, *Interoperable*, and *Reusable* (Wilkinson et al., 2016). These generic principles can, of course, be interpreted very strictly or loosely, but at their core the FAIR principles advocate transparency and openness at all levels. When it comes to implementing these principles for musical corpora, the central FAIR issues in music have recently been introduced and discussed in a special issue of *Empirical Musicology Review* (Moss & Neuwirth, 2021). To give an example, just uploading a corpus to a web page with no documentation may fulfil some of the principles, but the sheer amount of data carpentry and sleuthing work needed to make the corpus usable by others will deter its use and cause actual errors. Instead, depositing a corpus in a standard repository (*GitHub, Zenodo, GitLab*), using standardised, open, and non-proprietary formats (e.g., MusicXML, csv files) and documenting the structures of the data carefully and again using non-proprietary formats (e.g., RTF, pdf, or plain ascii text documents rather than Microsoft Word files, for instance), would be the minimal way to adhere to FAIR principles. Offering tools to access, analyse, link, and transform the data could be additional steps that will go further in adhering to the FAIR aspirations.

Many of the datasets and corpora released to the OSF do adhere to these principles, as the OSF advocates discovery, documentation, and, of course, accessibility of the materials. At this moment, the Python package called mirdata[4] is probably the most advanced handling of music corpus management, which offers simple steps to access the music, metadata, and annotations. Some of the corpora available within the mirdata protocol also contain success measures for assessing various musical properties (onsets, keys, etc.). These measures have been adapted from the standards developed in the MIR field.

The fact that FAIR principles advocate open access means that resources following these principles can reach scholars without access to well-equipped libraries, and this can be seen as a way of democratising scholarship.

Example Corpora

A great deal of Western classical music is available in a format that allows full scores to be used in computational analysis. The limited availability of non-Western music is far from ideal, but at least the situation is improving rapidly. There are excellent online link collections that keep updated lists of music corpora for computational musicology[5], music information retrieval research[6], and digital resources for musicology[7]. Let me highlight some corpora to convey the range and possibilities of the presently available corpora.

Table 11.1 lists sixteen corpora that are often used in empirical studies in some way or another. The range of music covered is broad, although the list is dominated by Western music (either classical, folk, or popular) but not exclusively so. The representation of music is typically as score or audio, although exceptions such as

Table 11.1 Examples of symbolic, event-based, and audio music corpora.

Name	Type	N	Description
RISM	S	>1M	Western classical music
KernScores	S	~100K	Western classical music
ABC sessions	S	~40K	Irish/Scottish folk music
JRP	S	340	Pieces by Josquin des Prez
ELVIS	S	~3K	Motets and masses
ABC	S	70 mov	Beethoven string quartets
Jazzomat	S	456	Performances of jazz
SALAMI	A*	2400+	Variety of Western genres
Million Song Dataset	A	1M	Contemporary Western popular music
McGill Billboard	A*	1.3K	US Billboard charts (Western popular music)
Cross-Era Classical	O	2K	Popular Western classical music
Da-TACOS	A*	15K	Western popular music cover songs
GTZAN	A*	1K	Ten Western music genres
Magnatagatune	A	~25K	Diverse range of Western popular music
RockCorpus	S	200	Western popular music
MAESTRO	E/A*	~1300	Piano performances of Western classical music
IEMP	E/A	~80	Performances from several cultures

A=Audio, S=Symbolic, E=Event-based information, O=Other (musical characteristic), and * indicates that the corpus is available within mirdata (see text). All datasets contain metadata and annotations.

event-based information or pre-calculated acoustic features are provided in some corpora. The size of the corpus often reflects the size of the population of that music. For example, the corpus called *JRP* contains pieces attributed to Josquin des Prez which are relatively small in number (N = 340), but this corpus contains most of the known population of repertoire. In contrast the corpus called *GTZAN* (Tzanetakis & Cook, 2002), which holds 1,000 recordings consisting of ten different Western genres, each represented with 100 examples, is a tiny fraction of the music recorded and published in these genres over the last 80 years. Moreover, this small sample is not particularly well balanced or specifically constructed to contain the most stereotypical examples of genres, unlike some later corpora related to genres (Bogdanov et al., 2019).

I will give more room to 5 of the 16 corpora from Table 11.1 to highlight the diversity of materials and representations for this approach.

RISM

For historical reasons, *RISM*, or as the full name goes, *Répertoire International des Sources Musicales*[8], deserves more than a mention as its scope and ambition has been unmatched in the history of music research. It was founded in 1952 in Paris with the aim of documenting all relevant sources of music across the world, probably meaning the Western world at the time. There are one million manuscripts documented in RISM after the year 1600 from Europe and more than 100,000 entries concerning printed music between the 16th and 19th centuries. The RISM website offers a search interface that can be used to find matches in the database covering parts of the RISM collection. The corpus is well documented and linked to various libraries and archives where the original manuscripts are held, although the full scores are not usually digitally available.

KernScores

An excellent collection of Western classical scores for corpus analyses is *KernScores*. KernScores comes with several score formats and contains more than 100,000 works in total. There are interesting subsets in the collection, such as a large number (10,000+) of monophonic songs that contain previously released datasets, such as the *Essen folk song collection* (8,000+ folksongs) by Schaffrath & Huron (1995), *Native American songs* (370, Densmore (1913)), and *Chinese songs*. All scores are well documented with information about the encoder, location, date, and many other details. Kernscores also comes with precalculated musical descriptors and harmonic analyses (Sapp, 2005). Scores can also be easily analysed with tools such as *music21* covered in an earlier section (Chapter 9) as they can be easily read from their online repository. Kernscores is also linked to a web service that allows one to find themes using various search options (see Themefinder[9]). A subset of KernScores has been used in many empirical studies as a reference set.

ABC – The Annotated Beethoven Corpus

ABC – The Annotated Beethoven Corpus is a detailed and rich corpus containing expert harmonic analyses for all Beethoven string quartets. Expert analysis indicates the key, scale degree, chord form, figured bass, pedals, and suspensions for each beat or half bar in each of the 70 movements of Beethoven's central repertoire (the string quartets). All this is offered in an accessible format at GitHub[10] with well-defined standards for labelling all chord properties. The very act of labelling chords is not a trivial task, and this corpus comes with detailed information about the decision-making behind the annotation and expertise wielded toward the task, and the whole process has been separately documented and described (Neuwirth et al., 2018). The size of this corpus may be characterised as small when we compare it to some other corpora described in this section, but in terms of giving us a detailed harmonic analysis of Western tonal music, it is, of course, substantial.

Million Song Dataset

The *Million Song Dataset* (MSD*)* is a compendium of data for one million contemporary popular music tracks that contains songs by over 44,000 unique artists (Bertin-Mahieux et al., 2011). The MSD corpus comes with rich metadata about each track (tags, genres, locations, artist names). Most interestingly, MSD comes with a snapshot of usage data from one million users that contains fascinating information about actual music consumption, and the sheer volume of this information makes this corpus particularly valuable. For example, there are almost 50 million play counts in the corpus that can be used to estimate popularity and liking of each track. Moreover, MSD comes with a representation of lyrics for a quarter of a million tracks. I say representation of lyrics as the full lyrics are not offered in the original format for copyright reasons, but are available as a 'bag of words', which is a sort of compacted collection of the most frequent and salient words with the redundant words omitted (not far from the popular word clouds). The corpus does not offer the original audio, as this would breach copyright laws, but pre-calculated audio features are offered instead. There have been other additions (such as cover songs) to the MSD corpus after it is initial release, and to underscore its profound impact on MIR, this corpus has already been cited more than 750 times since its release.

IEMP Corpus

Not every corpus needs to be massive or consist of Western music. Multiple non-Western corpora have been released over the last ten years, ranging from *Turkish makam music* that comes with over 6,000 audio recordings and over 2,000 scores (Uyar et al., 2014) to a corpus of Carnatic music with nearly 2,000 recordings[11]. Here, I want to highlight a corpus that captures multiple performances of small ensembles in several cultures, namely the *Interpersonal Entrainment in Music Performance* (IEMP). This corpus, published by Clayton et al. (2021), offers examples of musical performances that emphasise improvisation and learning music without scores. The IEMP corpus also contains multiple representations (video, audio, annotation of onsets and musical structures) and spans multiple cultures (jembe performances from Mali, Hindustani duo and trio performances from North India, candombe salsa and son ensemble performances from Uruguay, stambeli performances from Tunisia, and jazz performances from the UK), all in uniform formats and documentations, available from the Open Science Framework https://osf.io/sfxa2/. So far, the corpus has been used to demonstrate the boundaries of entrainment (synchronisation accuracy and its relation to structures of music, as well as ensemble type, culture, and other factors) across cultures (Clayton et al., 2020).

Corpus Studies Workflow

When empirical music research takes the corpus study approach, there can be various workflows that tackle the question at hand. Here, I have summarised a typical workflow, where attention is directed to (1) definition and sampling, (2) encoding and annotation, (3) cross-validation, (4) analysis and summary, and (5) interpretation. Figure 11.1 illustrates how separate parts of this workflow are connected, and here I am placing a special emphasis on aspects that I have not previously mentioned (sampling and cross-validation). Let me next expand on these new elements.

Starting with the definition of the corpus and sampling, I want to emphasise that a corpus does not usually contain all existing musical works of a given musical style. Most of the corpora are samples of musical genres, not exhaustive accounts of the population of works or performances. This bears similarity to the sampling topic covered earlier (Chapter 5) where we acknowledged that the actual population is only characterised through samples. The question arises as to whether the sample locked into the corpus offers a balanced representation of the genre that it claims to represent or if the sample is perhaps biased in some fashion. Are the works/participants chosen truly randomly or has the selection been driven by some other guiding principle? Does that principle allow sampling the potential population evenly – remember stratified or random sampling in Chapter 5 – or is the principle creating a bias, as in convenience sampling, also mentioned in Chapter 5?

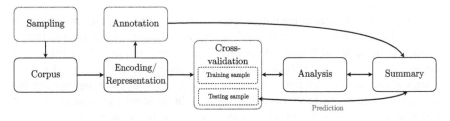

Figure 11.1 Corpus analysis workflow.

This is an important consideration, as any inference from the analysis of the corpus may be used to make general statements about the music in question and a biased sampling threatens the validity of these statements. If it turns out that only the most affluent composers were represented in the corpus because their scores were copied to multiple locations or that performers representing a specific ethnicity were over-represented compared to the distribution of ethnicities in the underlying population, the interpretations will reflect the biased sampling principles rather than the population. This sounds clear and logical, but the situations that we come across may be ambiguous; it may be that the reasons behind the selection of works or performances for a corpus are opaque, not known, or not well-articulated, as is the case in many folk song collections. This has also been a common problem in corpora representing the Western music canon, and decolonisation efforts have paid critical attention to this issue (Holzapfel et al., 2018; Tan, 2021). Once the representativeness – or at least some reasonable basis for a balanced sampling – is established, or at least the shortcomings of the existing sampling are acknowledged, the corpus can be considered defined.

Before heading on to analysis, especially if the purpose is to build a model that has predictive ability, it is a good idea to consider splitting the data into *training* and *testing* samples. This means that only part of the corpus is being used in building the models (training set) and the remainder of the corpus is stored only for evaluation purposes of the model (testing set). The purpose of this operation, called *cross-validation*, is to keep some of the data unexposed to models so that the test set can be used to test how good the models are by having them predict new data to which the model has never been exposed. This makes the models more realistic and more likely to provide sensible estimates outside the context of the data, and in technical terms, this is done to avoid overfitting. The split into training and testing sets can be done in various ways. A common strategy is to randomly allocate 80% of the pieces in the corpus to the training set and keep the rest (20%) of the pieces in the testing set. There are more advanced cross-validation schemes where the subsets are allocated repeatedly by switching the subsets systematically (called *k-fold cross-validation*), and one can also construct a cross-validation process based on other variations of splitting the data (e.g., *leave-one-out cross-validation* or splitting the sample into two halves, etc.). We will look at an example analysis of a small corpus that we already visited in the data analysis section (Relationships Between Continuous Variables), but this time we will add cross-validation to our prediction of annotated energy ratings using acoustic features from a small film soundtrack corpus.

In the final two parts of the corpus analysis process, the analysis and summary process depend on the type of research question, although we can usually divide these into three broad themes: descriptive summaries, inferential statistics, and advanced or exploratory statistics. In the first analysis, the analyst provides summaries of the data divided into meaningful units of analysis, often highlighting the correlations and internal patterns within the data. In the second process, the analyst provides an answer to the previously defined research question using statistical inference (t-test, correlation, regression, etc.). In this process, the need might arise for creating predictive models that will capture the parameters of the phenomena under investigation in a way that can be used to predict cases encountered in the future. This also means that such aims will benefit if a cross-validation is used in the analysis process, as it guards against overfitting the models to the specific idiosyncrasies of the sample.

In more concrete terms, if the aim is to explore synchronisation accuracy in actual music performances, a model that is aware of the underlying tempo, the type of instrument, and the genre of music can give a plausible range of synchrony in milliseconds that operates as a good benchmark and prediction for other studies. Or if the task is to understand how tags describing music are linked to audio features, the result of the analysis can be offered to other researchers as an 'autotagger' that is capable of populating probable tags to any audio it encounters (Bertin-Mahieux et al., 2008).

More advanced analyses or explorative analyses might go beyond descriptions and inferential testing by extracting underlying hidden organisation in the data. For instance, Fabian Moss and Martin Rohrmeier analysed the use of pitches in notated Western music over 600 years (Moss & Rohrmeier, 2021). They borrowed techniques from textual analysis, namely computational 'topic models' that can capture the essential 'topics' of pitches. In this case, these topics brought out the keys associated across lines-of-fifths and different degrees of chromaticism. The prevalence of these topics was also observed to vary as a function of time in a way that makes sense in the history of music and music theory such as increased chromaticism in the 18th and 19th centuries.

Corpus Analysis Examples

Case Example #1: Genres Classification Using Acoustic Descriptors

Let us explore the pioneering genre classification research by George Tzanetakis and Perry Cook (2002). They took 100 examples from ten different mainstream music genres of the time (classical, country, disco, hip hop, jazz, rock, blues, reggae, pop, and metal). Note that the selection of excerpts for this dataset was not particularly rigorous or representative, but it was what George Tzanetakis had at his disposal at the time. For this reason, the dataset has some quirks and imperfections, but I think it is still a fun and illustrative dataset to explore.

In the first step, we load the data (audio and metadata) using the mirdata Python package (Bittner et al., 2019). To keep this fast and simple, I will take a 10% sample of the dataset (100 excerpts from the 1,000). The actual Python mirdata library contains over 40 different MIR datasets that can be accessed with simple commands, and this makes it an ideal candidate for learning how classic studies operate.

In the second step, we extract the acoustic descriptors of these examples. These include descriptors related to loudness (RMS), tempo (BPM), timbre (spectral centroid, spectral bandwidth), and the ten first MFCCs using the audio analysis library Librosa in Python. In this process, we extract the features by calculating the mean values of each feature in the 30-second excerpt. There are other ways to sum-marise the features (e.g., median, or a trimmed mean where we have eliminated outliers by extreme quantiles before calculating the mean). Just to give you an idea

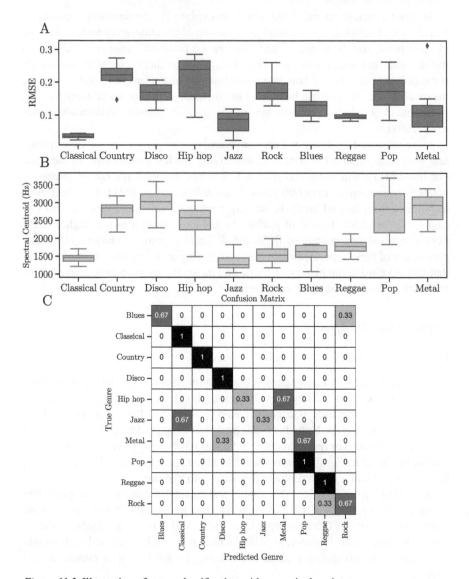

Figure 11.2 Illustration of genre classification with acoustic descriptors.

Panel A and B: Distribution of RMS and Spectral centroid values across ten genres in all excerpts. Panel C: Confusion matrix of the random forest classification model showing the proportion of cases predicted in the actual and predicted genres.

of how the extracted features will differ between the ten excerpts and ten genres, the upper panel of Figure 11.2 shows the distribution of two acoustic descriptors between genres.

In the third step, we run a simple hierarchical classification tree called a random forest. This technique creates a number of decision nodes based on the classification performance (i.e., how well the ten genres separate) by using a subset of the features and repeating this process many times over. It is a robust technique and does not really require the distributions to be normally distributed. Before we run this classification model, we want to normalise the features. We also want to cross-validate the model, which means that we split the data into training and testing sets. We first train the model on the training set, which here is a randomly selected 70% of the data. Once we have trained the model, we test it against the unseen data (the test set, 30% of the data) to assess how the model performs. Note that when we randomly split the data into training and testing sets, we might want to *stratify* the data according to genre, which makes sure that we have a similar proportion of excerpts from each genre within both sets. The results of this classification model indicate that it can correctly predict 70% of genres in the unseen data (the training set), which is a good predictive rate considering that 10% would be the chance level, and the original study achieved about 60% accuracy with 30 descriptors. Note that the accuracy varies across genres, and for several genres the model predicts all examples with 100% accuracy whereas some genres are consistently misclassified; jazz is misclassified as classical in 67% of the cases, and blues as rock 33% of the time. These errors can be easily seen in the *confusion matrix*, shown in the bottom panel of Figure 11.2.

Finally, as a fourth step, we can identify which acoustic descriptors are most important in this genre classification mode. For this classification technique, the process of building these classification trees keeps track of the degree to which the predictors increase the model. In this case, the top three acoustic descriptors are MFCC8, RMS, and spectral centroid. This is not such a surprise, as we saw from visualisation of the descriptor values across genres that dynamics and timbre seemed to separate many of the genres from each other. In fact, if we rebuild a classification model with just these three acoustic descriptors, the classification rate decreases from 70% to 63.3%. In other words, discarding 14 descriptors reduces the accuracy of the model by only 7%. For interpretability, this simpler model is much better. The *principle of parsimony* suggests that a classification model with just three descriptors can be characterised as a simple, yet effective model. There are formal measures to rigorously evaluate the trade-off between the simplicity and accuracy. By the way, this genre classification analysis can be run with the full dataset (1,000 excerpts) as easily as with the 10% sample, and the results will be similar. See the Python code in Chapter11.1.

Although this example focuses on audio and music genres, the task of classifying music based on descriptors is a general one; one could classify Renaissance composers based on descriptors derived from score analysis of harmony, melody, and rhythm (Cuenca-Rodríguez & McKay, 2021), or identify similarities in folk songs from across the globe (Savage et al., 2015), or even what the consistently used timbral descriptors in orchestration treatises are (Wallmark, 2019).

Case Example #2: Synchrony in Cuban Son and Salsa Performances

As a second corpus analysis example, let us complete the story of onset asynchronies we started in the earlier section (Chapter 9) when we compared how tightly synchronised each of the different instruments in a recorded Cuban son performance are (song titled *Palo Santo* shown in Figure 10.2). With the onsetsync library we can access a small corpus of son and salsa performances (namely five performances with a total of 26,867 onsets across seven to nine instruments). In the previous analysis, we observed how the bass was consistently (17.2 ms) ahead of the guitar but synchronous with the tres (3.7 ms). Were these patterns just specific to this song (*Palo Alto*) or a more generic trend related to the timing between guitars and bass in the salsa and son pieces in this repertoire? Well, the repertoire is not large, but we can compare these two instrument pairings across five available performances with a few lines of code. See the R code in Chapter11.2 at https://tuomaseerola.github.io/emr/

```
# Code 11.1
library(onsetsync)           # to handle onsets
library(dplyr)               # to handle summaries
corpus <- onsetsync::CSS_IEMP   # Cuban Salsa & Son
D <- sync_sample_paired(corpus,'Bass','Guitar',0,1,'SD')
RES <-summarise(group_by(D$asynch,name),M=mean(asynch*1000))
D2 <- sync_sample_paired(corpus,'Bass','Tres',0,1,'SD')
RES2 <- summarise(group_by(D2$asynch,name),M=mean(asynch*1000))
names(RES)[2] <- 'Bass_Guitar'   # rename for clarity
RES$Bass_Tres <- RES2$M          # rename also
print(RES)

## # A tibble: 5 × 3
##    name           Bass_Guitar Bass_Tres
##    <chr>              <dbl>      <dbl>
## 1 El Cantante        -5.24      14.6
## 2 Habanera          -11.3        6.60
## 3 Palo Santo        -16.1       -3.54
## 4 Tumbao Sangreao   -12.0        5.24
## 5 Yo Naci En  Un Sola -7.10     -4.36
```

In this example (see the output of Code 11.1) we can see the previously observed pattern (see Figure 10.2) where the bass plays approximately 16 ms ahead of the guitar. This offset is similar in other performances (from 5 to 12 ms). The synchrony between tres and bass is more varied as the tres onsets are behind the bass in three performances although the asynchronies are small (< 7 ms) in most of the performances. We cannot describe the synchrony between the bass and guitars simply as highly synchronous, since the two guitars are aligned to the bass differently. Perhaps the next logical step would be to explore the asynchronies across the beats in the cycle to discover a more nuanced pattern of varied synchronies and to relate the observed differences to the differentiated roles the two guitars have in this music (Poole, 2021).

Summary

It has never been easier to design and carry out corpus studies than now. There is a wealth of existing music corpora to draw materials from, and a great set of freely available open-source tools exist for executing the analysis operations. Reporting the results of a corpus study is no longer a rarity; published studies involving datasets in musicology are becoming increasingly common (e.g., Cottrell, 2018). This also means that the research community and journals know what to expect in the reports of such studies, and there is an expectation that the materials are available as well. The beauty of corpus analysis is that it benefits from the same transparency as computational analysis, but it can pose questions that involve hundreds or thousands of examples. Modern online notebooks and open repositories have made these aspects of corpus analysis particularly appealing, as it is not just confined to a few experts who have their own in-house datasets. Corpus studies can articulate answers to questions about the whole collection of music or any subset within the collection, and in doing so corpus studies can also be used to explore the issues of bias or representativeness that may be the shortcoming of many corpora. For instance, one can compare the impact of leaving out or including a particular geographic region encoded in scores (e.g., as the place where a folk tune was collected), or one could compare whether there is an appropriate balance between the genders of the songwriters or composers in the corpus compared to the known prevalence of these proportions.

This brief overview of the existing corpora suggests that more work is needed in corpus studies to offer a more diverse range of cultures, genres, and ensembles, especially those that go beyond Western classical and popular music. There is also a need to establish the links between different music representations, scores, audio, and event-based information (MIDI or motion capture) that capture the performances. In some rare cases such as the MAESTRO corpus, we have access to all three (performances as audio, as MIDI, and also links to the scores), and in other cases the notation is not relevant, but having a wide range of metadata to allow different questions to be explored with a corpus such as the Million Song Dataset (MSD) will grow in terms of the value it offers for scholars turning to corpus studies.

Corpus analysis in the symbolic domain has not established standard ways to encode and annotate corpora and implement analyses, and some colleagues have expressed their concerns (Neuwirth et al., 2018; Oramas et al., 2018) that this lack of coherence has impeded the development of corpus studies in general. However, it is very difficult to come up with an encoding scheme that would be optimal for all the possible cases that would be needed to capture the example corpora presented in this section. For this reason, perhaps the realistic solution is to adhere to the FAIR principles and migrate towards common solutions such as *MusicXML* and *music21* for the storage and analysis of scores. It takes a lot more than an agreement on standards and formats to establish firm solutions in a developing sub-discipline, and if such solutions are to be promoted, training and the publication processes are likely to be the key elements in getting them accepted and consistently supported.

For music research in general, a carefully curated music corpus can be a contemporary version of a critical edition of a composer's repertoire. Corpora can take the place of critical editions and become respected sources of authoritative information that are used by numerous scholars. The main difference to the critical editions of the past is that the information is likely to be more dynamic, containing the metadata and example scripts to load, filter and analyse the pieces in the corpus. As I mentioned earlier, some of the corpora such as Million Song Dataset highlighted above have already become widely used norms, and new ones are likely to be generated with opportunities for real uses in real situations.

Coda

This chapter has introduced music corpus studies and covered the main elements of the corpus, such as representations, metadata, and methods of access. An emphasis was placed on transparent principles covering corpus data management. A diverse range of example corpora was presented spanning traditional databases of Western music with score representations (e.g., RISM, KernScores, the Annotated Beethoven Corpus) and popular music relying on audio (Million Song Dataset) to multicultural datasets of small ensemble performances (e.g., the IEMP corpus). The corpus study workflow was introduced where the emphasis is placed on definition and sampling, encoding and annotation, cross-validation, analysis, and interpretation.

Discussion Points

1. A significant proportion of the corpora introduced in the chapter represented Western art or popular music. Is this well matched to the current academic interests of contemporary research communities?
2. If you have studied music history in any part of your education, were corpus studies ever used to promote an argument or line of thinking in music history? What kinds of uses do corpus studies lend themselves to for teaching?
3. A music corpus could be considered as a contemporary version of a critical edition of music that represents a genre, a composer, or a period of time. What does this analogy miss and what aspects of critical editions cannot easily be incorporated into a corpus?

Notes

1 https://imslp.org/
2 https://wiki.musicbrainz.org/Main_Page
3 https://theglobaljukebox.org
4 https://mirdata.readthedocs.io/
5 https://fourscoreandmore.org/musoRepo/
6 https://github.com/ismir/mir-datasets/
7 https://wiki.ccarh.org/wiki/Digital_Resources_for_Musicology
8 https://opac.rism.info/
9 www.themefinder.org
10 https://github.com/DCMLab/ABC
11 https://compmusic.upf.edu/datasets

Further Reading

Shanahan, D., Burgoyne, J. A., & Quinn, I. (2023). *The Oxford handbook of music and corpus studies*. Oxford University Press.

References

Albrecht, J. D., & Huron, D. (2012). A statistical approach to tracing the historical development of major and minor pitch distributions, 1400–1750. *Music Perception: An Interdisciplinary Journal*, *31*(3), 223–243.

Baker, D. J. (2021). MeloSol corpus. *Empirical Musicology Review*, *16*(1), 106–113. https://doi.org/10.18061/emr.v16i1.7645

Bertin-Mahieux, T., Eck, D., Maillet, F., & Lamere, P. (2008). Autotagger: A model for predicting social tags from acoustic features on large music databases. *Journal of New Music Research*, *37*(2), 115–135.

Bertin-Mahieux, T., Ellis, D. P. W., Whitman, B., & Lamere, P. (2011). The million song dataset. *Proceedings of the 12th International Conference on Music Information Retrieval (ISMIR 2011)*.

Bittner, R. M., Fuentes, M., Rubinstein, D., Jansson, A., Choi, K., & Kell, T. (2019). Mirdata: Software for reproducible usage of datasets. *20th International Society for Music Information Retrieval Conference*, Delft, The Netherlands.

Bogdanov, D., Porter, A., Schreiber, H., Urbano, J., & Oramas, S. (2019). The AcousticBrainz genre dataset: Multi-source, multi-level, multi-label, and large-scale. *20th International Society for Music Information Retrieval Conference (ISMIR 2019)*.

Brinkman, A., & Huron, D. (2018). The leading sixth scale degree: A test of day-O'Connell's theory. *Journal of New Music Research*, *47*(2), 166–175.

Brinkman, A., Shanahan, D., & Sapp, C. (2016). Musical stylometry, machine learning and attribution studies: A semi-supervised approach to the works of Josquin. *Proceedings of the Biennial International Conference on Music Perception and Cognition*, 91–97.

Bronson, B. H. (1949). Mechanical help in the study of folk song. *The Journal of American Folklore*, *62*(244), 81–86.

Carnovalini, F., Rodà, A., Harley, N., Homer, S. T., & Wiggins, G. A. (2021). A new corpus for computational music research and a novel method for musical structure analysis. *Audio mostly 2021* (pp. 264–267). Association for Computing Machinery. https://doi.org/https://doi.org/10.1145/3478384.3478402

Clayton, M., Jakubowski, K., Eerola, T., Keller, P. E., Camurri, A., Volpe, G., & Alborno, P. (2020). Interpersonal entrainment in music performance: Theory, method, and model. *Music Perception: An Interdisciplinary Journal*, *38(2)*, 136–194.

Clayton, M., Tarsitani, S., Jankowsky, R., Jure, L., Leante, L., Polak, R., Poole, A., Rocamora, M., Alborno, P., Camurri, A., Eerola, T., Jacoby, N., & Jakubowski, K. (2021). The interpersonal entrainment in music performance data collection. *Empirical Musicology Review*, *16*(1), 65–84. https://doi.org/http://dx.doi.org/10.18061/emr.v16i1.7555

Cottrell, S. (2018). Big music data, musicology, and the study of recorded music: Three case studies. *The Musical Quarterly*, *101*(2–3), 216–243.

Cuenca-Rodríguez, M. E., & McKay, C. (2021). Exploring musical style in the anonymous and doubtfully attributed mass movements of the Coímbra manuscripts: A statistical and machine learning approach. *Journal of New Music Research*, *50*(3), 199–219.

De Clercq, T., & Temperley, D. (2011). A corpus analysis of rock harmony. *Popular Music*, *30*(1), 47–70.

Densmore, F. (1913). *Chippewa music*. US Government Printing Office.

Frieler, K. (2020). Miles vs. Trane: Computational and statistical comparison of the improvisatory styles of Miles Davis and John Coltrane. *Jazz Perspectives*, *12*(1), 123–145.

Holzapfel, A., Sturm, B., & Coeckelbergh, M. (2018). Ethical dimensions of music information retrieval technology. *Transactions of the International Society for Music Information Retrieval*, *1*(1), 44–55.

Mauch, M., MacCallum, R. M., Levy, M., & Leroi, A. M. (2015). The evolution of popular music: USA 1960–2010. *Royal Society Open Science*, *2*(5), 150081.

Meyer, L. B. (1989). *Style and music: Theory, history, and ideology. University of Chicago Press*.

Moss, F. C., & Neuwirth, M. (2021). FAIR, open, linked: Introducing the special issue on open science in musicology. *Empirical Musicology Review*, *16*(1), 1–4. https://doi.org/https://doi.org/10.18061/emr.v16i1.8246

Moss, F. C., Neuwirth, M., Harasim, D., & Rohrmeier, M. (2019). Statistical characteristics of tonal harmony: A corpus study of Beethoven's string quartets. *PloS ONE*, *14*(6), e0217242.

Moss, F. C., & Rohrmeier, M. (2021). Discovering tonal profiles with latent Dirichlet allocation. *Music & Science*, *4*. https://doi.org/10.1177/20592043211048827

Moss, F. C., Souza, W. F., & Rohrmeier, M. (2020). Harmony and form in Brazilian choro: A corpus-driven approach to musical style analysis. *Journal of New Music Research*, *49*(5), 416–437.

Neuwirth, M., Harasim, D., Moss, F. C., & Rohrmeier, M. (2018). The Annotated Beethoven Corpus (ABC): A dataset of harmonic analyses of all Beethoven string quartets. *Frontiers in Digital Humanities*, *5*. https://doi.org/https://doi.org/10.3389/fdigh.2018.00016

Oramas, S., Espinosa-Anke, L., Gómez, F., & Serra, X. (2018). Natural language processing for music knowledge discovery. *Journal of New Music Research*, *47*(4), 365–382. https://doi.org/10.1080/09298215.2018.1488878

Polak, R., London, J., & Jacoby, N. (2016). Both isochronous and non-isochronous metrical subdivision afford precise and stable ensemble entrainment: A corpus study of Malian jembe drumming. *Frontiers in Neuroscience*, *10*, 285.

Poole, A. (2021). Groove in Cuban son and salsa performance. *Journal of the Royal Musical Association*, *146*(1), 117–145.

Sapp, C. S. (2005). Online database of scores in the Humdrum file format. *ISMIR*, 664–665.

Savage, P. E., Brown, S., Sakai, E., & Currie, T. E. (2015). Statistical universals reveal the structures and functions of human music. *Proceedings of the National Academy of Sciences, 112*(29), 8987–8992.

Schaffrath, H., & Huron, D. (1995). *The Essen folksong collection in the humdrum kern format.* Center for Computer Assisted Research in the Humanities.

Tan, S. E. (2021). Decolonising music and music studies. *Ethnomusicology Forum, 30*(1), 4–8.

Tierney, A. T., Russo, F. A., & Patel, A. D. (2011). The motor origins of human and avian song structure. *Proceedings of the National Academy of Sciences, 108*(37), 15510–15515.

Towse, R. (2017). Economics of music publishing: Copyright and the market. *Journal of Cultural Economics, 41*(4), 403–420. https://doi.org/10.1007/s10824-016-9268-7

Tzanetakis, G., & Cook, P. (2002). Musical genre classification of audio signals. *IEEE Transactions on Speech and Audio Processing, 10*(5), 293–302.

Uyar, B., Atli, H. S., Şentürk, S., Bozkurt, B., & Serra, X. (2014). A corpus for computational research of Turkish makam music. *Proceedings of the 1st International Workshop on Digital Libraries for Musicology,* 1–7. https://doi.org/https://doi.org/10.1145/2660 168.2660174

Wallmark, Z. (2019). A corpus analysis of timbre semantics in orchestration treatises. *Psychology of Music, 47*(4), 585–605.

Wilkinson, M. D., Dumontier, M., Aalbersberg, IJ. J., Appleton, G., Axton, M., Baak, A., Blomberg, N., Boiten, J.-W., Silva Santos, L. B. da, Bourne, P. E., et al. (2016). The FAIR guiding principles for scientific data management and stewardship. *Scientific Data, 3*(1), 1–9.

12 Reflections, Challenges, and Future Prospects

This final chapter draws together the main tenets of empirical music research and presents a view of the topics where such an approach is particularly fruitful but not often utilised. The chapter will first cover what kind of research and methods should be improved if empirical research aspires to carry a broader role in music research. Next, the focus is moved onto the barriers to and enablers of empirical music research. The final section briefly presents music information retrieval and music and well-being applications and ponders whether the empirical research approach could also be turned towards other big societal questions such as climate change.

Focus on Musical Processes

One of the central aims of this book has been to provide an entry into the empirical research processes that are explained and demonstrated in the context of music research. The range that I have covered has been broad, from research designs to sampling to analysis and inferences, but also more specific examples and demonstrations concerning analysis of music in its many forms. By now, I hope that the reader is convinced that there is an abundance of options available for approaches that either analyse music or seek to understand musical behaviours or processes. All of these approaches have the potential to be conducted transparently and in a manner that allows others to replicate them. I also hope that I have managed to convey the excellent availability of empirical data that can be used to explore musical behaviours, musical thinking, or traces of these in the music itself. I have emphasised the role of formalised models in implementing and testing the claims put forward and this is probably the most advanced part of empirical music research that completes the full research loop from theory, hypothesis, design, observations, analysis, interpretation, and revision of the theory in the form of a model.

Although empirical music research addresses musical structure or musical behaviours, it is worth bearing in mind that when we focus on music, these are the 'traces of music' that ultimately reside in people's minds, as tacit knowledge. Most operations that empirical music research designs explore use traces to infer

DOI: 10.4324/9781003293804-12

something informative about how we process, conceptualise, and embody music. This knowledge is embedded not only in the architecture of the human body but also in culture and traditions involving music. It is useful to consider these aspects as separate entities, at least to avoid the assumption that once we figure out how something appears on the score, in audio, as movement related to music, or as a physiological signal triggered by a change in music, we have understood something about music. In fact, we have gained some little insight into how our participants process the complex cocktail of biological, cognitive, and cultural elements of music, and the task of music cognition research is to determine the boundaries and main sources of these processes. Empirical research is at the core of these efforts.

A vital part of the empirical research process is the way research questions are posed using research designs that allow us to pinpoint the key aspects of music or behaviours directly, often involving experiments where one can manipulate the potential levers of these behaviours. The other part of the process is to be able to obtain information about music and behaviour in a way that is replicable, robust, and relevant to the research question at hand. This means asking questions that have concrete, operationalised concepts, assumptions of what musical reality is like, and which can be addressed with concrete operations. Sometimes this means tackling the question with measures combining behaviours and physiology, but in other cases, turning to self-reports provides the best information available. In all cases, the results of these research designs are assessed with known methods that often take the form of inferential statistics. Empirical research about musical behaviours often requires information about music or musical processes that warrant the use of computational tools. I have tried to demonstrate in the section about music analysis (sections titled Analysis of Audio and Analysis of Scores) that there are plenty of existing tools that do not require a great deal of specialist expertise to get a handle on musical qualities, whether this is done by annotations or by extracting quantities from musical scores, events, audio, or movements related to music. These tools should not be available to only a few specialists that have the programming background and the luxury of having been exposed to the tools, although the development of the tools and applying them to new questions and materials might require such competences. In my view, solid work in empirical music research can be done with modest technical competence by relying on existing tools and the basic functions that they provide. Developing the specialist competences involving computational analysis does allow oneself to be engaged in exciting new possibilities for music research.

One of the core elements of empirical research in music is that computational models built on any data can be used to predict future cases, i.e., what happens in observations that are not part of the dataset. In this way, the models go beyond descriptive research and allow for the testing of clearly formulated predictions. This is a distinction from music theory, which is largely descriptive, but of course useful and compatible with the way music historians and performers may describe and label formal aspects of music (Wiggins et al., 2010). Conversely, empirical research that acknowledges the many manifestations of music (as something that occurs in the minds of people, as sonic events, as performances, as movements and affordances, as personally meaningful events, as historical objects) can strive towards understanding how these labels are created by being able to make predictions to a sufficient degree. This could be a tall order for some questions, but even aspiring to tackle such questions in an open and transparent way will create dialogue between the traditional approach and the empirical one, which is vital.

Some aspects of empirical music research may be disruptive for specific established findings within various disciplines in music; what if empirical studies show that the sonata form is not really that accurate a representation of how we as listeners parse the structure? Are we then going to suggest to music theorists and analysts that their descriptive focus could be realigned with another annotation task? Or if empirical performance research demonstrates that seeing the musicians adds significantly to the enjoyment of music and moving with the music is another boost to decoding expression in music, are we going to continue to advocate research that looks at the full spectrum of these behaviours in concerts, dances, and other events?

In some cases, empirical research of music can consolidate and support existing findings and theories in musicology, music history, or music analysis. The challenge is to formulate and operationalise the theories in such a way that they are testable and to find suitable materials and design to put the theory under empirical scrutiny. One of the success stories of this kind is on tension in music by Lerdahl (2001), which has been explored empirically (Lerdahl & Krumhansl, 2007), resulting in various simplifications to the model and overall maintaining strong support for the theory.

These are the broad aspirations for empirical research on music. I will next turn my attention to the ways in which these aspirations may be achieved.

Increase Diversity

Empirical music research does not have to embrace Western concepts or materials or representations of music, although now the majority of research utilises all of these. A global perspective on music sets this default mindset of Western musical systems and values in a position where it should no longer be the default starting point and diversity in cultures, genres, and the types of musical process should be actively sought. Empirical music research is particularly well suited to tackling many of the generic processes in music that are not dependent on specifics of Western culture despite the long history of following this narrow pathway. Robust findings about human cognition of music should tolerate and incorporate the diversity of behaviours and responses across cultures, countries, groups of people, and levels of expertise into understanding these processes. The diversity itself will help us to realise which aspects of musical processes are subject to high levels of learning and culture and which are less so. Broadening the cultural scope of research is nevertheless a challenging task, as every aspect (e.g., literature, models, training, values) of past research is permeated with Western concepts, musical traditions, behaviours, and findings obtained with a culturally and socially narrow pool of

WEIRD (Western, Educated, Industrialised, Rich, and Democratic) participants. Expanding our scope beyond the West will require years of concentrated efforts in working through the theories and established findings that need to be expanded and reassessed with a broader set of samples. Undoubtedly, this line of work will also discover topics and issues that have not been addressed at all and will relegate some of the past topics as specific obsessions of the Western classical music tradition.

Another way of asking what the valuable questions in empirical music research are and who can provide valuable answers is to think of what music gets listened to and performed regularly. Should music that gets most of the attention in the real world be a better representation of music in empirical studies than music that is listened to by a minority (as some classical repertoires are)? Is this playing into the hands of consumerism and large international companies who can market such music to millions of consumers? Does this push the empirical research of music more firmly into media and popular music studies with the added twist of adopting an empirical approach? I think this is a simplification that has gone too far, and there will be room to explore all genres and traditions, including Western classical music, but the question is more about priority and balance; making decisions of what to study is a conscious and deliberate choice. The Western art music tradition has long been the default focus of music research in empirical studies of music, too, although at least emerging empirical studies about live concert experiences and health and well-being are breaking free of this default paradigm and following contemporary music genres.

A related dilemma is whether the broad range of interests and attention of different cultures, traditions, and genres of music will yield insights by means of cross-cultural comparisons, or whether it would be more effective to study one or two cultures or traditions more thoroughly to gain insights about the specific behaviours and processes. It is probable that both strategies will work, and although the dangers of comparative musicology are still well remembered, there will be a new opportunity to ask fundamental questions about music that are not merely footnotes of Western music traditions, but explore the nature of music making and values associated with music in non-Western cultures.

Equality and Diversity

The lack of diversity (gender, ethnicity, and social class) is a problem not only for teaching and research in the entire academic world but also for empirical music research, as increased diversity is good for the development of ideas and making progress on challenging topics. As I emphasised in Chapter 3, the scope of and interest in empirical music research are toward the issues of capabilities and processing music. Although much of the early music cognition and psychology of music used Western art music as a starting point, the scope of the music and of the participants has diversified during the last 15 years. In terms of scholarship opportunities, the field is far from diverse and equal, but the starting point in terms of gender is in my view positive as much of the pioneering work and leadership over the last 40 years in empirical music research has been done by women (Motte-Haber, Deutch, Deliège, Krumhansl, etc., see Chapter 3).

Change in diversity and equality is slow and is dependent on societal and cultural changes. But the change needs agents and activities from everyone in academia, especially from those high in the food chain (white males such as me) such as an awareness of equality and diversity in selecting students and staff members, making adjustments to workplace guidance to allow people with caring needs to contribute to work more flexibly, avoiding keeping work roles gendered, valuing contributions to diversity, and as a final example, declining to contribute to events/conferences with severe equality deficits.

In writing this book, I have attempted to diversify three elements of its sources: the gender and geographical/cultural region of the primary authors and the styles of music represented. As a diversity statement for this book, I have compiled some simple indicators from the references (N=482). In terms of gender, the first authors of the references are predominantly men (77.1%) despite my efforts of preferring to choose publications by women. The cultural diversity of the first authors is 59.1% Anglo-American and 40.9% non-Anglo-American. When the sources relate to specific examples or collections of music, 63.2% of the sources referenced represent Western art music. 36.1% of the studies reference music outside the western canon, and these are either Western folk music, but also reference non-Western music traditions. Offering statements such as these does help to trace the changes in diversity in this field, and I expect these indices to show more diversity over time.

Decolonialisation and Empirical Music Research

Empirical music research is subject to the same criticisms as most Western academic research that deals with Western art objects, concepts, or canons, in that it builds understanding of how we process and comprehend music using solely WEIRD participants, or where these research activities are mainly carried out by white, Western, privileged scholars. Empirical music research has become aware of these issues following the lead of ethnomusicology over the last 50 years and psychology over the last ten years concerning the overly Western emphasis in the data from WEIRD samples (Henrich et al., 2010). Diversifying the participant pool is a slow process for many reasons. Recruiting non-WEIRD participants requires hard work, new connections, and additional resources, language skills, and cultural competences. All this also means broadening the scope of research, methods, and the actual meaningful research questions.

Equally important for diversifying and decolonising empirical music research is the actual diversity of the scholars in the field. The normal efforts to diversify the discipline by paying attention to diversity in recruitment will take decades to have an impact unless more radical initiatives are adopted. At the level of scholarly societies, there has been a trend to reach out to Asia and the Pacific to broaden perspectives. Societies also have antiracism committees that are planning concrete steps to take, but much of this has to do with the university mechanisms and the values embedded within them. In terms of empirical research, this discipline conducts research that seeks to assess how people, albeit mostly in Western societies, generally use, produce, and consume music. This points out that we should not focus on Western art music or privileged traditions as such, since they typically have a very small prevalence in musical activities.

What about methods and techniques and the colonialist values embedded in these? Some argue that Western music notation is part of the colonial representational system. Relying less on this convention or eliminating it altogether would not hamper this discipline, as empirical music research does not always utilise Western notation as the basis of analysis, but utilises the timing and pitch information of the performance or derives features from the audio signal. These approaches do sidestep the colonial heritage of Western notation and may focus on more popular music and the music of non-Western cultures, but technology itself can be a source of other types of representational biases (Holzapfel et al., 2018), especially when the data is inherently culturally situated and, therefore, data and algorithms can support various ideological leanings while under the guise of being just algorithms and data (Dourish, 2016). Although ethnomusicology has talked about these issues in the context of folk music research (Stokes, 1997; Walden, 2014), there has not been much discussion about these issues in empirical music research, but it is safe to say that there is a massive amount of work is needed to even identify some of the latent values that sustain the inequalities in this type of scholarship.

Despite these existing caveats, empirical music research has the potential to contribute to our understanding of how knowledge in music is acquired and how inequalities in many of the mainstream music genres and social systems operate and are sustained. But this requires an active tackling of the issues outlined.

Challenges and Opportunities

How to engage humanistic musicologists in empirical approaches? There can be different routes and levels of engagement where training and education in musicology play a major role. Possessing basic knowledge of the empirical research principles for music research would be a minimal element in a broad musicology training, but how to motivate music departments to include such elements in their curricula? I would argue that any scholarly training comes with the expectation that the reader is able to comprehend common research issues and quantitative paradigms (experiment design, sampling, statistical analysis, and interpretation) which tend to be common research paradigms in the real world. I am not the first to say this, as it has been mentioned by others (Bryman, 2006; Deacon, 2008), but it is worthwhile repeating that there should be room for a wider ontological framework in music research; dismissing the quantitative approach as something that has no place in the humanities or music is an ideological relic from the past. Minimum awareness of empirical research possibilities in music should be a basic requirement in the training of musicologists. This training should cover the methods involved in empirical music research, including empirical experiment design and analysis, as well as computational tools for analysing music in its many forms (scores, texts, audio). Ideas about replicability and transparency in research should be an essential part of such training. These would allow students to evaluate the traditional theories and systems in music with a new perspective that is geared towards finding out more about the topic and asking questions which can be empirically tested. I believe that these themes will help students gain a wider understanding of scientific principles that are not necessarily otherwise part of the standard education in humanities.

Let's break down the themes where empirical music research requires skills, tools, disciplinary training, challenges, and opportunities for discussion and training, as well as interdisciplinary collaborations.

Bridging the Digital Skills Gap

There is a sizable gap between traditional music analysis and the empirical approach. In this book I have talked about the ways in which the empirical approach, computational models in particular, can strengthen traditional analytical techniques, but of course there is another issue at stake here, which refers to digital technology. Most musicology is now carried out by digital technology (scores, scans of scores, sound files, digital texts, and databases); as Laurent Pugin has said, 'the field is undergoing the same revolution as all disciplines in the humanities' (Pugin, 2015). The *digital humanities*, which is a broad umbrella term for everything that comes under digital (creation, publishing, dissemination, and analysis), have not captured the imagination of musicologists in the way that was perhaps predicted or envisioned to in the early days of the field. To give you an example, Ichiro Fujinaga and Susan Forscher Weiss expressed optimistic views in 2004 that musicology would shift to a digital approach and would routinely use corpus analysis as a routine (Fujinaga & Weiss, 2004), echoing David Huron's call to musicologists to shift from a 'data poor' to a 'data rich field' by undergoing a fundamental change in methodologies (Huron, 1999). This gap was not bridged ten years ago (Liem et al., 2012) nor more recently (Urberg, 2017), although there are pockets of musicology such as music theory and performance studies where the shift is clearly on its way.

Currently, music research does not fully exploit the digital tools in research. This situation is caused by a lack of training and awareness, which are signs of too little cross-disciplinary fertilisation and communication. The music research community needs to organise opportunities for scholars and students to spark their interest in the empirical approach, such as music hackathons, and to learn the basic competencies of computational score analysis, audio analysis, and other elements of empirical music research. There is a wealth of information available about empirical research, but the case examples of how these can help different fields of music research need attention. There are several areas where collecting and assessing annotations about music, or creating models that provide testable predictions, would help to clarify research topics and questions.

Competencies Required

The set of skills that I have promoted within these pages is one that more than one person can easily master. Skills in empirical music research require understanding about many research designs, methods, instruments, statistics, computational approaches, coding, and so on. This range is certainly too wide to be fully included in a music degree and too specialised to be the target of a psychology, cognition, or data science degree. But it is also quite clear that not every study needs all the different approaches, and when several approaches may be leveraged towards one research question, it is common to enter into collaborations where experts on specific methods and approaches contribute in their specialist area. However, the broad skill set promoted is a bottleneck for training, as mastering a single approach already requires considerable investment, not to mention developing a broader awareness of the literature and findings surrounding the topic and methods.

Computational music analysis, while it is just one part of the empirical approach to music research, is taught at a growing number of universities although the number is still small. Influential scholars in music theory such as Dmitri Tymoczko have advocated the use of a programming approach to make progress in the field (Tymoczko, 2013).

A mixed economy of computer languages such as *Matlab*, *R* and *Python* have been used to generate relevant computational tools and libraries for analysing music (*MIR toolbox*, *Librosa*, *Essentia*, *music21*, etc.). Asking prospective students to learn several languages is not feasible, so a decision about the most promising and widely usable programming language could be useful, although this would be nearly impossible to mandate and coordinate. Additionally, the diversity of language and solutions might allow for a richer set of possibilities. At the moment, it feels that Python has the best potential due to its prevalence, the ease of using notebooks for sharing analyses, and the flexible way that libraries can be created and imported to each project, but I am acutely aware that most languages can now offer similar solutions. On the other hand, having a mixed economy might also allow one to capitalise on the advantages of several languages, which all have their own strengths, communities, and supporters. And once you learn the basics of one language and a set of tools, acquiring the competences for the others becomes easier. But as a field, focussing our efforts on mutually compatible libraries and languages would be an asset, and at this moment I feel that the direction of travel suggests Python as the best candidate.

Interdisciplinary Stances

The term *interdisciplinary* broadly describes research that involves multiple disciplines, but the exact relationship between disciplines is often ambiguously defined. *Interdisciplinarity* normally refers to coordinating methods and approaches from separate disciplines towards a singular research question. In addition, there are other terms now equally often invoked, such as *multidisciplinary* and *transdisciplinary* research. An influential definition of these terms (Stember, 1991) suggested that interdisciplinarity signifies a collaborative work that combines the methods and approaches from different disciplines, whereas multidisciplinary is a stance where people from several disciplines work together on a topic, utilising methods from their own disciplines. Transdisciplinary is seen as a higher form of collaboration, where research initially combining different disciplines creates something that is beyond any combination of these. In empirical music research, I have mainly talked about either interdisciplinary actions or just adopting a more empirical approach to an existing discipline. This latter strategy does not invoke any of these terms if the scope of empirical research is already within the discipline (e.g., carrying out a corpus analysis using statistical measures is an example that already has a long history in musicology). In some complex questions of music, I have mentioned combining the methods and values of several disciplines, which can be read as a call for multidisciplinary action (chills induced by music, understanding emotions induced by music, etc.).

What I advocate is the kind of collaborative relationship between disciplines that Andrew Barry and Georgina Born have put forward (2013). Instead of one dominating discipline with a subordinating relationship to other disciplines, they suggest three possible interdisciplinary modes; the first mode is *additive,* where different disciplines are brought to the same discussion and allow each to contribute within their own terms. The second mode that Barry and Born suggest is *subordinate* interdisciplinarity, where one discipline is at the core, and others simply bring small elements to the collaboration but do not question or confront the core discipline. Born states that the subordinate mode is a common way physical and natural sciences bring in elements from social sciences or humanities when needed, and this seems to be the way MIR adopts elements from ethnomusicology without challenging the fundamentals of scholarship values (Born, 2020). This criticism is also relevant for music psychology. In many of the examples given in this book, I have advocated music psychology as the dominating discipline that asks the right questions and has the appropriate methods. I have also mentioned music psychology or the empirical approach in general as something that could also occasionally dip into music history or theory to obtain research materials, annotations, or historical or analytical phenomena as a starting point. This approach of empirical music research that I am advocating in this book probably also falls in part into subordinate interdisciplinarity due to my own position as a music psychology scholar. But I am wary of imposing empirical music research as a discipline because I prefer to offer it as an approach rather than a standalone research area or field. As a broad approach, it should not be seen as dominating even though I am hard at work promoting it for many issues and questions in music research. The third mode that Barry and Born have put forward is called *agonistic* interdisciplinarity, which has no hierarchy, and the scholarship contribution of the disciplines comes through new emergent and unforeseen transformations, methodologies, and theories. This interdisciplinary mode is characterised by awareness of the limits of each discipline and a desire to go beyond what each discipline on its own could achieve. This hybrid mode may lead to a new discipline formed out of the existing disciplines. No matter what the term is, such a step change would offer a profoundly new way of working together. Some of the more established areas of empirical research of music might have the possibility of working in an agonistic fashion. Computational analysis of historical documents, such as semantic analysis of historical texts (Newman & Block, 2006) could be regarded as something that is beyond what each discipline could achieve. Or a combination of ethnomusicology involving in-depth analyses of ensemble performances around the globe and empirical timing analysis of the same materials (Clayton et al., 2020) is another example of agonistic interdisciplinarity that has created something that is more than the sum of its parts.

Engaging Research Communities

There are some unique traditions in computational sciences and in MIR that have created a sense of community and have accelerated research and engagement among scholars. Since 2005, the MIR field has held so-called MIREX (Music Information Retrieval Evaluation eXchange) competitions, which are organised by the International Music Information Retrieval Systems Evaluation Laboratory (IMIRSEL) at the University of Illinois and led by Stephen Downie (2010). MIREX offers a set of technical and conceptual challenges (beat tracking, genre recognition, tempo estimation, score alignment, cover song identification, etc.) for the whole field to tackle. The competition runs a platform to evaluate the algorithms submitted on their servers, using the data specified for the tasks. The competition also uses commonly shared benchmarks to measure the success of the algorithm performance and organises the coordination of these tasks. Every submission is then run at the event and the ranked list of submitted performances makes it clear how everybody is doing in this annual challenge. It is an engaging and very transparent way of making progress in solving these tasks and has resulted in many known solutions for these problems. There has also been a similar public challenge through the *Performance Rendering Contest* (RENCON) in the past. This competition functioned as a Turing test for musical performance (Hiraga et al., 2004) and the assessment of performances generated by different algorithms was carried out by a live jury.

In addition to these events organised within the traditional conference framework, numerous informal events have created a culture of exploration and engagement with music data. So-called 'music hackathons' around the world – classical music hackathons, world music hackathons, remote music hackathons, music and health hackathons, etc. – have created opportunities for people curious about the possibilities of music data or technologies to build creative prototypes based on music, sensors, data, or a combination of all of these. These events are excellent ways to network and get people interested in music information retrieval and to allow the companies involved in these technologies to meet the future experts. These events can challenge participants to solve thorny questions about musical structure analysis, to connect various live sensors to interact with a performance, or to create a new dynamic visualisation of somebody's playlists on a streaming service. A future goal of these activities would be to get scholars and students of the humanities to join and participate in the events. It would also help if efforts were made to recruit participants for such events from diverse cultural backgrounds, social classes, and ethnicities. This must be combined with open discussions about what the valuable research themes and topics are. There is also room for informal events such as music hackathons to develop new tools and new directions for research that serve the wishes and needs of the practitioners, music industry, cultural sector, music education, well-being applications, or other stakeholders, but here again the connection between the academic community and the non-academic community needs serious time commitment to identify mutually profitable directions.

Applications

The empirical paradigm promoted in this book is aligned with applied research in music technology and developing music interventions related to health and well-being. These are the two areas which have already had some impact on society and there is potential to go further. I will also want to promote another use of music that tackles the changing of attitudes and behaviours that contribute negatively to climate change. Although music is not the most efficient way to combat this crisis, music can raise awareness, and encourage behavioural change by promoting eco-friendly habits.

Music Technology and Creative Applications

The whole music distribution chain has radically altered over the last 15 years, largely because psychoacoustics research made a breakthrough in discovering how to compress audio in a way that preserved the perceptually important parts of it for us (the birth of the MP3 standard in the early 1990s as part of the audio encoding standard in MPEG). This started the migration of music delivery to online through iterations, where we now have streaming services offering subscription-based models to access a massive (tens of millions of tracks) catalogue of music. Additionally, the management of the content of these services has speeded up the pace of research in music information retrieval, as there is a need to infer mean-ingful aspects of music from audio alone, such as mood recommendation, playlist curation, and genre recognition or tagging the properties of the audio. The industry has also given music researchers data about contemporary uses of music in streaming services and access to some of the data within the services (e.g., Spotify API). Identifying music from the sonic landmarks – using apps or services such as *Shazam* – has long since surpassed the human capacity to recognise music (Wang, 2003). Other technology start-ups such as *Chordify* have taken basic MIR tasks such as chord and beat estimation and turned them into a well-functioning service that helps budding musicians to get the chord annotations of any music available on YouTube (see de Haas et al., 2013). There are other services that go further in the content analysis of music, turning this into a teaching tool. For instance, *Yousician* offers tutoring in guitar (and other instruments too) by listening to the playing of the user; the service can detect all mistakes and assist in correcting them with a user-friendly and reactive visualisation that makes learning part of the game. Score following is another technical innovation that makes the lives of musicians easier, as this technology allows musicians to play from a single tablet where page turning is handled automatically by matching the score to live audio (*SampleSumo*). Most of these innovations – and many that I did not expand on such as *Songle* which automatically annotates the chords, beats, structure, and melody for a given song – started as empirical projects aimed at solving a research question about a specific issue and many of the early reports detailing the successes of the schemes can be found in the pages of ISMIR proceedings[1].

These examples above only relate to the delivery and consumption of music, but empirical research on music technology and the creation and production of music has offered similarly radical step changes to the creation of music. For editing, accurate F_0 detection (spearheaded by companies such as *Melodyne*) has allowed unprecedented amounts of artistic freedom to adjust performances. Also, automatic mixing solutions, software synthesisers, and virtual instrument libraries that are based on actual recordings of instruments instead of artificial samples have broadened the range of possibilities. The real shift has probably been in the affordability and portability of the studio environment that has allowed anyone with a laptop, microphones, preamplifiers, and software tools to record, edit, mix, and master music. In addition, creative software tools such as *Max/MSP*, *Ableton Live*, and *SuperCollider* offer another creative use of music technology (live music generation, technology-assisted composition, and performance) where links to empirical research findings and models are often strong.

It is important to note that these applications, companies, and services only partially follow the principles of empirical music research advocated in this book. They typically collect empirical data (annotation, ratings, etc.) and harness such systematic observations when building the system, which are formalised and implemented through computational models. These steps are in line with the type of research I have also advocated for empirical academic research. But here the similarity between commercial enterprises and academic research stops. Commercial enterprises usually cannot be transparent in the same way as academic research, as their business models and data are critical information and cannot be shared. More broadly, commercially driven topics may be far from academic interests and are usually geared toward short-term gain, rather than solving complex issues or addressing niche topics. Commercial projects can also have severe biases, and their algorithms can strengthen existing cultural and gender biases (Ferraro et al., 2021). However, they also have the potential to address these issues in ways that are far more wide-ranging than academic research due to the sheer volume of data and coverage that some of the content-processing companies have, but there needs to be either encouragement, legislation, or a sound business rationale to tackle this issue in music recommendation (Porcaro et al., 2021).

It is important to consider the implications of the changing music consumption landscape for music research and musicology in general. In my view, there are substantial practical changes needed to how music research is done to acknowledge and incorporate fully digital processes of creation and distribution. The history of music reception is now partially embedded in social networks and the role of critics, radio, and magazines has diminished. As a result, research on geographical and historical trends must find ways of capturing and analysing the wealth of information now embedded in different services (e.g., *X* [formerly *Twitter*], *Instagram, TikTok, YouTube, SoundCloud,* and streaming services). For instance, when considering the success of the remix of 'Despacito' (by Luis Fonsi and Justin Bieber) in 2017 to become the second most popular song on YouTube, the dissemination mechanisms and recommendation of the various services need to be central elements of the analysis. Understanding the role of recommendation algorithms in streaming services is an integral part of explaining what becomes popular and how cultural artefacts such as music spread globally and locally. There is a wealth of information generated every week and month about the actual behaviours of hundreds of millions of music listeners, often enriched with localised data and individual differences. Currently, there are no large-scale history projects that would attempt to store snapshots of these processes for academic study, but it would be important for music research (history, sociology, and music preferences) to be able to leverage the relevant parts of these precious data.

Health and Well-being

Research on health and well-being related to music has increased in the last 15 years. Research under these themes is usually fully empirical and has adopted many of the principles I have advocated for in this book (transparency, formalisation, etc.) years ago due to the pressure and practices adopted from medical research. Rehabilitation research involving music comes with the tradition of rehabilitation research in general, where strict protocols and well-planned study designs with preregistrations have been the norm for two decades or more. The role of music has long been recognised in rehabilitation involving certain types of injuries/disorders (Parkinson's, dementia/Alzheimer's disease, and stroke). Empirical studies that have evaluated the effectiveness of music intervention in any such disorder/injury have followed a strict study protocol set by the medical field. In essence, the principles advocated within these pages will work for health and wellness research involving music. In terms of discoveries, there are specialised books dedicated to summarising the findings of music interventions for health and well-being (MacDonald et al., 2013; Sunderland et al., 2018) and recent meta-analyses summarise the best practices (Sheppard & Broughton, 2020).

Influence of Environment-related Attitudes and Behaviours

Our species has been facing self-inflicted environmental catastrophe for decades now, but only during the last few years have we started to witness the direct impacts of climate change on our weather and environment. Anthropogenic global warming is already having a profound negative impact on everyone on the planet. Music research is not considered to be at the vanguard of actions mitigating change, but Helen Prior (2022) has persuasively argued that empirical research of music could and should be leveraged towards changing individual behaviours and attitudes towards the environment. She reviews the mechanisms (emotions, empathy, identity, influencing norms, altruism) arising from environmental psychology through which music in the broad sense could be used towards this, and calls for empirical studies that would test the effectiveness of these interventions for changing attitudes and beliefs. This is not the first instance where scholars involved in empirical research of music have suggested actions to reverse the ongoing catastrophe. An eminent scholar in music psychology, Richard Parncutt, has advocated for actions that decrease the release of carbon, and he demonstrated the human costs of burning carbon by converting them into meaningful units such as measuring different activities against the amount of carbon released in an average long-haul flight (Parncutt, 2019). He also spearheaded initiatives to minimise travel to conferences when he was the president of the European Society for the Cognitive Sciences of Music and organised the main events in the field in 2018.

Future Prospects

The empirical take on music research is a broad approach, but sufficiently specific to make this a positive and trustworthy approach to adopt. Empirical research allows one to learn from mistakes and invites colleagues from all over the world to evaluate, reassess, replicate, and comment on the research. This engagement with others under known rules and guidelines facilitates interactions and creates a common ground for assessing the robustness of research. It has the capacity to scale up from small-scale pilot or student projects to large-scale projects with multiple disciplines and measures, up to multi-site collaborations involving several teams in different countries. Empirical research of music is fundamentally collaborative and can also bring together different relevant disciplines of music research.

The empirical approach to music research can also steer focus towards questions and methods that provide research processes that can be evaluated with common yardsticks such as reliability, generalisability, and validity. The results of empirical studies have the potential to be accessible and understood by a wide range of readers and raising the level of competence of potential readers of research is one of the reasons why everyone involved in scholarly research of music should at least acquire at least some of the basic competences of this approach.

The promise of an empirical view of music has arisen during the last 20 years. Whether this view can reach and gain a foothold among students and scholars of musicology, music analysis, music history, performance studies, and ethnomusicology will depend on many factors. The availability of methods and appropriate support and guidance with specific examples and engagement related to different disciplines will likely affect the persuasiveness of the empirical approach. There are formidable challenges to bridging the gulf between those performing traditional analyses on music and culture and those already engaged in computer-driven analyses or empirical research designs, but the chasm may be narrowed through training, discipline-specific engagement, and availability of methods and tools, customised to the needs of the disciplines. I have tried to give examples of the empirical approach applied to ethnomusicology, musical experiences, music analysis, and various other topics, which should resonate among traditional disciplines involved in music research. Perhaps the most valuable aspect of the empirical approach comes from the way data may challenge or confirm existing theories and conjectures, no matter how well established they might be and how awkward refuting something we have all learned to believe to be true might be. I am excited every time I see classic topics of musicology being addressed in an empirical fashion, since such studies can inject energy and motivation into the traditional and may confirm or sometimes refute ideas that have been passed on for perhaps too long in the literature without a rigorous testing of them. I also think that theorising about musical processes and phenomena, which is a valuable part of research, needs to be done in a way that postulates concrete testable theories and allows for open assessment by the community.

I believe that the empirical take on music will allow us not only to provide answers to questions that are interesting and exciting about what music means to us and how we comprehend music, but also to questions that are important for society: understanding how music can be used in rehabilitation of some disorders, depression, dementia, and stroke, and how music is used to regulate our moods and emotions in subtle yet effective ways. The social aspects of music (empathy, togetherness, connecting with others, sharing narratives, emotions) are topics that are not only valuable, but inherently empirical and need rigorous methods to be explored in detail. And these topics will also have a significant impact on how music is valued in our society. This does not seek to undervalue the efforts of music making, cultural and historical research, or performance practices, nor diminish the sheer enjoyment of creating music. Any of these applied and health and well-being directions of research will require recognition and incorporation of these fundamental aspects of music in our cultures.

Note

1 www.ismir.net

References

Barry, A., & Born, G. (2013). Interdisciplinarity: Reconfigurations of the social and natural sciences. In A. Barry, & G. Born (Eds.), *Interdisciplinarity* (pp. 1–56). Routledge.

Born, G. (2020). Diversifying MIR: Knowledge and real-world challenges, and new interdisciplinary futures. *Transactions of the International Society for Music Information Retrieval*, *3*(1), 193–204. https://doi.org/http://doi.org/10.5334/tismir.58

Bryman, A. (2006). Paradigm peace and the implications for quality. *International Journal of Social Research Methodology*, *9*(2), 111–126.

Clayton, M., Jakubowski, K., Eerola, T., Keller, P. E., Camurri, A., Volpe, G., & Alborno, P. (2020). Interpersonal entrainment in music performance: Theory, method, and model. *Music Perception: An Interdisciplinary Journal*, *38*(2), 136–194.

Deacon, D. (2008). Research methods for cultural studies. In M. Pickering (Ed.), *Research methods for cultural studies* (pp. 89–104). Edinburgh University Press.

De Haas, W. B., Magalhães, J. P., Wiering, F., & C. Veltkamp, R. (2013). Automatic functional harmonic analysis. *Computer Music Journal*, *37*(4), 37–53.

Dourish, P. (2016). Algorithms and their others: Algorithmic culture in context. *Big Data & Society*, *3*(2), 1–11.

Downie, J. S., Ehmann, A. F., Bay, M., & Jones, M. C. (2010). The music information retrieval evaluation exchange: Some observations and insights. In Z. Ras & A. Wieczorkowska (Eds.), *Advances in music information retrieval* (pp. 93–115). Springer.

Ferraro, A., Serra, X., & Bauer, C. (2021). Break the loop: Gender imbalance in music recommenders. *Proceedings of the 2021 Conference on Human Information Interaction and Retrieval*, 249–254.

Fujinaga, I., & Weiss, S. F. (2004). *A companion to digital humanities* (S. Schreibman, R. Siemens, & J. Unsworth, Eds.). Blackwell.

Henrich, J., Heine, S. J., & Norenzayan, A. (2010). Beyond WEIRD: Towards a broad-based behavioral science. *Behavioral and Brain Sciences*, *33*(2-3), 111–135.

Hiraga, R., Bresin, R., Hirata, K., & Katayose, H. (2004). Rencon 2004: Turing test for musical expression. *Proceedings of the 2004 Conference on New Interfaces for Musical Expression*, 120–123.

Holzapfel, A., Sturm, B., & Coeckelbergh, M. (2018). Ethical dimensions of music information retrieval technology. *Transactions of the International Society for Music Information Retrieval*, *1*(1), 44–55.

Huron, D. (1999). *The new empiricism: Systematic musicology in a postmodern age.* Citeseer. www.music-cog.ohio-state.edu/Music220/Bloch.lectures/3.Methodology.html

Lerdahl, F. et al. (2001). *Tonal pitch space.* Oxford University Press.

Lerdahl, F., & Krumhansl, C. L. (2007). Modeling tonal tension. *Music Perception: An Interdisciplinary Journal*, *24*(4), 329–366.

Liem, C., Rauber, A., Lidy, T., Lewis, R., Raphael, C., Reiss, J. D., Crawford, T., & Hanjalic, A. (2012). Music information technology and professional stakeholder audiences: Mind the adoption gap. *Dagstuhl Follow-Ups*, *3*.

MacDonald, R., Kreutz, G., & Mitchell, L. (2013). *Music, health, and wellbeing.* Oxford University Press.

Newman, D. J., & Block, S. (2006). Probabilistic topic decomposition of an eighteenth-century American newspaper. *Journal of the American Society for Information Science and Technology*, *57*(6), 753–767. https://doi.org/https://doi.org/10.1002/asi.20342

Parncutt, R. (2019). The human cost of anthropogenic global warming: Semi-quantitative prediction and the 1,000-tonne rule. *Frontiers in Psychology*, *10*, 2323.

Porcaro, L., Castillo, C., & Gómez Gutiérrez, E. (2021). Diversity by design in music recommender systems. *Transactions of the International Society for Music Information Retrieval*, *4*(1), 114–126. https://doi.org/http://doi.org/10.5334/tismir.106

Prior, H. (2022). How can music help us to address the climate crisis? *Music & Science*, *5*. https://doi.org/10.1177/20592043221075725

Pugin, L. (2015). The challenge of data in digital musicology. *Frontiers in Digital Humanities*, *2*(4). https://doi.org/https://doi.org/10.3389/fdigh.2015.00

Sheppard, A., & Broughton, M. C. (2020). Promoting wellbeing and health through active participation in music and dance: A systematic review. *International Journal of Qualitative Studies on Health and Well-Being*, *15*(1), 1732526.

Stember, M. (1991). Advancing the social sciences through the interdisciplinary enterprise. *The Social Science Journal*, *28*(1), 1–14.

Stokes, M. (1997). *Ethnicity, identity and music: The musical construction of place.* Berg.

Sunderland, N., Lewandowski, N., Bendrups, D., & Bartleet, B.-L. (2018). *Music, health and wellbeing*. Springer.

Tymoczko, D. (2013). Review of Michael Cuthbert, Music21: A toolkit for computer-aided musicology. *Music Theory Online, 19*(3).

Urberg, M. (2017). Pasts and futures of digital humanities in musicology: Moving towards a "bigger tent." *Music Reference Services Quarterly, 20*(3–4), 134–150. https://doi.org/10.1080/10588167.2017.1404301

Walden, J. S. (2014). *Sounding authentic: The rural miniature and musical modernism*. Oxford University Press.

Wang, A. (2003). An industrial strength audio search algorithm. *4th International Conference on Music Information Retrieval, Baltimore, Maryland, USA, 27–30 October 2003* (pp. 7–13).

Wiggins, G. A., Müllensiefen, D., & Pearce, M. T. (2010). On the non-existence of music: Why music theory is a figment of the imagination. *Musicae Scientiae, 14*(1), 231–255.

Index

268   *Index*

Heggli, O. A. 79, 224
Helmholtz, von H. 1, 9–10, 12–13, 21
Helmholtz resonator 10
hemodynamic responses 91 *see* neural
Henrich, J. 101–102, 106, 250
Hentschel, J. 75
Hepokoski, J. 116
Herremans, D. 51, 193
hertz (Hz) 211
hidden Markov model 185, 220
high-level semantic descriptors 216, 217,
    222–225
Hindemith, P. 8
Hindustani classical music 71
Hiraga, R. 255
historical musicology 14, 28, 102, 248, 257
Hjermstad, M. J. 83
Holst, G. 58
Holzapfel, A. 236, 251
Homeostasis 90
Honing, H. 21, 28, 36
Hood, M. 182, 228
Hornbostel, E. M. 15, 77, 182, 215
Howell, D. C. 136–137
Huettel, S. A. 91
humanistic musicology 28–30, 33, 37,
    40, 172
humanities 1, 2, 27–30, 33, 37–39, 116–117,
    171–173, 251–252, 254
Humdrum 186
Huovinen, E. 27
Huron, D. 27–28, 32, 34–35, 40, 61, 90,
    167, 183, 185–186, 231, 233, 252
Hurwitz, E. R. 224
hypothalamus-pituitary-adrenal axis
    (HPAA) 89 *see* neuroendocrine markers
hypothesis 33, 45, 49, 56, 83, 117, 143–144,
    147–148, 161–162, 164–166, 164–166,
    168, 168; testing 143, 144, 148, 161,
    190, 246

IEMP Corpus 234, 235, 242
ISMIR 76, 107, 257
impact factor 173
improvisation 29, 53, 86, 184, 235
imputation 136
in situ 98
independent: observations 151; variable 56
indirect measures 44, 84; self-reports 83
individual differences 69, 79, 79, 102–104,
    102–104
inferential reasoning: 33; statistics
    143–144, 145, 147–148, 161–162,
    237–238, 247; testing 143, 145, 147

information dynamics of music (IDyoM)
    161 *see* modelling
informed consent 46, 168
inner hair cell 218
instrument classification 15, 77
instruments 4, 8–9, 15, 17, 31–32, 75–76,
    78, 103, 106, 159, 167, 183, 186,
    197–198, 201–204, 213–215, 217, 222,
    230, 240, 253, 256–257
inter-coder agreement 139
interaction 11, 20, 29, 196; effect (statistics)
    150–154
interdisciplinarity, agonistic 255; research
    28, 253–254; collaborations 174,
    178, 181
international music score library project
    (IMSLP) 230
interpersonal reactivity index 103 *see*
    personality
interpretative phenomenological analysis
    (IPA) 137–138, 140
interval: 7, 8, 19, 63, 82, 128; counts 35;
    distribution 189, 190; frequencies 35
intervention 59–60, 62, 88, 258 *see* music
    intervention
interviews 13, 45, 53, 63, 80–81, 178;
    semi-structured 137–138; transcription 138
intonation 93, 220
Izard, C. E. 55

Jackendoff, R. 18, 185
Jacoby, N. 86–87
Jakubowski, K. 71, 86
Janssen, B. 185
Japanese popular music 184
jazz 79, 103, 183, 194, 229, 232, 235,
    237, 239
jigsaw puzzle task 85
Jockers, M. 117
Jones, M.-R. 16
Joubert, E. 70
journal articles 164–165, 169–173,
    175–176, 179
judgement bias 84
Juslin, P. N. 53, 61, 106
just intonation system 220
Järvinen, T. 194

Kamehkhosh, I. 204
Kanizsa illusion 13
Karlsson, J. 53
Kayser, D. 85
Keller, P. 87, 98
Kelly, D. 86, 121